CREATURE COMFORTS

'I say only that I am bewitched by you,' Michael went on. 'I can't think of anyone or anything else since the first day of meeting with you.'

'Short acquaintance is not to be trusted.'

It did not seem at all like short acquaintance. How could she tell him that he had never been out of her thoughts, out of her dreams?

Moment by moment she was slipping towards infidelity with giddy indifference to the consequences. She hungered for the pleasure of yielding to impulse, of not being ruled by logic. If only she possessed an ounce of Anna's unscrupulousness, she might be in his arms now, might surrender to the passion that was in her. But she was not Anna . . .

About the author

Jessica Stirling was born in Glasgow and has enjoyed a highly successful career as a writer. She began with the bestselling Stalker trilogy: *The Spoiled Earth*, *The Hiring Fair* and *The Dark Pasture*. Novels set in England, eighteenth-century and late-Victorian Glasgow, and the Scottish countryside followed. Her most recent novel, *The Workhouse Girl*, is set in nineteenth-century Glasgow.

Creature Comforts

Jessica Stirling

CORONET BOOKS
Hodder and Stoughton

First published in Great Britain in 1996 by Hodder and Stoughton
A division of Hodder Headline PLC
First published by Hodder and Stoughton in paperback in 1996
A Coronet Paperback

10 9 8 7 6 5 4 3

A CIP catalogue record for this title is available
from the British Library.

ISBN 0 340 65793 6

Printed and bound in Great Britain by
Mackays of Chatham plc, Chatham, Kent

Hodder and Stoughton
A division of Hodder Headline PLC
338 Euston Road
London NW1 3BH

No one envies or hates one of his own party;
even the devils love one another in their way;
they torment one another for reasons other than
hate or envy; these are only employed against
the just.

William Blake

Contents

ONE

Men and Wives

Anna had bought him the monkey as a pet but to her disgust he had made of it a surrogate child. Clad in a tiny hand-stitched vest of blue cotton and a pair of nankin breeks the little creature, hardly larger than a tabby cat, perched on Matt's shoulder, chattering amicably and nibbling a piece of bacon rind which the young man had draped behind his ear.

Shirtless and barefoot, Matt sprawled in the box chair before a blazing fire. The kitchen was as hot as sin for it was Matt's habit to pile logs and soft coal so high upon the hearth that it was all Anna could do to sidle close enough to hang a pot on the chain or find a place for the kettle on the hob. When she accused him of being wasteful, Matt took umbrage and declared that she had no feelings; had Jacko not been born in the tropics and how could he be expected to survive a Scottish winter without a bit of pampering? Jacko was only an excuse for self-indulgence. Matt had always been fond of toasting his big, muscular body and now that he was master in his own home he saw no reason to deny himself the pleasure.

Thirty months of marriage had schooled Anna in dealing with her husband's foibles. Thirty months of marriage to Matt Sinclair had so coarsened her that, for the most part, she was unaware of the tense, graceless state of their relationship. She attributed her husband's moodiness to the fact that she had not borne him a son. If only she could conceive, she believed, Matt would instantly mend his ways and become loving and considerate. Even so, Anna was not altogether anxious to stumble into the pitfall of motherhood. Young though she was, just touching twenty in that spring of 1812, Anna's instincts told her that the error of an ill-wrought marriage could not be erased by love alone or by dividing what love there was with an innocent bairn.

It was all her sister Elspeth's fault. If at one time Elspeth had not been so damnably struck on Matt Sinclair, then she, Anna, would not have teased and trapped him into making fumbling love to her in the trees below the Nettleburn. Out of that act and out of her compulsive confession of it, disasters followed like stones clattering downhill.

Mammy had dragged her straight to the Sinclairs' house. Outraged and ashamed, the Sinclairs had been stung into agreeing on a hasty wedding. Banishment to the gloomy old cottage in the pine wood had followed and now it seemed Matt's prospects for advancement had been left to tarnish and rust. As if she had not woes enough, she had been daft enough to be taken in by a packman and to buy Matt a monkey!

Rain had drizzled across the country for weeks and it was rare enough, even in fine weather, to find one of the travelling kind on Ottershaw. Matt's father, grieve of the policies, gave strangers short shrift. But there he was, with his snap hat and moleskins soaked to the colour of ink, when she jerked open the door to the unexpected knock.

Drenched or not, the packman grinned cheerfully.

"Well?" Anna demanded.

"Buy a song-bird, leddy?"

From a pole balanced on the mannie's shoulder dangled two wicker cages, in each of which huddled a couple of canaries as drab and dank as their captor but lacking his professional chirrup.

"Good God, man, our woods hereabouts are alive wi' birds," said Anna scornfully.

"Aye, but mine are exotics."

"Get awa' wi' ye! Exotics indeed!"

"Buy one an' it'll repay its cost wi' a warblin' that will make your heart soar."

"It'll make my heart sore, right enough, when I find it stiff on its back come the mornin'."

The traveller squinted past her at the blazing fire and bubbling pots but Anna had no charity to spare and did not invite him in out of the rain. In fact she was on the point of slamming the door, since he clearly carried no trinkets or ribbons to entice her, when she noticed the paw.

"What," said Anna, "is that?"

"A monkey."

From the vee of the man's jacket struggled a sad little grey face.

"Is it a real one?"

"Livin' an' breathin', all the way from Guinea," said the packman. "He's of the capuchin breed. I call him Jacko."

"Let me see."

Instantly the packman clapped a protective hand upon the sombre hood. "Nah, nah, mistress. Jack's no' for sale. See the pretty wee songsters instead."

Blinking, Jacko stretched out his arms to Anna as if beseeching her to rescue him from endless roads and interminable rain.

"I'll give you five shillin' for the monkey."

She was aware that the packman might have trudged to Pine Cottage for no other purpose than to trick her into buying the monkey. Perhaps he had heard, while drinking in the Ramshead or the Bull, of the young man on Ottershaw who had a passion for taming wild creatures. It was true that Matt had kept martens and squirrels in cages but they had died quickly in captivity in spite of Matt's care, or because of it.

Anna did not wish to seem gullible but her caution was set against a desperate longing to cuddle the sad little creature to her breast.

She heard herself say, "Eight shillin'."

The offer was extravagant – three weeks' work in the dairy did not earn her such a sum – but she had a few pounds saved from her mother's legacy, money hidden in a stocking in her cupboard, money Matt knew nothing about. He would skin her alive, though, if ever he learned what she had paid for the gift, no matter how much he liked it.

"Ten shillin', take it or run awa'."

"I'll take it."

The packman scooped the capuchin from his jacket and handed it over to Anna. Tail wrapped around her arms, paws like hooks, Jacko clung to the girl, shivering. He smelled, Anna soon discovered, a great deal less appealing than he looked. Even so, she hugged him sentimentally to herself while she went into the cottage, fished out the ten shillings and paid it to the packman who went away, whistling.

Matt was overjoyed with the gift. He kissed Anna to show his gratitude but gave her little enough attention after that, distracted by Jacko's antics. It did not take him long to establish rapport with the animal or for Jacko to become impudent and spoiled.

By Christmas Anna detested the wee brute and cursed the impulse which had urged her to part with good coin to bring him into her life.

Matt Sinclair and his precious Guinea monk were star turns at the Ramshead and the Black Bull. Jacko was enormously popular with the men who gathered in the drinking dens. Jacko would perch on his shoulder and cling to his untidy blond hair and be petted by the boozers. Jacko, in fact, was popular with everybody except Anna and Matt's father; Lachlan Sinclair disapproved of 'alien stock' and the time his son wasted in aimless play.

Over the months Jacko became a source of considerable vexation to Anna. He cheated her of pleasurable hours of peace between her return from work at the dairy and Matt's arrival from the wooded slopes of Drumglass. Jacko, however, was crafty. He kept out of Anna's way when they were alone in the cottage. He would hide up in the beams or hang from the saddle-rail by his tail and spit cherry stones at her or even make water lightly on her hair, swooping and skipping away before the tide of her wrath. If she complained to Matt, her husband simply laughed and informed her that all monks were mischievous. Jacko did not absorb all of Matt's attention, however. Not even the monkey could distract young Sinclair from devising schemes for personal advancement. On that drizzling night in early April, Matt was at it again, chasing yet another rainbow.

"For eighty pounds I could buy enough stock an' all the furnishin's we'd need for a holdin' of our own," Matt said. "We could be shot o' this place as soon as we found a vacant steadin' with a bit o' land attached."

"Aye, so we could," said Anna.

"I'd give an arm an' a leg to watch my father's chops fall when I hand him a quit notice."

"Aye, so would I," said Anna.

Matt stretched one long leg and wiggled his toes, staring at his foot as if wondering how he might dance his way to independence. "Eighty pounds would set us up."

"Aye, so it would." said Anna.

She had removed her heavy skirt and blouse and was comfortable in spite of the heat in the room. Provided Matt had something to turn in his mind he would not notice that she was idle. Once he tired of the daydream, though, he would bark at her to stir her lazy derry, to make the bed, sew a tear in his shirt or even scour the pots with sand. Matt could not bear to see her enjoy a few brief moments of leisure and ease. He had been ruined by his saintly mother, Aileen Sinclair, who was never idle. When she found it necessary to pay a visit to the earth closet, she took with her a small piece of sewing, as if she considered it a mortal sin to sit even there, without domestic occupation. If Aileen Sinclair was not sewing, she would be cooking or cleaning or beating wet clothes or tramping her old spinning-wheel or, if all else was squared away, she would vigorously curry the poor old kitchen cat to keep it free of fleas. To Anna's way of thinking, such an obsession with industry was a frightful affliction which menfolk had no right to condone, let alone encourage.

"At this sale," Matt droned on, "the gear'll go cheap."

In the past eighteen months Anna had been shown dozens of bills and how Matt had heard that the stuff would go cheap was beyond her for the farm in question was at Blairgowrie which was miles away across the Water of Tay in remote Perthshire.

"Aye, if only we could raise some bloody capital," said Matt, "it would give us an opportunity to change our lives."

Realising what was coming next, Anna gave herself a little shake to prepare herself for acrimony. Carefully Matt removed Jacko from his shoulder and set the monkey on his knee where it squatted as on a rock.

"You could ask her for a loan," Matt said.

"Ask who?" Anna knew perfectly well.

"Your sister."

"Even if she had any money of her own, Elspeth wouldn't part with a ha'penny."

"Aye, but she could ask her husband. Moodie dispenses loans all the time. I'd pay him a full rate o' interest," said Matt.

"Matt, I'll not go beggin' to Elspeth."

"It's not beggin', woman. It's the transactin' o' business."

"In that case, talk to Moodie man-to-man."

"I'll not crawl to yon toad."

"But you'd have me crawl to Elspeth?"

"A different matter, a different matter."

"What way is it different?" said Anna.

"Elspeth's your sister."

"In name only. She's not my flesh an' blood."

"Don't carp," said Matt. "She's related to you, she has Jamie Moodie under her thumb, an' she'd wheedle a loan of money out of him if you asked her."

"I'll not do it, Matt."

Anna expected him to fly into a rage but he preferred to sulk. He stroked the capuchin with a gentleness which highlighted his obstinate anger. No matter how long he sulked, though, she would not ask Elspeth for money for a venture that would surely lead to ruin. Matt knew something about horses and, she assumed, about chopping down trees, but he was no farmer. He had been raised as the eldest son of an estate manager and his education had not fitted him to labour mindlessly in the dirt, to the sweat and scrimp and worry — which was the lot of all smallholders.

Since Mammy's death and Elspeth's marriage to a wealthy weaver, Anna had avoided her sister. She preferred to believe that it was Elspeth who was avoiding her and had convinced herself that Elspeth was ashamed of her impoverished relations. Compared with most folk in Balnesmoor and Ottershaw, the Sinclairs were not particularly hard-up. Compared to James Simpson Moodie, however, they were bone-gnawing paupers. James Simpson Moodie owned several lucrative properties, including the new woollen mill at Kennart and the hamlet that had sprung up around it.

It made Anna squirm to see how elegant a situation Elspeth had secured for herself. A foundling reared by a drover, Elspeth Cochran occupied the lady's life as comfortably as a cuckoo would a wagtail's nest. She had servants at her beck and call, a riding-carriage, private gardens and a house of ten apartments to hide in when she wearied of Moodie's doting attentions; all of which cast across Anna's existence a shadow of ordinariness.

Nobody in the parish would have classed either of Gaddy Cochran's daughters as 'ordinary'. Their girlhood had been marked by mystery and intrigue and both had grown into beautiful young women, so exceptional in looks that they could not avoid malicious tattle. Gaddy, then Gaddy Patterson, had first come to Balnesmoor in the company of a rough Highland drover. By sheer chance she had stumbled upon a dead girl on the moor's edge. Under the corpse was a baby, still alive. The dead girl had never been identified or her origins traced but Gaddy had laid claim to the baby, had christened her Elspeth, and had settled to live in a sheep hut leased from Sir Gilbert Bontine, the laird and landowner. If that were not queer enough, scandal had followed in the course of the years when Gaddy attracted a level-headed farmer, Coll Cochran, to her bed. Later, after Anna had been born and Coll's legal wife had died, Gaddy had married him, though that had not been enough 'recompense' for the goodfolk of Balnesmoor. When the Cochrans' home on the hill was washed out by floods, many thought that it was no more than divine retribution for a life of unpalatable wickedness. Only weeks after the disaster Gaddy followed Coll to the grave. Almost before her mother was cold in the ground, Elspeth married James Simpson Moodie and soared above the stigma, once and for all, of being naught but an orphan brat.

Anna could not make up her mind how much guile was in Elspeth, what opportunities had turned on fortune and which stemmed from calculation. No doubt her sister had become very grand but, to Anna's way of thinking, Elspeth had fulfilled her destiny while she herself still had her fate to find.

"Matt?"

Her husband lifted the sale bill and studied it as intently as Mr Eshner, the new minister, studied his Scriptures.

"Matt, will you not answer me?"

Pointedly, Matt ignored her.

Anna hesitated.

If she wished she might bring him out of his pique, take his mind off bankrupt stock and borrowings. His blood was too hot to allow him to resist if she applied her talent for seduction. In that office of marriage Matt was favoured. But making love with Matt was seldom satisfying, for he was quick and gruff and greedy. In a moment, though, he might notice the crusted pots on the hearth and decide to bully her into housework. Better to lure him from his sulk and spend the rest of the evening snug under the blankets in the back-room bed.

Stealthily Anna slipped from the stool and placed a hand on her husband's thigh. Matt flushed. It was a queer game the young Sinclairs played but Matt's desire was kindled by it.

"What's this, what's this?" he asked thickly.

"Matt, I'm fair wearied for my bed."

"Bed, is it?"

"Hmmm!"

Chittering, Jacko jumped from Matt's knee to his shoulder and bared his little teeth at the girl.

"Put him in his box," said Anna. "Quick."

Matt needed no urging. Stepping on to the chair he swung the monkey up and posted it into a wooden box with a wickerwork panel which was roped to the rafters. To the accompaniment of Jacko's angry screams and scratchings Matt stepped down again and, reaching for his wife, fondled her breasts and pressed his body against hers. She caught him by the nape of his neck and brought his mouth to her parted lips.

Farms were forgotten, ambition laid aside. Matt Sinclair burned with healthy desire. He pulled down the straps of her shift and bared her breasts. He nuzzled his mouth against them then impatiently lifted her in his arms and made towards the bedroom while Anna giggled and cried out in mock protest.

Abruptly, without warning, the cottage door flew open and Matt's father stepped into the kitchen.

Lachlan Sinclair's ankle-length greatcoat and cocked hat were pearled with rain. Now in his fiftieth year, his hair was streaked with silver and his face had filled out, relieving it of the gauntness which, a couple of decades before, had made him cadaverously handsome and had fluttered the hearts of many a lass in Ottershaw. But moral rectitude, which had not mellowed with the passage of time, had always been Sinclair's hallmark and he had never taken advantage of his attraction for the opposite sex.

"What's goin' on here?" he demanded.

His eyes blazed at this glimpse of detestable 'modern libertinism'. Outside, through the half-open door, the huge pale face of the grieve's horse peered out of the darkness and gave a feathery neigh which set Jacko ranting loudly in his cage.

Anna was the first to recover her wits.

16

"Matt," she hissed, "put me down."

Matt dropped her like a sack of thieved meal. Anna turned her back, laced up her bodice and pulled a shawl over her bare shoulders. She might have made a joke of it if Matt's frustration had not already boiled over into rage.

"Have you not manners enough to knock before bargin' into a man's privacy?" Matt shouted. "Is this not my home?"

Sinclair said nothing.

Deciding to pour oil on troubled waters Anna dug her husband in the ribs and enquired, "What brings you here, Mister Sinclair?"

Sinclair's indignation vanished. He removed his hat, bowed his head and solemnly announced, "The laird is dead."

"What?" said Anna, taken aback. "Old Sir Gilbert?"

"Aye, my master."

Matt relaxed. "God, but the old devil hung on long enough. How did he pop?"

Sinclair said, "He was just sittin' in his bed, eatin' supper, when he just slumped over."

Never before had Matt seen his father weep. He had assumed that the grieve's ducts were as dry as his heart. The tears nonplussed him. He glanced at Anna.

"Come, Mister Sinclair," said Anna. "Sit yourself down."

She led him to the box chair where he sat for several minutes with his long brown hand covering his face and his shoulders heaving with silent sobs.

Nudged by Anna, Matt awkwardly placed a hand on his father's back and administered a series of tentative little pats by way of consolation. In due course the sobbing dwindled and ceased.

"Aye, Mister Sinclair," said Anna, "you've been with the laird for a wheen o' years."

"Thirty years, lass."

Lachlan Sinclair was the son of the son of a grieve of Ottershaw. No mere foreman, he managed the thriving estate and had made more impression upon Ottershaw than all his ancestors put together. He had a diligent and scientific approach to farming and had been admirably backed by Sir Gilbert. Now, however, with the old laird gone, the prospect of progress was challenged, not by rebellious tenants but by the complications of family dispersal and the absence of the rightful heir, Randall. Sir Gilbert had been an easy-going fellow, content with his lot and conscientious in his duty to his tenants, a model of rustic *noblesse*. His younger son, Young Gibbie, though no fool, was too much influenced by a domineering wife while Randall, wedded to the army, had spent so little time on Ottershaw that he was an enigma to the folk there. Until Randall returned to Scotland, however, or formally renounced his claim to the lion's share of Ottershaw, there could be no forward advance.

True, barley would sprout, ewes would drop lambs, mares foal, trees fall in the plantations and bracken punch its soft green fists through untended soil; the spring calves would suckle blissfully unaware that one feeble old man had finally given up the ghost, that his sons were divided by a Continental war and that a change far removed from the axle of the seasons was about to turn over Ottershaw. Sinclair had good reason to shed tears that April night, for there was no saying what virtues might accompany old Sir Gilbert to the grave.

Anna whispered, "He's upset, Matt. Fair shocked. Give him a dram from your keg."

"What keg?"

"The whisky keg you keep in the hut."

"What do you know of kegs?"

"I'm not blind. I know it's whisky uncontaminated by a duty stamp. Never mind that now. Fetch your father a glass."

Matt grunted, left the kitchen and returned a minute or two later bearing a glass full of cloudy amber liquid which he thrust at his father. Having wiped his eyes and recovered some of his composure, Lachlan accepted the glass, sniffed it and drank a mouthful. His eyes screwed up as if he had sucked on a green lemon.

"What sort of poison is this?"

"Good honest whisky."

"Illicit whisky, I'll wager," said the grieve. "Have you been having dealings with Pad Tomelty?"

"Never heed where it came from," said Matt. "Drink an' be glad of it, Father."

Half the houses in the parish ran wet with the product of Pad Tomelty's illicit stills. It was preferred by discerning tipplers to taxed and tested distillations. The grieve had too many other things on his mind to challenge his son, however.

He drank the rest of the whisky without complaint and returned the glass to Anna. Colour returned to his cheeks and, with brusque formality, he got to his feet, extracted a letter-packet from the breast of his greatcoat and handed it to Matt.

Glancing at the writing on the wrapper, Matt noticed, to his surprise, that it was addressed to Major Randall Bontine. "What? Do you wish me t' carry it to Spain?"

"I wish you to ride to Glasgow and deliver the package into the hands of Colonel Wellman at the Cavalry Barracks in Port Eglington Street."

"Will it not do as well come daylight?"

"What if the regiments have a ship sailin' out of Port Glasgow on the morning tide?" said Sinclair. "Would you have us miss passage because you're reluctant to ride in the dark?"

The Ottershaw lawyers had been in communication with the aged Colonel Wellman as a precaution against the death of Sir Gilbert Bontine. Through Wellman's offices letters and official despatches wended out to the Peninsula for several Scots regiments who were serving there. It was an expedient route; the only route, in fact. Even so, it would be many weeks before Randall received news of his father's passing and signed his name to the documents that the package contained. The documents, when returned, would give Young Gilbert the power to act for the family and might, if Randall were so disposed, relinquish claim to the properties in exchange for a financial settlement.

"Take Sabre," said Sinclair.

"Master Randall's own stallion?"

"It's the fastest horse in the stable."

During his salad days as a stable lad the bloodstock stallion had been Matt's special charge and only he had ever established rapport with the big, skittish horse. Sabre would be sure to impress the cavalry officers at Port Eglinton Street with the fact that Ottershaw was no tuppenny sty and that the Bontines were quality folk.

"Am I to go alone?"

"You are. But hurry, Matthew, I beg you."

Anna had already gone into the back room to find Matt's riding breeks and his good black coat. It would be a wet and dirty ride and he would arrive dishevelled but at least he would start off looking smart.

It would hardly matter, of course, what he looked like, for the decrepit officers who staffed the Glasgow barracks would not take notice of a servant, even if he were riding a fine thoroughbred stallion. Their minds would be fixed on the faraway war in Spain. By comparison Bontine business would seem trivial and the letter would be consigned to an ordinary mail coach or a slow vessel out of Leith. Eventually, though, it might find its way to Randall Bontine who, Anna imagined, might very well read it with a shrug of indifference and go on to light his cigar with the document, leaving Gibbie to fret and fume for months or even years.

While Matt shaved and dressed, Anna stayed in the back room. She listened, head cocked, to the purl of male voices. It was the first time she had heard father and son communicate close and confidential. Perhaps there was hope for Matt's future yet. Perhaps Sinclair would soften and restore him to a rung of the ladder that would lead one day to Matt becoming the grieve of Ottershaw.

"Anna."

The girl rose from the side of the bed and at once went into the kitchen.

Matt looked well enough in the rig. He held his head haughtily and kissed her, without urging, upon the cheek. It was as if the damned great lump imagined that *he* was going to fight the French and find glory under the guns. She managed not to smile, though, as Matt solemnly shook his father's hand and, with the letter-packet safe in his jacket, strode out of the door and unhitched the horse that his father had ridden from the stables. Sabre would be saddled and waiting in the stable yard, champing in annoyance at having his night's rest disturbed. The grieve and the girl listened to the sounds of the horse fade into quiet, rain-hissing darkness. Even Jacko seemed caught in the hiatus, paws clenched to the wickerwork, face screwed up in enquiry.

Anna cleared her throat. "Would you care for another dram, Mister Sinclair?"

Although he had given her permission to do so, Anna could not bring herself to call him Father.

Sinclair shook his head. "Why do you burn such a wasteful fire?"

"To keep the monkey warm."

"Aye, him and his precious monk." Sinclair shook his head once more; his son's habits were quite beyond fathom. "Are you with child yet?"

"Nature'll decide when it's time for me to bear, Mister Sinclair." Out of devilment, Anna added, "It's no' for want of tryin', be assured."

Sinclair grunted and reached his hat from the table, his thoughts turning to pressing events at the mansion. Though funeral arrangements would be decided upon by Young Gibbie, Sinclair would be required to execute them. Certainly he would have to gather the servants and estate workers and inform them, officially, that the laird was dead. Word would be half-way to Stirling by now, of course, since news of that magnitude spread like wildfire.

Anna opened the door for her father-in-law then put a hand on his sleeve.

"Mister Sinclair?"

"Aye, lass?"

"Will he come home?"

"He'll be home tomorrow forenoon."

"I meant Mister Randall."

Sinclair hesitated. "He might. Aye, he might."

"I hope he does," said Anna.

The fact that she had an opinion at all surprised the grieve. "Why so?"

"He'll be a better master than Gibbie."

"You'd do well to remember that Mister Gilbert may be our new laird and learn to speak of him with more respect."

"Equally, though, Mister Randall might be our new laird," Anna insisted.

"It'll hardly matter in the dairy," said Sinclair. "The hands'll be treated fairly by either one since they're both Bontines an' their father's sons."

Sinclair pulled open the door. The conversation had made him faintly uneasy. Air flicked at his hair and flapped the skirts of his greatcoat. He turned and bade his daughter-in-law a curt good night. Sensibly Anna asked no more questions, but shivering a little, stood at the cottage door and watched the erect figure of the grieve merge into the trees. She closed the door and turned against it.

Letting the shawl slip from her shoulders, she permitted a broad grin to stretch her lips and, thrusting herself forward, performed an impromptu little jig around the kitchen table. Jacko scowled disapprovingly from above. The passing of the old laird affected Anna not one jot, except inasmuch as it might persuade Randall to return to Ottershaw and take possession of its policies and all the folk who dwelled thereon; herself, of course, included.

Several years ago, when she was little more than a child, she had kissed the handsome soldier. The memory of that evening had never been far from Anna's thoughts. She wondered if Randall Bontine remembered it too. Remembered her. Fancifully, she imagined he might think of her and weigh her a bit in the balance when he came to make his decision.

Suddenly the capuchin screamed, eyes glittering with inexplicable malevolence. The din made Anna start and immediately abandon her dance. Hands on hips she scowled up at the monkey in its box. She considered releasing it, for that was what Matt would want her to do, then changed her mind. Picking the lamp from the table she swept through to bed, leaving the litter in the kitchen untouched and Matt's pet to swelter in his cage in the rafters. With the door firmly closed Jacko's chatter would not disturb her unduly, not tonight when, at peace, she might uninhibitedly dream of a soldier lover and Randall Bontine's return to Ottershaw.

For many a gallant Highlander the night march to Almarez would be the last duty he would perform in the service of King George. Half the regiment would be dead before daylight. The lads carried that knowledge with them like extra bags of shot. They had been buoyed up by the recent capture of Cuidad Rodrigo and the surrender of Badajoz but their enthusiasm for the latest campaign waned as they trudged along the paths that the Spanish guides had picked out across the pitch-black mountains of the Lina.

Plans had already been evolved and finalised. Backed by a battalion of Portuguese caçadores, General Chowne's 'slashers' would storm the castle of Miravete which towered over the pass and protected the road to Madrid. General

Long's column would tackle the French garrison's war-works beyond the summit where stout gates and palisades bristled with muskets and cannon.

Composed mainly of Gordons and Highland Light Infantry, General Howard's brigade had been given the task of taking the French forts of Ragusa and Napoleon which defended the line of the river in front of the little town.

Sir Rowland Hill accompanied the Scots, riding with Howard at the head of the straggling column. Not far behind the commanders and their aides rode two seasoned officers, Iain Stuart and Randall Bontine. They were both of the rank of major and rivals for the honour of leading the dawn attack upon Fort Napoleon. The great attraction for the officers was the fact that the battle would surely become that most desperate and glorious of all military enterprises – a forlorn hope.

Bontine's application had been first into the general's hand but the charge would probably be given to Stuart who was favoured for his bluffness and blunt manner. Besides, Bontine was still regarded as an interloper, a Hussar, though he had served as liaison to the Highlanders for twenty arduous months. It would be Stuart who would wag the claymore at the head of the storming party, Bontine was a name that trailed no legends outside a wee patch of farmland west of Stirling, whereas Iain Stuart belonged to that race of kings and tinkers worshipped by the Gaels, and owned a castle in misty Kintail.

Bontine's value to the Scotch brigades lay not in the speed of his sabre but in the quickness of his tongue. He spoke fluent French and Portuguese and was versed in the ninety-nine variants of Spanish, from the red-rough jabber of sierra guerrillas to the soft sallow dialects of the Andalusian plain's folk. He could converse with priests in a Latin as formal as a cardinal's and could address nuns with a charm that was utterly at odds with his appearance, having features which might have been shaped by Satan to tempt novices from their vows. With tunic top discarded, shirt unlaced, Major Bontine looked more Spanish than Pedro Gomez, the matador turned desperado.

In contrast, Stuart cultivated a granite-like smoothness, all shaven and polished. He showed no scars to the world whereas

Bontine had scars in plenty, including one that quirked the corner of his lip into a wry smile. High cheekbones, a complexion the colour of walnut wood and hair worn curled in a style that the Highlanders abdured set the Hussar apart from his fellow officers. He did not much care for their manners and did not encourage friendships, except when out-piquet duty was on offer or there was a charge to be led, for Randall Bontine loved not just the heat of combat but the proximity of death and longed for the opportunity to rub close to death's pale garment time and again.

In Egypt and during the bloody months of struggle in the Peninsula, fate had dealt generously with Bontine's queer appetite for danger. As he guided his mare down the stumbling path between the woods of Truxillo and the river Tagus, with cassions and tumbrils rattling and groaning in the dark around him, Randall Bontine felt a little on edge, eager to be once more engaged with the oldest enemy of all. Somehow, though, he must attach himself officially to the storming party and be in the vanguard of the action. It was there that real glory might be found, that he might test his courage to its limit. He glanced slyly at the passionless Major Stuart riding flank to flank with him and turned over in his brain how he might persuade the fellow to let him take the claymore.

Almarez was hardly an inspiring location for brave deeds. The town was merely a handful of hovels backed on to an ancient stone bridge which had been ruined by bombardment. Some way downstream, the French had constructed a pontoon to link their forts. The first fort, Napoleon, was exceedingly well-entrenched and protected by heavy cannon and about three hundred troops. Sir Rowland Hill had explained to the officers that a surprise attack would be impossible. Chowne's 'slashers' would have to charge the garrison at Miravete first where the Frenchies would ignite signal rockets and tar-barrels to alert the river forts and bring them immediately to arms.

At length the Highlanders, weary and bruised, emerged from the foothills on to the flat pastures which spread to the river. Hardly had the last Gordon set foot upon level ground before the sky across the hill turned livid with flashes and flares as musket and cannon shot reverberated down the valley. The assault on Miravete had begun.

A flock of goats, which miraculously had escaped French

foraging parties, came bleating down the sward. Confronted by a priest and a couple of English generals, the animals unhesitatingly flung themselves into the river only to be tugged out of sight by coiling currents. Encumbered by weapons, hammers, levers and scaling-ladders, the soldiers sought to separate themselves and reform in some sort of order some little distance from the bank of the Tagus. Once in formation they would be given a few minutes' stand-down before being marshalled for the dawn attack. Randall Bontine stuck close to Major Stuart. He also tried to keep Sergeant McIver in sight while he fought the restlessness which the confusion roused in his wiry and unreliable mare. Fifty or sixty yards away, on the summit of a low hill, the staff officers' tent was being erected, giving centre to the bedlam. It would be a matter of ten minutes or a quarter of an hour before Stuart and he would be called to the general's table and the charge finally allocated.

Bontine slid from the saddle and calmly unpacked his breakfast. Stuart dismounted also. He watched the Hussar unroll a spotted kerchief and take from it a fist of beef, roasted black but appetising enough for a soldier after a hard night's march. Bontine tore off a bite and, without a word, offered the fist to the Highlander. Stuart shook his head, determined to go into battle on an empty belly, as the *Manual of Arms* advised, lest he was gut shot and the ball had to be extracted by surgeon's forceps. Bontine grinned and tore another mouthful from the meat. He also had a wine-bag full of dry Jerez. He offered it too to Stuart and was again refused.

"Och, aye, Major," said Bontine, laying on the accent thick, "it'll be a braw sort o' mornin' for a fecht, I'm thinkin'."

"That it will, sir," Iain Stuart answered.

Expertly Bontine sucked from the teat of the wine-bag and wiped his mouth on his sleeve. Stuart turned. His valet was waiting to be given instruction but Stuart waved him away. There was nothing, at this moment, for the majors to do. To assist in the work of the brigadiers would have been unseemly and they dared not intrude, until summoned, upon the deliberations of the generals. In formation soldiers lay about on the ground among a welter of equipment. To get away from the Hussar more than anything, Stuart picked clear of the sprawl and guided his horse to a sprig of the river to allow it to drink. With the wine-bag slung across his shoulder and a cheroot stuck in his mouth, Bontine, tormentingly, followed.

Across the river the vineyards and orange trees of Almarez seemed to be asleep. The abutments of the old bridge were visible against a lightening sky. Some distance downstream the sluggish current slapped and rippled against the floats of the French pontoon. Now that they were able to survey the terrain at first hand, both Stuart and Bontine saw how painfully exposed the storming party would be as it made its run on Fort Napoleon. Side-by-side, while the horses dipped to drink, Highlander and Lowlander stared at the scene that softly emerged from the May morning mist.

"It is," murmured Stuart, "ominously still, is it not, Bontine?"

"It'll be frantic enough below the trench walls if I know the Frenchies."

"If, sir, it was given to you to lead the storming party," said Stuart, "how would you approach the task?"

"It will not be my party, Stuart."

"Perhaps not; but how?"

Bontine pointed his cheroot to the right. "To gain a few precious yards of cover I would approach from the line of scrub. The German rifles would then be able to fire over the heads of our column as it pressed upon the *tête-du-pont*. The leader of the storming party must ensure that the earth ramps are surmounted and the French guns stilled before the main attack begins or there will be a fearful slaughter. It is the only possible approach.'

'I agree, Bontine."

The officers glanced behind them as fresh explosions rocked Miravete and flames shot, angry and profound into the sullen cloud which quilted the sierra.

"Powder kegs," said Stuart.

The officers were silent, thinking of soldiers caught by the blast, of the hellish agony of black powder burns.

Stuart cleared his throat. "Go on, Bontine."

"One must have a taste for simplicity, Major, to derive enjoyment from this prospect. God, a weasel could find no shelter on the sward between the trees and the rampart," said Bontine.

"How would you tackle it?" Stuart said. "If you had command."

"I would tackle it – as you will, no doubt – with a cry in my throat and my sword in my fist and the lads hugging my rump. I'd be first up the first ladder and would not turn my face from the front no matter how heavy the odds."

"Fine words for a Cavalry officer."

"I had no horse under me at the battle of Albuera; only rocks and dirt like every other Scot who fought there!"

"Were you not afraid?" said Stuart.

"No, Stuart, I was not afraid."

"Then you have no humanity, sir."

"That – sir – may very well be true."

"Or you are a teller of lies."

"If that's your opinion, Major, why do you not put me to the test? You will be given charge of the storming party, of that there's no doubt, but do you not appoint your own supernumerary?"

"What if I do?"

"Appoint me."

"So that's what you require, is it? To be my first officer?"

"It is."

"A desperate honour, Bontine."

"To be first over the wall of Napoleon will be honour enough for me."

"Aye, but will the clansmen follow you?" said Stuart.

"If you give them the chance they will follow even a Hussar when the fighting's fierce enough and their blood is roused."

From the assembly ground came the shouts of sergeants and the snapping voices of haughty young subalterns from the kennel by the generals' tent. In the bleary light it seemed that the field was sprouting soldiers like dragon's teeth.

"Come, Stuart, grant me the favour," said Randall Bontine urgently. "What harm can it do? I am, after all, a major too. Would you have a mere captain dogging your footsteps into the *Gazette*?" Bontine bit his lip. "Please, Stuart."

It appealed to Stuart's vanity to hear Bontine plead. He had not, in fact, considered whom he would invite to support him. He had no particular officer in mind for the appointment.

"Major Stuart tae the general's table," cried a voice from

the field. "Assemble for attack, sur, in five minutes. Major Stuart, sur, dae I have your ear?"

"Aye, I hear you, Sergeant," Stuart replied.

The Highlander drew his horse from the shallows, petted its muzzle and walked it away, side-by-side with Bontine and the mare. The tops of the mountains were clear against the milky sky to the east while the hovels of Almarez had emerged from the night. It would have been a scene of utmost rural tranquillity, except for the clank of war machines and the boom of cannon from the heights. Stuart paused. Bontine and he were boxed by the flanks of their mounts, brought into intimacy by the sleek, wet shoulders.

Stuart said, "It is at this hour that my thoughts turn to my homeland and my heart yearns for Kintail. Would that I could smell the heather on the fens and hear the lowin' of my fine cattle on the slopes of Elchaig."

Bontine had no stomach for such moist sentimentality. Elchaig, he suspected, would be a midden of rain-soaked peat and skittering scree, possessed of beauty for the six or eight days in the year when the sun managed to penetrate the mirk.

Stuart went on, "Would that I might spend but a moment now on the bonnie shore of Loch Alsh with my dear father at my side; then I could die content!"

Randall Bontine seldom squandered a thought for Ottershaw or the parish of Balnesmoor, hide-bound and petty, or for his feeble old father who had nothing on his brain but sheep, sheep, sheep. He gave a sigh, though, to indicate to Stuart that in spite of his flamboyance he was a lugubrious Scot at heart.

"Aye, Stuart, but we have chosen to be soldiers and must fight nobly. To die well in battle is the fate my own dear father would wish for me."

"You speak the truth, Bontine." Stuart wiped his shiny face with a granite hand. "You may have charge of the second rank of the storming party if that is your wish."

"It is my dearest wish."

"The appointment is yours," said Stuart.

"You have my gratitude, sir," said Randall Bontine, who had no intention of dying for anyone or anything, least of all for a parboiled notion of nobility.

Stuart offered his hand in manly amnesty. "Good luck to you, Bontine."

"God be with you, Stuart," Randall Bontine answered and, having gained his ends, stuck the cheroot back in his mouth and led the mare to tether without wasting another word on the pompous idiot from Kintail.

That part of Balnesmoor which lay east of the village was known as the Orrals, a name whose origin was lost in lore and legend. Sprawling between the enclosures of the Strath and the summits of the Campsie Fells, it was unfettered, uncouth country owned in part by the Bontines, though no posts marked the portion and it featured only nominally in valuations of the estate. Few local people ever set foot upon its acreage. Its grazing was callow and cattle there put to cud had the habit of dying without visible cause, giving rise to the rumour that the place was cursed.

Elspeth's childhood had been spent only a mile from the edge of the Orrals, under the shadow of the hill of Drumglass. But she did not know the eastern tract at all, though she had often walked its bordering road, holding Anna's hand, on the way to school in Balfron and had looked often enough upon its rough, uninviting acres from the hind side of Dyers' Dyke in the days when the Cochrans had tenancy of the farm. But residence in Moss House as the wife of James Moodie had altered her perspectives and the Orrals, lying just behind the house, had become a refuge from gentility.

Perhaps the wild moorland reminded her of her girlhood on the Nettleburn. Perhaps it offered contrast to the solid satinwood elegance of Moss House. Perhaps it sheltered her from knowledge of the proximity of Kennart where her husband's looms whacked out a fortune in wool goods and the mill-workers' rows were full of babble as if the men had taken on the faults of the jennies and scribbling machines to add to their human failings.

By stepping over the stile tucked at the rear of formal gardens, only a half-mile from the bustling backs of Main Street, Elspeth could be as cut off from Balnesmoor as if she had been whisked to a virgin continent. She would remove her slippers and stockings and hide them in a bush. She would tie up her skirts with a cloth belt and bare-legged and barefoot

29

like a fisher lassie would wade into the bracken and cross to the little glen where the burn dropped down from the hill.

It might well be that James knew where she spent her afternoons, though even her husband would hardly have a spy on the Orrals. No tyrant at home, James was aware of how much she detested Kennart. He did not insist that she visited the new community or interest herself charitably in the lives of his workers. Kennart was so changed from the days when the bridge spanned a calm, brown pool, and the village lads, Matt Sinclair among them, came down to bathe on warm summer evenings. Whether James did or did not know about her fondness for the Orrals, Elspeth pretended that it was her secret place. Cautiously she avoided showing herself on the ridge which was overtopped by Dyers' Dyke. The Cochrans' farm was now occupied by a shepherding family, employees of James, and if they saw her they might take word back to the master. She kept to the glen, a great sag in the contour, well coated and lush, where, below the line to which grouse laid claim, pheasants, horned in emerald, strutted in a stand of rye grass.

In fighting fig, the cocks were eager to attract as many hens as their territory would bear. Elspeth had watched the preliminary mating dances and could identify individual specimens, even among the dowdy brown females. In a frayed quarto volume from James's library, she had read that the laying season for pheasants stretched into June. But as a rule there was little enough science in the young woman's observations. She was no recorder, no list-maker, nor did she delve into the new sort of literature which sought to explain everything by rigid reasoning and evidence of fact.

The sky that May day was fresh, with scuts of white cloud moving against a bolt of pale blue and in the glen the sun beat down so warmly that Elspeth discarded her wrap. She sat cross-legged in the lee of a rock watching the cock pheasants confront each other.

The man was stationed, not thirty yards from her, across the neck of the glen. For a moment after she detected his presence she thought that it might be Matt, her brother-in-law, then, heart thudding, she realised that he was a stranger. He smiled and raised a finger to his lips.

Elspeth would not be stilled. She instantly rose and un-hitched her skirts to hide her bare legs.

"Wait," the stranger called. "I intend you no harm."

"Who are you, pray?"

"I am called Michael Blaven."

"What do you do here?"

"I might ask the same question of you."

Elspeth's instincts urged her to scramble up the slope and run through the bracken to the safety of James's garden; yet she sensed no malice in the man, and lingered, intrigued. Besides, the width of the glen still separated them.

"I'm Mistress Moodie. I live just there, on the Harlwood Road," she announced, like a warning.

"Are you, by chance, wife to James Moodie?"

"I am."

"I have heard of you."

"Have you, indeed?" said Elspeth crisply. "Now, sir, you have told me your name but not the nature of your business on the Orrals."

"I've come here to gather plants for my aunt. Perhaps you know her? Janet Blaven of Preaching Friar."

Elspeth relaxed her guard. Miss Blaven was a dabbler in green medicine, sufficiently independent and well-to-do to rouse no hostility even in those Philistines who scorned spinster healers and thought them to be agents of the devil. Miss Blaven's thatched cottage, which bore the odd name of Preaching Friar, lay in a dell beyond the Harlwood print-fields. James had once pointed it out to Elspeth as they rode back from dinner with Mr Rudge.

"I know of your aunt," Elspeth admitted. "But we have not met."

"May I extricate myself from this bush and come round to talk with you?"

"Talk of what, sir?"

"To exchange pleasantries, without unseemly bawling."

Elspeth nodded. "If you wish."

She took herself to the top of the slope and glanced anxiously towards Moss House. She could just make out the tops of the trees at the garden's end. She was nervous of meeting the strange young man though he was no tinker or footpad but a relative of a woman of excellent reputation. Unless, Elspeth

31

thought, he is lying, but it was too late to retreat. She stood her ground as he made round by the neck of the glen, stepped over the burn and waded through the heather to join her.

Michael Blaven wore an open-throated shirt and cutaway coat of burled tweed. His cuffs were turned up and fastened neatly with twine. Around his shoulder was a leather game-bag. Like Elspeth he was bare-legged and barefoot. His hair was dark brown and soft and his skin pale, except for a spot of colour on each cheek. As if to establish his *bona fides*, he immediately opened the game-bag and produced a linen pouch which he held out to her.

"Dandelion root," he said. "According to my aunt, best taken when spring sap rises in the stem."

Cautiously Elspeth sniffed the little sack. She did not know what dandelion root smelled like, but the odour was faint and she was willing to take the stranger on trust. He popped the pouch back into the bag, gave her a bow and offered his hand. In town society the gesture would have been considered a flagrant breach of etiquette and Elspeth would have been obliged to treat the gentleman coldly. But the Orrals was far removed from Edinburgh's salons and she gave him her hand without hesitation.

"Madam," he said. "It is an honour."

He held her fingers lightly for a moment and did not smarm over them with his lips, a custom which Elspeth deplored. It surprised Elspeth how appealing she found the stranger's attentions. She was used to brittle, insincere flattery, to the application of cold charm, the coin of many of James's associates. Mr Blaven, however, was friendly without being forward. Even so, Elspeth could find nothing to say to him. She had no common ground with the gentleman. She could not enquire about the state of crops or the prices of wool or the speed of the new coach to York. She knew nothing at all about Michael except that he was related to Janet Blaven and collected dandelion roots.

As if appreciating her difficulty, Michael said, "Pheasants never cease to give me amusement. They remind me of Glasgow dowagers."

Elspeth seized the lead. "Are you from Glasgow, then?"

"I am currently residing in Harlwood with my aunt."

She could not be sure whether or not he had intentionally

evaded her question. "Are you a cuckoo or a bird of passage?"

"I'm a sparrow in the attic," said Michael. "Just a simple town lad lost in the confusions of the countryside."

"But you're not ill-versed in country matters," said Elspeth. "At least you can tell a pheasant from a peacock."

"And a hawk from a handsaw."

"I beg your pardon?"

"It's a line from a play."

"I've never been to a play," said Elspeth.

"Well, you've missed little," said Michael. "Theatres are stuffy, vulgar places."

Elspeth said, "Are you an apothecary?"

"Lord, no!"

"But you do assist your aunt?"

"Perhaps I should become an apothecary, a pupil of Aunt Janet. In fact, I'm without a profession. I have abandoned all ambition to forge ahead in the world and have settled for the life of a recluse."

"Have you no family, apart from your aunt?"

"I've no wife and no children." He dismissed the question airily. "What of you?"

"What of me?"

"I am, I confess, surprised to find the wife of James Moodie alone on the Orrals in the middle of the afternoon."

"I'm not kept under lock and key, Mister Blaven!"

"I did not mean to suggest it. But are there no tea-drinkings, no calls for you to make as part of your duties as a wife?"

"Not today," said Elspeth.

"I am glad of it."

"Are you? I'm puzzled as to why it should make you glad or sorry how I spend my afternoons."

"If you had had a tea engagement, Mistress Moodie, I should not, in all likelihood, have met you."

"I think, Mister Blaven, I must return home now."

"I didn't intend to be forward."

"It's not that," said Elspeth. "It's simply – simply time for me to go home."

"May I walk with you to your gate?"

Quickly Elspeth said, "No. I prefer to go alone."

Michael gave a gentle shrug of understanding. "In that

case, with permission, I'll go back to grubbing along the burn bank for more wild Taraxacum."

"Is your bag not near full?"

"No, alas. My aunt requires vast quantities of spring root. Dried and powdered it constitutes a wonderful specific for disorders of the liver and kidney."

"My mother used to take it from time to time, for purifying her blood," said Elspeth.

"I'll ask my aunt to deliver some to your mother, if I may."

"My mother died these two years since."

"Ah!" Michael paused respectfully. "Do you have children, Mistress Moodie?"

"No, I have no children," said Elspeth. "Now, I must go."

"Perhaps we'll encounter each other again."

"I fear not, Mister Blaven. I seldom come to walk on the Orrals. My 'duties' keep me o'er busy."

"That's unfortunate,' said Michael. "I've enjoyed our conversation very much."

"Good afternoon to you, Mister Blaven."

"Good afternoon, Mistress Moodie."

Swiftly she turned and walked along the indistinct path that would carry her to the shoulder from which she might see not just the tree-tops but, solid and safe, the chimney-heads of Moss House. Although she did not pause to glance behind, she sensed that Michael was standing at the edge of the glen watching her, watching over her until the hunch of the moor put her finally out of sight.

Four girls knelt on the floor. Two were dairy-maids from Ottershaw. The second pair were sisters from the hamlet of Eardmore which lay three or four miles into the hills.

"Go on then, Anna, will ye ask her for a readin'?" said Brigit Tomelty. "I haven't got all day t' loiter here."

Shafts of sunlight penetrated the broken roof of the ruined hut in the bramble thicket and dappled the earth floor with shadow. A candle flickered, smoke rather than light adding to the atmosphere of conspiracy. The sisters, Wynn and Marian Sylas, had brought the red-wax candle stump along with other paraphernalia.

Anna said, "First tell me if he's still alive."

Brigit Tomelty said, "Ye'll need t' give him a proper name. It'll not work wi'out a proper name."

Anna drew in a deep breath. She was reluctant to reveal her secret but had no alternative. She caught Brigit's arm. "On pain o' death, tell nobody outside this place."

"Nah, nah! You can trust me, Anna."

"Well," Anna took the plunge, "his name's Randall Bontine."

"Bontine!" Brigit let out a wicked chuckle. "Damn me, you have gall, Mistress Sinclair, so ye have."

In a dead, flat sort of tone Marian, the dummy's sister, said, "Haud yer tongue, Brigit."

"Is Master Randall Bontine o' Ottershaw still in the land o' the livin'?" Anna solemnly enquired.

The girls fell silent. Even Brigit Tomelty's eyes grew round as Wynn Sylas's head began to thrash about on the cabbage-stalk neck. The dummy wore a bright print-cotton dress, sizes too large for her. About her throat were strings of carved wooden beads which clucked and chuckled as her head rolled.

"Is she havin' a fit?" murmured Brigit.

"Let her do her wark," said her sister.

It was weird work, indeed, for half a crown. Anna regretted having ventured into this game which the sisters from Eardmore had transformed into something more serious and possibly dangerous. She could not withdraw from it now, however, not without insulting Brigit who had arranged the meeting.

Brigit Tomelty was one of the many children of Pad Tomelty, the whisky smuggler, and nobody could understand why Sinclair had ever agreed to give her work on Ottershaw, unless Sinclair too had been intimidated by her evil eye. But Brigit was gentle with cattle, could coax an extra quart out of the slackest teat and was also punctual at the milking stool, which was more than could be said for some lassies. Brigit was also possessed of all sorts of arcane knowledge, quite beyond the ken of the simple village girls, who held her in awe. The 'new' generation might be godless but the sinews of superstition were strong in them. Besides, they loved inducing 'the shivers' and discovered in Brigit a brashness that was easy to confuse with evil. Not knowing quite what she wanted or expected, Anna had approached Brigit about three weeks after old Sir Gilbert had been put into his grave in the Balnesmoor kirkyard. The affair had been disappointingly dull and, like Matt's ride to Glasgow, had promised more diversion than it delivered. Brigit was quick to sniff mischief in Anna's tentative request and relieved Sinclair's young wife of a shilling in exchange for arranging a full-blown 'reading'.

Anna did not know what a 'reading' entailed. She thought it would be cards or hazel sticks. She had not expected it to be done by Wynn, the deaf-and-dumb lass from Eardmore, who was reputed to speak the truth; or rather to record the truth upon her scratched school slate. The mute's prophetic gifts were scorned by cynics who pointed out that her sister Marian was the biggest gossip in the county and that Wynn's amazing predictions were vague things open to all sorts of interpretations. Whatever the truth might be, Brigit Tomelty professed a belief in the dummy's powers and that was recommendation enough for Anna.

Eyes half closed, lashes flickering, Wynn mouthed the name, "*Randall Bontine*", without uttering a sound.

Anna could see the stunned tongue taking a big lick out of the words. The dummy's hand rose. In it, held like a dagger, was a wedge of cloth-cutter's chalk. On the dummy's lap, leaning against her breast, Marian placed the old school slate. The hand slashed at the slate. Letters appeared with incredible rapidity.

LIVE

"He's alive," said Brigit. "We've learned that much."

"Where is he?" Anna asked.

It was impossible to make sense of the writings of Wynn's tongue but the word fisted on to the blackened board was clear enough.

SPAN

"Spain," said Brigit. "Is that no' right, Anna?"

"I'm askin' *her*, Brigit, an' payin' sweet for *her* answers."

Anna was uneasy, feeling that she might be the victim of an elaborate fraud. So far, she had been given nothing but the word *Spain*, which anybody in the county could have surmised since Randall Bontine was a soldier.

Wynn's mouth was a crinkled line, head cocked to one side as if she were puzzled by the images that floated behind her lids. Letters flicked off the chalk in what seemed to be an

36

illiterate jumble which only became readable after the hand had lifted away.

FLAG SORD SUN WATER SMOK DETH

Anna sat bolt upright.

"Death?"

"It's a battle," said Brigit; Marian nodded agreement. "Randall Bontine's fightin' a bloody battle."

Wynn glanced, puzzled, at her sister and shook her head.

"That's all she can see," Marian announced.

"A wee bit of a battle," said Anna, "is not enough for half a crown. I could've predicted it m'self without leavin' the kitchen."

Brigit Tomelty tended to agree that an element of deception had been put upon them. "Come on, Marian, get her t' dole out a drop more, eh?"

No signs or signals passed between the sisters and Anna wondered if the dummy was not truly mute or if she had learned to read from the lips by careful study.

"More, Wynn, eh?" Brigit cajoled.

Resolutely the deaf-and-dumb girl shook her head.

"It's a damned cheat," Anna declared.

Wynn was staring at her, her gaze even more disconcerting than the Reverend Eshner's pink-rimmed stare. It seemed to penetrate right to the truth in Anna's heart.

Wynn groped behind her and produced a book, a Holy Bible.

Flat and thin, Marian smiled. "Wynn says she'll make a bindin' for you, Anna Sinclair, since you're not satisfied wi' her readin'."

"A bindin'? I hope it's better value than a readin'."

"Aye, far better value," Marian Sylas promised. "Wynn likes fine t' do bindin' spells."

"Get on wi' it, then," said Brigit.

The dummy handed the Bible to Marian. It was a perfectly ordinary volume with a grained cloth cover, an edition distributed to young people when they became fledged members of the Kirk. But the unexpected appearance of the Holy Book at such a convention disturbed Anna considerably. It raised in her a terrible dread, as if the power of the mute from the hills had been put above suspicion. Within the Bible was a long, iron door-key, head and handle projecting from the

Book's ends. Marian Sylas opened the Book at the place marked by the door-key and beckoned Anna to come closer.

Anna, on her knees, shifted reluctantly.

"Here." Marian placed her fingernail on a verse in the Book of Ruth. "Read this part aloud an' try to remember it."

"What for?"

"Read on 'til I tell ye to stop."

"I'm not readin' –"

"The words will bind you to your loved one," said Marian.

"Maybe the spell'll no' work on a laird," Brigit suggested.

"This spell is powerful enough to work on anybody," said Marian. "You, Brigit Tomelty, take the handle o' the key an' place it on the tips o' your fingers."

"Me? What for are ye needin' my assistance?"

"You're a neutral pole," Marian answered.

"No. I –"

"Do it, Brigit," said Anna.

The handle of the key was placed gingerly on Brigit's fingertips, the head of the key rested on Anna's, the Bible held open where she could see it.

"Now," said Marian, "read an' remember."

Anna read, "*Entreat me not to leave thee, or to return from following after thee: for whither thou goest, I will go; and where thou lodgest, I will lodge: thy people shall be my people: where thou diest –*" Anna hesitated, lifted her gaze to Wynn who smiled reassuringly; she continued, "*thou diest, will I die and there will I be buried: the Lord do so to me, and more also, if ought but death part thee and me.*"

"Can ye remember it?"

"Aye, I'll try."

Carefully Marian Sylas placed the Bible over the key and closed it. She bound it with two grey cotton tapes and adjusted it into balance again on the girls' fingertips. With new fervour Wynn wriggled forward on her bottom and touched the upper cover of the Bible with a gesture as light as thistledown. By now Anna was desperately afraid. In seeking the service of the mute from Eardmore she had not imagined that, before the afternoon was over, she would be calling on the power of the Lord to invoke love in Randall Bontine, if love it was.

The Holy Book was quite horizontal.

Marian Sylas said, "You're the enquirer, Anna Sinclair."

"What . . . what do I do?"

"Entreat awa'."

She had paid a tidy sum of money for 'contact' with Randall Bontine. She had longed with all her heart for the laird's soldier son to remember her with the same pervasive force as she recalled him. But she had not, until that moment, ever believed that he would. A sensible part of her character knew that the likes of Randall Bontine had kissed, and God knows what else, hundreds of girls and that he would hardly be likely to recall an incident on the banks of the Lightwater all those months ago. Now, however, that sensible core was silenced by the precision of the ceremony.

"Entreat," Marian ordered.

Anna began hesitantly but found that the verses slid from her tongue as if she had rehearsed them for days.

"*. . . will I die and there will I be buried: the Lord do so to me, and more also, if ought but death part thee and me.*"

"Again," said Marian.

"But why?"

"It hasn't taken yet."

"*Entreat me not to leave thee, or to return from following after thee: for whither thou goest, I will go; and where thou lodgest –*"

The Bible tilted suddenly on the key. It hung from its spine for an instant then clapped down to the floor, plucking the iron key from the girls' fingers. Brigit cried out and snatched her hand away as if it had been burned. She scowled at Wynn, but the dummy had exerted no pressure at all and only the natural little pulses in the girls' fingers had disturbed the Book's balance. Not Brigit, who had no more religion than a doorpost, and certainly not Anna, would have accepted such a rational explanation at that moment. To the Ottershaw lassies a deep old magic had clinched the spell.

Anna's upper lip was dewed with perspiration. She felt exhausted, as if she had sent her spirit in pursuit of Randall Bontine and the chase had been long and arduous.

"I'll . . . I'll need to be makin' awa' now," stammered Brigit, who had been shaken by a ceremony which she had not witnessed before and which lay outwith the range of vices to which she normally subscribed. "Are ye comin', Anna?"

"Go, then," said Marian. "Wynn can do no more for ye. It's all set an' dyed into the cloth. Indelible."

Huskily Anna said, "I give ye both thanks."

Wynn sat like a great raggy doll, legs stuck out, head cocked, a tiny crease of satisfaction on her lips. Slate and chalk lay by her thigh, Bible and key on the ground between her feet. It was the last image that Anna had of the mute from Eardmore for, with Brigit tugging at her hand, she got to her feet and quickly left the bramble hut, hurrying away down the overgrown path towards the cow pasture. Wynn, smiling still, watched the dairy-maids depart.

Touching Wynn's soft, unhealthy cheeks with her fingers, peering eagerly into the colourless eyes, Marian knelt by her sister's side.

"You saw somethin' else, did ye not?" she whispered. "Tell me, lovey, tell me what else you saw."

The dummy giggled and, lifting the slate once more, chalked one word upon it: BLOOD.

When the regimental colours were broken to the wind the storming party rose from hiding in the scrub and raised the scaling-ladders to point at the walls of Fort Napoleon.

"God keep you, Bontine," Stuart said.

"Safe through the day, Stuart," growled Randall.

Stuart hoisted his arm. The old basket-guard claymore glinted in the first rays of the morning sun.

"Now, my gallant laddies," he roared. *"Charge on to victory."*

Randall had shed his heavy riding boots in favour of soft leather sandals. He had wrapped his throat with a red bandana and had knotted a silk kerchief about his brow to keep sweat from trickling into his eyes. Crossed about his chest were two sheathed bayonets and a holstered pistol. If Stuart disapproved of the informal trim he gave no sign. In any case it hardly mattered what opinion Iain Stuart had of the half-mad Lowlander for neither man was likely to survive the charge.

From the line of the breastworks came a stutter of musketry. Garlands of fire showed up the caps of the French grenadiers.

"Vive l'Empereur." Randall, half-way across the open ground, heard the hoarse French voices from the angle of the epaule. *"Cannoniers, commencez. Commencez le feu."*

The roar of nine twenty-four-pounders shook the river bed. Grape and canister swept like iron rain over the storming party and carried half the Scots into oblivion.

Weapons, ladders and bleeding corpses were strewn everywhere. Behind the survivors the British muskets barked in reply but Stuart and Bontine, ducking and weaving, avoided the worst of the crossfire from the *tête-du-pont*. Outstripping the Highlander by several yards, Randall was first into the dry ditch. He hauled himself up the bank, sprinted to the base of the wall and flung himself against it. Looking back he could see how terrible had been the carnage wrought by the French cannon and almost despaired of finding any Scots survivors to give him support.

"Come along, damn you. Come along, come along," Randall shouted.

Iain Stuart's visage appeared above the rim of the ditch. His jaw was set, his eyes blazing. He lifted himself and waved the claymore to rally the lads who were cowering in the ditch. The ball penetrated the exact centre of Stuart's brow. He tottered and fell dead with the sword still in his fist.

Randall felt no grief whatsoever. Sentiment could not pierce his excitement. He saw no point in risking his neck to drag the major's body out of the gunfire. Instead he spun his sabre into both hands and raised it high so that the sun would catch it like a heliograph.

"To me, lads. Rally to me."

And, damn them, if they did not obey. The Highlanders clambered past Stuart's body as if it were nothing more than a dismembered branch. Their eyes were fixed on the Hussar. He would tell them what now was to be done and how best to do it. He would perform for them the service of thinking. Randall stepped away from the wall to make way for the first of the wooden ladders.

"Set it here and set it firm."

Four other ladders waved out of the ditch. Red-faced Sergeant McIver, still with his pipe in his mouth, directed the bearers as calmly as if he were taking a stroll on the sands of Morven. The ditch was piled with wounded infantry. French gunners were jabbering like parrots at the top of the wall. With ladders planted against the glacis, however, the sight-lines for the French defenders had become awkward. They scrambled to change position, to find loopholes and embrasures and, soon, would drop back on to the bulwark parapet. Randall could not see the parapet for the wall seemed to slide into the tinted sky, but he had the architecture of the fort imprinted in his mind and felt no doubt or uncertainty as he rapped out his commands. He knew what he would have to do, how he would have to be first up the first ladder and first on to the parapet.

"Steady it, lads. Steady. Hold the ropes now."

Randall unholstered his pistol and stuffed it into the breast of his tunic. The ladder was braced and the soldiers were staring at him. They were mere boys, farm-hands and shepherds, tanners' sons and candle-makers. They looked to him because of his breeding. They knew that he was made of finer stuff than they but, in battle at least, they did not resent it. Randall swung himself on to the ladder and raced up the rungs as nimbly as a squirrel, up to the lances and bayonets and swords which bristled at the top of the wall.

The assault was falling into place, however. British muskets had attained the ditch and their fire kept the French on the hop. The din was deafening. Grape pocked the earthen face of the wall as Randall hauled himself up the last few feet and, without hesitation, vaulted on to the parapet.

When they saw that Major Bontine had gained the fort, how the lads cheered and shouted and rattled on to the ladders. Major Bontine seemed immune to the shower of shot around him and, with sabre and bayonet, cut a swathe through the grenadiers like a reaper through corn. Those who saw it would later talk of the courage and strength of the Lowland laird, speak in awe of his single-handed attack and how he had held the parapet long enough for a dozen ladders to be cracked against the glacis and for the Highlanders to mount and clamber and flood into the roof of Fort Napoleon.

The redoubtable Sergeant McIver somehow found his way from the base of the ditch to the top of the scaling-ladder. He joined the major and the pair plunged onward, the sergeant's pike making short work of the handful of grenadiers who had tarried around the cannonades. Randall's sword passed through the breasts of old guardsmen with great bow-shaped moustaches and crimson cheeks and soon French blood plastered the sabre's hilt and trickled thickly down his arm. All around there was fighting. Roaring guttural war-cries, the Gordons swarmed on to the parapet so the boards were slippery with blood and, within minutes, cluttered with dead and wounded.

Randall glanced to the far end of the pontoon. The blaze of

French artillery from Fort Ragusa glared on the river but, through the bedlam around him, he could hear the drone of the pipes as the 92nd breached the fort's inner talus. The Light Infantry's right wing had poured into Napoleon and the Frenchies were driven back into the narrow yard in front of the barracks, hard against the bastion from which the flagstaff sprouted, gathering for a final stand around the tricolour.

The major punched McIver's arm and gestured. The sergeant needed no urging. He leapt down the steps from the breastworks into the thick of the fray below, with Randall on his heels.

Ahead, Randall could see the hedge of steel that protected the rag of French honour. When the flag was taken the surrender of Fort Napoleon would be inevitable. Between him and the inner yard, though, was a pit or demi-gorge filled with billets of timber and baskets of earth. The Hussar would not be deterred. Leaving the sergeant to protect his back, he ran forward and onto the tottering surface of the demi-gorge and was, for a minute or so, the only British soldier there, though eight or ten Highlanders crouched twenty yards behind, firing into the hedges.

"Give them Egypt!" Randall shouted.

In the sandals he was nimble on the debris and crossed the demi-gorge alone. Pikes and bayonets pointed at him fifty feet away, and he was target for a dozen guns. But the French had an officer who was as brave and resolute as Randall Bontine, just as willing to sup the rough red wine of glory.

He was, Randall reckoned, a dragoon of rank no higher than a captain. Tall and lean and agile, he wore a corselet and plumed helmet and was armed with a heavy sabre and a dagger. Randall felt a strange wave of happiness that caused him to throw back his head and laugh at the appropriateness of it all. It was as if he had finally encountered himself, in French garb, and must battle to survive not against an equal but a twin. The dragoon sensed it too and, grinning like a wolf, tipped his sword in salute. Randall stepped forward and raised his sabre.

The blades met, rang, parried by dagger and bayonet. Randall could smell the dragoon, smell the odour of Spain, earthy and corporeal, spiced with garlic and gunpowder. He locked the Frenchie's dagger hand at the wrist with the back of his right, reared on tiptoe and stabbed the bayonet into the fellow's back. The steel slid from the corselet then caught, tore upon cloth, then, under cloth, upon flesh. The dragoon kneed him and thrust him away. He sliced with a horizontal stroke, making the major dance backward. Blood, however, was spurting across the corselet. Randall shifted in for the kill. But the dragoon was also nimble and clever; Stuart would have called him 'a bonnie fechter'. He changed the pattern of the attack and without warning swung low. The French blade tore muscle clean to the bone from Randall's knee to his hip. He let out a cry of agony, sagged and fell.

Sergeant McIver's pike, swung like a flail, broke the French officer's neck before he could deliver the *coup* and the dagger caught Randall just below the ear. He hardly noticed the sting for he had lifted himself on hands and one knee and was roaring in triumph as the dragoon slumped stone-dead before him.

"McIver," Randall said. "Help me to my feet."

The sergeant, however, had gone charging on, anxious for his share of glory too, and just as ambitious as the officer. He cared not much of a jot for a man who was merely a Hussar and a damned Lowlander and was, in McIver's judgement, anyway as good as dead.

44

TWO

The Binding

High scudding cloud and blinks of sunlight were scattered over the Orrals by a warm, strenuous breeze from the west. On the moorland, gorse was stripped of its flower and petals clung to the heather like flakes of yellow sleet. The burn curled back on itself at the head of the glen making a horsehair crest which wetted the withered bracken for half a furlong. Michael had settled himself below the wind and had tied a plaid to two saplings for shelter. Today he carried no game-bag to hold herbs and plants, but instead had brought a basket from which he had unpacked a dish of cold chicken, a bottle of elderflower wine and two glasses.

It was their fifth meeting. Neither Michael nor Elspeth pretended that coincidence had a hand in it now.

Elspeth made her way down into the glen.

"Is there no dinner for you at Preaching Friar?"

Michael raised a wine-glass in greeting.

"It's a tidy step from Preaching Friar," he said. "I'm in need of sustenance before attempting a return journey."

"Why, tell me, do you subject yourself to such arduous exercise?"

Carefully he decanted wine and handed her a filled glass. "To bring you refreshment. My aunt has had this bottle in her cellar for three seasons. Give me your opinion of its flavour."

Elspeth sipped. "Delicious! But how do I know it doesn't contain a sleepin' draught?"

"Perhaps it does," Michael said. "Perhaps it's my intention to drug you, wrap you in my plaid and steal you away, never to be seen again."

"How would you transport me?"

"Across my shoulder."

"Like an old carpet?"

45

"I might carry you in my arms, if you'd prefer it."

The image, the thought of the closeness it would entail, warmed Elspeth. No matter how playful she might pretend to be, she had a plain need of Michael Blaven. She yearned for him, not yet as a lover, but to fill the hollows of her heart, to give her the youthful, intimate sort of friendship which James could not provide. Love, she was learning, had many shades and varieties. She had not been in love for long, not long enough to understand how love between two respectable, decent people should be expressed. She went on in the same slightly silly vein.

"I fear you would not get far," she said, "with me as a burden."

"I would carry you to the ends of the earth," said Michael.

"The ends of the earth, I imagine, might very well look just like the Orrals," said Elspeth.

Michael laughed, then, seriously, asked, "Did you not come yesterday?"

"I trust you're not chiding me."

"No, it was more of an observation."

"My husband took me to ride."

"I see."

"He is my husband, and does have call upon me."

"Of course," said Michael.

"I should not meet with you at all, here, in secret."

"I can hardly come rapping upon the door of Moss House," said Michael.

"No," said Elspeth. "It would not be the same."

"Have you informed your husband of my existence?"

Elspeth hesitated. She had no standard by which to judge Michael's intentions. James had not 'courted' her in any sense of that word. She had gone into the marriage as a contract, calculatingly.

There had been other men; the labourer at Dyers' Dyke – Peter Docherty – for instance, who had loved her and would have married her if she had wished it. Sometimes, just a little, she wished that she had taken up with Peter and not James. Though the life would have been harder, at least there would have been more honesty to it. Then there was Mr Rudge who, when tipsy after too much claret, would whisper to her in low, suggestive tones. She was both repelled and flattered by

Rudge's injudicious propositions but she did not resent Rudge as she resented James and, oddly, as she somewhat resented Michael. The young man from Preaching Friar had ruffled her, shaken her settled existence. She did not know yet if she could allow herself to love him, only that the possibility had been offered, not denied as with James.

"No," Elspeth said. "I haven't told James anythin' about you, not even that you exist. It would not be advisable."

"Would he prevent you seeing me again?"

"What would you expect? Of course he would."

"He would be a fool to do otherwise," Michael said. "I think, however, that I'm the greater fool."

"Oh? Why?"

"For allowing myself to be bewitched by you."

"Surely you don't suppose that I've bewitched you out of malice — if I've bewitched you at all?"

"I cannot say what reason you may have, Elspeth. You come here, you give me hope, you don't spurn me."

Elspeth had no answer, no remark which might lightly deny the truth of it.

"I say only that I am bewitched by you," Michael went on. "I can't think of anyone or anything else since the first day of meeting with you."

"Short acquaintance is not t' be trusted."

It did not seem at all like short acquaintance. How could she tell him that he had never been out of her thoughts, out of her dreams? Moment by moment she was slipping towards infidelity with giddy indifference to consequences. She hungered for the pleasure of yielding to impulse, of not being ruled by logic. If only she possessed an ounce of Anna's unscrupulousness, she might be in his arms now, might surrender to the passion that was in her. But she was not Anna and her vulnerability remained protected by stern common sense. She believed in duty, cared for comfort, and approached other natural desires with caution.

"Can you deny that you want me to take you in my arms?" Michael said.

"I could not trust you to stop there."

"Would you want me to stop there?"

He was forcing her into inviting him to make love to her. How could she possibly explain that she was still a virgin, that

47

her husband had not consummated the marriage? Michael might suppose that she was to blame. She saw suddenly and very closely how James had demeaned her, how he had tarnished their relationship. Anger and guilt, feelings as insidious as they were inevitable in the bizarre circumstances of the marriage, had changed her already.

Michael took her silence for rejection.

"I'll not ask that question again," he said.

"I don't wish you to think that I'm – I'm –"

Now, suddenly, Michael understood – or thought he did.

"Never would I think such a thing," he said, emphatically. "I have too much respect for you, Elspeth. I can't separate you, for both our sakes, from your husband."

Confused, Elspeth hid behind a spat of anger. "How dare you even suggest it, Mister Blaven."

She played the love game as ladies were supposed to do, and hated herself for it. Modesty was only inch-deep in the aristocratic women whom she had met. Under their pale, sweet powder the great ladies were not at all refined but hung like field-lassies on the pleasure of being loved. There was a hypocrisy in them which Elspeth despised; but it was a hypocrisy which it seemed she must share.

"Even if you became miraculously free of your husband, I would not wish to separate you from your settled life in Balnesmoor," said Michael, ambiguously.

"I'm glad to hear it," said Elspeth. "You are takin' an excessive amount for granted, sir."

"I wish to be allowed to love you," Michael went on, "because there is no help for it. It has happened without my willing it. But I would not and will not, disadvantage you."

"Oh, but you *have* 'disadvantaged' me," replied Elspeth. "Can you not see? If I was a byre-lassie you'd not be so considerate of my feelin's, I fancy. You'd take me without a qualm."

"Is that how you regard me; as a heartless rake?"

"You put it too strongly but – yes – it's close enough to what I feel."

"Why?"

"Since you've told me nothin' of yourself and because you think that spinnin' pretty words will gain you your way."

"The words are not particularly pretty. Besides, I asked

only for a kiss as a token, not as a preliminary to – to –"

"Aye," said Elspeth. "Have you no pretty word for *that*, Mister Blaven?"

"I want to remember you with a kiss." It did not sound insincere; she was tempted to believe him. "You see, I'll not be here for long."

"Leave now, if you wish," Elspeth said.

Michael glanced at the wine-bottle on the grass and at the dish of chicken which his aunt had painstakingly prepared, upon which sauce had congealed and petals of gorse had settled, with little black flies stuck and drowning in the gravy. Elspeth regretted her priggishness but she could not bring herself, however, to plunge into an affair even under the guise of love.

"Elspeth, I thought you cared for me."

"I do. I'd like to remain your friend, to meet –"

"It isn't enough."

"I cannot become anythin' more. A kiss won't change my mind, Michael," she said. "I canna. I'm wife already."

"Do you love him?"

"Aye, I do." She lied convincingly.

Michael put his head on one side and smiled with such wistfulness that all doubt fled from her mind. She felt as if she had deceived Michael Blaven and not James. The look on his face was so sad it near broke her heart.

"I came too late," Michael said. "Yes, I can see that. I came too late."

He knocked the bottle with his ankle and let the wine gurgle on to the grass, then stooped and swept aside the dish into the burn and snatched the blanket from the tree, tearing it from its strings. The movements were not angry but had an air of haste as if he had to attend to duty elsewhere.

"It was wrong of me," he said. "Yet I'll offer no apology. It's a careless fellow, not a trusting one, who would let his wife run wild on the moor."

"You don't know James or –"

"Ah, but I do, Elspeth. I know his sort too well."

"Michael?"

She moved to him, put her hand upon his shoulder and, lifting herself on her toes, kissed his mouth. The heat of his skin surprised her. She let her lips linger, hoping that he would

49

toss away the plaid and wrap his arms about her, draw her tightly against him and never let her go again. But he accepted her kiss modestly, reticently.

When Elspeth separated from him, Michael sighed. In his eyes Elspeth still saw the sadness that she had not managed to diminish only, for a split second, to share.

Mother Moodie sat in the painted wood pergola looking wrinkled, inscrutable and wise. Her special high-backed chair, upon which she was toted about Moss House and its formal gardens, was padded with embroidered silk cushions. A richly-patterned shawl was tucked in crenellated folds across her knees. Draped around her shoulders was another shawl, heavy with scarlet tassels. Ranged close to her were three little ebony tables which bore dishes of sweetmeats and raisins, and decanters which contained her favourite cordials. No longer, however, did Mother Moodie use the symbols of plenitude to wreak havoc with the servants and exercise her ounce of power over them. Her expression of sagacity was a sham. The shrunken body under its burden of clothes was nothing but a receptacle for a brain as shrivelled as a winter pippin. Mother Moodie had turned senile.

Days went by when no word escaped the old woman's lips. On others, however, she would mutter, moan and snigger for hours on end and attain little peaks of excitement which would cause her to cry out – though whether in rage or in joy nobody, not even her son, could decide. For everyone who came into contact with her, including Carstairs, the smart young doctor from Blanefield who had replaced the venerable Rankellor, Mother Moodie's spasms of loquacity were only dotage drivel. James, however, was fascinated by them. He spent much time in her company, patient as a dog at a rat-hole, waiting for truth to emerge so that he might pounce on it, kill it and carry it away.

On that afternoon of wind and cloud James had ordered that his mother be taken outside and placed in the shelter he had built and furnished for her comfort.

Seated on a stool, James had been at his mother's side for an hour. She had said nothing and he doubted that she would that day since the features were shuttered and her eyes as remote as glaciers. What went on in her head was unfathomable and, every so often, James would lower the sheets of the *Glasgow Herald*, through which he browsed with an uncharacteristic aimlessness, and would contemplate the woman's implacable face, searching for signs. He feared that her condition might portend his own eventual decline, the irrational twilight in which only vague outlines of the personality could be defined and in which state, without guile, he might give up his secrets. At length James got up, stretched his arms and took a stroll down the strip of lawn which lay like a skittle-board between the hedges.

The wind was gusting strong and he was a little anxious about Elspeth who, so Tolland had informed him on his early return from Kennart, had gone walking upon the moor track. But, James reminded himself, Elspeth had been an active lass, used to the wide spaces of the Nettleburn and he could see no harm in her being out on the rough but protected track that backed the gardens of Moss House.

James showed no evidence of the slowing processes and flagging energies that affected some men in their middle years. His hair was dark and thick and he was careful at table not to let his appetite carry him into excess. Besides, he had a muscular frame, developed through thirty years of hard manual labour at his loom. He expected to live long. His maternal grandparents, in their nineties, were still alive, residing in a tithed cottage near the border town of Selkirk. He had called upon them on one occasion while visiting a stapler in that town, though his mother had not clapped eyes on her parents since the day of her marriage, sixty years since. James had sisters, married and settled out of the county, whom he hardly saw at all. No doubt, after his mother's death, communication between them would cease. He would not regret it. After all, he had found Elspeth. Elspeth was his present comfort, his future, his one and only love, the core and centre of his being.

James had just reached the stile which climbed the drystone wall when he saw her a quarter-mile or so out upon the moor. She was running. James stiffened, jumped to the stile and stood upon it. Shading his eyes he scanned the cloud-patched moor. There was nothing and nobody in pursuit of the girl, thank God. Smiling slightly he relaxed at the realisation that she was young enough to be filled still with what the French termed *joie de vivre*, the vital principle. He lifted his arm and waved. Elspeth did not notice him. She ran swiftly through the bracken away from the glen. She did not direct herself straight towards the stile but cut to the east, out of sight behind the pillared yew hedge. James had to wait five minutes for her to reappear. She was surprised – startled? – to find him by the stile.

"James, what's wrong?"

"Not a thing, dearest. I came home early today, there being little to occupy me at Kennart. I had it in mind," he helped her over the stile, "to travel out to Salter's to look at his lambs; but that chore can wait 'til tomorrow when, perhaps, you might care to accompany me."

"Aye, of course," she said.

James studied her, puzzled by a quality he could not identify. "Did you have a pleasurable excursion?"

"Very pleasurable," she said. "It's such a bracin' day."

He offered his arm. She took it, linking her elbow with his. She did not rub herself against him, stroke his hand with her fingers, offer any of the pleasant, intimate contacts which, in a normal marriage, a wife would freely accord to her husband.

She was, however, trembling.

"Have you caught chill?" said James.

"No, I – I ran a little because I – because I thought the rain might be comin'."

It had become his habit to doubt only himself, not Elspeth. For a brief, cold moment anger hovered on the edge of his consciousness. Did Elspeth not realise that she must be beyond reproach, that she must epitomise an integrity that could not be contaminated by suspicion?

Casually he said, "Is the glen wet?"

"I didn't go so far as that," she answered.

She was an inexpert teller of lies. He could have schooled her in that art too if it had been his wish. They had walked the length of the boxed-in lawn and Mother Moodie lay ahead of them. James was glad of the excuse to release Elspeth's arm, to break contact.

Rather too eagerly, Elspeth asked, "How is Mama today?"

"Sayin' not a word," James answered.

There was in the girl a natural tenderness. Even if she was shy of the old woman, she could respond sympathetically to her helplessness. It would have been a different sort of tale, of

52

course, if Elspeth had been a cottar's wife and poor and the old woman had been cluttering the chimney corner and she, Elspeth, would have had to do all for her, lifting and laying and feeding, changing her soiled linen. Money made tenderness possible.

"Mother Moodie?" Elspeth knelt by the old woman's knee and peeped up into her expressionless features. "Would you like a wee drink now?"

Mother Moodie stared straight through her son's wife.

"It's one of those sort of days," said James, still watching Elspeth closely. "She needs no attention."

"Mother Moodie?" Still on her knees, Elspeth turned to look up at her husband. "She is so —"

Suddenly the old woman was keening, her withered hands waving as if to push away an unseen assailant. Elspeth leapt back from the base of the chair and sat down hard upon the grass.

For two or three seconds the old woman spoke intelligibly. *"Och, Jamie, no. No, Jamie. No. Och, no, no, Jamie."* Then, twitching, she fell back into the cushions with her arms akimbo, still crying and dry-sobbing.

"Mother." James was by her immediately. "Mother, what is it? God, what ails you now?"

"Jamie, Jamie?"

"I'm here. I'm here."

But he was not there. The man who stalked the old woman was a figment from the past, someone out of the shadows. She fought feebly as James tried to calm her. Saliva ran down her chin instead of tears. It was the first bad fit she'd had for months. James was severely shaken by it, though, as soon as the memory passed like a cloud across the hill, the old woman was calm again except for a fretful, almost inaudible mutter of recrimination.

Awkwardly James placed his arm about her shoulders and glanced at Elspeth who had scrambled to her feet.

"What shall I do? Shall I send for Doctor Carstairs?" Elspeth said.

"No, it's over. She's forgotten it."

"It was so — so horrible."

"Aye." James sighed.

"She cried out for you, yet she didn't want you."

James lifted his forearm from his mother's shoulders and shook his head. "Not me. My father."

"She was frightened of your father?"

"I remember no hurt he gave her."

James spoke without conviction. It occurred to him that he had been privy to an incident of such intimacy that he could not bring his mind to dwell on it; nor could he stand there contemplating the husk of the woman who had once been pretty and desirable, irresistible to a bridegroom. He stepped away from the chair and started down the skittle-board lawn, calling over his shoulder, "Stay with her. I'll find Tolland and have her brought in."

"James?" Elspeth called.

But her husband had gone indoors.

Dinner was arranged for eight o'clock, the customary hour for the evening meal at Moss House. Having seen his mother settled and ensured that Betty would be in attendance in the chamber, James excused himself and retired to 'accounting' in the spartan study at the rear of the ground-floor corridor.

It was by no means uncommon for James to lock himself away for an hour or two before or after dinner with his ledgers and little cartularies. Elspeth had absorbed a deal of information on James Moodie's wool-cloth empire. She understood cash bargains, even the value of notes of credit and promissories, but the pyramidal nature of commercial finance, with transactions conducted on paper for commodities and stocks, seemed quite alien to the weaving trade.

James, however, had something other than commerce on his mind that night. He did not, in fact, go down the servants' corridor into the cell-like study. Instead he went out by the 'gun-room', a hexagonal inspiration of the architect of Moss House who could not believe that an occupant of his grand dwelling would care nothing for sport. The 'gun-room', devoid of sporting paraphernalia, contained a rack of stout boots and shoes and a pegged board from which hung tweed coats and capes, together with some weathered hats. Here James donned leather boots and a half-jacket and, hatless, slipped out of the door into the kitchen yard.

Stables and carriage mews lay a short distance from the house, separated from the kitchen gardens by a high wall.

James usually travelled in a gig or comfortable, well-sprung carriage. Tonight, however, he ordered the head horseman to saddle a sturdy pony for a trot. Mounted, James snecked the pony from the stable yard and swung it on to a track which led towards the quarries on the spur of the Orrals.

The pony was sure-footed and made swift passage across the heather scrub. Away towards Fintry the sky was dark with weather and coming dusk. James absorbed the gloom of the evening as he rode towards that quarter of the ridge from which he had seen Elspeth return, running, that afternoon.

Streaming over the moor the wind buffeted the weaver and wetted his neck with a few spots of rain as he guided the pony along the shoulder of the glen. He sat up tall and noticed the bottle immediately. Its regular shape made it obvious. James grunted, "Whoa," reined the pony to a halt and dismounted. He climbed down into the glen and crossed the burn. Hunkering, he examined the bottle then gingerly lifted it and sniffed the neck. The bottle was no relic of a tinkers' carousal; the dregs had not soured in the air.

Getting up, James poked about in the shrubs. He found the strings tied to the sapling and stared at them as if they were rare butterflies. They puzzled him and gave rise to depraved imaginings. He pried about beneath the small trees, but found nothing further there and extended his search upstream.

After ten minutes, the weaver decided that he had discovered all the 'evidence' that remained. He was convinced now that his wife had been here, had met with some person and enjoyed the assignation enough to bless it with a cup of wine.

Leaving the bottle where it lay, James climbed back to the pony. Spots of rain had thickened into drizzle. A haze veiled the summits and blotted out the lights of the villages. He gripped the saddle and swung himself into it. As he did so he caught sight of a man on pony-back, a man who had lingered just a moment too long. The rider was across the head of the glen, on a rock-crumbled knoll, prominent against the wet grey sky. The instant that James turned his head, the rider fled.

Fury welled up in James Moodie. He stabbed his boot-heels into the pony's flanks to start a pursuit but realised that the rider would be fast away before he could negotiate a crossing of the burn. Crippled by frustration, he slumped in the saddle, hand over his eyes, while the rain wound about his shoulders like wetted flax. The fact that the bottle found in the glen had contained wine and not whisky did not seem material, did not prevent James Moodie from leaping to a wrong conclusion.

It took the weaver several minutes to gain control over his emotions. Eventually he wheeled the pony's head into the rain to circle back to the stables, back to Moss House.

He would say nothing of his ride on to the Orrals, of his discovery. He would not remonstrate with Elspeth, demand explanations. But, by God in Heaven, he would watch over her so closely that she would never again have an opportunity to slip away to meet her brother-in-law, Matt Sinclair.

Anna's best efforts at being a good wife were spoiled by a kind of incompetence which Matt would have found laughable if he had not been its victim.

Stockings, clotted with suds, dangled from a sagging string over the hearth and dripped steadily into the pots which the girl had propped on the baking stones. Smocks, shirts and a pair of shapeless under-drawers were suspended from rafter nails making Matt obliged to steer a careful course through clammy garments to find his seat at the supper table. Out of the pots Anna ladled a feast fit for a king; yet somehow she had managed to over-salt the broth, singe the potatoes and leave the heart of the barley loaf as sticky as clay. She had done, however, her best. Liberal helpings of kail broth were followed by a mound of stovies, a mash of potatoes enriched with flakes of meat scraped from the bones of a hare they had had three days ago. Matt ignored the cinders and spooned the stuff greedily into his mouth. He washed it down with whisky and water; he no longer had any reason to be shy before Anna about his taste for Tomelty's smuggled malt. He was as hungry as a wolf tonight. He had worked damned hard all day long, not planting trees for the Bontines but delivering empty kegs to the bothy known as Tomelty's Well where Pad had installed his still in preparation for the cereal crops which would come off the fields in ten or twelve weeks' time.

Matt's deliveries were usually made without incident as he had been schooled in the lie of the land by Pad himself, a man to whom stealth was second nature. On the last drag down of the day, though, he had been sighted by somebody. He had beaten a hasty retreat into the plantations just in case the stranger was a King's officer strayed over from Aberfoyle. Matt was not particularly disturbed by the appearance of a rider on the Orrals. The mannie had only been paddling about in the glen, two miles or more from Pad Tomelty's hide.

Jacko, who had an aversion to soapsuds, was seated on Matt's foot, clinging to his shin. The monkey, Matt noticed, had been given a bowl of walnuts to crack, which showed that Anna had softened in her heart towards the wee creature. Matt had no clue as to why his wife had changed so. He put it down to the fact that she had realised that, after all, he might come into a position of power on Ottershaw. After serving, Anna took a chair and ate her own supper.

Matt pushed away his plate, belched, and leaned back. Jacko rubbed a dry nose against his knee and received in return a lackadaisical scratch on the brow.

Anna said, "I'll do it if you like, Matt."

Matt had been thinking of nothing in particular. Drowsiness was creeping over him from the strenuous day and the effects of the *aqua vitae*. Imagining that she meant something intimate, he shook himself out of languor, blinking.

"Wait a wee bit," he murmured.

Anna propped her elbows on the table and rested her chin on her fists. Matt had seen that look before. He sighed. There were times when not even a clout on the ear would dissuade his wife from her pleasure.

"Och, no," Anna said quickly. "I mean I'll talk to Elspeth about a loan of money."

"Loan?"

"For buyin' farm stock."

"Farm?" Matt pulled himself together. "Aye, why not? A loan might come in handy."

"I thought you were eager."

"That was – I mean, the sale's long over."

"Are there no other sales?"

"I thought you were dead set against talkin' to Elspeth."

"I see it as my duty, Matt."

Matt shrugged. The notion of escape from Ottershaw had been knocked out of his mind by acceptance into Pad Tomelty's band of smugglers.

Bontine's foresters, led by Kenneth McDonald, were into

every money-minting trick. They operated with a cleverness that would have astounded Lachlan Sinclair. It had taken McDonald the best part of two years to decide that Matthew was no sneak sent in by the grieve to uncover their ruses. When he realised what was going on, Matt was delighted. Apart from anything else, division of the profits meant that he could begin to salt away shillings and pounds. In a year or two, he calculated, he might earn tenfold more from running whisky for Pad Tomelty than he would in wages.

"There is no sale right now, is that it?" said Anna.

Matt smiled, stretched lazily across the table and took her hand. He had been tempted to brag about his exploits, though they were tame enough, but he knew his wife too well to suppose that she could be depended upon to keep a tight lip. One murmur, one hint to old Lachlan and the grieve would not rest until he wrung the truth out of somebody, probably his son.

Matt said, "It's the war with the French."

Anna frowned. "What's Napoleon got to do with us lookin' out for a steadin'?"

"In a year or two, when the Frenchies are beat, when the affairs o' Ottershaw are put straight, my father says they'll see me raised."

"They?"

"He means Young Gibbie."

Anna made sense, somehow, of her husband's explanation. She nodded and brought his hand up to her cheek. Below the table Jacko clung more possessively to his master's ankle as if sensing what the courtship would lead to, namely him being stuck in his box. The drowsy, inattentive expression passed from Matt's face. He sat up and disengaged his hand from Anna's.

"But," Matt said, "if you think the time's ripe to put the tap on Elspeth, I'll not prevent you."

"For what, though?"

Matt stroked his chin thoughtfully and said, "Aye, speak wi' her. Butter her bloody paws. See if she'll cajole the weaver into partin' wi' some money; a loan, that is."

"How much?"

"Twenty guineas."

"Elspeth might do it, but the weaver'll need a reason."

"Why are you so eager to help me, all of a sudden?"

Flustered, Anna would not meet his eye. Matt was too intent on his own ideas to detect the guilty confusion in his wife. He would not have understood it in any case, since he had not been told of her rendezvous with the sisters of Eardmore. He would only have dismissed their readings and binding spells as daft lassies' cackle. It was, however, fear that had changed Anna, fear of the strange magic wrought by the dummy and her awful sister; fear that she would be bound by the spell and that Randall Bontine's unknown destiny would somehow be inextricably woven with her own.

"I'm sick o' Ottershaw," said Anna. "I want out o' this dismal place."

"To go where?"

"Somewhere far away."

Matt laughed wryly. "Take Jacko back to Guinea, eh?"

Her anger caught him by surprise. "I'm not makin' jokes, Matt."

"Verra well," he said. "If you wish to help me in my enterprise, Anna, speak with your sister."

"Only if you'll back me up, Matt."

"Aye, of course I will."

Anna snuffled and suddenly burst into tears. Taken aback, Matt detached the capuchin from his leg and hurried round the table to put an arm about his wife.

"Are ye sick?"

"I'm sick o' Ottershaw, that's all."

"I thought you liked Ottershaw."

"I *hate* it."

Matt put his cheek against her hair, shielded her with his chest and clapped her shoulder as if she had hiccoughs and not a queer black mood.

Anna said, "If I get Moodie to advance us a loan o' twenty guineas, will you look for a steadin' far from Ottershaw?"

"Aye," Matt answered. "If you raise the wind, I'll do the rest."

He meant it too – but not quite as his wife intended. Certainly he could find a use for twenty guineas. Given a measure of luck he would turn the sum into a small fortune, not by investing it in a patch of sour ground, not by breaking his bloody back for thirty years, but in a stroke, by a clever

59

deal with the whisky-maker supreme, Mr Padric Tomelty himself.

On the north bank of the River Endrick, near the spot where women congregated to beat sheets and blankets, a clump of common comfrey flourished in the May-month sun. Miss Janet Blaven went on her own to select the best broad-leaved specimens which she uprooted intact with a trowel. Tinged with mauve, the white bell-flowers were pretty enough to grace a decorative spray but Miss Blaven had other less frivolous uses for the herb.

She carried the plants straight from the river walk to a work-block in the malting-shed at the back of Preaching Friar. There she extracted sap from roots and stems and preserved it in a globular bottle with a few drops of Hollands gin. Miss Blaven believed that there was a special potency in preparations made from new vernal growths. To relieve her nephew's distress every atom of restorative power would be required; however, she was only too well aware that Nature produced no substance which would heal the livid concretions in her nephew's lungs and extend his days on earth much beyond mid-winter.

If Michael had remained in Glasgow, lodged amid the stink and vitriol and bleaching gas, he would have been in his grave months ago. Janet Blaven could not understand why Michael's father – her brother Robert – was so stubborn as to insist that the boy must tread in the family's footsteps. It must have been apparent, even to Robert, that his youngest son was not fit enough to undertake intensive study in chemistry at Glasgow University and, later, at Leiden in The Netherlands. There were three other sons, all older and more robust than Michael, to manage the future of the St Cyrus Manufacturing Chemical Company, men already trained for the task and infected with the obsession that had possessed Robert and his father before him. There was also the spectre of disease in the Blavens' great square mansion in St Cyrus Street. Michael's mother had died of an internal abscess. Four of Robert's eight children, the entire female strain, had not survived to marriageable age. Janet's mother, also, had been seized by a wasting illness and been taken while she, Janet, was still in swaddling frocks. Asthmas and consumptions were, it seemed, destined to be the counterweights to wealth, balancings against which the Blavens must forever weigh their progress. Grief and loss had plated Robert and his sons. They could no longer see out of the cold clenching fog of commerce and chemical process and had, to their shame, written Michael off like a bad debt or a failed experiment.

She had rescued him from the sick-room in St Cyrus Street, whisked him away to Preaching Friar which had been her refuge from contamination for almost thirty years. Yet it had been 'vitriol' that had given her freedom, her share of the fortune which her father had amassed through his dedication and industry in the '70s and '80s. Preaching Friar, she occasionally reminded herself, floated on a sea of chlorine on a raft of dry bleach. It seemed a suitable sort of irony that Michael should find a sanctuary there.

In the past months Miss Blaven's locks had turned from grey to snow-white. She had not enough vanity to hide them under a wig. Hair apart, however, she did not look fifty-four. She was slender and still quick, and of resolute character. Though she attended kirk every Sabbath and never missed saying evening prayers, she did not believe in miracles. Consequently she did not expect God to unblock the impostume in her nephew's lungs. She had a leathery conviction that all things were written by divine hand. She put her trust in the promise that Michael would find the happiness which had been denied him when, at last, he was called to join the Host in Heaven. She prayed, though, that he would not suffer an excess of pain and would slip from her as lightly as a thistle seed plucked away by the breeze.

When Michael finally wakened from his long slumber it was wearing close to dusk. Thin humid rain had persisted intermittently throughout the week and no time seemed lost to the young man who, coughing, called out to her from the snug, whitewashed room beneath the eaves.

Miss Blaven went at once, carrying a tray with the bottle upon it and a jug of barley-water warmed from the kettle. She had been prepared for his wakening, for a rise in his fever and the torments of doubt that came with the sweat. But, to her surprise, he was not soaked in sweat. He sat upright against the bolster, waiting to speak with her.

"How long, Aunt, have I been incapacitated?"

"Five days."

"Ah, these summery colds. How they do persist."

"Aye, and not helped by catching a soaking on the Orrals," the woman said firmly. "Had you not brain enough to come home at once?"

His neck seemed as slender as a comfrey stem, his shoulders high under the crumpled cambric shirt. On the bolster were spots of blood, dried like tea-stains. Now that he was a little better she could sit him in a chair and change the linen on the bed. She had a daily maid but would not permit the girl to do anything for her nephew. She attended to his needs in person.

"I came home at once," Michael said.

"Nonsense, boy! Why, I could trot off the Orrals in an hour. Did you not *see* the clouds approaching?"

"I was — occupied."

"Searching for dandelions, I suppose?"

"Have I really been asleep for five days?"

"Yes."

She did not elaborate. It was quite usual for a period of deep sleep to wipe away the memory of the pain and restlessness which preceded it.

"I must be up soon. Abroad in the air. Taking my exercise," said Michael.

"When you are well again."

"I'm well now."

"I will tell you when you are well."

"I have to be — want to be abroad again."

"Why?" Aunt Janet enquired, bluntly.

"Is that barley-water? May I have a sup, please? I feel as if I had been wrung out like a clootie."

She poured him a glass, added ten drops of comfrey and held the vessel for him. He took it from her, his fingers shaking. She sat on the side of the bed, ready to assist, but he was determined to demonstrate that he was on the path to recovery and would be able to tramp again upon the high moor very soon. He drank the liquid in three gulps, sighed and let Aunt Janet take away the glass. She refilled it with cloudy barley-water and said again, "Why?"

He lay back against the bolster. She brought the glass to his lips and fed him more of the refreshing liquid. He did not protest or struggle to help himself.

"What sort of business have you devised that requires your presence?" she said.

"I have no business," he said.

"By the number of occasions you have trudged on to the Orrals –" Miss Blaven jerked the glass away as her nephew coughed. She scanned his face anxiously but the spasm was brief and not scouring. She went on, "– I thought you must have business there."

He laughed and shook his head. "I like the wild moor. I like to be upon it, under the sky."

"What do you do there? Pursue shadows – or something a trifle more substantial?"

Michael looked surprised. He could hide nothing from her in his weakened condition but she must be careful not to excite him.

"Macfarlane, the shepherd at Dyers' Dyke, has pretty daughters –" she said.

"Shepherds' daughters?" Michael interrupted.

"Perhaps a drover's lass?"

"Never!"

"Are you too genteel for country girls, Michael?"

"Oh, dear me, no!"

She saw that he had a need to confess, but was uncertain of her reaction. So it *was* a lass that had lured him out on to the moor. She felt a little stab of envy, followed instantly by a sorrow that she did not care to define.

She said, "Will I have to consult my mirror for an answer, Michael?"

He laughed again, nervously. "Yes, it is a young woman. But, truly, it's nothing."

"I'm intrigued," said Miss Blaven lightly, "by the place of the rendezvous."

"Hardly a rendezvous."

"What sort of young woman dwells on the high moor?"

"She does not dwell there. She walks there."

"Ah!"

"You sound disapproving."

"Not in the least."

"It's nothing," he said again. "Chance encounters, no more."

"Do you find her appealing?"

63

"Fair," he said, shrugging and pursing his lips. "Fair, as company."

"Fair of face?"

"Oh, indeed, indeed. That I cannot deny."

"Is she from Harlwood?"

It was out before he could prevent it. "Balnesmoor."

"And what, pray, would a respectable young beauty from Balnesmoor be doing upon the Orrals?"

"I told you, Aunt; taking the air, as I do."

"May I enquire the name of this smothered creature?"

"Her name is Elspeth."

His cheeks were fired by embarrassment, not fever. Nonetheless Miss Blaven's anxiety was immediate and palpable.

"Elspeth?" she said. "Of what family?"

Michael paused. Though he appeared jocular and relaxed, the woman sensed his tension. If he had not just passed through a bout of consumptive fever, he would not have told her at all.

"It's nothing, Aunt. How can it be?"

Miss Blaven ignored his question.

"What is her family name?"

"She is wife to Mister Moodie, if that's answer enough."

"Weaver Moodie's wife! Oh, Michael!"

She got to her feet, planted the glass on the tray by the bed, then, with a firmness that lay perilously close to anger, wagged her forefinger at him. "No more, Michael. Do you attend me? You will not meet with Moodie's wife, no matter how pretty, no matter how 'innocent'. You must not meet with her upon the Orrals or anywhere else again."

"Aunt." He struggled to lift himself. "I did nothing improper."

"Meeting her at all was improper. She's wife to another man."

"We only spoke together, that's all."

"Spoke of what?"

"Conversational matters."

"It must stop, Michael. No more rendezvous upon the moor. You will not see Mistress Moodie again."

"Aunt, I – I think I may be in love with her."

"Do not be a fool, Michael Blaven."

"I cannot help myself."

"You *must* help yourself. You must be strong in the matter. If she seeks to entice you –"

"How can you understand? Elspeth is not –"

"Whatever she may be, she is a married woman. Weaver Moodie would have every right to seek redress against her, if –"

"What are you telling me, Aunt Janet?"

She tried to control her outburst but could not. Even she could not be certain what so appalled her in Michael's admission. Perhaps it was the accumulation of gossip which had drifted out of Balnesmoor, stories which had had her maid all agog. She could not say that she had ever known Gaddy Cochran or her daughters, though she had seen them upon the road between the villages now and again. But she had a slight acquaintance with James Moodie and feared his cunning and his power. In Moodie was a similar sort of affectlessness to that which spurred on Robert Blaven and his sons. There was, however, also a moral consideration and, above all others, the thought that Michael might waste the last few precious months of his life in fruitless yearning for a woman who would bring nothing but misery.

"I tell you, Michael, you must not meet Mistress Moodie again."

"Aunt, I beg of you."

"I'll brook no argument, Michael."

"But she will think I have abandoned her."

"Elspeth Moodie may think what she likes. Besides, she's not yours to abandon. No, she's wedded to Moodie in the eyes of God."

"I would not harm a hair of her head."

The unfortunate conversation came to a sudden end, exploded by a spasm of coughing. Excitement had occasioned it; the body would not be denied.

"Lie back, Michael. Lie back."

Miss Blaven knew how to cope with corporeal crises. She ministered tenderly and devotedly to her nephew for the four nights and five days during which the hectic fever raged again; and first love was forgotten in the burning.

Randall hardly knew where he was or the name of the town into which he had stumbled twenty hours after parting company with the Highlanders.

Sir Rowland Hill had marched the division on, turning its face towards Castile, famous and romantic Castile, of old the land of warrior and troubadour, of love and chivalry, battle and song. There was no song in Randall Bontine's throat, though, and he did not give a Spanish damn now about love and chivalry. His one thought was to hold himself on the horse long enough to reach a surgeon who could repair his leg.

Pus and tabs of gangrenous flesh surrounded the wound and stained the bandages brown and green. Fearful spasms of pain threatened his sanity and made him useless as a fighting major. Besides, he had to find an adjutant of the 18th Hussars, one of the senior officers, Seaton or Hardy or Newberry-Price, who might ratify his period of leave and lay a trail which he might follow when he was healed and hearty once more, a trail to lead him back into the thick of battles yet to be fought. In the meantime, however, it was all he could do to cling to the saddle and nudge the beast onward. He kept telling himself that all would be well once he found a surgeon who was more than a bloody saw-bones, that all would be as it was before, that nothing about him had changed.

Dusty, stained and dishevelled Randall reached the town an hour after dark. A cold summer rain added to his misery. He found the town filled with French and British wounded, men brought down from forts and fields, though there had been no momentous battle in the past month. Erosion kept the hospital community busy and, as the Hussar swayed through the narrow streets, he could hear cries and groans of suffering coming from the open windows. On the piazzas of the marketplace, biers of the dead and beds of the maimed were laid out like goods for sale. 'On with the tourniquet and off with the limb' was the mode of medicine practised here. His swollen leg throbbed in sympathy. At length he brought the horse to a halt and shouted down to a poor crippled wretch who was struggling to learn how to stand upright with an improvised crutch.

"You. Is this Vacol? Have I reached Vacol?"

"Aye, sir. You have, sir," said the soldier, a Scot.

"Where's the surgeon's office?"

"Everywhere, sir."

"Are there no regiments here? No officers?"

"In the café by the Santa Clara gate, sir."

"Which direction is the gate?"

"Yonder, sir."

The soldier had propped himself up with the crude, olive-wood crutch. Out of pride and respect for rank, he kept himself upright while he conversed. He tried to salute and to point at the same time and fell, yelling, into the stone gutter at the base of the piazza steps.

Randall stared down at the crumpled heap.

Useless. The man was useless to the army now. He would be given a shilling or two, packed off home and left to fend for himself. It might take him a year to wend his way north to the glens unless he had charitable relatives who would send him the price of the coach. God, but he would have to learn quick how to spin himself about on the olive-wood stick or he would not survive even as a beggar in the streets.

The soldier, groaning, rowed himself into a sitting position and began the laborious process of hoisting himself upright. Randall saw that the man's leg had been hewn off from mid-thigh. Involuntarily he placed his hand on his own limb, as if to reassure himself that it was still in place.

"Who did this to you?" Randall asked.

"Frenchies, sir."

"The name of the surgeon, I mean."

"I never kenned his name, sir."

Fumbling, Randall fished a handful of *pesetas* from his pouch. A month ago he would have flung them into the gutter, uncaring; a month ago he would have spurned charity. The man crabbed forward at Randall's signal and took the coins gratefully. By the light of the flares on the walls, Randall saw that he was no man at all, just a boy of eighteen or nineteen who could not have been in the field for long. He had a wheaten stubble on his chin and round brown eyes like those of a milk-calf.

"Are the Hussars here?" Randall asked quietly.

"Some, sir. I was wi' the 40th."

"Thank you, soldier." Randall straightened in the saddle as the youth tried again to salute him.

"Sir?"

"Aye, lad?"

"Keep awa' from the surgeons, sir. They'll tak' no trouble,

67

even wi' a gentleman. Any cure but the saw, they say, is a waste o' their precious time."

"I'll heed your advice."

Randall rode on in the direction of the Santa Clara gate but did not turn around when he heard a cry of pain behind him; the soldier had fallen again.

The café, bright-lit and rowdy, was built out from the wall of the town only a few steps from the gate. Painfully, Randall dismounted. He felt nauseous and hung on to the saddle for a moment or two until the lights stopped spinning and the ground steadied beneath his feet. The heat in his leg reached up into his groin and belly. Squinting, he fastened his gaze on the door of the café. Within would be soldiers, brother officers. He was determined that he would not collapse across the threshold, would not show unmanly weakness.

The horse snickered.

"Be patient, old chap," Randall muttered. "You'll have your feed, for you've a piece to take me yet if I'm not mistaken."

He tethered the animal to the rail and, making an immense effort, climbed the wooden steps and pushed through the moth-wing doors of the café into the heat and stench which if he had been hale would have revived him immediately.

The drinking-room was crowded with officers, some of whom had had their wounds dressed and, in defiance of the orders of *el medico*, were quaffing horn after horn of native wine. Little interest was shown by the assembly in the stranger and Randall insinuated himself into a position by the door. He leaned against the wall, waiting for pain to subside and his concentration to return so that he might study the faces in the room with attention.

Sweat beaded his brow and stippled the mixture of mud and grime upon his cheeks. He fought against the untenable indignity of crashing in a swoon before officers from three nations, for there were Frenchmen too, prisoners, mingled with the Britons and Spaniards. He had enjoyed many an evening in such company but tonight the merriment dinned in his ears and the reek of tobacco smoke and wine made his gorge rise. After several minutes, however, the pain diminished a little, sufficient to enable him to take control of it. He spotted Seaton, arm in a sling, seated in a corner close to the fire.

Seaton was engaged in uproarious conversation with an

officer of the 50th whose head was bound in a bloody turban. Most of the officers wore bandages but their injuries did not dampen their enthusiasm for war and talk of war. Spanish officers were hunched over chess-tables, absorbed in their favourite game, forgetful of the conflict which was so vital to the liberty of their country. They seemed to bear out the cynical observation that if a Spaniard were given a cigar, sunshine and a flagon of Jerez, it would be all one to him whether Spain were ruled by Solomon or Caligula.

"Seaton, I say," Randall called, after clearing his throat.

Treading carefully, he hobbled between the tables and casks. Seaton turned, grinning.

"What paltry excuse is this you wear? Is it an elbow diseased through lifting too many drinking-horns, uh?" Randall said.

"Bontine, you old warhorse, you scallywag! Damn me, I thought the Highlanders had 'capitated you for their trophy room."

"God, but it's good to see the face of a fellow Hussar, even if it is one so ugly." Randall braced himself against the back of Seaton's chair.

Seaton looked in no better shape than he was himself, though quantities of wine had given the man's gaunt cheeks a simulation of health through heat and heavy sweating.

"Have you the acquaintance of Carfax?" said Seaton.

Carfax was a deal older than either of the Hussars and had begun to shed his hair. Disdaining a wig, he dipped a shiny forehead in greeting and gave Randall a wink. Carfax was deep in his cups, eyes as red and fiery as a boar's.

"Drink," he roared. "Ye'll take drink, will ye not, sir?"

"I will," said Randall, because it was expected of him.

He was handed a horn of hot brandy punch which he sipped with apparent relish.

Seaton was not so drunk as he appeared to be and, seeing Randall's condition, rose from the chair and put a hand on the major's epaulette. "What brings you here?"

"As with yourself, a touch of steel."

"Where? In the organs?"

"The height of the leg."

"Not too high, I trust; not so high that it imperils your performance."

"Fortunately not. But I am septic, I fear, and need attention."

"Was the field surgeon no good?"

"A leech. He would have had both legs off from the waist if I had not prevented it."

"And I would have been minus my fin." Seaton nodded at the sling in which his arm was cradled. "It proved to be little enough."

"Who is the best surgeon here?"

"Mendez."

"A Spaniard?"

"Aye, but a better surgeon than he is a barber."

"Where may I find him?"

"There."

A Spanish colonel was seated with a napkin and brass basin under his chin while the senior surgeon of his regiment – Mendez – delicately trimmed the pointed beard that graced the officer's face.

"So much for the dignity of the medical profession," said Randall. "Will he attend me?"

"If you ask him with an infusion of your customary charm," said Seaton, "perhaps he might be persuaded."

"Intrude, do you mean?"

"Aye, before he tackles his dinner," Seaton said, gesturing with his drinking-vessel.

Enveloped in a cloud of tobacco-smoke a snub-nosed British captain was busy preparing a German dish, the ingredients of which spilled from a haversack on the table beside him. He was shredding cabbage vigorously into a large tin trencher, adding pinches of pepper and sprinkles of vinegar from a bottle.

"Mendez has a British cook, does he?" said Randall.

"They are close friends. One cooks, the other eats."

"How will I –?"

"Approach and be haughty, Bontine," Seaton advised.

Randall nodded and made his way across the room to the place where the surgeon worked. He let phrases form themselves, a salmagundi of arrogance and humility which passed for courtesy in this country and to which the Spanish officers responded. The colonel was generous. The colonel agreed to release his surgeon-barber and Mendez led the major out of the crowded room into a side chamber.

Mendez was built like a fighting-bull, swarthy, muscular and impatient. He spoke no English and did not seem to be impressed by Bontine's fluent command of Spanish. His hands were covered with dark hairs from the colonel's beard. His tunic was stained with dinners past and, Randall noticed, with dried blood.

The Hussar did as bidden, though, without hesitation or protest. He hoisted himself on to a vegetable rack and let Mendez cut away the padding of the wound with a dagger. Mendez incised the leg of his riding-breeks almost up to the waist. He peeled away the cloth. Randall smelled the stench of the wound and after a hasty glance at its green oozing turned his head away and stared into the lantern that gave the chamber light. Mendez used the dagger tip as a probe. There was no pain. However much like a bull the surgeon might be in appearance he was dextrous and gentle in his professional work. The examination took no more than a minute.

In Spanish, Mendez said, "I will remove the limb and you will live."

Randall's mouth was as dry as a cornkist.

He cleared his throat. "What if I do not give you permission to remove the limb?"

"It will not serve you well, that leg."

"Will I, however, succumb to it?"

"How much will you pay me?" said Mendez.

"I beg your pardon, sir?"

"I am surgeon to a Spanish colonel, not a lackey to Wellington's army."

"It's your damned country we're here to save."

Mendez shrugged. "Have you English money? Gold coins? I will save both your leg and your life, Hussar, for the sum of twenty guineas."

"What if I cannot pay?"

"You will die, quite slowly and extremely painfully."

"Unless I find an English surgeon."

"Mendez laughs at your English surgeons."

"Can you really save the limb?" Randall asked.

"It will be a leg of wood."

"What?"

Mendez corrected himself. "It will not be wood, of course, but it will be as stiff as a piece of oak."

71

"Will I be able to ride?"

Mendez shook his head. "Only across the saddle, as ladies in your country do, and not at all for many months."

"Damn you!"

"Damn me if you wish," said the surgeon. "I will take my dinner now if you have nothing to offer me but curses."

"What can you accomplish that I cannot have done free by another surgeon?"

"I will unite the muscles with a stitching. It is expert work and difficult. I am skilled and have done it for many men. It will then be necessary to cleanse and anneal – do you understand me?"

"In what manner?" Randall asked.

"With heat."

"Cauterise it?"

"Yes."

"I've seen it done," said Randall. "It's not twenty guineas' worth."

"You will scream with the pain of it, sir, though I will not plunge a poker into the opening. No, that is not how Mendez seals wounds. I will attend to each piece of rotted flesh as if it was my own. The work will be prolonged and you will swoon. If you do not swoon, Hussar, I will be obliged to have my assistant knock you on the head lest the pain turns you mad."

Randall smiled. "You do promise value, Señor Mendez."

"I promise you life. I will leave you with a limb of sorts, enough to fill your trouser and put into your boot."

"When can it be done?"

"As soon as is convenient to you. Tonight, if you wish, after I have eaten my dinner," said Mendez.

"Where?"

"Here," said Mendez. "Unless you would prefer to put your courage on display before half a hundred intoxicated gentlemen who will no doubt wager on whether you will live or die under my ministrations."

"So be it," said Randall. "I will await your attention when you are ready, Señor Mendez."

"I await sight of my twenty guinea pieces. I have no intention of sharpening my knives until I see the colour of gold upon the table."

"Twenty guineas," said Randall, fishing a leather purse from his pocket and tipping out the heavy coins.

"Excellent," said Mendez. "We will commence in one hour."

"Mendez, what if I do not survive?"

The surgeon laughed and fluttered his sturdy hands.

"I will give you your money back," he said.

Anna hesitated at the iron gate which separated Moss House from the public highway. She brushed the front of her dress and adjusted her bonnet before she slid back the bolt, pushed open the gate and apprehensively entered the garden. She walked gingerly up the path to the front door. As sister, no less, to the lady of the house it would not be seemly to present herself round the back like a common servant.

Ivy rustled on the old walls and swallows darted under brooding eaves. Bees droned in a swarm-hole under an ornamental rose at the base of the chimney. Sunlight turned the oriel windows to copper. Even so, Anna refused to be impressed. It was a plain house, she told herself, not so ancient as it pretended to be, and not so very large either.

She reached up and gave the black iron bell-pull a vicious tug.

One minute later the door swung open and Tolland confronted her.

"Aye, madam? Is there something you are requirin'?"

"I'm requirin' conversation with Mistress Moodie," said Anna, scowling.

"Does madam no' have an appointment?"

"No, I do not."

"Who, if one may enquire without offence, is madam?"

"You ken fine who I am."

Tolland peered down his nose. "Madam Sinclair, is it not?"

"Fetch my sister here, Mister Tolland, since you seem bent on keepin' me on the stoup like a bacon-seller."

The reprimand was delivered with snap, though Anna was, in reality, awed by the stiff-mannered man in cream vest and broad-striped shirt.

"Anna? Anna?"

Tolland turned, a shade nonplussed. Elspeth appeared at his side.

"Why, it is Anna. I thought I heard your voice. This is a most pleasant surprise. Come away in, dearest." She gestured in welcome, then, to Tolland, said, "What's wrong with you, Tolland? Did you not recognise my sister?"

Tolland had dignity and sense. He did not protest or try to defend his negligence.

He bowed.

Anna gave him a black glance as she whisked past him.

"We'll take tea, Tolland. Please ask one of the maids to bring it," said Elspeth. "We'll be in the parlour."

"The drawing-room, madam?"

"Aye, the drawing-room."

"Will madam also be requirin' bread and butter?"

"Of course, Tolland. And cake."

Three or four years ago, when they were girls on the Nettleburn together, Anna would have nudged her sister and made some cutting remark about the pompous steward but she had lost that sort of intimacy with Elspeth long since. She could not be sure that Elspeth did not approve of Tolland, would not regard her criticism as a sign of vulgarity.

Elspeth pushed open the doors of the drawing-room and let Anna enter first.

Although Elspeth had not expected company, she was dressed as for a ball in a frock with an untrained skirt and a bodice of forget-me-nots. On her feet were sandals of gold cloth laced with two minute, pale-blue tassels – so exquisite that just noticing them made Anna feel as lumpy and lame as a heifer with a festered hoof. Elspeth's hair-style had been altered since last the sisters had met. It was now cropped quite short and loose, with an air of arranged casualness to it. The lightness suited Elspeth who, in spite of being tall, had a fineness and delicacy of feature that had emerged with womanhood.

Anna clumped behind her sister into the sun-filled drawing-room.

The furniture was dainty and unpretentious, chairs and a couch in pale-green velvet, an oval table waxed to a deep brown shine, side tables, a fender of painted iron and, since it was summer, white muslin curtains wafting at the long windows. To Anna's way of thinking the room demonstrated her sister's softening presence and gave evidence of a taste which

74

she, Anna, did not possess. On the other hand, she reminded herself, Elspeth did not have to crawl on her knees to polish the skirting, haul out the rugs to beat, nor have to balance on a stool in order to burnish the curtain rings every morning without fail. By God, what a time of it Jacko could have in a room like this!

"Do sit yourself down, Anna."

Elspeth seemed to be excited at Anna's unannounced visit. She was never all 'swanny', inhibited by manners, when in her sister's company, yet Anna felt that the welcome was over-effusive.

"You're lookin' very fashionable," Elspeth remarked.

"It's only my old Sabbath dress," said Anna. "You've seen it often enough."

"Sit down, please."

"Where'll I sit?"

"Take the couch."

Uneasily Anna settled herself on the couch.

"Tea will be along in a moment," Elspeth fussed, then seated herself by Anna's side and took her sister's hands. "It *is* good to see you, Anna. I miss you."

Anna extricated her hands and folded them in her lap.

"Very nice of you to say so, Elspeth."

"How is Matt?"

"He's fine."

"Were you working this morning?" A certain formal correctness elevated Elspeth's speech. "At Ottershaw, I mean."

"Aye."

Four maids attended to the morning milking and did other chores, mainly sluicing and shifting, until three o'clock. Four other lassies, married women, took over for the evening milking, a system which Sinclair had introduced and which was unique to Ottershaw.

"Have there been many changes since old Sir Gilbert went?" Elspeth trundled the conversation along.

"No, hardly any."

"What of Mister Randall?"

"What of him?"

"Will he come back?"

"How would I know? I'm not privy to Ottershaw secrets."

"I thought maybe Mister Sinclair –"

"Bloody Mister Sinclair; he'll hardly cross the time o' day with Matt or me." Anna sniffed and shifted an inch further away from her sister. "You seem to be doin' fine."

"Yes," said Elspeth. "Yes, I am."

"It was a grand catch ye made, Elspeth, no denyin' it."

"James looks after me very well."

The stilted conversation limped to a halt; three or four seconds of silence, with just the *tock-tock-tock* of some solemn big clock in an adjacent chamber.

Anna said, "Is he not pressin' you for a bairn yet?"

"No, not yet," said Elspeth.

"At his age he canna wait long."

"Anna," said Elspeth, "is that why you've called today? Are you carryin'?"

"'Deed I'm not," said Anna. "'Deed I am not."

Silence again; three, four, five, six seconds of it counted out by the timepiece invisible.

Anna said, "I've come here to request a favour."

"What sort of favour?" said Elspeth.

"Matt an' me have –"

Much to her consternation a discreet knock upon the door interrupted Anna's pitch. A silver tray, big as a cart-wheel and worth more than Matt earned in a year, was carried in by a young girl, Moira Kerr, who was not one of the resident servants but came daily from the village. She was sister to a lass with whom Elspeth and Anna had gone to school, one of a large family of Kerrs, several of whom were now employed at Kennart. Elspeth had grown used to her role as mistress to old acquaintances but it startled Anna to see Moira there, acting menial and humble.

"Thank you, Kerr." Elspeth had finally learned that it was proper to address servants, in the Edinburgh fashion, only by surname. "Put it upon the oval table an' I will do the pouring presently."

The girl set down the tray and turned towards the door, eyes cast down.

"Kerr."

"Aye, Mistress Moodie?"

"I believe you are acquaintit with my sister."

Kerr squinted suspiciously at Anna.

"You may wish her a good afternoon, Kerr."

Obediently Kerr gave a bob of recognition. Anna responded with a nod. No words were exchanged, in contrast to the hearty, strident sort of greeting they would have given each other 'outside' Moss House. The distortions of normal behaviour which Elspeth's marriage to James Simpson Moodie had generated suddenly became apparent to Anna. She felt resentment rise in her gorge but she said not a thing as Kerr was dismissed. Next Elspeth went through the ritual of pouring tea, offering silver water jugs and sugar lumps and milk, slices of fine bread spread with butter, seed cake the colour of a marigold. It was a fussy, prolonged palaver. Anna suffered it only because she did not wish to antagonise her sister or to seem gauche in her eyes.

Soon the girls were seated with teacups and saucers, bone-china plates and silver knives no heavier than grass-blades balanced on their knees. Thus fettered, Anna felt even more awkward.

"I believe you were goin' to ask me for a favour," Elspeth said.

Anna swallowed a lump of bread and butter, coughed, sipped tea. "Aye, I was."

"What is the nature of this favour?"

Anna disposed of the crockery, putting the items on to a side table by the couch.

"Matt's of a mind t' leave Balnesmoor."

"Ah!" Elspeth cocked her head and went on snipping at a limp slice of bread with her teeth. "Is it the animosity between him an' his father that's at the back of it?"

"Aye, that's the cause. The quarrel's been festerin' for years," said Anna, relieved of having to invent motives.

How could she possibly explain to her sister that she was here not at Matt's urging but because she was afraid of Randall Bontine, afraid of a daft curse laid by the Sylases of Eardmore? Cocooned in luxury, Elspeth would not understand. Best, therefore, to follow Elspeth's lead and let her think it was all Matt's doing. Besides, Elspeth had always had a soft spot for Matt and might do for the man what she would not do for her sister.

"Matt's of a mind," Anna continued, "to buy gear for a steadin' of our own."

"Not, I take it, in Balnesmoor or Ottershaw?"

"Far away," said Anna. "Out of reach o' Mister Sinclair."

"Does Matt not have prospects on Ottershaw?"

"Not since his marriage to me."

"This steadin'," said Elspeth, sitting forward, "it surely would not be large?"

"It would be as large as we could furnish."

"I have no money of my own, Anna."

"Moodie – James, I mean – he'd lend it to you, would he not?"

"I wouldn't dare ask him."

Anna frowned. "Why not, tell me?"

"I'm his wife, Anna. A wife doesn't ask her husband for money."

"I would if I were you."

"Perhaps you would. But if you did, your husband would be right to be angry with you."

"I canna understand why," said Anna.

"I'm part of his property," said Elspeth, without a whimper of self-pity. "I belong to him."

"He shares –"

"He gives. He doesn't share. It's not right for a man to share. I'm here in Moss House only because James took me in."

If Anna had been raised more conventionally she would not have remained deaf and blind to the clatter of how marriages were forged, the new processes, the new beliefs. She regarded herself as Matt's equal, if not his superior. She was astonished that Elspeth subscribed to such an unnatural division between man and woman.

Anna said, "Ask him if he'll make a loan then, a loan of capital to Matt."

"How would the loan be repaid?"

"Out o' earnin's."

"Earnin's from a steadin'?" said Elspeth.

"Mammy managed it."

"Stuff!" said Elspeth. "Mammy wouldn't have managed at all if it hadn't been for Daddy, for Coll. We would have wasted to bone, you an' I, if we'd depended on income scratched from the patch by the Nettleburn. Mammy sold cattle, an' Daddy paid her to do it."

"Matt could sell cattle."

"Matt knows nothin' about cattle."

"He could learn."

"Could he? How long would that take?"

"Sheep, then."

"Sheep? I doubt if Matt can tell a Leicester from a Suffolk."

"Aye, an' what *is* the startlin' difference, then?" cried Anna, to show, stupidly, that breeding did not matter when it came to raising. "A sheep's a sheep."

"Leicesters provide long wool an' are excellent for cross-breedin'," said Elspeth. "Suffolks give short wool an' rare mutton."

"Matt could learn that, the way you've learned it."

"I learn from an expert," said Elspeth. "Who would teach Matt?"

"It's me, is it not? You'll not lend money to me because I won Matt for a husband instead of you."

"That might have been true three years ago, but it was only childish infatuation. Anna, dearest, you've got to realise that my husband's an entirely practical man. He started with a handloom an' built the Kennart mill."

"Would James not give Matt an opportunity to prove himself? Nobody else will. Not even his father. How can Matt learn if nobody'll let him learn? How can he advance in life if nobody'll encourage him to take one forward step?"

"Advance where?" said Elspeth. "James would say Matt has advanced enough for a young man. Better if Matt put his quarrel with his father to rights an' settled for being a future grieve of Ottershaw."

"Twenty pounds," said Anna, almost pleading. "Twenty pounds would do it. We could go off wi' just twenty pounds. Start anew. Begin properly. If not a loan, a gift, Elspeth. I beg it, for Matt's sake."

"If I had capital of my own, more than the few guineas Mammy left, I'd let you have it willingly, but I'm as poor as you are. It would have to come from James an' I'll not even put it to him."

"Mean!" Anna hurled herself to her feet. "You're mean-spirited, Elspeth Cochran. You always were. It's out of spite you're doin' this to me an' my husband."

"I'm only giving you the sort of answer James would give me," said Elspeth.

"Aye, an' he's mean. He's graspin'. Everybody knows that."

Elspeth rose to her feet too. She put down the saucer and plate carefully. Her cheeks were flushed with embarrassment.

"Anna, I canna do what I've no power t' do," she said, lapsing into the rough accent of her girlhood. "James'll have none o' lendin', an' none o' givin', not least to Matt Sinclair who is well fitted in life as it is."

"Aye, if you call bein' a tree-planter well fitted; if you call bidin' in a dank cottage in the deep woods well fitted; if you call bein' ignored –" Anna gathered her skirts in her hand and swung towards the door with a toss of her head. "Never heed! Never heed! I apologise for takin' up your precious time, Mistress Moodie. You'll ha'e no more bother from me, never fear."

"Anna, please. Don't you see how it is?"

At the drawing-room door, Anna paused, an expression of injured pride upon her face.

"I'll be biddin' you good day," she said.

"Anna." Elspeth spoke softly. "I'll – I'll talk to James."

"Och, don't trouble yourself. We'll manage, Matt an' me."

"What do you want?" said Elspeth. "Is it just twenty pounds?"

"I want to be far away," Anna cried. "Somewhere other than Ottershaw an' Balnesmoor. I'm stifled here. Smothered. Sick of the Lennox."

"I'll – I'll put it to James."

Abruptly Anna was once more composed. She did not permit Elspeth to approach her, however, or to touch her.

"Suit yourself," Anna said and, without another word, left the drawing-room and Moss House.

THREE

Breaking the Will

Hildebrand droned on, "Now, as I understand it from your letter of introduction, it is your wish and charge that I inform you in confidence of the procedures of the law in relation to inheritance specific to the deed and testament issued from the hand of the landowner of the estates of Balnesmoor and Ottershaw – to wit, Sir Gilbert Bontine, late deceased – of which you have provided me with fair and accurate copies for scrutiny. Is this a fact?"

Alicia Bontine gave assent with a sweeping motion of her slender hand, since breeding would not permit a mere nod of the head.

"Is this a fact, sir?" Angus Hildebrand required a double assurance, it seemed.

"Certainly, certainly," Gilbert answered.

Hildebrand had stopped his infernal pacing and leaned over his table to search the clients' faces as if to detect in them some trace of prevarication or evasion. Finding none, the lawyer continued, stepping off on another march up and down the floor in front of the long, rain-speckled window. Gilbert groaned inwardly.

"Whenever the succession to property is not left to the operation of the law but is contained in a deed of settlement, one heir being, as it were, substituted for another, the estate is said to be entailed and the heir may be deemed the heir of entail. The person upon whom the estate is first settled is known as the 'institute' and the remaining person or persons as heirs of entail or 'substitutes'."

Up and down, up and down, as if the fellow's mental faculties only operated in conjunction with his feet; Gilbert had recognised the style of the Dumbarton lawyer; the fellow was a fair and accurate copy of a master of Greek and Latin who had made his life a misery during his two years of study at the infamous High School of Edinburgh.

Gibbie had retained virtually no Latin, even less Greek and was about as interested in the mechanics of the law as he was in the mechanics of windmills. He was interested, however, in the *outcome* of the law, what the law might do for him in besting Randall. He therefore put up with Alicia's scheme to seek the aid of an independent and unbiased gentleman of the law, separate from the Bontines' traditional legal advisers, Mr Dixon and Mr Royle.

"The effect of deeds depends upon the terms under which they are conceived. Three divisions are set down under the law, each possessing, as it were, a different degree of force."

Nothing would stop Hildebrand. Such men were irresistible.

"The divisions are – first, entails containing a simple destination. Secondly, entails with prohibitory clauses. Thirdly, entails that are guarded with irritant and resolutive clauses."

Dead flies, victims of monotony perhaps, decorated the narrow ledge under the panes. Dust like oat chaff coated the books and deed boxes which were mounded on the cabinets that lined the chamber. The chamber itself was perched on top of a close in the Cross Vennel and shared a stair with brothers from the Freemasons' Lodge whose premises were adjacent to it.

"Let us consider, then, the effect of the first two kinds in relationship to the deed and testament before us." Hildebrand had his thumbs hooked into his vest and marched with a strut. "When a proprietor settles his estates upon a series of heirs, substituted one after another, but without laying restraint upon members, or heirs of entail, as they come to succeed, or prohibiting them from altering the course of succession which he has nominated, the deed is a simple destination."

"Did my father do so?" interrupted Gilbert, wishing, on the instant, that he had held his tongue.

Alicia and Hildebrand both gave him such ferocious stares that he might have cowered beneath the table if he had had the space to do so. But Gilbert was tall and angular and, even at an age short of life's prime, was hardly sinuous. He stiffened on the uncomfortable chair and mumbled apology.

"Pray continue, Mister Hildebrand," said Alicia.

Hildebrand sniffed.

"Without interruption," Alicia added, threateningly.

Did she not know that Hildebrand would take her at her

word? The only method of dealing with fellows like the lawyer was to prod them along. But he was no prodder. He had no ounce of push in him, a deficiency which Randall and his sisters, even his amiable stepmother, had been at pains to remark upon when he was growing up.

Hildebrand began again. "A deed of simple destination has the effect that the order of succession pointed to in the entail is to be observed so long as no alteration is made by any of the heirs, or heir, succeeding to the estate; but as the heir in possession is an unlimited fiar, he is entitled to alienate the lands and to alter the order of succession in the same manner that the maker might have done."

It was on the very tip of Gilbert's tongue to cry out, "Can Randall do that?" when he received a sharp tap upon the kneecap from his wife's reticule.

"The clause of destination, therefore, merely grants to the substitutes a hope of succession which is entirely dependent on the will of the heirs of first succession." Angus Hildebrand stooped. "Is this fact clear?"

"Perfectly, perfectly," said Gilbert.

"Besides the destination, the deed may contain different prohibitions upon the heirs, intended for the purpose of preserving the succession to a series of heirs nominated by the maker." Hildebrand paused. "No such a prohibitory clause exists in the settlement set forth by Sir Gilbert Bontine's hand. We will, therefore, not embellish the clause with further exhibitions."

That, thought Gilbert, should save an hour or two at least.

Alicia gave Hildebrand a signal and Hildebrand, who was a gentleman of some perspicacity, deferred to the woman who was, in his opinion, instigator of the consultation and would probably be the one who had his fee paid.

"May I enquire, Mister Hildebrand, how much of this fascinating elucidation is pertinent to the deed and testament of my late father-in-law?"

"In the matter of 'elucidation' all things are pertinent, Mistress Bontine."

"Is there, however, in the testament, a prohibitory clause at all, anything which may legally prevent Randall, the eldest son and apparent inheritor of the estate, from doing as he wishes with it?

"Not," said Hildebrand, "that I can see."

"Am I to take it that, having perused the documents carefully, you can find no means of preparing an appeal to a court?"

"An appeal, Mistress Bontine?"

"To redeem for my husband that which is – morally, shall we say – rightfully his?"

"To wit?" said Hildebrand.

"To wit, Ottershaw."

The question, though hardly direct as Gilbert recognised it, was direct enough.

It gave the lawyer pause.

From outside came the rumble of a cart and an exchange between two mongers, vociferously peppered with oaths. A large bluebottle, on its last legs, stammered against a corner of the window and, as Gilbert watched, dizzied down and fell to the window ledge where it lay on its back with its legs kicking; an analogy for his claim to the mansion and lands of Ottershaw which he sensed was also dying on its feet.

"Can," Alicia went on, "a case be prepared for challenging the legality of the deed?"

"Not when it is taken in conjunction with the testament," said Hildebrand.

Alicia sucked her teeth. It was an ill-mannered habit which she had never been able to break, a sign that she was perturbed. It ruined the elongated line of her profile which, in candlelight and shadow in particular, was handsome, and also made the wisps of dark hair which lately had appeared on her upper lip more evident, like the whiskers of a cat. Gilbert wished that she would not suck her teeth, but he did not chide her, not even gently, at this moment.

After all, what Hildebrand had to say about the deed and testament was crucial to his future. He would not be left homeless or penniless; Father had not been so cruel and remiss as to exclude him, or any of his children, from an inheritance of monetary value. But it was Ottershaw that Alicia wanted. Anything less than the whole pudding would not do.

"Is it impossible?" said Alicia.

"How many offspring, living, survive Sir Gilbert?"

Gilbert answered, "Eleven."

"Eleven? Is that a fact? Male issue?"

"Three," said Alicia before her husband could open his mouth. "Randall, Gilbert and Robert."

"Robert," Gilbert put in, "is my half-brother. He is the son of my father's second wife, and a good deal younger than Randall and I."

"What age is he?"

"Thirteen."

"Does he reside at Ottershaw, in the bosom of the family?"

"He resides, mainly, in Ireland with his mother and my uncle," said Gilbert. "Since my father's demise my stepmother has been much away from Ottershaw and, indeed, plans to make her home in Marinwood in Ireland."

Gilbert did not embellish these simple declarations of fact. It was no business of Angus Hildebrand that Alicia had successfully driven his stepmother out of Ottershaw, not by demand but, rather, by an excess of devotion; devotion coupled with discipline and authority.

"There is, I see, a sizeable settlement of money laid upon the widow," Hildebrand stated, lifting the bulky testament. "I assume that such legacy, and others mentioned, can be met from resources without the selling of land or leases?"

"Yes," said Alicia, who had personally gone through the documents with a bone-comb. "It has been established that it will not be necessary for my husband, or for any inheritor of Ottershaw, to sell property or tack. Sir Gilbert was wise enough to ensure that there was money in the banking houses, sufficient to meet the legacies, without recourse to selling part of Ottershaw."

"Does that include the seven thousand pounds which is allotted to your husband?" said Hildebrand who, whatever his failings as an explicator, had certainly studied and mastered the testament.

Gilbert glanced at Alicia; he had not thought to ask.

Alicia answered promptly. "It does, Mister Hildebrand."

Hildebrand said, "It is therefore clear that the disposition of the moveable property, which affair is in the hands of the appointed executors, is fused with the deed. The will and testament cannot convey heritage; that is the business of the deed and document pertaining. But, according to my reading of it, the paying-out of legacies precludes the disposition of further moveables attached to the estate itself – to wit, the whole goods, gear, tack and household furnishings – which are to be handed with the land and buildings to the full-blood, senior, male heir."

"Randall," said Gilbert, nodding.

In his latter years his father might have appeared a wool-gathering dreamer, reclusive and unworldly, but the blood of the Bontines still oozed through his aged veins and suffused a Bontine brain. Sir Gilbert had redrafted the testament, along with the heritable deed, six years ago.

"The intention and stipulation of the testator is clear," said Hildebrand. "He wished the elder full-blood son to have Ottershaw, its lands and its rented properties, intact, and to preserve them intact."

"It's unfair," said Alicia, a phrase she had been repeating at regular intervals since the will of old Sir Gilbert had been made known.

Gilbert tended to agree with his wife. It was not that he wanted the power or the income that came from Ottershaw, just that he, and not Randall, had given it his attention during the past decade.

Randall had chosen to turn his back on Ottershaw and Balnesmoor, to forsake the life of a laird of the parish in favour of the roving, adventurous life of a soldier. Randall had mocked the stay-at-home. Yet it was Randall who would inherit Ottershaw, who would turn Gibbie and Alicia and their children out, who would have to learn the arts and crafts of landownership from the beginning and take responsibility for the tenantry. Alicia was right; it was unfair.

Gilbert said, "It was, however, how my father in his wisdom wished it to be."

Hildebrand said, "I take it as a fact that the testator was of sound mind up to the date upon the testament?"

"A matter of definition and opinion," said Alicia.

Gilbert leaned forward urgently. "My father's mind was as clear as spring water right to his last hour."

"Therefore his reason and competency might not be grounds for challenge?"

"Certainly not," said Gilbert.

Alicia tutted but did not disagree with her husband. There were far too many reliable witnesses to attest that Sir Gilbert had been of sound mind and disposing judgement when the documents were drafted.

Hildebrand said, "That being the case, I regret that I can offer no immediate, practical assistance in the matter of obtaining redefinition of the deed or the testament. The law, unfortunately for some, is not like a horseshoe which might be bent and recast at will."

The lawyer began again to walk up and down. He did not notice, or elected to ignore, the bluebottle's death dance or the battle royal between the mongers in the street outside the window.

Hildebrand went on, "The authorities are strict upon several points of the law of inheritance. If I might cite a case of note for the interest it contains – to wit, the action of Lord Strathnaver versus the Duke of Douglas."

Gilbert had had enough. To Alicia's surprise and Hildebrand's consternation, the man got to his feet and interrupted the speech.

Gilbert said, "We're grateful for your advice, sir. May I ask in conclusion if there is anything at all to be done, if not to secure the estate of Ottershaw for myself, to secure it for my children, of whom I have four?"

"Nothing can be done expediently and directly."

"I see. Well, you have our thanks." Gilbert shook the lawyer by the hand.

Hildebrand, Gilbert thought, looked unwarrantably glum. Perhaps it had been his intention to milk Alicia's determination to have Ottershaw for their branch and draw fees for months to come. Gilbert had never shared Alicia's belief that the estate's lawyers were prejudiced in favour of Randall. They were merely executors and fulfillers of the wishes of his father. Unfair it may be; Randall had no interest in the Lennox estate, no interest in the continuation of the traditions attached to the family and the place. But it was how Father had chosen to dispose of it. Rank and power must continue to accompany wealth and, by leaving such odd distinctions open to ambition, would not repress exertion by narrowing the field for competition. Randall and he had always been in competition, and Randall had always proved superior. Had that been in Father's mind when he summoned Dixon and Royle to draft and notarise his will, deed and testament?

"There is," said Hildebrand, "one glimmer of hope."

Alicia stopped sucking her teeth and perked up.

"Do you mean hope of inheritance, Mister Hildebrand?"

"Indeed, I do."

"What is it that we might hope for?"

"Randall, the oldest son, has no issue, has he?"

Alicia nudged Gilbert, as if she were too modest to give a complete answer.

Gilbert said, "None that we know of. None legitimate and baptised."

"That being the case," said Mr Hildebrand, "if–and Lord knows we would not, I'm sure, wish it – but if the oldest brother and nominated heir does not survive long enough to marry and bear issue then, and only then, will you or your surviving heirs come into full and complete possession of the estates of Ottershaw and Balnesmoor."

"Is that the law?" said Alicia.

"That indeed is the law," said Mr Hildebrand. "One would not, of course, wish Mister Randall an early and untimely death."

"Indeed it would be most un-Christian to nurture such a tragic hope," said Alicia piously. "Nevertheless we must acknowledge the fact that Randall is a serving officer at present engaged in the Spanish campaigns and that he must be constantly at risk."

"At risk," said Hildebrand, "and without legitimate issue."

At that moment Gilbert noticed that the bluebottle had struggled to its legs again on the window sill and, with wings buzzing loudly, had risen up the glass. Gilbert did not know whether he was relieved or disappointed that Hildebrand had held out hope. How could he, her husband, tell Alicia that Randall resembled that bluebottle, stubborn and indestructible? He would sound like a fool.

"Mortal man," said Hildebrand, "may be powerless to tamper with the Scottish laws but God, if He chooses, may break or bend the horseshoe at any time."

"Alicia, I –" Gilbert began.

But his wife paid him no heed. She was shaking hands with the lawyer, rewarding him for his help and advice with one of her enigmatic smiles.

What that smile meant precisely Gilbert did not dare imagine.

The sun sank in a welter of blood-red cloud and stretched the shadows of the olive grove out like great velvet fingers towards him. Between the trees, framed in laurel, was the end of a winding river, molten gold in the afterglow. From the horizon came the chanting of ecclesiastics and the slow, solemn tolling of a chapel bell. He seemed to be standing just above the ground, floating motionless in the last rays of that sunset, unable to tear himself away, unable to exert any sort of volition at all.

She came out of the trees in the middle distance, a girl dressed like a peasant but with a sash of white silk about her waist. He had the uneasy feeling that he knew her but he could not put a name to the face nor place her in the scheme of his existence. He saw now that she carried a taper in her cupped hands and, though she was running, that the flame did not waver or go out. She stared straight at him as she approached and her lips parted and her head was thrown back and he felt that she might be crying a warning except that there was no sound in his ears but the chanting and the knell of the chapel bell.

He cried out but made no sound.

Who are you? Tell me your name.

She ran towards him. She came no closer.

Straining every muscle he broke the terrible, sticky inertia and tore himself from the landscape, striving to reach her since it seemed that she would never reach him.

She was an angel bearing the Light of Salvation.

He desired her with a strange pure passion.

From the trees galloped a brigade of French officers. There were twenty or more in the company, magnificently accoutred with full, swaying plumes and tricolours as large as hayfields floating away behind them from the tops of their lances.

The girl was oblivious to the charge and ran as before, without motion, the taper offered out to him. He saw her vividly outlined against the wall of horsemen and he cried out to her again as she had to him; but still there was no sound except the ineffable solemnity of the bell and the rhythmic chanting.

He tried to cover his eyes, to blot out the horror, but he could not even perform that simple action and, paralysed, watched the lances lower and point at her, then bend. He saw her lifted on the tips. She thrashed and screamed and threw up her hands and the taper blossomed into an orb of golden light and floated, light as thistledown, up and up and up into the darkening sky. Involuntarily his eyes followed its soft flight until it vanished into the heavens. When he lowered his gaze again the horsemen had gone and nothing remained but the girl, still now, with her clothing all torn and bloody, and her neck thrawn.

Randall screamed aloud at the terrible loss that smote into his heart, screamed and struggled – and jerked himself suddenly wide awake.

"Bontine, for the Good God's sake!"

Sweat trickled down his face and his neck was rigid. He thudded back against the long bolster as he saw the light again. The light was no figment of his imagination but only a candle held by an aged nun and before it, huge and bloated, was a familiar face thrust close to his own.

"Bontine, do you not recognise me, man?"

Pad of cloth upon his brow wiped away sweat.

"It's Seaton, your old companion."

"Seaton?"

"Aye, who else would bother with a tramp up the hill to call on a scallywag like you?"

"Seaton, I was – I was dreaming."

"It's the fever again."

"No. No, I've been better," Randall declared in a voice that did not encourage credence.

But he had been better. During the hours of daylight he had been remarkably well, without unendurable pain in the leg, only a clawing sort of itch which in its way was worse than the spasms. It was the hours of the night that he found difficult. He was tormented by a strange recurring dream, the dream of a girl to whom he could not put a name. He had spoken of the dream to Mendez, before Mendez had moved on with his Spanish colonel. Mendez, however, was not a doctor of the mind; he had declared the repair of the leg to be successful but had made no promises for its function. "Dreams?" Mendez had said.

"Dreams of women are better for you now, Hussar, than dreams of glory in the field."

Randall had no need to ask the surgeon to explain. He was not so free of pain as to imagine that the leg was as good as new. When he first climbed out of the truckle bed in the bare ante-chamber of the nunnery on the hillside above Vacol, three miles higher than the bivouacs, the limb would not support him. It would not bend to his demand. It splayed out, let him down, pitched him to the floor. The nuns – only two of whom he had encountered, both old – were amused. Their apparent lack of sympathy roused his anger. The women of the cloth were, however, excellent nurses and the food, what he could eat of it, was nourishing. Seaton, he later learned, had arranged the hospital and paid for it out of his own pocket.

Seaton clasped him by the arm and drew him up from the bolster. He was not nearly so weak as he had been and took further strength from the comradely grasp.

"Randall, I am on my way again," said Seaton. "My wound has healed sufficiently and I hear again the skirl of the pipes from over the mountain. We are awa' to hunt Soult's divisions through the sierra."

"I'll – I'll join you in a week or so."

Randall swung himself out of the bed. He wore drawers and a compression band about his stomach but nothing else. The wizened old nun was not shocked, nor did she giggle. She stood quietly in a corner holding the candlestick so that the officers might have light. Upon a chair, Randall's uniform hung empty. It seemed leeched of colour as if it, like his career, had faded rapidly in the wake of his injury.

"There's much talk of your deeds at Almarez, talk coming down from the brigade," Seaton said.

Randall felt no pride. Almarez was over and done with, together with all the battles he had fought in and survived. He had not joined with death, only with pain and injury. The rest seemed hazy and touched with a peculiar boredom. He did not wish to be reminded of it, not by Seaton at any rate.

"When do you leave?" Bontine asked.

"In the dawn light."

"What is the hour now?"

"After ten of the clock."

"In a week," Randall said, "I'll be fit in a week or so."

"Och, man, you'll not be fit for many a month. I spoke with Mendez. You're fortunate to be lofted on two pins at all."

"Give me a horse –"

Seaton shook his head at the vanity of his fellow officer, the irrational belief that he was cut from different stuff from other men.

"Brigadier Coltart is in office at Requena, on the route to the ports of Valencia. There is a regimental establishment there," said Seaton.

"Are you telling me I must report to Coltart?"

"We are away, Randall."

"Aye, I suppose you are, Seaton. I give you thanks for all that you have done for me."

"I have a final gift," said Seaton. "Brandy. French bottled at that. A trophy." He placed the bottle upon the table. "And I have brought you letters from the mail-bags which came up three days ago. You have several missives from Scotland. I envy you your letters from home."

"You envy me nothing else, I'll wager."

Seaton's bluff features softened. "No, nothing else, Bontine."

The men shook hands, Randall still seated on the bed. The final greeting was stilted. The jests and badinage fell flat. The nun watched, her head on one side.

Then Seaton was gone. It was improbable, Randall realised, that their paths would cross again, though he had bid hail and farewell to so many amiable officers in his career that he felt no more than a momentary pang of regret at Seaton's departure. The door closed. The nun remained.

Upon the table, by the brandy bottle, were four packets of mail, eight or nine letters in all. Diffidently Randall stretched out his hand for them. He could not reach.

The nun shuffled to assist but he growled, "No," and held up his fist threateningly. She stopped, the candle-holder extended, bathing the table and the bed with its light.

Randall grimaced, pushed himself upright and, balanced like a rope-walker, tottered to the table. He did not sink on to the chair but held its back, waiting for the stitch of pain to draw out of his thigh. He was bound still, and the linen was clean; no oozing, no poison. What lay beneath the padding was a mess of scarred, knotted flesh with the fatty blisters of the searing-iron still raw. He leaned into the chair and took the brandy bottle into his hand. He drew the cork with his teeth then, the bottle poised, glanced at the nun. She was very old, very wrinkled, winnowed by the years. He wondered how much she understood of the war, if she admired him for fighting for the Spanish cause.

"If you would be so good, Sister, as to set the candle down upon the table, I would be obliged to you," he said softly in her mother tongue.

It wearied him to charm her. He wanted to give her orders, snap at her like an arrogant subaltern. But he might be here for days yet, weeks perhaps, until he could find a method of revitalising the muscles of his leg and fitting himself into a saddle. If he could not march, he would force himself to ride. He would live on horseback, eat and sleep on horseback, would become a Minotaur; or did he mean a Centaur?

The nun put down the holder. The candle was tallow and gave a glabrous light, stinking as the wick spluttered and uncurled. It was long enough, fat enough, however, to provide several hours of reading, though he imagined that he would be bored by Gibbie's trivialities and his father's essays on sheep before a quarter-hour had passed.

"Thank you, Sister," he said.

The old woman bowed and, still without a word, shuffled out of the room and closed the door.

Randall swung the brandy bottle and drank deeply.

It was fiery and quite smooth and he drank again, twice, before setting the bottle back upon the table. He felt better, stronger. He inched his way around the chair and hoisted himself on to the table, letting his legs dangle. He had discovered a certain comfort in that position, with the weight relieved. He moved the candle-holder and the bottle and, with his left hand, spread out the packets beside him. They were sealed and stamped but without legible date.

He picked one packet at random and broke it open.

Three letters.

He picked one of the three and ripped it with his thumbnail, unfolded it and, holding it low to catch the light, began to read the latest, belated news from home.

At home James Simpson Moodie presented the image of a man who straddled the pinnacle of worldly success. In Edinburgh society, certainly in London, Mr Moodie might have been considered a trifle 'rustic'. In county towns where much of his business was conducted, however, and in the marts of that coarse but vital centre of the new commerce, Glasgow, Mr Moodie's conservatism was respected, his no-nonsense style admired.

Marrying a young beauty without pedigree plucked from the fields had done the merchant's reputation no harm. James and Elspeth made a handsome couple. They appeared entirely well suited. She possessed youthful poise to offset his mature stolidity. That he loved her there could be no doubt. If certain cynical gentlemen – Rudge and Scarf, for example – murmured that bouncing with a girl thirty years his junior had certainly benefited James Moodie's health, they did so out of earshot of their employer.

Tales that came from servants at Moss House, chits of girls who fastened on anything they did not understand, were given little credence. After all, many a married couple in spacious circumstances kept separate bedchambers. It was becoming quite the fashion and, it was said, added spice to games of chase-the-goose. It also freed a husband from a clutter of paint pots and ribbons and from tripping over little slippers when he advanced his conjugal rights.

It did not, of course, occur to anyone – not even the all-seeing Tolland – that James Moodie had never bedded his wife, that Elspeth remained as virginal and pure as she had been at the altar step on her wedding day.

Dinner, or supper as it was called when guests were not being entertained, was the final event of the day. Afterwards there might be a half-hour's reading in the library or a hand or two of jaggs or cribbage played between wife and husband by way of fellowship. But Elspeth was expected to be off upstairs by half-past nine at the latest to leave her husband to his accounting or letter-writing or to deciphering the published bills and acts that stemmed from an over-active parliament, all of which seemed, according to James's grumbles, designed to bring wool merchants to ruin.

Ten was a late enough hour for a girl used to beginning work at dawn and being wrapped in her blankets not long after the sun went down, but Elspeth, like her husband, was no sleepy-head. She would prop herself on the bolsters and by the light of an oil lamp or a branch of candles would read far into the night. Most nights she would still be awake when James came upstairs. She would listen to his tread upon the boards of the landing, listen with hope and anxiety, her face turned towards the unlocked door. But the footsteps did not falter. She would hear his door open and unhesitatingly close and, night after niggling night, be left to wonder what she had done or not done to turn him against her in that way. Why did he not want her?

There was, however, an undercurrent of relief in her bewilderment. She had no more desire for James than he for her. Her feelings for Michael had forced her to recognise the truth, that she was locked into a marriage in which desire had no part.

Dinner that particular night was as lavish as always. James set a full table. The board groaned with dishes to suit his taste; plain fare but an excess of it, as if it gave him satisfaction to survey dishes of meat and tureens of soup, cheeses and fillets of smoked fish, comfits, cream puddings and imported fruits ranged all about. When master and mistress had had their fill the rest was taken off by the serving-girls. What would not keep was scoffed by the domestics or handed out to gardeners and stable-men in the morning. Mr Moodie might be shrewd and hard in business dealings but he was not, in small things, mean.

Little was said during the course of the meal and when it was over James ordered coffee to be served in the library. A bright fire had been lighted in the grate and four or five posies of garden flowers, selected by Elspeth that afternoon, adorned the mantelshelf and heavy furniture. James poured coffee from a plain, octagonal pot of solid silver which he had purchased along with other valuable pieces from a dealer in Perth. To be sociable, Elspeth accepted a little cup, laced with fresh cream and sugar. She was alert for a pause in James's desultory complaints against manufacturers in Yorkshire's West Riding who had again permitted their workers to rise up in demand for a minimum wage and to demolish valuable property, including a couple of gig mills.

"Twenty minutes," James said, "and the foul work of musterin', destruction and dispersal was over."

"Aye, dear, I read of it," said Elspeth.

"Luddites, they call themselves." James shook his head.

"Give rioters a name an' you dignify their mutinous causes. God, but hangin's too good for them."

"Are you worried it'll happen at Kennart?"

James hesitated. "There will be no riots here. For some reason, for which we may be thankful, the folk of the Lennox have no fear of marchin' on with progress."

"Perhaps they haven't learned yet," Elspeth said.

"Aye, well, the labourin' class is always slow to learn anything." James rested his shoulder against a corner of the mantelshelf. "I regard the Yorkshire louts as wretched and deluded. I could almost pity them, near enough, if it was not for their barbarity an' the ravages of disorder which they equate with the expression of grievances. I wish they were sensible enough to realise that what benefits the masters equally benefits them. Investors of capital are not their enemies. Would they prefer to be cast out into the cold, wet fields again to scrounge ha'pence howin' cabbages and toppin' neeps?"

Elspeth gave him no answer. It had occurred to her, though, that the building of mills and similar manufactories was of itself a dangerous thing. Out in open rows and cold rigs, there was no congregation, no concentration of discontents; men and women suffered more stoically in small communities. She had, however, not explored this line of thought, certainly not enough to challenge her husband in discussion. James's question had been rhetorical in any case.

Elspeth wondered when she should bring up the matter of the loan to Matt Sinclair, how she could best introduce the subject. To her surprise, James gave her a lead.

"What did your sister want?"

Tolland, of course, had informed James that Anna had been to call at Moss House.

"She came t' request a favour."

"What would that be?" said James.

He was studying her with odd intensity, the little coffee-cup lost in his hand. He had put the saucer on the shelf by the flower bowl.

"She wondered if we — if you — would be prepared to lend Matt money," said Elspeth.

"On what security?"

"I don't know if there is any security."

"What answer did you give your sister?"

James seemed angry; not in the manner she would have anticipated. It was as if he were angry at her.

Elspeth said, "I told her you'd not make a loan without a security."

"Do you want me to give money to this man?"

"It's of no great importance to me, James."

"But you have – feelin's for him?"

"He's my sister's husband."

"His father's grieve of Ottershaw and no pauper. If there's an urgent requirement for cash, why does the lad not ask his father?"

"He wishes to leave Ottershaw, to strike out on his own."

"Doin' what, by way of profession?" said James with something close to a sneer. "Sellin' withy baskets to auld wives?"

"A steadin'," said Elspeth. "A smallholdin' of his own is the objective."

"Where you would be free to visit?" said James.

It did not dawn on Elspeth what troubled her husband. She had no tie, except the fact he was married to her sister, to Matt Sinclair. Her fancy for him had long ago vanished; a childish affectation, no more.

"I'd hardly be likely to visit at all if they settle out of the Lennox," Elspeth answered. "Matt wants away from Ottershaw, to be his own man."

"He told you so? He spoke with you intimately of his plans?"

"I knew nothin' of it until this afternoon when Anna called."

"Yet you informed her there would be no loan from me. Why did you do that, Elspeth?" said James.

"Because I –"

James put the coffee-cup into the saucer, came to a short-legged satin chair and seated himself upon it, leaning his fists on his knees.

"Do you not think he should leave Balnesmoor?" said James. It was hardly a question at all.

"Anna's keen to be away."

"Oh, so it's Anna who must carry the blame."

"Blame? Who must carry blame for –"

"Why does your sister want away from here?"

97

"I don't know, James. I assume she's tired of Ottershaw."

"Sinclair's no farmer, you know."

"I told her so."

"Wiser and better men than him have foundered on a smallholdin'," said James Moodie. "How much does he ask for?"

"Twenty pounds," Elspeth answered, "to purchase stock an' farm furniture."

"Twenty pounds, indeed! God, when I was his age it took me a six month crouched over the loom to make that sort of sum; aye, and precious little of it was profit. It seems these days that the young have no patience." James reached between his knees and dragged the chair forward. "So – twenty pounds is Sinclair's price, is it?"

"It's as much as you care to lend him."

"It's ten times what I'd care to lend him."

"Very well, James," the young woman said. "I'll inform Anna to that effect."

"Unless you insist, I'll give him nothing."

"I'm only a messenger." Elspeth was confused. "Anna would have come to you but she holds you in awe."

James snorted. "Why did Sinclair himself not come to see me?"

"Because I'm Anna's sister."

"Could he not meet my eye?"

"I don't know what you mean."

"Could he not face me?"

"He hardly knows you, James."

"He knows you better, does he?"

"We attended school together. We're of an age."

James got to his feet. "If I give Sinclair a loan of twenty pounds, will he clear out an' leave Balnesmoor for good?"

"That seems to be his intention."

"If I do this, you'll not see him again?"

"It's unlikely, unless Anna needs me."

"Unless *Anna* needs you?"

"If she falls ill or, perhaps, if she has a confinement, and I'm obliged to be with her, then I would ask your permission –"

"Is she with child?"

"She says not."

"You, by some chance are not –" James did not complete

the question, sensed that it was excessively vindictive and unjustified.

"How can I be with child, since you've not seen fit to consummate our vows?" Elspeth snapped.

"It was an ill-considered, ill-timed remark," muttered James. "I was thinkin' of your sister, not you."

"I'm your wife, James, the kind of wife you elect to make of me."

"Is it so hard?"

"Sometimes it is hard."

James returned to the fire and retrieved his coffee-cup and saucer. He fussed with the silver pot, his back to his wife who, however, did not lapse into her seat again.

Part of her shrank from pursuing the question of her unnatural marriage; another part of her longed to bring it into the open. James made her so comfortable, though, treated her with such affection that she could find no small stick with which to beat him. How could she tell him that she needed to be loved as a man loves a woman? She had come to him, come to Moss House to join in a mercenary union, to give him pleasure and access to her body in exchange for the security that his wealth promised in abundance. He had cheated her of that, had somehow made it all seem dishonest by ignoring her femininity. And, she realised, she was lonely.

James turned, forced a smile, cocked his head. "I'll talk to young Sinclair. I'll give him a chance to put his case."

"Don't talk to him," said Elspeth. "Please don't bother."

Suspicion again. "Why should I not, since it's Sinclair who'll have my money, if I choose to give it?"

"Let me tell Anna you have refused. I warned her you might. Let the matter remain as it is."

"Why did you ask me at all, in that case?"

"I don't know. I wish I'd never raised the subject."

"Leave it to me, my dear," James said. "I'll disentangle the fankle you seem to have got yourself into."

He was humouring her now, patronising her. Oh, yes, James would defend her against every offence – except his own incomprehensible reluctance to treat her like a grown woman.

Though a carriage clock stood on the table in plain view, James drew his watch from his pocket and consulted it ostentatiously.

"Ah!" he said. "I see it's growin' late. Off upstairs with you, dear."

"And what of you?"

"I have work to do," James said.

She gathered her skirts and turned from him.

"Elspeth?"

"What?"

"Have you not forgotten somethin'?"

"What?"

"My kiss."

He offered his cheek.

She kissed him brusquely and obediently then left him alone in the library to ascend, alone, to her bed.

James had come up and gone into his room and closed the door. She had not stirred at the sound of his footfall on the stairs. It was warm in the bedroom. The casement was open. Lace curtains wafted in the balmy night air which drifted off the hillside and carried the sharp little sounds of the moor into the silent house. She had been reading the latest novel to arrive from Menzies' Circulating Library, an innovatory scheme which James had paid fee to join. *The Italian*, a later work by Mrs Radcliffe, had gripped Elspeth at first. It seemed so in tune with her audacious daydreams that she could not lay it down. But her eyes had grown tired in the candlelight and the thread of the story had become confused. She had put the volume aside, her mind tumbling with thoughts far removed from the pilgrims and *banditti* of Italy's Inquisition.

She wore the lightest of shifts. In it she felt weightless as she slipped from the four-poster. When she confronted her image in the cheval-glass, with the glow of the candles behind her, she seemed to have no substance at all. Tentatively she cupped her breasts, feeling the nipples stiffen instantly under the thin silk. She was taken by a longing to strip off the garment and fling herself nude upon the bed. Breathlessly she hurried to the window.

The first of the harvest moons silvered the evergreens and cast fat shadows over the lawn. The drystone walls which slithered over the pastures were sharply outlined and the great humped shapes of Drumglass and Dumgoyne showed every crag and cranny in coal-black silhouette. Elspeth sighed and stretched out her arms as if to embrace the hills and the moorland. Cool air soothed the throbbing in her body, reduced the errant and unfamiliar need. Out on the Orrals a vixen cried hauntingly and a colt in the stables near at hand snickered; then all was still and silver once more.

If he had not wished it she would not have seen him. He was well hidden by the bole of a sycamore, close enough to look up into her bedroom, close enough to admire her by the back-light of the candle within the chamber. He had no hesitation in showing himself.

"Michael?" she said.

His sway-brimmed hat was as old as sin and he wore a greatcoat loose about his thin shoulders like a cloak. He behaved without a trace of embarrassment and with jocular candour swept off the hat and delivered a bow so deep that his brow almost touched the grass.

She felt a huge surge of joy at the sight of him, relief in the knowledge that she had not lost him or that he had not abandoned her. It gave a sharp edge to his declaration of love. She knew that he had not come to spy upon her but only to be close. She wanted so badly to call down on him, to tempt him upstairs by the servants' corridor, to bring him to her here in her bedroom. She felt no remorse and no shame in allowing him to look at her figure. How it would have ended was a mystery which had no solution. At that moment a light gleamed in the window of James's room and dappled the broad stone ledge of the corner. It was too obvious, too threatening a sign to ignore.

Michael vanished as if he had been consumed by the sycamore tree. She felt cheated, robbed of the moment and its infinite possibilities. She would not be driven by James from the open window and lingered there for fully ten minutes. But Michael had gone, had slipped away into the darkness and would, even now, be skirting the edge of the moor on his way home to Preaching Friar.

How many nights had he visited the garden in the hope of seeing her? Perhaps being close was reward enough. Had James seen him? She doubted it. There would have been a hue and cry for sure; ruffians had been abroad in Balfron and Killearn, thieves and housebreakers. Michael was a stranger to her husband, would always be a stranger to James Moodie.

She was comforted by the knowledge that he came to her in the night, that he had not held it against her that she had rejected him that day upon the Orrals, almost two months ago, and had not ventured one step upon the moor since then. She was disturbed, however, by the fact that her need of him had not diminished in the intervening weeks, but had grown stronger, had become desperate and undeniable. He seemed to be everywhere around her, as if the moor itself reached out to caress her. By her side, only a few feet away, the lamplight in James's window receded. She was once more alone. She waited, trembling and breathless, for Michael to return, her heart breaking with her longing for him.

After a time she was driven from the casement to the bed. She sank down upon it, yielding and solitary, and let the breeze from the moor brush her limbs and stroke her body. She could not resist now. How long could she resist Michael? There was no answer, only her own little moaning cry, and out upon the moorland the whimper of the vixen like a child afraid of the dark.

It had come as a fearful shock to Alicia when the letter from Harwich had reached Gilbert's hand. Randall was back in England. Randall had been discharged of his commission, honourably it seemed. Randall would be banging his fist on the table in two or three weeks' time. Randall had no intention of relinquishing his estate or his title to anyone, least of all to Gibbie. Randall wanted Ottershaw's rent books and income, not to mention the mansion, all for himself. He advised Gibbie, in straightforward terms, to begin a search for a suitable domicile for himself and his family. Randall even had the gall to suggest that Gilbert might prefer to reside in Ireland, to put down roots on a small agricultural estate near Uncle Alexander's in the ring of Kerry. Gilbert was not well pleased and Alicia was black affronted.

"Am I to be turned out of my house like a gypsy from a field, left on a cart in the rain with my poor children starving and shivering around me?" she had cried.

"Come now, Alicia, Randall has given us six months to find a suitable dwelling. Villain he may be but he won't have us bodily thrown out."

"I would believe anything of that person," Alicia had gone

on. "I always took him for a man of some honour, a soldier who would put commission and country before personal benefit and gain."

Gilbert had nodded. "Indeed, it's strange that he seems eager to return. He's never cared a jot for Ottershaw. Why, suddenly, should he embrace it?"

"To spite us."

"Have you heard no more from Hildebrand concernin' the deed?"

"It appears that nothing is to be done about it."

"Oh!" Gilbert was not unduly surprised.

"But what, I want to know, is to be done about Randall?"

"Perhaps," Gilbert had said lamely, "Randall will change his view after he comes home. Ottershaw hardly seems the sort of place for an active and adventurous fellow. Perhaps he will see the folly of trying to be a laird, will accept a sum of money in lieu, and go his own way to perdition."

With such fond optimism Alicia had to be content, and bide her time until Major Bontine severed himself from the ties of his King's Commission and steered north across the Scottish border again.

In the villages, word spread quickly: Mister Randall's going to become the new laird after all. Mister Gibbie's flung out on his lug, lock, stock and biscuits. Wild rumours stimulated the conversation of tenants and servants, giving rise to excuse for heavy drinking among men who obscurely felt that their security was threatened by the return of the military enigma.

On the Sabbath morning, Reverend Eshner offered a prayer for the laird's safe return and, in the family pew, Alicia Bontine screwed her face into a mask of fury and glowered from under the knob of her bonnet at the minister who, being one of those who prayed with his eyes closed, did not notice the lady's ire. In his secret howff up on the moor, Pad Tomelty offered a toast to Major Randall for the increase in the local consumption of whisky; but nobody knew who it was who had leaked the news of the laird's return. It could hardly be Hunter, Tolland's equivalent at Ottershaw, for Hunter, like a true-born steward, was the soul of discretion. It could not be Lachlan Sinclair for he had told nobody except his dear and trustworthy wife, Aileen; and Aileen had told nobody except her son, Matt, who had in fact come to her for the express purpose of having the rumour confirmed. Matt, in due course, told Anna and Anna flew into a panic.

Matt, however, had no time to spare to placate his silly wife whose moods and fancies struck him as childish, not the sort of things a man should be bothering himself with, not when there was money to be made now the cereal crops were in and Pad Tomelty's pot stills were steaming night and day. What Matt did not tell his wife was that he had been approached by no less a personage than James Moodie and that the damned weaver had tried to bribe him to leave Ottershaw.

Moodie had caught him coming out of the back of the Ramshead inn, behind the pig mews, late on a Wednesday night. Dressed in black he merged into the shadows about an hour or so after the sun had gone down. Matt had had a dram or two from the contents of the kegs which he had spent the afternoon cargo-ing down the hillside, instead of clearing out a coppice of old beech trees as he should have been doing. How Moodie had got himself into hiding, for the Ramshead was all eyes and ears, Matt could not imagine. It gave him a shake, though, to be called to out of the mews.

"Sinclair."

"Who's there?"

"Calm yourself. I'm no Exciseman."

Weaver Moodie showed himself. He had his hands in the pockets of his coat and the collar turned up as if it were already chill winter and not a mellow September evening.

Matt said, "What are you doin' in such a place as this?"

"I wish words with you, Sinclair."

"Could ye not have sent one o' your messengers, since it's private discussion ye seem t' require?"

"It's private enough here," said Moodie.

"How did ye know I'd be –"

The question died on Matt's lips. So, also, did his urgency to be away up the fork road by Dyers' Dyke to return the cart and pony to the shed by McDonald's cottage.

There was noise from within the inn, the scrape of a fiddle and three merry songsters trying to adhere on the melody of *Fare Thee Well, My Dame*. There was light too from the windows, enough to show Matt the heavy leather purse that Moodie had removed from his pocket and held up, chinking, in his fingers.

"Fifty guineas," said James Moodie. "Guineas of the good, old-fashioned, solid sort."

"Aye, I've seen guineas before, Mister Moodie."

"But have you ever owned one," said Moodie, "let alone fifty?"

"What is this?"

"The loan you requested through the intercession of your wife," James said. "Fifty, not twenty."

"On what terms is it given?"

"When you have settled an' turned the ground to profit, you may repay me as you can."

"It might be years an' years."

"I'm aware of that fact. Nonetheless, here is the cash you asked for." James Moodie gave the purse a little, almost impatient shake.

Matt did not reach out for it. He was suspicious and arrogant. "Is there no condition?"

"I informed you that there was no condition. The loan is to aid you in findin' a steadin' of your own, for the stock and the furnishings," said Moodie. "Take it."

"Strikin' out on my own is an easy thing to talk about, more difficult to accomplish," said Matt.

"Damn me!" Moodie snapped. "Am I to dangle this purse before you all night?"

"What if I take the money to put to other purposes? What if I repay you, with accumulation of interest, in – say – a six month?"

"The money is for a farm. Ground," said Moodie. "In fact, I have enquired about a vacant rent of sixty acres –"

"Where?"

"Cromarty."

"Cromarty!" Matt exclaimed. "Why in God's name would I be wantin' to make a home in Cromarty? It's a thousand miles away."

"Hardly so far," said Moodie. "It is, however, a sweet parcel of ground with a sound cottage upon it, so I have heard on good authority."

"What if I don't want to go to far-off Cromarty, but prefer to find a steadin' of my own elsewhere?"

"I'll hold the fifty guineas until you do."

"Are ye bribin' me to leave the Lennox, by any chance?"

"I was led to believe it was your wish to leave here."

"Ye were led to believe incorrectly," said Matt.

"Do you not want my money?"

"I'll take your money, certainly," said Matt, stretching out his hand for the purse.

"And leave Balnesmoor?"

"Nah, nah!" Matt shook his head. "I'll not be told by you or anybody how I must direct my life, Weaver Moodie."

James Moodie's fist swallowed the leather purse but he held his hand raised so that the bag might reappear at any moment. "You may never have such an opportunity again, Sinclair."

"I may have better," said Matt with a smirk.

"Running whisky for Tomelty?"

"I canna understand why ye have this interest in my welfare, on a sudden," Matt said. "Pitchin' guineas at me. Pryin' into my business."

"I have been reminded," said James Moodie, "that you are a relation, albeit by tenuous connection. I feel I have a responsibility to you, Sinclair."

Matt made an unflattering sound with his lips.

"I need no man to look out for me or mine," he declared. "If you'd made this offer – aye, and it's a generous offer I'll admit – three months ago I might have taken it an' gone. I have somethin' to hold me here now. I'm not givin' it up, Weaver Moodie."

"I see," said James Moodie, "that you are naught but a stubborn fool." The fist with the purse in it returned to James's pocket.

"Why do you want rid o' me?" said Matt.

"I think you know the answer."

Matt stuck his tongue into his cheek. "Perhaps I do. Perhaps I do not," he said, endeavouring to cover bewilderment with youthful bravado. "But I'm not goin'."

"Then you may rue it," said James.

From the side door of the inn a knot of Moodie's mill-hands spilled on to the cobbles of the yard, shouting and cursing jovially. Moodie's name was on their lips, slurred and slanderous. If they had known that the weaver was within earshot they would have sobered immediately with the shock of it. But James Moodie had no ears for the jolly insults and ribaldry.

"I saw you upon the moor, Sinclair," he hissed.

"Aye, then you know," Matt stated.

The young man and the weaver were close together and neither would relent.

"If you stop now," said Moodie, "I'll say no more about it."

"What if I do not?"

"I'll be your enemy."

"Hoh!" said Matt, shrugging.

James Moodie broke off the conversation. There was no more to be said, no further appeal to be made to Matt Sinclair.

Matt felt a warm suffusion of triumph as if, somehow, he had bested the well-to-do weaver in a contest of wills. He was tempted to brag of it to McDonald an hour later when the woodman came out of the cottage to see the cart and the pack animal safe home. Prudence stayed Matt then and slyness stayed him later when he had returned to Pine Cottage to find Anna in her usual guddle of pots and platters.

Aye, if he could have gone without Anna to Moodie's promised croft in distant Cromarty, if Moodie had offered to take her off his hands, perhaps he would have been more sorely tempted. He found that he had no desire to talk with his wife, to tell her that her plea to Elspeth had been well made and had borne fruit. He had no energy left that night for argument and quarrel. He knew that Anna was keener than he was to get out of Ottershaw and far away from Balnesmoor. Matt did not associate it with the laird's return, with Randall Bontine, the illustrious, mysterious eldest son of the man who had owned him since the day he'd been born.

Saying nothing of his work that day, or of the strange encounter with James Moodie, Matt greeted Jacko lovingly and with the monkey perched on his shoulder sat down in good humour to eat.

FOUR

Citizens All

High tide at Broomielaw, combined with a sudden sharp drop in temperature, brought October mist oozing from the river into the heart of Glasgow. Redolent of salt and brew-wash, fish and horse-manure, the mist browned like gravy as it poured across the meadow flats and over the roofs of the villas that flanked Queèn Street and elegant Exchange Square. Although it was not yet the rasping winter fog which would prowl the town for weeks on end and draw its rope through the lungs of many a citizen, the mist could hardly be classed as mellow. Certainly it had bite enough, come seven o'clock, to bring a wheeze to the chest of sturdy Trina Cunningham.

Big-boned and fleshy, Mistress Cunningham seemed far too robust to suffer from a delicate chest yet her health was sufficiently suspect to require her to nip frequently from the flask of gin which her 'husband' George had brought along with the rest of the truck from their lodgings behind the stables of the Lord of the Isles. It also necessitated an extra layer of shawls about her enormous shoulders, a blanket tucked around her enormous legs and a deal of concerned fussing from George in intervals of business at the hand-cart.

It being a Tuesday and the bill at the Queens being an interim company without a decent comedian or an exciting play to carry it, custom at the stalls along the south side of the street was hardly brisk. Trina was not much troubled by having to replenish the crusty pies or soused herring or the russets or green marble pears on the trays. Hot pease pudding or sweet chestnuts roasting on a glowing brazier would suit the change in the weather and a change in venue might have found more customers. But the farthing crowd no longer appealed to the Cunninghams who, having defied constables and the theatre's bully-boys for the privilege of setting up opposite the pillared frontage of the Queens, intended to stay there through thick and thin.

In addition to the Cunninghams' cart, the pavement gave space to flower and confectionery stalls, to trays of combs, pins and handkerchiefs and an antlered rack of gloves attended by a sedate 'lady' recently abandoned by a caddish earl. Riff-raff and beggars were deterred from invading the pitch in theatre street, chased away by George and several other fellows who attended the women there. Queen Street was too remunerative to queer with undesirables.

In the ten months that the Cunninghams had occupied the stance they had reaped a handsome reward for their enterprise. Indeed they had money to spare and George had even opened a modest account at the Ship Bank, which was a rare thing for street people to do. Living had become easy for the Cunninghams. Trina had regular doses of gin to keep her tubes 'liquidated' and George now bought his tobacco in pigtails. For all that, the Cunninghams were not content. They found that they had precious little time to savour the fruits of their labours. Traipsing round the food markets in search of cheap cuts and cheaper fruits, lugging purchases back to the stable building for Trina to garnish, hand-carting the stuff to Queen Street – all consumed much time, in addition to the long cold hours of attendance on the stall.

There were occasions when George and Trina wondered if it was worth the effort or if they would have been happier as they had been before, tagging the city fairs for a shilling or two, and living idle on the knuckle.

On that particular Tuesday, with winter barking in the mist and the pavement chill upon the toes, George and Trina were bored and disgruntled and ready for challenge, for the opportunities that chance was about to throw their way.

It was some four or five minutes after curtain-rise and those citizens who had ventured out to see a nobody named Parish perform the role of Captain Absolute had cleared the foyer. Only a few well-to-do patrons would roll up to the columns now and the stall-owners would either move off to other corners or while away the slack period by chatting and taking a bite of supper.

The late-comers did not come in a carriage. Walking, they appeared suddenly around the street's south corner. There were two ladies, a female servant and a muscular young footman. George and Trina were able to tell at a glance from which strata of society the ladies had sprung.

Taking the pipe from his mouth, George muttered, "Trade money."

The footman had no buckles on his shoes and the maid was plain stuff too, though the ladies both wore opulent gowns which rustled under fur-trimmed mantles. Obviously they had not come far, possibly from one of the new villas in Ingram Street.

It was the elder of the ladies who called out in a vulgar voice, "Marzipans. I really must have marzipans. Thomas, see what's on the trays, lad."

The women followed Thomas the footman towards the stalls.

"Apples look choice, m'm," Thomas said.

"Fresh from Lanark this very morn," confided George. "Pears too, drippin' with juice. Four fruits for tuppence."

"No, I want marzipans." She turned to her young companion. "Elspeth, my pet, what catches your fancy?"

The young woman, hardly more than a girl, approached the Cunninghams' cart and studied the trays by the light of the lantern which George obligingly tipped forward on its pole.

At that instant Trina Cunningham rose from her stool like a hot-air balloon, crying, "Good God, it's Bell Harper!"

Frowning, George glanced at his distraught wife and lost touch with the customers who, steered by the old lady, had gone down to the sweetmeat tray and were buying papers of marzipan in preference to fruit. The group swung towards the theatre and were on the edge of the coping before Trina found voice.

"You, lady. You, come back," she cried.

Thomas squared his shoulders and prepared to protect his mistress and her guest from harassment.

"Take an apple, lady. It costs nothin'. It's a gift for somebody pretty," Trina called, offering a pippin in her big fist.

Thomas would have relieved the stall-owner of the apple but Trina would have none of it. "Let her come an' take it hersel'."

And the young woman returned, hesitantly, into the puddle of lantern light.

"It is you. Bell, how can it be you?" Trina leaned her astonished bosom upon the trays and stared at the girl as if she were a ghost.

The footman gruffly put an arm about the girl's shoulder and steered her away from the half-daft fat wifie with her offer of apples and her air of derangement. Slumped on the trays Trina stared round-eyed until the young woman disappeared into the theatre.

"What is it, dear one?" George asked anxiously.

He placed a hand on his wife's shoulder. In response she twined her arms about his waist and laid her head on his stomach. She was shivering. George feared that she had contracted a fever. When she rolled her eyes to his, however, he saw that she had been stunned by an amazement. Bending, so that the nosey stall-holders on either side could not hear, he asked again what was wrong.

"Lord, Lord!" Trina answered. "I believe I just seen a ghost."

"A ghost?"

"Aye, her. The young 'un."

"She looked solid enough t' me," said George.

Trina shook herself free. "What age would ye say she was, yon lady?"

Humouring his wife, George shrugged. "About twenty, I'd hazard a guess. Twenty at the most."

"I worked by her in the wash-tubs o' the Tontine. Full twenty years ago."

"Impossible," said George. "Trina, you're mistook."

"It's her, I tell you. It's her. No mistake."

"Who is she, then?"

"Bell Harper. Forty if she's a day."

"Forty? She's never forty. Nah, nah!" said George. "Besides, yon's a lady. She never tramped suds in her life."

"Georgie, I tell you it's the self-same lass."

George relieved his wife of the gin flask and, uncapping it, sipped a mouthful of the reviving liquor.

Trina sank down upon the stool once more. She stared at the frontage of the Queens as if the solution to the mystery was being played out on the stage within. She too realised that the fine-dressed lady, with a maid-servant and a footman in her entourage, could hardly be the poor bedraggled slattern she had been acquainted with two decades ago. Memories stirred in her mind. She grunted again, nodded again, as explanations occurred to her.

"Her daughter, then," she declared.

Bewilderment left George Cunningham's features, replaced by a slanting slyness.

"She had a daughter, this washer-lass?" he asked.

"She'd a pie in the oven, last I saw."

"An' a husband?" said George.

"No husband, only a courter."

"What happened t' this Bell Harper lassie?"

"Flung out," said Trina, as if the answer should have been obvious.

"Where did she go?"

Trina Cunningham shook her head. "Can't say."

"To find the courter, the father o' her bairn, perhaps?" George suggested. "Or back to the bosom o' her family?"

Balanced against the woman's knees, he passed her the flask and watched her drink as if gin might ignite memories and illuminate the dark corners of the past.

"She had no family. She came t' the Tontine orphaned."

"To find the man, then," George stated. "The daddy."

"I wonder," said Trina, "where she bides now."

"If that lass *is* her begotten daughter then your Bell Harper bides in a mansion house an' eats her dinner off silver plate."

"It's her daughter," said Trina, flatly. "I just know it."

George Cunningham wriggled closer, an elbow across his wife's lap, his mouth only an inch from her ear.

"Who," he whispered, "might the daddy be, eh?"

"I saw him," said Trina, "three or four times, at the backs o' the tavern, waitin' for her. Handsome he was, if small built."

"Wealthy?"

"Ragged poor," said Trina. "A country lad, a weaver."

"His name, his name? Can ye recall his name, dearest?"

Chapping her knuckles on her forehead as if to shake down facts like walnuts from a stunted tree, Trina pondered.

"I canna. It's forgot, plain forgot," she said, at length.

"Never heed," said George. "Maybe it'll come back to ye."

"It's her, though, Georgie. I'm not mistook on that score."

"I'll take your word on it, Trina, 'til it's otherwise proven."

George Cunningham got up and with his hand on the

woman's shoulder, as if posing for a formal portrait, joined her in staring across the road to the Queens. He had no need to explain himself to his woman. They were of like mind and like intention. Both were stimulated by the coincidence and alive to its possibilities.

"First step?" said George.

"Follow her home," said Trina.

Mortifications administered by the management committees of the sundry Incorporations and Guilds of the City of Glasgow were invariably bequeathed to assist the poor and needy. Charity had become as much a mark of prosperity as the erection of a new mansion in the deep green fields beyond the Kelvin. Custodians of these charitable trusts were invariably dignified men, upright as steeples. John McCracken, nine years deceased, had been a fellow of different stamp. Canny in business as a woollen draper, in private he had been a ranting, hard-drinking, rubicund reprobate who had formalised his vices by founding a society – the Stocking Club – of like-minded bon vivants who met fortnightly in the Buck Head Hotel in Argyle Street.

The current Chairman of the Stocking Club, son of the founder, administered the interest on the sum that old Johnny had left and, having regard to the wit and wisdom of the father of the feast, blew it annually on a rip-roaring dinner for drapers, hosiers and their friends who were in serious need of 'cheering up'.

It was as the guest of draper John McCracken that James Moodie found himself at the top table in the Buck Head Hotel, involved in a round of healths and merry toasts. James had no particular fondness for revelry and nurtured a definite dislike of crowds. But he had refused McCracken's invitation year upon year, on some excuse or another, and now felt that it would be churlish, not to say bad for trading relations, to refuse yet again. Besides, McCracken had generously invited James and his good lady wife to spend a day or two in the city, lodged in considerable comfort in the McCrackens' new town house in Ingram Street.

James was apprehensive about leaving Elspeth alone in Balnesmoor. He had sense enough to realise that he might in part be at fault for prompting her to find companionship in secret assignations. When he put the matter of a jaunt to Glasgow to her, Elspeth showed immediate enthusiasm and, thereafter, the arrangements fell snugly into place. Shopping and a visit to the play would be Elspeth's entertainments. She would be escorted by Nettie McCracken while James attended the Stocking Club dinner with John the draper and went to the Trade House on the following afternoon, to listen to a debate on laws relative to the imposition of tax on foreign wool imports. Elspeth, and simple chaps like McCracken, might imagine that James visited Glasgow to have sport but, as always, James's brain was ticking like a clock. Even in the rumbustious atmosphere of the Buck Head, surrounded by wholesalers and retailers of woollen goods, James could not relax the fretful tension which had become dominant in his character and from which, even now, there seemed to be no release.

James, of course, had made sure that the clutch of drapers with whom he had once done tuppenny business as a handloom weaver were either dead or so dwindled that they could not afford the Stocking Club's subscription. He had a fear that some low-grade customer, kept in bond for twenty years or so, would surge out of the company, point a finger at him and heap scorn upon him for his humble origins. The vast majority of drapers and hosiers in the room had also started small, had pulled and tugged at opportunity to drag themselves from hovels and reeking vennels into respectable prosperity; yet none knew Moodie, none had had acquaintance with the pious kirk elder of the past. Even so, James did not feel comfortable in Glasgow. It was here, not a mile from the Buck Head, that he had yielded to the temptations of the flesh. His sin was that of the town itself, an ugly and expanding entity, most fierce and frightful in its offerings. He could not forget it.

Though whisky flowed like water, wines and brandy too, James drank only enough not to seem stand-offish. He ate the viands and grilled salmon and a whole sweet tart, however, to have something to do and to absorb the alcohol in his stomach which countless comical toasts had put there, sip by sip.

By midnight James was the only sober man in the long, low-beamed room. Even he had a thickness in the head and a faint, annoying buzz in his ears. But the members of the Stocking Club, most of whom were indefatigable, were ranting loud as ever, led by one puce-complexioned draper or another through choruses of the old ribald songs, or treated to speeches and impromptu renderings of poems from swaying orators who climbed unasked upon the tables. The maids, James noticed, were still hard at work; not a rosy cheek among them, only drained-white exhaustion, as they hurried from tap-room and cellars with more bottles and jugs and tried, as best they could, to clear the plates away before breakage forced the Buck Head into bankruptcy.

The weaver reclined, head against the panelling, feet on a stool, and studied the poor enslaved girls and their tap-room masters. He was not temperamentally inclined to enjoy herd-pleasure; the omission weighed upon him further. McCracken, his host, had hopped away from the top table and was lost in a gaggle of younger men about the fireplace. Forty lost souls, James thought darkly, seemed to have swelled to a hundred or more. The formality with which the dinner had commenced had long ago vanished. He would have slipped away, gone back to bed in McCracken's house, except that he had seen the four-poster there and knew that Elspeth would be in it.

Rising, James pushed himself from behind the table and clambered over the legs of two fat drapers who, with arms about each other's shoulders, were crooning a weepy dirge about Fair Chloe and the Thorn. It would be an hour or two yet before the evening's celebrations ended and the drunken gang rolled into the night to find their carriages and wend away home for a few hours' slumber.

"Jamie, Jamie, whaur d'ye go?" McCracken sang out.

James did not have to reply. Vulgar suggestions came from several parts of the room. James grinned unconvincingly, waved at the Chairman and acknowledged the hoots of the company as he weaved between the tables to the kitchen exit as if heading for the earth closets at the rear of the carriage yard. He paused at the end of the short passage, however, to glance into the room where lassies in sodden smocks were sluicing mugs, glasses and bottles in wooden tubs as if it were a morning hour. They laboured in a wet and oily haze, barefoot and bare-legged, hair straggled into rats'-tails, skirts tied up. They paid him no need at all; the bold and buxom ones had, perhaps, already been beckoned away to earn a few extra pence in the darkness of the backs. If he wanted a woman, he could find one out there. He might have her without preliminary or aftermath for the price of a mug of ale or a loaf of bread. He pushed into the air and crossed the cobbled yard where a handful of carriage servants lurked. He went out by a lane to growing-ground by the hotel's west gable. An oppression of the spirit weighed heavily upon him.

Trees in autumn drapery; beyond them was the wall of a new dwelling, chimneys and slates, a perfectly square window lit by a candle. James caught the whiff of the mist, not dry now but pearled with moisture, redolent of damp vegetation. Off to his left he glimpsed movement, heard a woman's laughter, the curse in a man's voice. He hurried on under tree boughs to the place where the lane ended, as furtive as any of the nocturnal lovers, as much in need of solitude as they were of coupling.

Stopping – he could go no further – he leaned against the trunk of a little beech which clung to the mud in the corner like an urchin in search of shelter. His head ached. He put his hand to his face and kneaded his fingers into the flesh. The dark corner reminded him of the backs of the Tontine, transported him through twenty-two years. Isobel Harper had slaved like one of the tub-girls in the Buck Head. But he had not been a client of the tavern, had not had money to 'buy' her, to take her once and put her out of his thoughts for ever. He had defiled her with selfishness. He had believed himself to be 'in love' with her, while despising her for her low caste, despising himself for wanting her so. The shy touch of her breasts, her retracting loins, his own heavy demanding flesh; what pleasure was there in such an experience? How could he ever separate it from the vision of her under the tree boughs in the half-light where she waited, dotingly, on his instruction? Five times he had walked from Balnesmoor to Glasgow holding that sere, sweet image in his mind's eye. Five times he had forced himself into her, crouched and afraid and desperate; then he had abandoned her.

Weaver Moodie had cared more for his good name than for Bell Harper. When, months later, he saw her dead in the hut by the Nettleburn, he had felt a great wave of relief. If Bell had tracked him down, had confronted him with his bastard, he would have been ruined. He had so much more than Bell; less to give but more to lose. Now, though, after carousal, blood fired by meats and strong wines, he had deliberately sought out the memory, to relate it to Elspeth, Isobel's daughter. His daughter. He could not accomplish the transference. Elspeth was image, not reality. His love for her was different. If every woman were a daughter or a mother, how the life of a man would be eased. He would not be vulnerable to the distractions and demands that nature fixed like a horsebit into the heart and soul.

From under the limp leaves that remained on the trees, a draper emerged. James watched longingly. He saw how casually the man adjusted his clothes and strolled back towards the kitchen door; a man of the world, a sophisticate, gratified by his minor adventure. The servant-girl, tall and raven-haired, was casual too. She was no mirror vision of Bell Harper, however. She had no love in her. She tugged down her skirts and tied the ribbons of her bodice. He might call out to her, softly, and she would come to him. He might have her, and no harm to anyone. But the connection would not bring back Bell Harper, would not inch him towards the ultimate degradation, the pretence that his daughter was his wife, that loving Elspeth might absolve him from the sin of murdering poor Bell by ignorance, lust, selfishness and pride.

How he wished he had steered clear of Glasgow in this melancholy October month. He might still take the road out of the city and tramp home in four hours. For an instant he was tempted to surrender to his need to be back in the sanctuary he had created in Balnesmoor; Moss House, Kennart, a chaste marriage.

Elspeth was the only person in the world he loved now that his mother had grown old and senile. How he longed to shed the complex subterfuges of respectability, to walk away from everything, everyone. Duty and niggling doubts about his sanity stayed him, forbade him from yielding to impulse. Hidden by the beech, he lingered until the whore had gone back into the kitchens, then he slipped out of the lane and returned to the oppressive room, to McCracken and the rest of the devil-may-cares, to endure the dying hours of the night.

Tomorrow, however, he would concoct a plausible excuse for quitting Glasgow, for cutting short the visit. He would be home, safe home – with Elspeth – before dusk drew down over the hill of Drumglass.

*　　*　　*

A tom-cat covering a mouse-hole has an instinct for timing. It knows by nature when to spring and when to watch and wait. George Cunningham was blessed with a similar instinct. He did not need Trina's nagging to keep him to his post near the front door of the McCracken house in Ingram Street. Though he might harbour some doubt about the eventual value of the proceeding, he, like his woman, was a born opportunist. He had followed the ladies hence after the theatre performance and, after going home to his lodgings to snatch a few hours' sleep, had returned to his look-out shortly after dawn.

It was a murky sort of morning so George wore a heavy pea-jacket and a long muffler against the chill. He arrived in ample time to observe the house servant, a tousled, yawning girl of fifteen or sixteen, unlock the front door and set about to sweep the step and the narrow cobbled path that split the miniature garden down to the wooden paling and the gate. By the time the lass reached the gate with her broom, George just happened to be passing, just happened to raise his cap and bid her a good morning, just happened to stop and strike up a conversation while the girl leaned on the broom-handle and sized him up. If she had been older she might have spotted a charlatan; but she was young and daft and outgoing and, before you could say knife, was answering the stranger's questions unstintingly.

The house belonged to Draper McCracken. He resided there with the wife, Nettie. Visitors were in residence, which made a deal more work for everybody. Visitors up from the country. Visitors? Moodie, him a manufacturer, with a young wife. Moodie and the master had been out most of the night at a meeting in the Buck Head. Meeting? Supper for the Stocking Club. The servant-girl prattled on about the work and the quarters and the mistress of the house, to all of which the stranger listened sympathetically, interjecting a question now and again. A shout from the hallway and the appearance there of a stout woman in a linen apron ended the pleasant chat and the maid-servant was all of a bustle again, whisk-whisking away with the broom. George Cunningham topped his cap and smiled before strolling away, amiably, pipe in mouth, into the curtain of mist that draped the street's end.

Trina found her man, a half-hour later, seated on a horse-post fifty yards from the McCrackens' gate. She had brought him a nibble of breakfast wrapped in a cloth and he broke the bannock and folded it over the slice of cured ham. Talking between mouthfuls, he told Trina what he had learned.

"Moodie," Trina muttered. "Aye, that name chimes wi' me. But I'll need to be seein' him afore I can be certain."

"Draper McCracken had him at the Stockin' Club in the Buck Head last night."

"So Moodie might be connectit wi' the trade."

"Might be a weaver," said George.

"Up from the country. I wonder which part o' the country," said Trina.

"The lassie didn't know."

"What about the girl we saw?"

'Moodie's wife, younger by a lump than her husband."

"Wife, not daughter?"

"Wife."

"Aye, it's peculiar," said Trina. "I'll need to see them both wi' my own eyes."

"Trade's lost for the day," said George. "If you're willin' we'll settle to the task."

"I'm willin'," said Trina. "Who can tell, Georgie, it might be worth the loss o' a day's trade. An' a lot more, forbye."

"Sit here, then, dear one," said George. "Keep warm-wrapped an' snug."

Already the centre of the city was coming vigorously alive. Carters were out, hurrying pedestrians. The confluence of streets and lanes about the new Exchange created a clot of wagons and horses which, by half-past eight, almost blotted out the Cunninghams' view of Draper McCracken's villa. If George had not gone closer, close enough to see that the curtains had been furled in the upstairs' chambers, he might have missed the incident that occurred in the half-hour to nine o'clock. As it was he had to hasten to summon Trina from her seat at the horse-post in time to catch sight of gentlemen as they emerged from the villa and set off down towards Argyle Street. Trina was not built for speed. But her eagerness gave her wings and she danced through a flock of a dozen sheep and through a herd of fourteen milking-cows which had been driven up from the Stockwell and joined her husband just in time to start after the men. One, Cunningham surmised, must be Draper McCracken and the other, in all probability, his visitor, Moodie.

No clear sighting of the pair was possible, short of a confrontation face to face, a situation which had to be avoided, but McCracken did not race away at his usual rate down to Argyle Street and his retail premises. He walked sedately, almost mincingly, as if his head were a great wobbling bladder which required careful balancing. By his side, moderating his stride, was a strong-built man in his forties, swarthy and grim-seeming, wrapped tight in a tailored greatcoat and with a stiff, round, beaver hat on his head.

The city was strident with the din of trade and commerce, with the clack of engines emanating from the windows of cellar and attic workshops, the bawling of street folk, the trundle and groan of big-wheeled carts and the roar and bellow of animal voices rising above the general operatic chorus. The Cunninghams walked with the shuffling gait of born Glaswegians, displaying a sort of ambulatory conceit which stated, in the manner of it, that they would give way to no one. They were so much part of the street parade in the morning hour that neither gentlemen would have remarked them even if they had had occasion to look round.

In due course the draper and his guest swung into Argyle Street and entered the door of John McCracken's shop which was flanked on the right hand by two bow windows of bull's-eye glass. Behind the glass, artistically draped over little teak dressers and ladders, tartans were displayed, together with stockings of various hues and a variety of other garments from the weaving looms. There were two aproned 'lads' within, each armed with measuring strings and enormous metal shears, and, already, several customers poking about in the long trays of stockings, the mainstay of the retail trade.

George and Trina did not enter the shop. They took up a position at the centre window, George with his back to it, his flint tin in his hand and his pipe cocked as he went through the process of finding a spark to light the plug in the clay bowl. He seemed as nonchalant and easy as any man in Argyle Street and Trina, arms folded across her bosom, no more than a casual scrutiniser of the draper's wares.

"Aye," said the woman after two or three minutes. "It's him, the self-same chap from all those years ago. Moodie.

Jamie Moodie. I remember now. He's changed, but not so much as the calendar warrants."

"Are you certain?" muttered George.

"I'd stake my neck on it."

George nodded, collected his wife on his arm and led her back by the way they had come to another period of waiting and watching outside the Ingram Street house.

In due course, an hour or so after Jamie Moodie had returned from Argyle Street, the gentleman and his young wife re-emerged into daylight, and the Cunninghams' patience was rewarded with sight of the quarry. The stalk was properly begun.

At payment of two and a half pence per double mile, the Harlwood Flyer's trips along the road to Glasgow netted the McGowans a tidy sum per annum, particularly as Wattie had established the routes long before Post Office mail contracts had been dreamed of.

Speed was the McGowans' watchword, speed and the ability to forge through, no matter the state of the weather and the roads. In the 'normal' course of events, which meant any day on which the hedgetops stood clear of snow and the floods were less than nostril deep, wee Wattie and one of his sons would be on the board of the light, high-wheeled conveyance. Five passengers could be carried in comfort, plus two more hardy types on top but on that morning there were only two passengers awaiting the Flyer's departure in the ring of the Fosters' Tavern in the Candleriggs.

Coachman McGowan was surprised to see Moodie there. The weaver, Wattie knew, had come to town in his polished cabriolet and would not have sent it back to Moss House if he had intended to return after only one night's sojourn in the city. It was not, however, for the likes of wee Wattie to question the motives of the mighty Mr Moodie and Wattie nudged his eldest son who sprang to receive the valises from the servant and to stow them securely in the boot of the rear of the coach.

In a twinkling, young Wattie had flung open the passenger door, kicked down the drop step and was handing Mistress Moodie into the interior. Old Wattie leaned down from his perch. "Good day to ye, Mistress Moodie."

"Good day t' yourself, Wattie," the young woman answered,

but Moodie himself said not a word and looked grim and indrawn as he hoisted himself into the coach.

Minutes later, at a brisk pace, the Flyer bounced out of the tavern yard and headed uphill to the north-west, along a route that would take it through the suburbs into the rolling fields beyond the Saracen's Cross and the smoke-stacks of the St Cyrus Chemical Works.

Elspeth sat by the rattling glass of the off-side window, watching the fragments of the new Glasgow suburbs flit past. She made no attempt to engage her husband in conversation or to discover the true reason, not the excuse he had offered the McCrackens, for their abrupt departure.

James was taciturn and she was wary of riling him since his temper seemed to be smouldering damply like a pile of autumn leaves. She was not particularly sorry to be going home to Balnesmoor. She had enjoyed her visit to the Queens but thought the play itself silly and unsatisfying and had quickly found Nettie McCracken's effusiveness wearing and her vulgar remarks embarrassing. She was also glad that she would not have to spend another night in the Ingram Street house, for sharing a bedroom with her husband – he dozed in a chair by the fire, wrapped in his greatcoat – rubbed home the hollowness of their marriage. Besides, in Glasgow she felt very far away from Michael.

Soon after Wattie made his mail-stop at the Post Office cottage at the Saracen crossroads, the coach would climb a long hill by the mill at Calderbrae and she would see Dumgoyne peeking over the horizon, as if on the look-out for her return. But the Flyer made another halt, to pick up a passenger from St Cyrus.

She heard his voice and, an instant later, found Michael staring at her, hands braced upon the sides of the little door and his face pale. He gave her no greeting by name and Elspeth averted her eyes in confusion lest she too give away what was in her heart.

She stared out of the window at a paddock where carriers' cuddies cropped, at a hideous sod cottage with chickens on the roof and at seven or eight small, ill-clad children who stood dumb as calves by the raddled fence. Beyond the little tableau of poverty, sunlight gilded the distant pastures and lit the beautiful shedding birch trees.

Michael settled himself into the far corner seat.

"Good day to you, sir," he said to James.

But James, who had given the stranger hardly a glance, grunted to indicate that he was not in the mood for chatter.

"Is it not a fine spell of autumnal weather?"

"It is, sir, it is indeed," said Elspeth.

James glared at her and she said no more but sat tense and uneasy.

Michael looked different, changed, very thin and white, though he wore rather formal garb and held a tall hat on his knee.

Outside, young Wattie could be heard bawling at an urchin who had run under the horses' bellies, a dangerous and insane game in which the wild tribes of this impoverished hamlet engaged, much to the McGowans' irritation. There came the thud of a clod on the side of the Flyer and a barrage of curses from driver Wattie, the crack of his long whip, the furious scream of some child or other to whom punishment for stupidity seemed entirely unjust; then the coach was on the move, brisk and crisp, pulling away towards the Lennox boundary.

Michael had removed from inside his coat a small, parchment-bound volume which he pretended to study, though the book wagged and bobbed and the reading of it would have turned him blind if it had been more than a ruse for avoiding Elspeth's eyes. The girl too had turned away, her brow pressed upon the cold glass pane, as if the finger of near-pain in her forehead would freeze the clamour in her heart. Though his eyes were open, James seemed to be asleep.

It was an hour later, eight miles along the turnpike, when the Flycr again reined to a halt. The wayside station was Wattie's hire. Here he would relieve himself, drink a pint of mulled ale and share a half-cheese or a plate of mutton with his son while the horses were given a little feed and water and allowed to rest for a quarter of an hour before tackling the last stage of the journey to Harlwood.

"Do you wish to refresh yourself?" James said gruffly.

"No, I am comfortable here," Elspeth answered.

"I'll stretch my legs, I believe," James said.

There was a deal of shuffling and repositioning as Moodie got himself out of the coach. Michael remained where he was, the book lowered just enough to be polite. No sooner had

James left the Flyer, however, than Michael was at the window.

"Has he gone inside?" whispered Elspeth.

"He has, he has."

"Are you certain?"

"Certain enough." Michael stepped to her and, with his hands on each side of her throat, gently, very gently, tilted her face upwards to meet his lips. He kissed her brow then her mouth. His skin was cold, her own warm.

"Michael, no."

"Does he not know me?" Michael asked.

"He has no occasion to know you."

"Is he always so surly and silent?"

"No. But we should be thankful that he is today. If he had engaged you in conversation –"

Michael kissed her again, drawing her from the seat with his arm, pressing her body against his.

"I must see you. Alone. Soon," he murmured.

Elspeth clung to him. Never before had she felt as she did at that moment, transfused with excitement, borne beyond all sense and reason. If Michael had taken her across the seat of the coach, she would not have raised a cry or done anything to prevent it. Michael, however, drew away from her. He seated himself again by the window.

"Come to the glen tonight," he said.

"No, Michael, I can't."

"Tomorrow?"

"It's not possible."

"Do you still deny that you love me?"

"It's not –" Elspeth was interrupted by the appearance of young Wattie's broad, weather-beaten features in the window. She started guiltily.

"Is the ride soft enough for ye, Mistress Moodie?" Wattie enquired ingenuously.

"Aye, it's fine." Elspeth managed a smile for the coachman's son. "How – how long 'til we reach Balnesmoor?"

"Och, on a day like today, I'd say about an hour," Wattie answered.

McGowan gave no particular attention to Michael Blaven who had retreated behind his book again. There was no doubt, though, that the McGowans knew who Michael was, knew that he lived with Miss Janet in Preaching Friar. All it would take would be a casual word to James and Michael would be identified. Elspeth prayed that her husband would not discover that Michael was no stranger in the Lennox. She feared, without reason, that James would somehow uncover the truth.

"Can I fetch ye a glass o' ale?" said Wattie.

"No, thank you kindly, Mister McGowan."

"Ye'll be home for your tea, I reckon." With a little slap of his hand on the glass by way of farewell, the guard vanished. He could be heard shouting cheerfully to a horseman who had emerged from the stable by the farm cottage.

Michael did not approach her again.

"I must visit you tonight," he whispered.

"Where?" Elspeth said quickly. "Visit me where?"

"I'll come to the garden."

"Please, Michael, no."

"You sleep alone, do you not?"

"He – James – he may be –"

"I cannot bear to think of him with you."

"Don't think of it then," said Elspeth.

"You saw me. That night. In August?"

"Yes."

"You are more lovely than –"

Impulsively Michael reached for her hand before she could withdraw. He tugged her towards him across the width of the coach and kissed her once more upon the mouth.

Every moment increased the chance of discovery. Elspeth could not predict how her husband would act, not this day of all days when he seemed so queer and indrawn. She fumbled for the strap of the carriage door. She had to separate herself from Michael, to be away from him or every shred of rectitude and caution would be thrown to the winds.

"Don't go, please," Michael begged.

Resolutely, Elspeth opened the door and, disregarding the mud, slipped from the coach to the ground. She walked unsteadily around the rear of the conveyance and looked across the rise of the fields to the dear, familiar hills. Now they offered her no sense of security and comfort, no protection. She could not escape from her emotions, from her need of Michael Blaven. Then she saw James, her husband, distanced from her by the sward before the cottages. He plodded over the rutted mud from the rear of the dwellings, the greatcoat about his shoulders. He appeared so strong, so pugnacious, without any degree of suavity; a country weaver in the afternoon of his life. She had never seen him so before, coarsened, thickened. She moved towards him nonetheless, welcomingly.

"Are you unwell, James?"

"Hm? No, no, I'm just glad to be nearin' home."

She offered him her arm. Stiffly, he took it and walked her back the few yards to the coach. She hated herself for what she was doing, demonstrating to Michael that she belonged to James Simpson Moodie who would protect her even against the kind of love that Michael offered, a love which could consume and destroy her by its physical intensity. From that fate only James could defend her for she had no will of her own.

Defiantly Elspeth sat by her husband's side, clinging to his arm throughout the rest of the journey, her face scarlet with the shame of the double deception.

It had not been Randall's intention to tease his brother but the opportunity somehow arose and he could not resist it. Gilbert was such a fool with a gun that there was a certain danger in the sport too but Randall, who had hardly left the house in the weeks since his return, revelled in the hazards of following Gibbie, unseen, out on to the sprig of shorn ground where pheasants were occasionally to be bagged for the pot.

Gilbert carried his father's ancient muzzle-loader and was accompanied by Todd, a toothless fossil but as close to a keeper of game as Ottershaw chose to support.

Gibbie's marksmanship was notoriously erratic. To be within a mile of Gibbie when he had a gun in his hands was an experience to jangle the nerves.

"God, man!" Todd would grumble to his chums. "It is safer bein' the prey than the keeper, since a man is larger than a bird."

Quite aware of his brother's failings Randall was exceedingly careful to keep himself not only out of sight but below the range of the gun, under the hill which dived from the grazing, in a luxuriant wimple of weeds, into a little meandering burn. Here spring-mad bullocks often took wing, thinking they were larks, and broke their backs in bellowing astonishment. There were no bullocks in the field that afternoon, however, and all would have been well with bird, beast and man if a leggy and inexperienced half-grown hare had not stopped to cock an eye at the creature which crashed along the edge of the corn stubble.

Randall saw the hare before Gibbie did and prudently eased himself against the trunk of a young birch which had found root on the burn bank just before the hare sprang and darted downward in a zig-zag flight.

Later it was claimed that Todd had saved the laird's life and prevented a horrible act of fratricide, but this was quite untrue.

Todd had come to the edge of the fall and had just glimpsed the glint of Randall's brand-new, lightweight No. 7 bore detonator, which required the lugging of no awkward ancillary equipment, when Gibbie raised the flintlock and wagged it in the general direction of the hare.

"No, sir, no!" Todd bawled out.

Distracted by the keeper's outburst Gilbert snatched the trigger and the flintlock exploded.

The hare, relieved, stopped, sat on its hind legs and offered a little prayer with its paws while, by the birch, Randall Bontine slumped forward and, with a hand pressed to his breast, raised an accusing arm and pointed an accusing finger at his brother on the slope above him.

"Murderer," Randall gasped. "Mur-der-er."

Then the new laird of Ottershaw and Balnesmoor rolled on to his back, to all intents and purposes a goner from this world.

"God in Heaven, sir, you have kilt him," Todd hissed in horrified amazement.

"Killed who?"

"Mister Randall, sir."

"Devil take me, so I have," said Gibbie.

What Gilbert did not confess, then or later, was that he felt a little twinge of elation at the sight of his brother in a position of demise. There had been many occasions in the past weeks when he would willingly have shot the damned man, not out of spiteful jealousy but just to open him up. Fear, of course, swiftly replaced pleasure. Todd was already sledding down the hillside on the seat of his breeks and Gilbert followed him in a frightful panic at what he had done.

Randall was discovered on his back, injured knee stretched

straight, the other bent, both palms pressed against his chest where, presumably, the ball had entered to deliver its mortal wound. His eyes were closed.

"Todd, have I killed him? God, have I killed my own brother?"

Gilbert flung himself to his knees by the side of the corpse and leaned over, searching for blood.

"Is he dead? Is he dead?"

Hands closed suddenly about Gibbie's throat and a voice growled, "Not quite, Gibbie."

Gibbie sagged. "You pig, Randall."

Randall said, "If it had not been for a timely warning uttered by your trusty servant, however, I would have been the victim of your pique."

"No, no, Randall. I intended you no harm." Gibbie struggled against the fists which had slipped down to the collar of his coat. "Do you imagine that I would do you an injury?"

"I imagine, dear brother, that you might."

The servant had stopped close by.

"But – but why?" Gilbert asked.

"Don't play the innocent, Gibbie. I've seen how your wife looks at me. God, man, if she could shoot a dagger as deadly as she shoots a glance I would be a sieve by now."

"Alicia? What does she – Randall, it was an accidental mishap," said Gibbie, in a state of ire, confusion and guilt. "Will you not believe me?"

"Help me up."

Randall accepted Gibbie's support.

"You, what's your name?"

"Todd, sir."

"Well done this day, Todd. You shall have a dram or two as your reward."

If Todd was amazed at this interpretation of the events of the past few minutes he gave no sign of it. He had experienced Bontine promises before. When the laird returned to the house the promise would most like be forgotten and he would have no reward at all.

"Todd, I am weak in the leg, as you've no doubt observed," said Randall. "I'll need your shoulder to help me to the top of the brae."

"Aye, sir."

"Gilbert, gather the guns and accoutrements."

"What?"

"It's too damp in the air to leave valuable shooting-pieces out. Do as I say."

"Randall, I'm not your lackey."

"Gibbie, you have been poaching my game."

The change of tack caught Gilbert off-guard.

"What's that you say?"

Wisely, Todd had already begun to divest himself of gear. Now he left the brothers to clamber up the slope to retrieve the equipment which had been shed on Gibbie's panic-ridden descent. He, if not his master, could see what sort of sport was being made by the laird. It gave the servant grim amusement to be part of it. He listened to the raised voices which floated like an argument of fowls above the burn.

"Poacher? What do you mean?"

"I am the laird and landed possessor –"

"Randall, I cannot credit my ears."

"Is it not my game too?"

"Randall, I –"

"I let you eat at my table, warm yourself at my fire, but I see no reason why I should permit you to discharge a fowling-piece at my head."

"I explained that –"

"It's time, Gilbert, that I paid you off."

"Paid me? Paid me for what?"

"Paid you the sum specified as your portion," said Randall. "I will draft a note on the bank for immediate settlement of the full amount. I will do it tonight, in fact."

"And then, what then?"

"If you and your wife will join me for dinner –"

"Where? In the library?" said Gilbert.

Like his father before him, Randall had made the library the hub of his existence. He lived in solitude within the long chamber, eating there alone while the rest of the family gathered in the dining-room on the ground floor. He seldom left the divan by the fire or the chair at the long table which, so Gibbie had discovered, was littered with rent-books and commercial documents going back two or three decades. The tale of the estate was written there and seemed of more moment and merit to Randall than the reality which lay beneath the leaded windows or beyond the carved oak doors.

"We will dine at seven in the dining-hall," said Randall, "if it is convenient."

"It is," said Gilbert, now thoroughly flummoxed. "It is, of course, convenient. We would be dining –"

"Good," said Randall as Todd returned. "Now, load yourself up like a good fellow. Do not walk before us, in case the flintlock happens to go off across your shoulder. Follow at a safe distance behind, please."

"I will help you. Let Todd tote the –"

"Come, Todd." Randall pushed himself from the tree. "Give me your arm, if you will."

With the aged little keeper tucked under his shoulder like an improvised crutch, Randall tackled the hillside while his brother, fuming, struggled with the welter of equipment which had previously burdened the servant.

Unlike Todd, Gibbie received no gratuity, no sixpence in the palm for his pains.

All Gibbie got was the unequivocal order of the boot.

Alicia resembled nothing so much as a giant floribunda. After swithering for hours in her dressing-room between mourning-garb, which would have been rather appropriate, and a court-dress so replete with swaying hoops that it made Gilbert quite giddy just to watch her walk in it, Alicia had chosen a gaudy thing of lace and rose embroidery. Into the bosom of the dress she had inserted waxen 'artificials' which she powdered to match her own not insignificant protruberances, a version of lily-gilding which left Gilbert flabbergasted, though it did, he had to admit, give Alicia astonishing Amazonian authority. Even so, as he accompanied her down to the dining-room, he could not help feeling that his wife had abrogated all reality in the name of fashion.

"Be calm, my dear, be calm," Gilbert muttered.

Alicia snorted and sucked her teeth nervously.

Hunter flung open the door of the dining-room and the couple entered like strangers the room in which they had dined night in and night out for years.

Randall, however, had changed the friendliness of the long room. He had gone for drama and the table glittered with the family's best silver and crystal, treasures which had hardly been out of the safe-cabinets in a lifetime.

Gilbert bit his lip and took his seat at the dining-table without a word of protest at the sacrilege. Randall had gone the whole hog, had dressed in the uniform of an officer of Hussars, all except the swagged sword and tall, polished hat. It occurred to Gibbie that if he had been a Frenchie confronted with a line of fellows so attired he would have flung heroics to the wind and set off for the horizon at the gallop.

Hunter, in cream-coloured gloves, waddled to his master's side. Though well into his sixty-fifth year, Hunter knew how to be obsequious and gave the impression that if the new laird so desired he would fold himself naked on an enormous platter and stick an apple in his mouth.

Candles burned in silver holders and, though the October night was mild, a great log fire crackled in the hearth. All the servants were in attendance as if Randall were entertaining two score house-guests and not merely his brother and wife.

During the course of the meal, which was wholesome rather than exotic, Randall exchanged vacuous pleasantries with Alicia who replied, effortlessly, in kind. Gilbert was annoyed; did Randall suppose that they were such shallow, rusticated folk that they could not be spoken to without that patronising smile?

When the meal was finally over the long table was swept clean except for bowls of nuts and a silver box which held decanters. The entire operation was performed with such efficiency that Gilbert glanced often at the servants' faces to remind himself that they were the same people who waited on him so languorously every other night.

Without asking Alicia's permission, Randall took a cheroot from a leather wallet and lit it from a candle.

Randall paused, head thrown back, as if he were savouring the moment as well as the rich inhalation of tobacco smoke. He held the pose so long that Alicia's patience expired.

"Have we nothing to discuss, Randall?" she snapped.

"Ah, yes," Randall answered softly. "We have much to discuss."

"Can we not get to it, in that case?"

"Of course, Alicia, of course."

He clapped his hands and called out in a voice that made

the decanters vibrate, "Hunter, show the gentleman in."

"What gentleman?" Alicia demanded.

Randall let her wait for an answer.

Hunter, who had only just closed the dining-room door, flung it open again and ushered in an angular man attired in rusty black knee-breeches and a coppled coat that had been out of fashion when Plato was a boy.

"Mister Angus Hildebrand," Hunter announced.

"Good evening to you, Madam," Hildebrand bowed. "Good evening to you, also, Mister Bontine."

Alicia slapped a hand to her wax bosom as if it had suddenly begun to melt. She gave a short bark of astonishment and dismay. But Gilbert's anxiety vanished in that instant and, to his surprise, he felt a tickle of laughter in his throat.

Randall was such a showman, so devious, so conniving, so thoroughly on top of everyone and everything; Gilbert could not but admire his style.

"I believe you are acquainted with Lawyer Hildebrand?" said Randall affably. "Come, sir, sit here by me."

Hildebrand carried with him one of the cases that Gilbert had last seen lining the dingy chamber in Dumbarton town. Hildebrand took the chair on Randall's right, untied the buckram straps from around the box, laid out a copy of the will and a single-page document which seemed short-weight for the magnitude of the business that would stem from it.

"Where are the lawyers?" said Alicia suddenly.

"Mister Hildebrand is a lawyer," said Randall.

"I mean the Ottershaw lawyers, your father's agents."

"Oh!" Randall innocently blew a ring of smoke from the cheroot. "I received the impression that you did not trust the intregrity of Dixon and Royle. Otherwise, why would you take counsel on the conditions of the will and testament, not to mention the breaking of them, from Mister Hildebrand?"

"It seems there's no integrity, especially among members of the legal profession," said Alicia, glaring at Hildebrand.

"I was not, Madam, retained by your esteemed person," said Hildebrand, "and did not deem it, therefore, a matter of either breach of confidence nor of conscience to accept fee from the rightful laird of Ottershaw."

Gilbert cleared his throat. "We are aware, Randall, that the will and testament cannot be altered to permit my wife and me to share in Ottershaw. Mister Hildebrand made that perfectly clear."

"Candidly, Gibbie, I've no particular objection to sharing the house with you," said Randall. "But I do object to sharing it with your wife, particularly as she made such strenuous efforts to rob me of my entitlement."

"You are not competent," said Alicia. "In three years or five you will ruin Ottershaw."

"I'll not ruin Ottershaw at all," said Randall. "However, you've placed your finger on the sore spot, Alicia. You see, I'll make Ottershaw pay. Damn me, Gilbert, have you examined the accounts?"

"Of course," said Gilbert. "Ottershaw is profitable."

"Ottershaw is piffling," said Randall. "I admit that my father managed to salt away a goodly sum. How otherwise could I pay off his bequests and still hold on to the lands of the estate? I admit, too, that Father had certain progressive inclinations, especially in the way of sheep-breeding. But it is not enough."

"Not enough for what, pray?" said Alicia.

"Not enough for me," said Randall. "I intend to expand."

"Expand? How and in what direction?" said Gilbert.

"To repossess the ridiculously cheap leases as they fall due, for a beginning," said Randall. "To shift the use of the land from rearing, at least in fair part, and cultivate more acres."

"But why, Randall?" said Gibbie, interested in spite of himself. "I cannot understand why management is not enough. Surely it is not the role of the Bontines to grab and devour. Only to hold and to maintain."

"I care not a toss for the name of the Bontines," said Randall, "the illustrious mediocrity of our past. Good God, Gibbie, in a generation we could be swallowed up unless, like the python, we increase the width of our jaws."

"What does this have to do with us?" said Alicia. "Do you believe that we would hinder you?"

"Alicia, you would do anything to possess Ottershaw."

"Come to the point, regarding the future," said Gilbert.

"Father left seven thousand pounds, a very considerable sum," said Randall. "As close perusal of the will should have shown you, it was a lump sum to be paid to me should I choose to forfeit claim to Ottershaw."

Alicia's head flicked up. "Are you taking the money, is that it?"

"If, however," Randall went on, ignoring the question, "if I chose to return to Ottershaw, then a similar sum was to be paid to you, Gibbie. Poor little Robbie comes thin out of it all. But poor little Robbie will not starve; I'll see to that. Besides, poor little Robbie is only our half-brother and will share in Irish money from Marinwood in due course of time, or partake of the sum that Father left for Mother Elizabeth's comfort."

"Quite!" said Gibbie. "If you are the new laird, we'll not see Mother here again, I fear."

"That must be her choice. I would not deny her a place here," said Randall.

"She despises you, Randall," said Alicia.

"Well," said Randall, "I do not despise her. She is a fine woman and may marry again. I wish her well for her future."

"What of our future, my children's future?" said Gibbie.

"Sooner or later, Gib, that old muzzle-loader of yours might point at my head in earnest."

"Ridiculous!" Gilbert shouted.

"Besides, you would not be comfortable here with me. Seven thousand pounds will buy you a house and land which is better than moor and bog. It will be for you to make of it what you can. I prefer to have Ottershaw for myself."

Gilbert could see wisdom glimmering behind Randall's insults. It wasn't, however, a simple yearning for independence that moved his brother. It would not be liberty that Randall desired but licence, room not just to manipulate the future of Ottershaw but to exercise power in ways that were alien to the old lairds of the Lennox. If Randall intended to turn tyrant, then he was right to thrust his brothers and sisters from him; it was a law of tyranny that tyrants must stand alone.

Gilbert said, "How soon do you wish us to take our leave?"

"As soon as you have found a suitable accommodation," Randall answered. "Mister Hildebrand, would you be good enough to give my brother the document for signature."

Hildebrand, Gibbie noticed, no longer seemed so loquacious as he had been those months ago in Dumbarton. If his guess was correct Messrs Dixon and Royle would soon find themselves discharged in favour of the stork-like Angus Hildebrand.

There was, first of all, a convertible note on the account of the Estate of Ottershaw for the sum of seven thousand pounds, drawn on the account of Gilbert Lawrence Bontine from the offices of the Bank of Scotland in the Lawnmarket of Edinburgh, countersigned by Randall and already attested by Hildebrand as to authenticity. To accompany the note were two certificates, also attested, confirming the death of Gilbert Lawrence Bontine, *et cetera*. Receipt for the sum and an acknowledgement of settlement of the clause of the testament made up the rest of the papers. With a quill pen and inkstand brought in by Hunter, Gilbert did his business with signatures there and then and wrote off Ottershaw. It was a strangely perfunctory rite for such a final result.

Tight-lipped, Alicia watched. She felt victimised by the turn of fortune and furious at her husband, even though he had only buckled to the inevitable.

Randall poured himself a bumper from the decanter and drank it off in a swallow. He groped for the thick, polished stick that he had placed by the table-leg and hoisted himself to his feet, stiff after the prolonged period of inactivity. He motioned to Hildebrand who, still without uttering a word, rose and gathered the papers into the box.

"If you will pardon us," Randall said, with dry formality, "I will avail myself of Mister Hildebrand's presence to discuss several matters of a private nature."

Gibbie scrambled to his feet. "Shall Alicia and I leave?"

"Stay where you are, Gibbie. I'll be more comfortable in the library. Come, sir."

Followed by Hildebrand the laird of Ottershaw limped out of the dining-room.

Hunter paused in the doorway. "Will there by anythin' else for you, Master Gilbert?" he enquired.

"No, Hunter. Nothing."

The door closed.

Alicia let out her breath, the edges of the 'artificials' breaking free from her breast and forming two scalloped lines, like gills. She picked the frontage out with her fingers and dropped it upon the table, contemplating it as if Randall had unmothered her at the stroke of a pen.

"Well, dearest," said Gilbert, with a sigh, "that would appear to be that. We had better begin our search for a new home. Do you have a fancy for Ireland?"

"I have a fancy, Gilbert, for nowhere in the world but here."

"Now, Alicia, that cannot be."

"Harlwood, then. Killearn or Blanefield," she said. "Randall has done all he can to us, Gilbert. Your brother's wish is different from your father's will. He cannot prevent us settling nearby."

"He won't like it."

"All the more reason to do it."

"Alicia —"

"I want to be close enough to keep an eye on your brother. And on Ottershaw." She got to her feet. "Look for land, Gilbert," she commanded, as if she expected him to stride out into the night with a lantern. "Look for land in the Lennox. Land that may be worked, and a comfortable house. Oh, and approach Sinclair."

"Sinclair?"

"Sinclair is the best grieve in the county, is he not?"

"Well, yes, I suppose —"

"Then, whatever the cost, we must not leave Sinclair behind."

Elspeth listened to the creak of the big kitchen door as Tolland pushed it shut. Seated on the edge of the bed, already dressed in a warm frock and with a shawl about her shoulders, she heard the steward slap the bolt into its socket. Then there was silence below, a silence through which Tolland would stroll back to his cubby in the one-apartment abutment to the kitchen quarters which James had had constructed the year he had bought Moss House.

Usually James undertook the nightly ritual of securing the house himself. Until recently there had been no need to make doors and windows fast but of late there had been a spate of thefts in the district, much stealing from houses after dark, and James was afraid for the safety of his silver. Tonight, however, her husband had been too weary to sit up. He had given instructions to Tolland and had retired to his room immediately after supper. Elspeth too had gone upstairs early. She had dismissed her night maid to the attic where the females slept, segregated by the height of the house from male servants on the ground floor. There had been 'trouble' with servants in the past. But it was not one of the lassies who would steal downstairs tonight to join with a lover. It would be the mistress of Moss House herself.

The clock on the dressing-chest told Elspeth that it was eleven o'clock. When the tiny, hardly-audible tinkle of wires rang out, the girl got up and went to the casement, unlatched it and eased it wide open. There was no moon. The air was moderately warm for October, stirred by a rustling wind. The shrubbery was very dark. At first she could see nothing, then, with a catch of breath, saw Michael step from the protection of the evergreens.

For a heart-stopping moment Elspeth imagined that it was not Michael at all but her husband. She flinched and stepped back until the flicker of a lantern, screened by a cheesecloth, gave her a glimpse of Michael's features. She understood the signal, though it had not been arranged. She was no longer calm. The implications of her action crowded upon her, making her tremble. She did not, however, hang back. She gathered her courage and slipped quickly out of the bedroom. She sped on tiptoe along the corridor, down the broad staircase and across the hallway into the passage that led her to the door which separated the kitchens from James's private study.

The kitchen door had a plate-sized lock and a long, iron key. She paused, leaning her forehead against the grained surface, listening. Tolland's lair was far across the kitchens. Luke McWilliams, the arrogant little boot-boy, had grown too mature to billet in the house; now he slept in the stable loft. She felt for, found and turned the long key. It clacked deafeningly in the lock and the base of the door grated against the flagstone when she tugged it open. She extracted the key and dropped it into a scarf which she pushed into the pocket of her frock. She paused again, listened again. She heard nothing except the empty appeal of the wind about the garden and, irrevocably, stepped outside and closed the door behind her.

The wind had grown stronger in the past few minutes. It tossed the branches vigorously, manipulated the massy shrubs, and carried the enquiring yap of a stable dog to her. The draughts of air, though, were to her advantage, would disperse any sounds which she might make, confuse them with the bangings and knockings of the restless night.

Michael touched her.

She started and almost cried out. He drew her to him, kissed her mouth. Elspeth had never been kissed with such demanding tenderness before. She felt the tip of Michael's tongue touch hers and instinctively parted her lips. Now she realised that what she had endured in the bedroom had not been indifference or stoicism but a mounting desire which demanded no instruction, only opportunity. Michael put his hand under her breast. Romance was willingly exchanged for passion. After that first embrace loving would never be the same for the girl off the Nettleburn. She was caught in a tide of sensation.

"We mustn't stay here, my darling," he murmured."

"Where then?"

"Come with me."

"It's cold upon the moor, Michael."

"We will keep each other warm," Michael whispered. "I have brought plaids. We'll be snug as drovers since there is no frost tonight."

Elspeth did not protest. She trusted him. Besides, she was eager, incredibly eager, to experience love. The need freed her, it seemed, from ownership. Michael would not possess her as husbands possessed their wives. He would take only what she offered him, her heart, her love. It was love she owed Michael, not loyalty, not a dutiful submission to his will. He took her hand and led her through the shrubs towards the high straight hedges, to a corner of the lawn by the Chinese pavilion. Elspeth would, after all, have preferred the wild moor. But the moor was shuttered in moonless darkness. The boxed lawn was far enough away from the house to be safe. Michael had already spread the plaids on the grass behind the pavilion's steps. The close-knit hedges baffled the wind. Michael pulled her down. Kneeling, he kissed her again and again, stroking her body ardently with his hands.

"I love you, my darling. I have never loved anyone as I love you. I did not believe that it was possible to need someone so much," he whispered. "I want you so desperately."

She had no breath, no words to tell him how she felt. She worked her fingers down the fastening which held the bodice of the frock to her body. She let it part so that he might slip his fingers beneath her undershift and caress her breasts. She felt the softness of his mouth upon her and held him, cradling his head with her hands, pressing him against her while her body ran with fire. She was astonished by her lack of fear. Even when he stretched her back upon the plaid and laid himself upon her, furling up her skirts and touching her thighs, she did not struggle or resist but aided him with frantic urgency.

Michael could not know that she had not been loved before. She bit her lip when pain came, a scalding little sting, not severe, soothed by her readiness. Arms laced about his shoulders, she lifted herself against him. She gasped not with pain but with pleasure, then lay back once more, surprised by the ease with which he had entered her. Closing her eyes, she sighed until the breath caught in her throat and swelled in her bosom. She could hardly bear it, hold it, then in a sudden, unexpected surge of relief, heard herself utter a strange soft growl that hardly seemed to come from her lips at all.

Michael lifted himself a little and, reaching, found a corner of the plaid and brought it over them. Joined still in utmost intimacy, the couple kissed and toyed with each other. Across the hedges the great sloughing draughts of air dipped and swirled. They seemed to lift her up, fill her with their sourceless energy.

"Love me," she pleaded. "Love me, Michael, love me."

She had no shame in asking it.

In that hour Elspeth had no more thought of consequence than had the wind on the hill and, later, no more regret at what came of it.

FIVE

In Love for Long

The laird of Ottershaw did not cultivate the appearance of a
new broom. On the contrary, he sported the look of a very old
one. He had rummaged in the chests for apparel which
his father had stored and had put together a style which he
would stamp his own, a mixture of hand-me-down rig and
military which, with only changes of linen, he would wear
in all seasons except full summer. His only concession to
elegance was a long straight cane with a silver handle and
an iron tip which was seldom out of his hand in those early
months.

Dressed thus in heavy herring-bone and dour tartan trews,
the laird stumped out of the back door of Ottershaw to meet
his grieve in the October morn, to make it known that he
would be no recluse but master of the show and out and about
at all hours.

"Now, Sinclair, show me round my menagerie."

"Is it the beasts you're wantin' to see first, sir?"

"All of it."

"It'll take much time, laird."

"Time? God, I've naught but time, Sinclair. Let us begin
with the dairy. I've a notion to find some new domestics."

"Surely the house has sufficient servants, sir."

"They are mostly occupied with Gibbie and his brats and
are trained in Gibbie's ways. No, I want lively faces about
me."

Sinclair did not argue. He was not responsible for the house.
He had a notion that the kind of servants Randall would select
would be pretty young women. He had heard of indecencies
that besmirched the name of families in other quarters of the
Lennox.

"Many of the farm servants, the females, are married," said
Sinclair casually.

"I want them to work, not to bed," Randall snapped, as if reading the grieve's thoughts.

Sinclair flushed. "I meant only that we follow a policy of employin' wives in a day capacity. We prefer a system of split workin', in the dairy for instance."

"What is split working?"

They were walking towards the dairy yard, away from the house. Randall's progress was brisk. He stabbed the iron of the cane into the dirt and screwed himself forward on it. There was impatience in the movement which indicated pain. Try as he might, though, Sinclair could feel no pity for the soldier-laird.

"The mornin' milk is taken off by four wives," the grieve explained. "The evening milkin' is done by four others. The females work each a half-day, and are paid at a rate accordin'."

"Why do we not employ them in the ordinary manner?"

"Because it is wasteful of labour."

"You must convince me of that, Sinclair."

"Your father –"

"My father was more credulous than I am. However, we will put that aside until this evening. I shall be obliged if you will take supper with me, Sinclair, at seven o'clock. You need not waste your time, since you seem to be so conscious of the value of each and every minute, by dressing and grooming. There will be only you and I and we will take food in the library, without ceremony."

"Will there be a particular subject under discussion, sir?"

"Why do you ask?"

"In order that I might furnish myself with the necessary papers."

"Many subjects will be under discussion, particularly the land survey," Randall answered. "But I have copies of all the papers to hand. I wish mainly to hear your opinions on general farming matters."

"My opinions, sir, are held for the benefit of Ottershaw."

"I do not dispute it," said Randall. "In the meantime let us survey the young crop and see what the dairy has to offer."

Gloomily Sinclair led the way into the parlour where the girls, Anna included, were already stroking what milk was to be had from the teats.

*　　*　　*

There had been a moment, a fleeting instant, when Anna felt sure that Randall had recognised her. It was a day she would never forget, that forenoon of his home-coming, when Mr Randall had climbed down from the coach at the front door of Ottershaw and the grieve had solemnly taken off his hat and, on the signal, all the field-workers and the dairymaids, the horsemen and the little contingent of foresters who had herded out of the plantation for the event, all had cheered each time Lachie Sinclair had thrust his bonnet skywards.

The new laird had seemed oblivious to the welcome of the tenantry, the assembly of 'his' people. He had not raised his hand in acknowledgement, had not even turned to glance back at them. He had brushed Gibbie aside, Hunter too, when they came to assist him from the lopsided coach.

He had come down like an otter with a broken spine; still lean, still lithe, still quick but hampered by one part of his body, the left leg, and by something else that none of the women and girls could quite place at first and only later, prompted by McDonald, identified as pure, white pain.

The leaves had been swept from the drive and stone terraces. The borders had been trimmed, hurdles and feeding racks and the other untidy appurtenances of farming tucked away out of sight, everything made neat and tidy for the coach's arrival. There was no rain, though it threatened every minute of the ninety that the crowd waited, lined up by the driveway, and came only a minute after Randall had limped indoors.

Brigit had whispered, "By God, will ye be lookin' at the state o' him. Is the mannie drunk?"

"No, no," Anna had said through pursed lips. "No, no, no."

Inch by inch he had descended from the coach, defying anyone to offer aid. He looked worn out, worn down. From him emanated the only real breath of war that most of the good folk of Balnesmoor and Ottershaw would ever have, a whiff of the suffering and courage that soldiers in the foreign fields were forced to live with and thrive upon.

Anna felt the flutter in her breast, a fearful relief that the ball or blade had not taken Randall's life, lest in some intricate supernatural manner, stemming from the dummy's spell, she too had sickened and on that day died.

The wound did not diminish Randall in Anna's eyes, did not rob him of the aura which her imagination had put around him. On the contrary, even from forty yards away Anna had felt closer to him than ever, now that he was here in the flesh before her. When the new laird turned suddenly and stared direct at her, Anna's throat had closed in a kind of sob. She had stared straight and direct back at him, unaware of the real reason why he had selected her out of the fifty-odd folk who were gathered there, not vain enough, not with all the rich emotions that were floating in the air that day, to believe that it was her beauty which had caught and held his eye.

Randall Bontine had recognised her! Randall Bontine had remembered her! She could settle now, be patient, be certain that the binding spell would take its course, progress in stages like a fever. She was sure in her heart of hearts that Randall would seek her out and confront her, though the poor wounded man might not know why.

Later that night, with Matt sprawled across her, she had stared at the roof of the wee back room in the cottage in the pines and had imagined that she was floating away, rising like a wreath of mist to alight at the path's end, drift through the half-open window of *his* bedroom, lie by *his* side.

Later still, Matt on his back by her had said, "Aye, he's a queer-lookin' tyke, right enough. Him an' that corkscrew walk."

"He was injured fightin' the French. In single combat."

"Tripped o'er a keg o' ale, more like."

"Hold your rotten tongue, Matt."

"Och, an' what's wrong? Think he'll hear us?"

"He's our laird. We're his servants."

"I'm no bloody servant. Not Bontine's, anyhow."

"Just Pad Tomelty's."

She had not cared if Matt lost his temper with her. She needed to commence the process of release, not even to commence but to complete. She had never 'belonged' to Matt Sinclair, had never cleaved to him. Now that Randall was ensconced again in Ottershaw, Anna knew that it would only be a matter of time until the binding spell was fulfilled.

Beef was the prime produce of the Ottershaw cattle herds which, of course, took precedence over the sheep flocks. For all that, with butter selling at seven pounds per hundredweight in the wholesale markets of Glasgow and cheese at thirteen shillings each stone, this source of profit was not neglected by Lachlan Sinclair who ensured that the cows were kept in good health and that the dairy was run along 'modern' lines to keep the daily yield as constant as nature would allow. The parlour was clean, the buckets scalded before and after use and the big flat tubs used for creaming and separating were scrubbed every day, habits which the dairymaids did not understand but had grown used to. Sweet milk was taken off to feed the calves and Sinclair would have no casual slopping done by the stockmen. Woe betide anyone, woman or man, who brought laziness and dirty manners into the yard, for they would be blamed if the cows gave less than eighteen hundred pints each in the course of the season, as if cleanliness had anything to do with fat teats.

To Anna it began like any other day. She milked her allotment of cows and took the buckets one by one to the stone-glazed chamber through the tunnel where they were measured by weight by Mr Pryde and his boy. She returned to the steaming, cow-lowing interior of the parlour from which the animals were being led away by the herd laddies.

And there was Randall, along with her father-in-law and Hearn, the head dairyman, in the strewed stall at the parlour's nether end.

Anna dabbed her nose with her sleeve, tucked straggling hair under her bonnet, gave a discreet spit into her palms and rubbed her cheeks then came on, swinging her hips sonsily.

Randall had picked her up the moment she had entered the parlour by the narrow door. He followed her with his gaze as she wended through the cows into the cleared stretch where the lads were already raking muck into a ridged heap. Randall did not falter in his conversation with her father-in-law, nor did he give the least sign of recognition. But his eyes never left her until she went past him and out of the wide door into the yard.

In passing she glanced at him. She did not nod or drop a curtsy or flutter her eyelids or scowl and grunt a greeting, none of the responses that dairymaids and farm labourers would have contrived to cover an encounter with the laird. She just glanced at him and walked, swinging, on. But as soon as she cleared the open doors she had to stop to catch her breath.

She leaned against the post by the door, out of sight of the three men but not out of earshot.

"Yes, that one," she heard Randall say.

"She's no domestic, sir. She's never been trained to the house," her father-in-law said.

"The work," said Randall, "demands no special skills."

"I cannot recommend her, laird."

"Can you not, Sinclair? I want her. That's an end of it."

"Laird, she's – she's my son's wife."

"In which case I'm sure she'll be honest and loyal. Tell her to come to the kitchen tomorrow morning. Has she infants or children at home?"

"No, no she has not."

"In that case," said Randall, "Hunter will offer her the full day rate. What does the husband do?"

"He's my son, laird."

"Ah, so he's studying to be my grieve in course of time, is he?"

"He – aye – he's with the foresters now."

"Bring the girl to Hunter in the morning. She'll have a better rate than in the dairy and be warmer in the winter, indoors. Altogether more congenial for a member of your family. Is there something amiss, Sinclair?"

The grieve was silent, lips compressed and eyelids hooded, signs which anybody in the district would have identified as indignant anger.

"Is there?" Randall insisted.

"No, sir."

"Very well," Randall said. "You will be pleased to inform the girl of my wishes and see to it that she understands."

"Aye, sir. Will you be requirin' other girls from the byre?"

"Yes, one more. And a boy."

"A boy?"

"A boy old enough to wipe his nose in the mornings," said Randall. "Who is there about the place that might suit?"

"Another girl," said Sinclair, in a tone of stern disapproval, "and a boy? Might I enquire, sir, what will be required of the 'new' domestics?"

"Hunter will see that they know their duties," said Randall. "Come along now, let's get this done so that we might turn our minds to less trivial matters."

The voices diminished. Anna came away from the doors and walked diagonally across the yard, catching her father-in-law's last remark, "There's the Tomelty lass, sir. A very willin' worker," as she went.

She glanced over her shoulder. The three men, Hearn still tagging along, were strolling down the aisle of the parlour while the muck-lad stood with his rake and broom to arms, as if he were a sentry put to guard, not dispose of, the dung. As if conscious of her attention, Randall stopped himself with the cane and swung suddenly round.

Anna did not look away; this time she smiled.

Randall Bontine, however, did not smile in response but, with a strange indifferent shrug of his shoulders, turned back to face the hindquarters of the last of the departing cows.

It did not matter; Anna was elated.

He had asked for her, demanded her. He had brought her into his house and, if she was half the woman she supposed herself to be, in time he would bring her to his bed.

Preaching Friar was not Moss House, being smaller and more cosy, and Miss Blaven was more astute than a husband when it came to reading signs. It had shocked her to discover that Michael had not returned to his room until four of the clock. She could not decide whether she was concerned mainly for his moral welfare, or for the injury to his health that might result from spending the night hours out of doors in Heaven knows what conditions. She also believed that discovery was inevitable and that it would only be a matter of time until Moodie descended on Preaching Friar, ranting and raging and creating a loud, and justified, fuss. To soothe her nerves, Miss Blaven made a concoction of skullcap and valerian and sipped the nasty-tasting cordial slowly as if in penance for her carelessness in allowing Michael to run wild. Perhaps, though, her nephew had tried to untangle himself. Had he not gone off home to Glasgow without proper explanation, hinting that it was time to make peace with his father? Michael had been in an elated mood when he returned unexpectedly to Preaching Friar. But he was too ingenuous to keep the reason from his aunt for long.

"I met her on the Flyer," he blurted out. "By chance, by coincidence."

"Do you refer to Mister Moodie's wife?"

"I do."

"Ah, so now you have also met Weaver Moodie."

"How do you know that Elspeth was not travelling alone?"

"Do not be a fool, Michael. Women do not have the sort of enviable freedoms that bless males in our society."

"She might have been accompanied by a maid or female relative."

"Michael!" Janet Blaven lost patience.

Confusion made the spinster cross. She did not grudge Michael a few months of happiness, a taste of the sweetness of love. But why could he not have lost his heart to an unwed girl, even one of the wild-maned harlots who roved about the bothies and drove the ministers to distraction with their flouncing, pagan ways? She might have excused him such an irreverent fling. She could not, however, condone adultery. The affair might ruin the life left him and bring her – yes, she was selfish enough to consider it – condemnation in the eyes of the parish.

Michael was quick to sense that his aunt was not to be won round and took himself early to his room. Miss Blaven sat up late by the kitchen fire and, when the time came for her finally to retire, softly opened the door of her nephew's room. He had, of course, gone. The half-open window told its own tale.

There was no sleep for the spinster of Preaching Friar that night. It was after four o'clock before she heard him return, by the kitchen door this time, and go stealthily upstairs. She contemplated challenging him there and then but concern for his health was still paramount and she put off until morning the inevitable confrontation.

It was after nine before he came down, clad in a thick, flowing dressing-robe. He was tousled and smug, and in search of breakfast.

Thinly she said, "You look well this morning, Michael."

"I am excellently well, Aunt."

"Perhaps all the doctors are wrong and night air agrees with invalids."

"Night air? What do you mean?"

"Please do not pretend."

He came swiftly from the door and kissed her on the brow. She felt suddenly very old, separated from her nephew by a great gulf of years. His insouciance was no longer infectious. She did not respond to it with a lightening of the heart, only with an enormous sadness that he had reached a singular peak of experience from which God would cause him to topple. He had no more future, her poor, happy nephew, than a moth.

To hide her grief, she busied herself with crocks and kettle. She made him coffee and mutton ham and bannocks, while he sat uncertain and silent at the table. Upstairs, the day-maid was thumping bolsters and singing to herself, the sound cheerful in the rainy grey air of the morning. The fire crackled. Coffee-grains rattled in the roasting-pot.

At length Michael said, "Very well, Aunt, I'll not prevaricate or tell an untruth. Yes, I spent a night with Elspeth."

She did not face him. "Where?"

"At Moss House."

She whirled. "Within Moodie's house? Michael, how did you dare?"

"In the garden."

Janet Blaven shook her head. "What sort of insanity is it, Michael, that possesses you, that you would risk your health –"

"Damned be my health, Aunt! What health? I am not, at this moment, an invalid. I have the use of my limbs. I can still walk. How I choose to travel and who I choose to walk with –"

"Is she – is she your lover? Answer me."

"I will answer you, Aunt. Yes, Elspeth is my lover."

Miss Blaven plumped herself down on a wooden stool.

The kettle steamed gently on the hob and the coffee-jug steamed gently on the table. She had never known a man, never been loved as Michael loved the girl from Balnesmoor. Would it be right to deny him and send him away? No other course would separate Michael from Elspeth Moodie. Even that dire measure might not be sufficient now that he had joined with her! Miss Blaven was not blind to the power of physical passion.

Michael was beside her, all charm, all contrition.

"Aunt, I cannot help myself."

"You can," the woman said. "Oh, yes, you can help yourself."

"How long will I live?"

He had played the one card that would win the game for

him. Never before had he asked that question of her; the timing of it was cruel.

"Elspeth Moodie cannot cure you, Michael."

"Do you not understand that it's no adventure, Aunt? I have sincerely lost my heart to her and will not, under the circumstances, have time to transform myself into a suffering swain. No, nor to find another girl who might ease the pain of denial."

"It seems that you have not been denied anything."

"I did not force or cajole her, you know."

"Young women are foolish, Michael. It's a man's place to –"

"Aunt, please, give me your blessing."

She glanced up, scowling. "Blessing! That I will not do, Michael. I know right from wrong, even if you do not."

"Is it right that I should be chosen to die?"

There was no true conviction in his tone. He was using the threat to blackmail her, to gain her sympathy and her collusion. Michael did not, in his heart, believe that he would die at all. He was still of an age when immortality seemed possible. Lungs rotting in his chest and fevers never far away – these were transient misfortunes. But she knew the truth, better than anyone, better than poor, deluded, wilful Michael.

She got up from the stool.

"If you meet near Moss House, if you continue to cuckold the weaver, Michael, you might die sooner than you think."

"I will keep warm, I promise."

"God rest you, Michael! Do you think a scarf and a wool vest will protect you from the fury of a deceived husband? Particularly a dour, proud man like Jamie Moodie? It's not night vapours that might terminate your life, it's shot from a gun or a club upon the head."

"Come now, Aunt Janet, you cannot expect me to believe that Moodie –"

"I care not what you believe, Michael. I speak the truth. Moodie might well kill you. She's a young wife, he an aging man. Jealousy might lead him to murder."

Michael laughed uneasily. "This is not a silly play, Aunt."

"I only wish that it was, Nephew."

He seated himself on the table, close to her. "Do you really suppose that Moodie would do such a thing?" and then answered his own question. "You know, I suppose he might. If Elspeth was mine, my wife, and another man – Yes, indeed, I do see what you mean."

"You may be prepared to die for love, Michael, but if you die one day sooner than the Good Lord intends then it will be at Moodie's hand. And your lady love will have to suffer all the consequences."

"What shall I do? I'll not give her up."

"Not even for her sake?"

"She, I believe, would not want it. Elspeth is aware of the dangers. Probably more than I am."

"Does she know that you have an illness?"

"Of course not."

"So it's a matter of caution and duplicity, of which, it appears, you have now made me a part," said Miss Blaven.

"I will not involve you, Aunt."

"Bring her here."

"What?"

"Bring her here; or, rather, I will bring her here. I will strike up a tea-taking sort of acquaintance with the young woman. She may come here as often as prudence permits."

"How often?"

"Not more than once in each week."

"It's not –"

"Her visits will be undertaken with caution and some subtlety. If we have good fortune, Moodie will not suspect my social advances. I wonder if he has any inkling that you stay here with me."

"Elspeth says that he does not."

"So much the better."

"Aunt, I feel awfully guilty about involving you in this deception."

"It's rather too late for guilt, Michael."

"I do not wish to seem ungrateful, Aunt, but I need to be alone with –"

"I will leave you with her, never fear."

"For how long, and how often?"

"Michael," the woman snapped, "this is not a contract. Is it not enough that I've agreed to help you in making assignations of which I do not – be clear on the point – do not approve?"

"Yes, Aunt, of course it is."

"No more nocturnal prowlings."

"I promise. When will I see Elspeth again?"

"As soon as it can be decently arranged. I will call on her this afternoon."

"You are," Michael kissed her on the cheek, "a most marvellous aunt."

"No, Michael." She would not be charmed, not today. "No, I'm a fool, a sentimental old fool."

"This afternoon?"

"Yes."

Jamie Moodie's mill stretched beyond the base of the auld brig at the Loup o' Kennart and occupied a great narrow step on the west bank of the Lightwater. It had not long retained the appearance of a new building for moss, dampness, and soot coughed from the cottage chimneys had rapidly aged its stones and timbers. Inside the wood-floored, low-beamed rooms the air was clotted with flecks of wool in varying states of density, wreathed by smoke from warming-stoves and strong with the stench of the grease with which the mobile parts of the mules and carding devices were lagged. The separate chambers were not partitioned but, thanks to contour and construction, stepped down two or three feet, each descending from the other as if the whole place were trying to steal into the river to lave away the lather of ceaseless activity.

At the mill's high end was a lade of stone and logs which trapped a coil of the Lightwater and diverted it into a race across which was bedded a single large water-wheel. The wheel provided only a portion of the power required to rotate the axles and spindles within, for Weaver Moodie was not sufficiently confident of innovation to dispense with hand-jennies.

The weaving of the cloths was done on handlooms attended by craftsmen. They were paid, as in domestic arrangement, by the finished piece. The men who crouched over the looms had been culled from villages all across the Lennox and had trudged to sign their names on Moodie's book in the belief that he would somehow protect them against the inevitable sag in the trade that would occur when the war against the French was over. Many had worked for Moodie in the past so now the mill-owner offered them an attractive shelter, a sense of community, in addition to ready work for wives and children. Happily they traded pride for convenience, exchanged the bondage of paying rent to a laird for the privilege of being tied to James Simpson Moodie, all under one roof, all congregated in the beetle-browed oblong cottages that flanked the road above the mill.

Moodie had two managers, experienced agents who had been with him for many years. Mr Scarf was responsible for acquiring substantial crops of wool, for making sure that it was packed briskly to Kennart and properly stored in the 'dumping-den', a wooden shed of considerable volume which leaned out from the mill gable like a fallen buttress. Mr Rudge was manager of the mill itself. He had an office perched above the wool store that was reached by a flight of rickety steps. Scarf spent most of his year upon the road. But Rudge was confined to Kennart now and missed his travelling. He was much under James Moodie's eye and detested the crowded hamlet and enforced association with the vulgar herd. He was, however, exceedingly well paid for his suffering and was not, thank God, required to actually reside in the God-blighted place but maintained his house in Harlwood in high bachelor style.

It was not Rudge but McAlpin, his clerk of accounts, who first spotted the ruffians.

McAlpin was a youngish man, skinny and short in the leg, with dark hair, thin lips and a pair of sharp brown eyes. He hailed from Lenzie and had had an Academy education and had earnestly sought a position in Mr Moodie's enterprise. He inordinately admired his employers. He was industrious and respectful and placed himself firmly on the side of gentlemen. In course of time he hoped that he might ascend to the position which Mr Rudge now held or, if fortune smiled on him, that he might set up a manufactory on his own account.

On that particular afternoon McAlpin was not at his desk but had sought a breath of fresh afternoon air by walking to the mill-head room to collect the cloth tallies from the previous day's labour. It was more customary for the tallies to be delivered by a boy but McAlpin liked to bully the overseer, Slade, who was twice his age and size but had no intelligence to speak of. Having exercised both his legs and his tongue, McAlpin returned to the office steps, the tallies neatly folded in his left hand like a spray of paper flowers. He had climbed to the little landing by the door of the offices and paused to look down at Kennart from this perch, to enjoy the proprietorial feeling that it gave him, when the pony-cart hove over the brow of the hill on the Drymen road and came down into the mill community.

There was nothing unusual in travellers making use of the road between Drymen and Balnesmoor. But there was something about the couple, a man and a woman, with the laden cart which made McAlpin lean his stomach against the guarding-rail and watch more intently.

The woman was larger than the pony, near enough, a great squat lump, wrapped in shawls. She was seated upon the cart's edge with a rope-rein in her hand, balancing the long two-wheeler against the pyramid of sacks, tubs and boxes that towered behind her. She wore a strange hat, oval-brimmed, of dyed straw and, even as McAlpin observed the entry into Kennart, she lifted from her lap a flask and sucked from its neck like a calf at the teat.

At the pony's head was a man on foot, a tiny clay pipe jutting from his mouth, and his shoes – shoes, not pattens, McAlpin noted – flapping from broken straps. It seemed almost as if the fellow were dancing, coming down the hill, crimping the loose shoes to his feet, dancing and shuffling as mad folk do. He was clad in a pea-jacket of Amsterdam blue.

The couple obviously were not vagabonds or troublemakers. McAlpin, however, immediately marked them as town folk. His eyes narrowed with dislike and suspicion. He watched the cart trundle down into the muddy dip at the heart of the mill-hamlet and halt there. Puffing, the woman hoisted her bulk from the board while the man tied the pony-rope to the road's only hitch-rail, a slat nailed to a stump by the earthen walk at the cottage doors. The man ambled to the woman's side, put his arm around her waist and kissed her on the cheek.

Behind the pair, four old women and a young girl lumbering in the last weeks of a pregnancy came up the path from the riverbank with washing-baskets under their arms. The wives stopped, stared at the cart then moved on more quickly, chattering with excitement. Four or five very small children had materialised on the earthen walk and the sly, shy faces of others were visible in half-open doors. Strangers inevitably attracted attention in the newly-hatched community of Kennart. It was time, McAlpin decided, to report what he had seen to Mr Rudge before word leaked into the mill building and looms and spindles were abandoned as the workers flocked out to see what treasures the tubs and sacks contained. The accountant-clerk let himself into the office. But the manager's desk was bare, the chair behind it unoccupied. McAlpin returned to the stairs to resume his observation of the strangers.

Possibly they had come here, innocently enough, to seek work. Somehow McAlpin doubted it. They had not the servile manner of servants or field-workers, nor the cocky conceit of a craftsman and his lady. They behaved as if they intended to make purchase of the place. The woman pulled from the flask, wiped her mouth on her sleeve and passed the flask to the man who toasted the four corners of Kennart, grinning, before he drank.

Anger welled in McAlpin's chest. He flung himself down the stairs, shouting, "You there! I say, you there!"

The couple, arms linked like lovers, were strolling towards the mill head, ignoring the crowd of children and women who had crept up to the back of the cart to prod at the sacks in curiosity.

"You. Stop where you stand."

Chin thrust out pugnaciously, the accountant-clerk pranced towards the strangers who, still with arms linked, waited without a shred of surprise at being thus accosted.

"No pedlars here wi'out permission," McAlpin cried.

"Sir, we're no' pedlars," said the man.

The wives were pecking about the cart like pullets now and the enormous woman glanced over her shoulder and emitted a soft, deep, warning growl, like a mastiff.

"What are you then?" McAlpin demanded. He was dwarfed by the strangers, by the woman more than the man, but had become used to looking upward at folk and was not daunted by the weight mustered against him. "What do ye seek in our mill?"

"We're provision merchants, sir," said the woman.

"Provisions? Damned if you're not pedlars!"

"Is there a law agin sellin' here, a law we've not heard about, sir?" said the woman.

Attracted by the noisy conversation and by the sight of

somebody squaring up to wee McAlpin, who was much detested by the Kennart folk, the wives made a ring about the strangers. Already, even then, there was an air of magnetism between the women and the merchants.

The nearest shop was four miles uphill, in Balnesmoor. It was a weary trail for the wee luxuries that made long hours of toil at the looms worthwhile. Besides, the cart was whacked high and there was from it, so more sensitive noses claimed, a delicious effluvium of pickled herring and salted bacon. Unlike the farmers and their hands the weavers had no beasts to slaughter and no meal to grind here in Kennart; a man could not eat a blanket nor a length of kilt-cloth. Money was the tangible product of the looms, money that could be exchanged for provender and for drink. Now here was a cart groaning with good things and only bloody McAlpin to stand between them and the pleasures of purchase.

"Law!" said McAlpin. "When the manager's no' here, I'm the law in Kennart."

"Ha-ha!" cracked somebody in the crowd. "Ha-ha-ha!"

McAlpin pretended not to hear the jackass jibe.

"An' where, sir, would the manager be?" the man asked.

"In the privy," came an answer from the crowd.

McAlpin's face burned. He did not quite know how to cope with such reasonable behaviour. So far the strangers had done nothing except tie up their pony-cart.

"You, lad." The accountant-clerk singled out one of the older children with a stab of his forefinger. "Run this instant to the forge and fetch the smith."

Both a shoe-smith and a mechanical expert, William Baynham was one of the new breed of Vulcans who had taught himself to cope with the latest devices of industry and, his fears to the contrary, had found more than enough work in Kennart to keep him in red meat and whisky. The forge was separated by the bridge from the cottages, set on a shoulder of ground above the lade stream. Baynham was James Moodie's 'constable', too tall, too strong and too brutal to brook opposition. If there was a brawl, Baynham was summoned to disperse the culprits and usually managed to break the odd finger or wrist in the sorting. If there was recalcitrance within the manufactory, it was Baynham who appeared at Rudge's side, a great glowering threat to back the manager's commands. Everybody in Kennart, including McAlpin, lived in awe of the smith.

The boy, six years old at most, went off like a cat. He would not, of course, venture within thirty yards of the open door of Baynham's forge, with its hot fire and black-horned anvil, but would yell out Mr McAlpin's instruction from a safe and respectful distance. The strangers, it appeared, were not familiar with the threat that the smith implied and the crowd of females and children did not for the moment sidle back, though they would be fast enough on their feet when Baynham stepped over the gates and tramped on to the street. Until that occurrence, McAlpin and the newcomers appeared quite prepared to do nothing.

Disconcerted by the strangers' silence, McAlpin in a deceptively friendly tone asked, "What do you have on your cart?"

"Herring. Trotters. Hard apples." It was the fat woman who deigned to reply. "Provisions for the store."

"Store? A store here? Hah, ye'll need to think again. There'll be no merchanting hereabouts. Mister Moodie'll never stand for it."

"We'll see," said the woman.

"Where is Mister Moodie?" said the man.

"Mister Moodie is up in his house in Balnesmoor. He'll not be at the beck an' call o' the likes of you."

The woman glanced at the man, who extracted the clay pipe from his mouth and spat, quite delicately, on the cobble that lay between McAlpin's shoes.

McAlpin jerked back while the womenfolk in the gathering sniggered.

The cry went up from the little boy racing back from the bridge-end, "*He's a-comin'*."

The crowd shrank back, isolating McAlpin, the merchant-pedlars and the pony-cart.

Baynham wore a flapping leather apron and short wide shirt untaped to show an expanse of matted chest flushed by the forge fire. His hair curled with sweat and his eyes seemed to have a coal in each pupil. In one hand he carried the brass-studded plough-trace with which he meted out punishment when he was so instructed by Mr Rudge. Baynham, however, was not well pleased at being called away from twisting with tongs and a hand-vice a flat bar that he had spent a half-hour patiently nurturing to blood-red heat.

McAlpin licked his lip. "Mister Rudge isn't here. He left me t' look after the offices."

Baynham said nothing.

"These vagabonds'll not leave the road," said McAlpin.

"Aye, for what're ye wantin' me?"

"To – to remove them."

Baynham considered. He towered over the accountant-clerk, who managed only by the most strenuous effort of will to hold his ground, while the trace brushed and brushed back and forth restlessly against the thick leather hem of the apron.

"Remove them where?"

"O'er the bridge'll do fine," said McAlpin.

The smith stepped past the clerk and extended his right hand, the studded trace hanging from it like the hide of a flayed felon.

"Get on the cartie an' ride awa'," Baynham said, quietly, to the strangers.

It was the woman, who in bulk if not strength was nearly the smith's equal, who stepped forward. She protruded her stomach and breasts as she drew in her breath. "We'll move for no man, smith."

"Then I'll throw yon cartie in the water."

"An' if you do, m' mannie, ye'll be followin' it downstream e'er night falls," the woman said.

"For why?"

"For the reason, smith, that Mister Moodie'll discharge you from his service afore ye can suck three breaths," said the woman.

Baynham hesitated.

"Move them, Baynham. I'm givin' ye an order," McAlpin shrieked.

Baynham had more sense than the clerk. The couple had invoked the name of the highest power in the little kingdom above the Lightwater and Baynham would not take action against it, not on the word of an inky wee pipsqueak.

He shook his head. "I'm thinkin' we'll wait for Mister Rudge."

Stepping close to his woman's shoulder, the stranger said, "Bide with us for a while an' I'll give a solemn oath we'll sit quiet on the cart an', except for waterin' the pony, make no claim from the property. No, nor endeavour to press trade wi' the spinners or weavers or their spouses."

Baynham nodded; a solution.

McAlpin said, "Sit quiet for how long?"

"Until a message can be taken to Mister Moodie," the woman said.

"What message could ye be havin' for a gentleman like Mister Moodie?" said McAlpin.

McAlpin sensed in the pair the sort of implacable power that he craved. It was sufficient to give the clerk serious pause. Baynham, whose simple brute mind easily grasped such simple brute issues, glowered at him.

"Let a laddie tak' the message. Let Mister Moodie deal wi' them," said Baynham, sensibly but with a hint of threat.

McAlpin brooded for a moment. The crowd of onlookers hung on his decision. He spun round on his heel, looking down to the path behind which the earth privies were situated. He had the feeling that Mr Rudge had gone off somewhere. Perhaps he had taken one of the younger girls out to the sheds for a lesson in commercial diplomacy. McAlpin did not approve but he put his prudishness aside when it came to Mr Rudge and told himself that it was a necessary part of privilege.

He sighed. "Fetch me Laurence," he told the six-year-old runner and the little boy started off for the carters' den on the lane by the Drymen roadway where Mr Laurence and his horses would be found.

McAlpin gestured towards the pony-cart. "You'll not shift from there."

"Not 'til Mister Moodie gets here," said the stranger.

"Aye, you're fair sure o' yourself on that score," said McAlpin. "Now, what is this famous message?"

"Tell Mister Moodie," said the woman, "that Bell Harper has arrived in Kennart."

"Is that it all?"

"Bell Harper: the name will be enough."

A peculiar confluence of circumstances made deception easy by distracting James's attention from the woman from Preaching Friar who had turned up in his drawing-room unannounced. Tolland fetched the master from the library before sending a maid upstairs to bring the mistress from her room. James came

158

at once to the drawing-room and introduced himself to the upright, respectable lady and asked what he might do for her, asked with a certain restrained suspicion.

"I have come," said Miss Blaven, "to enquire if your wife might care to take tea with me."

James nodded. He had no objection to such a thing. But the woman seemed to believe that the invitation required an explanation. "I have been meaning to call upon your wife for some months now. My nephew, my brother's child, resides with me from time to time, however, and demands, as boys will, a great deal of me. It's refreshing, is it not, Mister Moodie, to have youthful exuberance about one in later life?"

James seemed oblivious to the implications that lurked behind the remark. He nodded again. He had heard of Janet Blaven, for even in Harlwood she was considered not a little eccentric, though she was not 'sinister' in any manner and attended kirk regularly. He had seen her there, in the high pew tucked away to the west of the pulpit, but had never addressed a word to her until that afternoon.

"I thought," Miss Blaven went on, "that perhaps Mistress Moodie might care to give me her company on occasional afternoons, particularly during the dull season, provided that the weather remains clement and the road betwixt Moss House and Preaching Friar is not rimed with ice or snow. The long wintry afternoons can be so tedious, can they not, sir?"

Weaver Moodie agreed.

"Is your wife at home, Mister Moodie?" the woman asked.

"She's resting in her room. She has been sent for and will be with us presently, I'm sure," said Moodie. "I feel certain she will welcome your kind invitation, since she does find it wearyin' to be stuck in the house all day long when the winter's with us."

"We shall take tea early, in order that she might be home before dusk," said Miss Blaven.

"Is your nephew with you at present?" said James.

Miss Blaven did not hesitate. She lied glibly. "Oh, no. Not at present. I expect when he grows older I shall not see him at all. He will forget his ancient aunt."

Before Elspeth could enter the drawing-room, and before James could enquire further about 'the nephew', Tolland knocked on the drawing-room door and entered.

"Aye, what is it?" James asked the steward.

Tolland advanced, stooped, whispered into James's ear.

At that moment Elspeth, flushed and uncertain, appeared at the drawing-room door. She glanced nervously at the woman and then at James. Had her love and love-making been revealed by the spinster from Preaching Friar? Elspeth's guilt increased as James shot from his chair, features contorted and complexion ashen. Muttering an apology he rushed from the room, quite oblivious to Elspeth's presence by the doorway. Anxiously Tolland followed his master.

Nonplussed by her husband's behaviour Elspeth drew a deep, steadying breath.

"You are, I believe, Miss Blaven." Elspeth came forward. "I have heard much good of you, though we haven't met before."

The woman studied her, and did not return her smile.

Elspeth said, "I ask you to pardon my husband. It's apparently a matter of urgent business – at the mill, I imagine – which has called him away so suddenly."

Miss Blaven inclined her head to acknowledge the polite apology. She still had not relaxed and seemed to Elspeth as prickly as an old hedgehog. Elspeth seated herself on a little satin divan.

Miss Blaven said, "I did not come, in fact, to speak with your husband, though I should have been quite justified in doing so in the light of the circumstances."

"What circumstances are those?"

The woman tutted and made a gesture as if brushing crumbs from her sleeve.

"Young woman, do you know, I'm Michael's aunt; old but neither blind nor deaf."

"I see," said Elspeth.

"Devil take chit-chat, girl," said Miss Blaven and, in a tone of voice that permitted no argument or interruption, outlined the scheme she had devised for furthering the affair.

Elspeth listened, hardly able to believe her ears.

Miss Blaven concluded, "Can you be discreet?"

"Yes. Oh, yes."

"Will you be expected to take a maid with you?"

"Sometimes, perhaps. But I can drive the gig myself an' have done so once or twice."

"You may come to my house then, but no oftener than once in the week. It would be unwise to arouse your husband's suspicions unnecessarily. One afternoon each week must suffice."

"Why do you do this?" Elspeth asked.

"Not for you. For my nephew. Out of love for Michael." Still the spinster was unrelenting. "I do not approve of deceit and connivance, and I would have no part in it if it were not for the fact that my nephew, that Michael – that he believes himself to be in love with you. Tell me, do you love him?"

"I do. I love him with all my heart."

"It is not just a game, hmmm?"

"Certainly not," said Elspeth. "I am not that kind of person, Miss Blaven."

"Ah, but it seems that you are. If you were not in some measure 'that kind of person' then I would not be on this unfortunate mission."

Elspeth opened her mouth to protest but found that she could not deny the accusation. She must, at least, be honest in sin.

It had not before occurred to her that she was already damned in the eyes of decent society, that there could be no forgiveness for what she had done, nor for what she was about to do. It would be furtive, a thing of stealth, but if loving could be found no other way then she had no alternative but to square herself, to admit what she had done. She had salve for the wounded soul, however, in the secret that she shared only with her husband, that she had come to Michael as a virgin, almost a bride, and that her marriage was no better than a contract on paper. She felt more like an errant, wilful daughter than an erring and unfaithful wife.

"What," said Elspeth, "what will happen in the future?"

"The future?"

"What will become of us?"

"Let the future look after itself, child. Take what is offered and be grateful. Put tomorrow entirely out of mind."

"I'm half afraid," said Elspeth.

"So you should be." Miss Blaven glanced towards the drawing-room door. "It seems that your husband has gone out."

"In that case we will have an opportunity to talk," said

Elspeth, "if you have the time to spare; and the inclination."

Miss Blaven sighed. "I suppose we had better get to know each other. Yes. Is tea to be offered?"

"Tea is to be offered," said Elspeth, and rang the little silver bell.

The stairs shook beneath the woman's bulk. She seemed barely able to squeeze herself between the rails and toiled slowly upwards as to a gibbet. James waited on the landing by the office's open door while the woman laboured, assisted by an occasional indecorous shove from the man who claimed to be her husband.

The abrupt, tempestuous arrival of the owner had dispersed the crowd, sent them slinking away to their homes, but now they crouched in doorways and by the windows, watching.

McAlpin had taken the rein of James's lathered horse and had hitched it by the pony-cart while Baynham, not daft enough to leave the strangers unguarded, hung about by the bridge-end, watching too.

As he had whipped and spurred the big horse down the road from Balnesmoor, James's mind had been in turmoil. Reason wrestled with imagination, hope with terrible fear. He had spared no time to question the boy who had carried the message up from the mill, except to ensure that it was indeed a woman who had delivered it and that the woman waited, in the flesh, at Kennart.

Divested by shock of all aloofness James had clattered the mount over the bridge and had flung himself from the saddle as soon as he spotted the strangers seated on the back of the loaded cart.

"WHO ARE YOU?" he shouted so violently that his voice could be heard within the mill building even above the din of the looms. "DAMN ME, WILL YOU ANSWER!"

"Do ye not recall me, Mister Moodie?" the fat woman said.

"I've never seen you before in my life."

"Aye, sir, but ye have. Long, long ago. In Glasgow."

"Never, I say."

"The years have takit their toll, right enough. But well do I recall how ye came t' see my friend Bell Harper behind the old Tontine. She was fair smitten wi' ye, Mister Moodie. She

162

talked of her weaver Jamie night after night while we lay in our beds."

The woman spoke with a sly wistfulness, softly. But McAlpin's ears were pricked like a fox's and James believed that the stranger's speech could be heard by everyone for miles around, like an echo carrying out of a cavern.

He was relieved, however, that the strangers came only from Glasgow and not from some black limbo beyond the grave. He had seen Bell dead and he had seen Bell buried and all that truly remained of her was the child, his child, his wife.

"What nonsense is this?" he said.

"It canna be nonsense, sir, when she left a bairn behind her, a bairn that's livin' still."

Before James could protest that he did not know what the woman was talking about, the man intervened. "Be that as it may, dearest, I'm certain Mister Moodie has no time t' spare for mullin' over the olden days, not here an' not now."

"What do you want in Kennart?"

"We've come with a purpose. Mutually beneficial."

"For money, is it? To extract money?"

The fellow seemed hurt by the suggestion. "Mutually beneficial, sir. If ye can spare a moment, in a bit of privacy, we'll tell ye what the purpose is."

James hesitated, then said quietly, "We'll talk in the room at the top of the staircase."

The room reeked of Rudge's scented tobacco and vibrated with the jerking engines in the long building to which it was attached. The sounds of industry were muffled but the thrill of the machines was transmitted through the boards. James closed the door at once and dropped the latch. He stepped to the window and looked down into the road. Cottars had crawled out again, whispering among themselves, agog, watching the high office intently, watching the staircase, watching the door as if they expected him to fly out and soar above their heads, scaled and horned and breathing fire.

Uninvited, the fat woman seated herself upon McAlpin's stool while her man stood by her side, pipe in mouth, hands in pockets. James stood behind the table, arms folded imperiously.

"Speak your piece, packman," he said.

"We're no packmen, sir," said the man. "I am named

George Cunningham an' this lady is my goodwife, Trina. We are Godfearin' citizens of the great city of Glasgow an' there, this many a year, we've served the populace as provision merchants and victuallers."

"What of this woman?" said James. "What was her name? Harper? Is she also in the victuallin' trade?"

The fat woman snorted derisively. "Bell Harper's been dead for many years, as well you know, Mister Moodie."

"I know nothing of the sort," said James. "What makes you suppose I'd ever heard of this girl before today? Candidly, Mistress Cunningham, I have no recollection of her at all. Nor of you, for that matter."

"I'm sure you recall the backs o' the Tontine well enough, Mister Moodie, since you spent such a deal o' time waitin' there for Bell to finish work an' come to you."

James was well aware of how he was being manipulated. He dared not relax, even though his heart was pounding and his chest constricted. If he showed even a trace of fear the Cunninghams would, like mongrel dogs, be at his throat in an instant. At all costs he must appear to have the upper hand. He thought of Elspeth back up the hill in the security of Moss House. She was so like her mother, so like Bell Harper. Fine clothes and fashionable grooming could not disguise the physical resemblance. There was little doubt that the Cunningham woman had seen Elspeth in Glasgow and had recognised her. To see Elspeth was to see Bell. Though there could be no shred of proof of his daughter's true identity, the implication of the Cunninghams' arrival was terrifying. Accusation alone would be sufficient to bring him down.

James stepped to the mark. "You claim, Mister Cunningham, to have a purpose in seeking me out. Let's hear of it without more ado, please."

"We've a mind to set up a shop," Cunningham said, "in the pure fresh air of the country. Kennart seems to be a spot ideal."

"There are no vacant accommodations in Kennart at present."

"Any old bit of a shed or barn will suit," said Cunningham. "We'll take it upon ourselves to make it neat an' habitable."

"I'm sure, sir, you'll find us a dry corner, for auld times' sake," said the woman.

"I see," said James. "You claim that your purpose would benefit me, but I see no benefit in the settin' up of a shop. Am I to charge you rental for the premises or to draw a certain percentage from the profits of your venture?"

"Findin' a shop at their doors will keep the labourers contentit," said Cunningham. "It'll prevent them wanderin' far from the mill place in search o' provender, fallin' into the temptations places the likes o' Balnesmoor offer."

James would hardly have called Balnesmoor the Gomorrah of the north, though, by the lights of some in the Lennox, Fintry or Balfron might qualify.

"See, there's the benefit," said the woman.

James said, "Hardly! Kennart's workers have managed well enough so far without a shop. Besides, if I wished to have a shop in Kennart I would open one on my own account."

"We have experience. We have sold foodstuffs an' fuels, all sorts o' things, for twenty years."

"In Glasgow," James said. "Kennart's requirements are not the same as those of the city."

"Bellies growlin' for tasty sup," said Cunningham, "sound the same everywhere."

How far would he have to push them before they raised the dreadful name of Isobel Harper again, until the woman thrust more 'recollections' at him, until Elspeth's relationship was exposed? James closed his eyes for a moment. It was not his heart that was pounding now but his head, a swelling, stabbing pain.

"What do you propose to sell in this shop of yours?"

"Everythin' needed by the folk hereabouts."

"For example?" said James.

Immediately the woman rattled off a list of foodstuffs and goods that seemed endless. James allowed her to indulge her fantasy, taking note of the fact that she included beer and spirits among the pies and candles, cheeses and smoked fish. He could not imagine such edible delicacies suiting the palates of his labourers but he could, with ease, imagine their delight at having drink available a stone's throw from the mill.

"How will you purchase all this stock?" he asked, when, at length, the woman had completed her inventory.

"We've money," said Cunningham. "Capital."

"Indeed!" James said. "Sufficient to furnish such an ambitious scheme?"

"We also have trusted friends from whom credit can be obtained," said Cunningham.

"See, Mister Moodie, there's nothin' to prevent it," said Trina Cunningham.

"But yet, where is my benefit?"

"We'll pay a tithe in the stead of a rent," said Cunningham. "The sum of one shilling in each twenty."

"Two shillings," James said.

"One shilling an' sixpence."

"Two," James insisted. "Not a farthin' less will I accept."

The woman reached up her hand and tugged on the pea-jacket and the man capitulated. "Aye, you shall have your two shillings, Mister Moodie."

"Who will keep the account, however?" James said.

"Has the account not been kept?" said the woman sleekly.

"I do not understand your meaning, Mistress Cunningham."

"We'll be keepin' the account," said the woman.

James laughed mirthlessly. "It would hardly be fair to ask or expect me to trust you quite so far."

"We're reliable," said the woman. "More reliable than many another."

James sensed that the name of Bell Harper was on the tip of the fat woman's tongue again and blurted out his agreement to prevent the utterance. Never before had he buckled under less pressure, given in to such woeful terms. The Cunninghams had him in flight, and were increased in arrogance because of it.

"When – when would you wish to commence?"

"We brought our pony an' our cart, as you saw," said Cunningham. "Show us the accommodation ye have in mind for us an' we'll have crusty pies and soused herring scentin' the air by dinner-time tomorrow."

But the woman would not let James Moodie surrender so easily. "Aye, Bell was fair fond o' pickled herrin', as you'll no doubt recall."

James's temper broke. "You're here only under sufferance," he snapped. "I've given you your wretched terms. I'll see to it that you have your damned cottage too. Now hear what I

166

have to say. My stipulation. Hear it well or I'll order my blacksmith to burn you out and break your pony's back into the bargain. Never in my hearing will either of you mention Bell Harper's name again."

"I thought the name meant nothin' to you," the woman said.

"Never, *never* again."

Cunningham patted his wife's shoulder. "Trust us, sir. The name you abhor will never be breathed betwixt our lips from this moment forth. Is that not so, my dearest?"

"Aye, that's so." Trina Cunningham got ponderously from the chair, supported by her husband. "Now, Mister Moodie, if you'd be good enough t' show us our bit corner, I'll set out my bakin' boards an' griddles in preparation for tomorrow."

Cunningham offered his hand.

To his eternal shame, James Simpson Moodie shook it — and sealed the devil's bargain.

The boot-plate by the hearthside in Sinclair's cottage was made of hard brass, polished to gleam like gold. Firelight shone on it and on the copper kettle which was used only to make medicines, and on the miniature warming-pan which had been a bridal gift to Aileen from her grandmother but was now no more than another pretty object to burnish. Lachlan Sinclair used the boot-plate carefully, waggling off the half-calf boots and setting them precisely on the board by the fire where they would dry gradually without flaking and stiffening and without shedding dirt upon the whitened flagstones.

The grieve sat back. Tonight he would welcome a taste of whisky, done with water and sugar perhaps, for he felt drained by the long evening in the company of the new laird. Rent books, stud books, tallies of yields from plantings, records of wool sales, beef sales and milkings; it was the grieve himself who had inaugurated the keeping of accurate records so could not complain at the new laird's fascination with facts and figures. He was surprised at the nimbleness of Randall Bontine's brain, however, for the laird was full of shrewd and penetrating questions.

But there had been another happening that afternoon which was of equal significance to Lachlan Sinclair. He had been approached by Mister Gilbert with a suggestion that he might care to leave Ottershaw and accompany his, Gilbert's, family on their exodus to pastures new.

"Where are these new pastures, sir?"

"I haven't found land to purchase yet," Gilbert had answered. "But when I do, Lachlan, I'll come to you again and ask for a decision."

Lachlan had been non-committal but the suggestion had set his thoughts racing. In fact he had already begun to wonder if his loyalty had ever really been to the lairds at all and not to the land itself. In prospect he could not imagine himself being comfortable anywhere else in the world.

He had his family to consider, however. What would become of Ottershaw under Randall? Would it, as Gibbie seemed to believe, quickly fall to ruin? So far he had seen few signs that Randall was a wastrel. If he went along with Mister Gilbert he would, of course, insist that places were found for his children, also for Matt and Anna. Thus would Matt be saved from the bad company of Pad Tomelty and Anna from the lascivious interest of the laird; or was he, perhaps, making too much of it?

He looked over at Aileen. She was busy with her needle, patching a pair of Sandy's breeks. Dearly would he have liked to share his worries with her but she would not understand the half of it and would only worry about matters that were, after all, man's business.

Lachlan Sinclair closed his eyes, though he was by no means drowsy, and turned the sundry anxieties over in his mind.

A few minutes later he was disturbed by a rap upon the door.

"Who can that be at such a late hour?" said Aileen.

The latch rattled and the door opened and Matt entered the kitchen. His cheeks were blushed and his eyes bright which suggested that he had been boozing, though he was far from inebriated. He tossed his hat on to the top of the chest by the door and came towards the fire, palms spread to soak up the heat. Matt needed no invitation, no welcome. Though relations with his father might be strained the home hearth and its comforts would never be denied him so long as his mother was alive.

Aileen was naturally delighted to see her son. She whisked

away her bits of sewing and instantly bustled a cog of hot leek soup and a plate of bread and butter on to the table.

Carefully, Sinclair said, "Aye, so it's yourself, Matt. You're out and about at a late hour tonight."

"I took ale with McDonald an', since he was the worse o' it, felt obligated to see him safe up the hill to his door. I came down by the pine bridge, so I thought I'd call in t' visit Mam."

Pleased by her son's explanation, Aileen said, "You'll be hungry?"

"Famished."

"Have you not been home at all?" Sinclair asked.

"Anna'll feed my monkey," Matt replied, as if that was all the answer his father needed.

"Have you not spoken with your wife today?"

"She's not spoken wi' me," said Matt.

"She has news for you."

Matt glowered. "What news?"

"Tell him, Lachlan," said Aileen. "It's no secret, such good news."

"Anna's been 'made up'," said Sinclair.

"Made up t' what?"

"Picked for a house servant."

To his parents' consternation, Matt threw back his head and bellowed with laughter.

"I see no humour in it," said Sinclair at length.

"A domestic? Bloody Anna?" Matt hooted again. "God, she can hardly boil water wi'out floodin' the kitchen. She'll not last more than a week inside the big house, mark my words. Anna – a servant!"

"It's good advancement, Matt," said Aileen uncertainly.

"Aye, and you should not talk so disparagingly of your wife," said Sinclair. "If you have a poor opinion of her fitness it should be kept to yourself."

Still shaking his head in amusement at the notion of Anna let loose in Ottershaw, Matt seated himself at the table. His mother served him with soup, bread and a rasher of boiled ham. He fell to eating with relish. Aileen watched him fondly, frowning.

She said, "It'll be more money too, will it not, Lachlan?"

"Better wages than a dairy-lassie makes, certainly."

"Longer hours each day, though," said Matt. "Aye, wi' any luck I'll hardly see her at all."

"What a thing to be sayin' about your wife," Aileen chided.

Matt shrugged with apparent indifference. He lifted a slice of ham between his finger and thumb, folded it into his mouth and chewed thoughtfully. "Is this the new laird's doin'?" he asked after a pause. "Is it him as wants her in the house?"

Sinclair chose his words with care. "Anna is only one of several."

'Who are the others, then?"

"Brigit Tomelty for one."

Once more Matt hooted with amusement. "By God, but he's keen, is Randall. Brigit'll have the bloody silver out from under Hunter's snitch, one piece at a time. Did you not think t' warn the man, Father, eh?"

"Brigit is a diligent worker," Sinclair said.

"Diligent on her back, right enough," Matt murmured.

"Enough!" said Lachlan Sinclair. "I'll not have that sort of talk in my house." He got to his feet. "It's late. When you've eaten your fill, you should be on your way home. You've a hard day's work ahead of you, if I'm not mistaken."

Matt wiped his mouth. "Aye, if the river stays low enough an' the bank soft, we'll be startin' shore-work the day after tomorrow."

"Are the props an' brakes all cut then?"

"Cut an' stacked for length," said Matt. "McDonald'll be sendin' for the horses."

"Has he told Craigie?"

"He has. Provided there's no heavy rain, the work'll be done by Saturday."

"I'll come round tomorrow. I wish to have a word with McDonald in any case," said Sinclair. A half-hour of his discussion with the laird had been devoted to the plantations. "It seems you'll be kept busy cuttin', if I can find a buyer."

"Cuttin' what?"

"The thirty-year acres," Sinclair said. "Three lots are to be sold. The value's about two thousand pounds sterling for each lot. Can we separate about twelve acres from each of the lots?"

"Aye, there's that an' more. The old laird was wise when it came to trees," Matt admitted. "He had the plantin's done for the sake o' the sons. Will Randall skin the whole forest?"

"Not him," said Sinclair. "He needs capital, though, since he has payments to make to the family."

"Is Gibbie departin'?" Matt asked.

"He'll be gone by Whitsun, I expect."

"Will you go wi' him?" said Matt.

Aileen, who had been removing the cogs from the table, froze over her task.

"What makes you suppose Mister Gilbert would want me?"

"He'd be daft if he didn't try to lure you awa' from Randall," said Matt. "You're the best damned grieve in Scotland, Da."

"Well, if Gibbie does propose it," said Sinclair, evasively, "I would have to give it much ponderin'."

"You'll never quit Ottershaw," said Matt.

Aileen Sinclair put one bowl into another and slowly straightened. She kept her back to the men and did not intrude, though she was dizzy with the desire to shout aloud that she wanted no other home but this one and no shift at her time of life.

"If, for the sake of hypothesis," said Sinclair, "I was offered the management o' Gilbert's estate, somewhere, would you come with us?"

"One grieve is all Gibbie'll need."

"There might be plantations."

"Plantations!" said Matt with derision. "Is that what you hope for me, Da, that I'll become a forester like Kenneth McDonald?"

"There are worse occupations."

"Nah, nah," said Matt. "I'm content where I am."

"It's yourself that has no ambition," said Sinclair.

"When I'm prepared, then I'll strike out for myself, but it'll not be on your coat-tails, Father."

"Strike out?"

Matt smiled, smugly, but would not be drawn further. He quickly brought the conversation back to the repair work which was pending on the banks of the Lightwater and distracted his father from further enquiry into his plans for the future.

Aileen took the cogs out to the tub by the back door and washed them in cold water. When she returned her husband and son were deep in discussion of estate work, so caught up that their enmities were forgotten.

She kissed her handsome son upon the brow, her husband

on the cheek and went through to her bed leaving the men clacking until after midnight. She was disturbed by what she had heard but blissfully unaware of the gathering shadows that threatened them all.

One o'clock in the morning, Jacko shivering in his cage, the fire near out, the table littered with pots and crocks and a tangle of damp wash dumped on each of the room's four chairs; Matt snorted wryly at the notion of Anna under Hunter's thumb where her sluttish ways would earn her stick and, probably, speedy dismissal.

Though Matt had been out and about since six that morning he was not in the least weary nor daunted by the thought that he must rise again in four hours or so for another day's labour. He had not told his father and mother the whole truth about his doings that evening. He had not lugged McDonald home at all, though he had been, for a time, at the Ramshead.

Kneeling by the hearth Matt built up the dying fire for the morning, placing big resinous logs with care, as he would shore up the crumbling bank of the Lightwater. It gave him pleasure to shape the fire, thumbing small coal into the cracks. He sat back on his heels, watching smoke reek evenly from the ramp and purl up the chimney as thick and grey as a kirkman's prayer. Rising, he untangled the washing and hung the items one by one across the ropes that webbed the rafters and, that done, treated himself to a final dram of hill-run whisky from the green flagon hidden in the dresser. It had been months since he felt so relaxed and at ease with himself and he had no wish for the day to end. He fished Jacko down from the cage and, clasping the monkey as he would a baby, padded softly about the kitchen, crooning to the creature who, at this hour of the night, was passive and without playfulness.

Glass in hand, the capuchin in his arms, Matt made his pet a bowl of warm cornmeal mash and, seated in the box chair, fed Jacko from a spoon. With the door of the bedroom closed he could blot Anna from his thoughts, push away the droll prospect of having his wife dance for Randall Bontine.

Thinking of Brigit's advancement to house servant, however, made Matt grin. By God, if Bontine had searched the Lennox from stem to stern he could not have picked himself a less reliable servant, though Brigit might put Anna to shame when it came to neat work – aye, and to pleasuring a man in other ways too. A little stab of jealousy touched Matt's heart, not for Anna but for Brigit Tomelty who, this past three weeks, had given him more fun and more affection than ever his wife had done, tumbling in barns and hay sheds and along the backs, anywhere where they could find a modicum of privacy.

Cradled in Matt's arms Jacko had fallen fast asleep. Matt laid aside bowl and spoon, tenderly wiped the half-open mouth and little round chin with his knuckle, and settled back in the box chair, too considerate to disturb the wee creature.

When the time came for him to escape from Balnesmoor only Jacko and Brigit would accompany him on his travellings. Every other thing and person would be left behind without a qualm; his father, the cottage, the tedious job, everything that leeched away his happiness, including Anna.

Anna too would be abandoned.

Anna most of all.

In the meantime let Hunter suffer her laziness, and the laird, if he was fool enough, sniff about her skirts.

Matt no longer cared.

Henry Hunter had started his career as a pot-boy in the Ottershaw kitchens and had been footman, valet and butler before attaining the august position of steward to the Bontine household. He had never suffered under his master, Sir Gilbert, but had had his patience tried to its limit by the mistresses of the house.

The first wife of the laird had been reared in the Tartar school of housekeeping and applied herself to domestic economy with the meticulousness of a German mathematician. Hunter had endured the woman for the first two decades of his service and regarded her behaviour as the norm; lavishness in public, obsessional parsimony in private.

The second wife had been quite different, a bright, gay, personable woman, thorough but trusting, and not unduly concerned with the fate of the bones from the stock-pot. Her rule had been cut short by the arrival of Gibbie's wife, the dreaded Alicia who, within a couple of years, had wrested the House Book from her mother-in-law and drove the servants to distraction by quibbling about every hobnail, button and duster. It had taken all Hunter's diplomacy to prevent the servants melting away under Alicia; even Mrs Lacy, the cook, had threatened to pack her bags and depart on more than one occasion. It was very satisfying to see Alicia stripped of power on Mister Randall's return, to take such umbrage that she abandoned all her duties and left the mansion without a female head.

Hunter had never married and, unlike Tom Tolland at Moss House, did not play the rooster in the hen-run. It did not surprise the downy old steward, however, when Randall picked two girls and a young boy to add to the staff. What the new laird wanted was a clutch of servants that he could call his own, servants who would not go tattling to Mistress Alicia behind his back.

Dunn was to be trained as a valet and resided in the servants' hall. Brigit Tomelty and Anna Sinclair, on the other hand, were to be hired as day-maids and released after six each evening to return to their homes. The boy was paid a pittance of two pounds in the year and given one day off each month to go home to visit his mother in Blanefield. Brigit and Anna received five pounds and dinners but got no allowance for clothing, being provided only with caps and aprons. Hunter would not have been surprised if he had had problems with Brigit Tomelty, though he kept a close eye on her, but it surprised him greatly when trouble stemmed from Anna Sinclair.

Anna had been in Ottershaw for just five weeks. It was Friday morning, a quarter of an hour after her arrival when Dunn's shrill voice commanded a pot of hot chocolate to be brought upstairs to the master's bedroom.

In the dining-room Gilbert, Alicia and three of their children stiffened as the cry rang down from the laird's quarters to the west of the staircase that climbed from the main hall. Anna saw little of Mister Gilbert's menage. Hunter had shown her the tunnel-like stairs that coiled up from behind the table-linen cupboard, stairs that she and Brigit must use to reach the library and the first-floor bedrooms.

"Chocolate, chocolate." Dunn loved the echo and impression of authority it gave and the laird egged him on to let it rip and damn the solemnity of the bell. "Chocolate for the master."

Mrs Lacy already had the tray set and quickly poured boiling water into the silver pot, snapping shut the lid. Hunter was in the dining-room attending Mister Gilbert and his family but Anna needed no special instruction as she had performed the rite almost every morning for weeks now. She tucked the curve of the tray into her elbow and headed for the back stairs.

Above Anna the door to the first-floor corridor opened and Brigit appeared, cheeks smudged with soot, empty pail clanking in her fist.

"Brigit, go back. I'll never get through wi' you there," hissed Anna.

Brigit retreated, holding the door. Anna tilted the laden tray and cautiously edged past her friend.

Brigit whispered, "He's in the bedroom. An' wait 'til ye see what he's doin'."

"What's he doin'?"

"Half undressed."

"Eh?"

"Waitin' for you."

"*What?*"

Brigit shot her eyebrows high, sniggered, pursed her lips in a grotesque kiss then flounced off, letting the door close and causing Anna to dance forward into the corridor. Tutting under her breath, Anna hurried to the door of the bedroom, knocked and waited.

Dunn opened to her and she went in, making for the octagonal table by the window, her head demurely lowered. She was aware of Randall, seated on a queer wee stool close to the bed. For once, Brigit had not exaggerated. Anna placed the tray on the table, turned.

"Will I pour for you, sir?" she asked.

"If you would be so good," Randall grunted.

He had clenched his fingers under the edges of the stool and had extended his leg before him, raised near straight. From the ankle hung a wooden bucket – a plain, dairy-milk container – half-filled with sand. The handle of the container was of white rope and there was a second bucket close by with a gardener's trowel in it. Randall was clad in his shirt and what appeared to be knee-length underdrawers.

Anna stared. She could see the shape of him clear beneath the clinging material as he deliberately lowered the leg until the bucket touched the floor then, with another grunt, raised it steadily and evenly upward again.

Though the morning was cold and the fire in the grate smoked black after fresh setting, there was sweat on Randall's upper lip. Dunn watched with almost as much fascination as the girl, though he had witnessed the performance a dozen times or more in recent weeks.

"Are you wantin' another spoonful in there, Mister Randall?"

"Come now, lad, would you have me crack the bone?"

"Och, no, Mister Randall, but you're doin' fine," said Dunn with an easy familiarity which Anna found puzzling. "Up higher, sir, eh? Up an' down."

Randall dipped his leg, rested, then raised the bucket higher than before, tilting his hips until his back touched the side of the bed behind him. He was quivering with muscular exertion. Sweat dripped from his brow. The long, cord-like muscles of his thigh and calf seemed to vibrate.

Dunn counted in a loud voice, "Ane, twa, three, fower, five, sax —"

The strain was too much. Randall sagged, letting the sand-bucket thud to the floor. He unhooked his ankle from the rope and fell back on to the unmade bed. He gave a great sigh, then propped himself on his elbows, and looked at Anna.

"Well, girl, are you going to pour my chocolate or are you waiting until it turns to ice?"

"Sorry, sir. Sorry."

She was trembling, as if she had shared his strenuous exercises. She was not mystified now. It had to do with the injury that made him walk so oddly. He was determined to bully the wasted flesh back to health.

Her fingers shook, the big cup chittered on the saucer as she took it to him. He made her wait, sizing her up, smiling.

"Taste it, girl," he said.

"What?"

"Taste it. Is it sweet enough?"

She juggled the saucer, lifted the cup and put her lips into the thick, dark liquid. It was sweet and appealing. She drank a little, watching the laird over the rim. In turn he watched her, amused.

"Aye, it's sweet, Mister Randall."

"Excellent!" he held out his hand and she gave him the cup.

Dunn had pulled away the sand-bucket and hauled it into

a corner of the room, indicating that the period of exercise was over.

Anna turned towards the door.

"Wait."

She swung round.

He was holding out the chocolate-cup. "I recognise the taste of your lips. We've met before, have we not, before I went off to fight Napoleon?"

Anna did not reply.

He said, "Are you not the Cochran girl who used to frequent the woods above Kennart on hot summer evenings?"

"Aye, laird. My name was Cochran before I marrit."

"Do you not remember our meeting?"

"I – I remember it, sir."

Eyes hooded, he laughed. There was no malice in it. Much of the coldness, the cruelty which she, as a young girl, had remarked in him had softened away. Whether this was due to her maturity or to some change in him, Anna could not be sure. She was not afraid of him now, however. Her fingers had stopped trembling. Somehow she had known that eventually they would speak in this manner of the past.

"I did not imagine that one day you would be a maid in my service." Randall stretched his legs. "I did not imagine that I would ever be laird of Ottershaw, for that matter."

He got to his feet, wincing a little, drank the chocolate in three gulps and handed her the saucer and cup.

"I asked Hunter," he said. "In truth, I didn't remember your name. It's Sinclair now, is it not?"

"Aye, sir. I'm wed to the grieve's son."

Randall seemed uninterested.

"Am I t'go now, sir?"

"Presently." He motioned to Dunn who had already taken a waistcoat and coat from a wooden cupboard and was flapping the garments to fill and air them. "There were two of you, were there not? Another pretty girl; your sister?"

"She's wed to James Moodie, him as owns Kennart."

"Ah!" Randall exclaimed.

"She fell lucky," said Anna.

Randall was quick to take up the remark. "And you did not? Being a servant in Ottershaw is not the same as being the lady of Moss House?"

"It's not, sir," said Anna. "Indeed, it is not."

Dunn brought forward the vest and coat and laid them across the bed-end.

"You had better go, both of you," Randall said. "I must dress now and show my face about the policies."

Anna picked up the tray and headed for the door. She was not embarrassed by Randall's questions but she was wary of her own loquacity and feared that she might misconstrue his interest in her and overstep the mark, become too familiar too soon.

Dunn opened the door for her and let her out into the corridor.

She heard the laird say, "Wait for me in the stable yard, Dunn. I'll be there presently."

"Will ye be wantin' a stick, laird?"

"Yes, alas. The cane."

Dunn came out of the bedroom and closed the door. He glanced at Anna and winked.

"He likes you," the boy said.

"How d' you –"

But there was no opportunity for Dunn to give a reply. At the corridor's end stood Mistress Alicia with a face like a vinegar sponge, a puling child hanging from each hand.

Dunn was off down the back stairs like a shot and Anna followed before she could be snared by the gaunt, acerbic woman and pumped for information on the state of the laird's health.

It did not take Pad Tomelty long to contact the Cunninghams and deliver occasional lots of illicit whisky to supplement their stocks of mild and heavy beer. Licence would be required when the couple openly came to selling wines and spirits but the Lennox folk had no scruples about diddling the Excise. Indeed, the only people who might be tempted to drop a word to the King's Officer were the landlords of other drinking establishments but they were too wary of Pad Tomelty to do him harm. True, the stiff-necked McAlpin might have had a shot at spiking the Glaswegians' guns but McAlpin was amazed to discover that Mr Rudge approved of the Cunninghams and thought it a sign of progress that Kennart should have a shop of its own. What McAlpin did not know was that

Rudge had been taken aside by James Simpson Moodie and told, in no uncertain terms, that the Cunninghams were to be given every possible assistance and encouragement, including free use of mill labour to improve their raw, ill-knit cottage on the shoulder of Rowan Hill.

Rowan Hill was hardly more than a knoll which marked the back of Kennart but the pathway was wide enough to take George Cunningham's pony-cart and bear the foot traffic which daily increased as the air became impregnated with the aroma of gingerbread and hot meat pies and the coffee-berries which Trina craftily roasted in a copper pan on an open fire outside the front door.

The cottage itself was a single-room affair with a half-loft, floored for a bedstead. Onto its gable, however, a wide, slope-roofed shed had been constructed by Kennart carpenters, made strong by iron clamps forged by Baynham, and even given a roof of chipped slate. Draped with fruits and strings of vegetables, dumpy with sacks and gleaming with jars, the shop within a two-month was an attraction in itself, a higgledy-piggle of common and exotic comestibles which brought women down from Drymen, Balnesmoor and Croft-amie and yielded the Cunninghams a turnover undreamed of in the streets of Glasgow.

The shop did not close at dusk. Lanterns soon adorned the posts and gave the place the appearance of a fairy cave. Menfolk came to buy beer and, with a back-of-the-hand mutter to George, to be slipped a dram in a glass or have their little dented flasks filled. Profit there was in foodstuffs, but real profit lay in the sale of drink. Profit was returned as stock, stock converted quickly into profit.

It was partly contrivance and partly accident which caused the Cunninghams' enterprise to bloom so verdantly and which brought debt, drunkenness and discontent to the industrious community of Kennart and, in due course, tore James Moodie's empire apart.

If Elspeth had been asked to give an account of her affair with Michael Blaven she would have found herself at a loss to describe it in any detail at all. In retrospect it seemed far too transient to have had such a devastating effect upon her and, by its brevity, to be hardly more than a passing flirtation. Of course it was more serious than that, much more serious, but the stretch of time from her first love-making until that shattering afternoon in January seemed, on the surface, calm and radiant and, in Elspeth's eyes, without sin, guilt or deception.

Nine times in all Elspeth drove a gig to Preaching Friar. Nine times she climbed the little straight staircase to the bright, white bedroom and undressed there and slid into the narrow pine bedstead with Michael and joined with him in an act of love. But there was a strange paradox in the circumstances, a price to be paid for the ease with which their meetings were arranged and brought to pass; the more intimately she knew Michael, the less he revealed himself to her.

Her memories of that brief period were of sensual pleasure, of the contact of his body, her startling responses, episodes of passion which swept away her need to know more of him. They hardly talked at all as they lay entwined under the bedclothes listening to the sounds of Harlwood and the house stroke upon the whitewashed walls like gentle sea waves. It did not seem dangerous or immoral but, when she thought of it, it did not seem real either.

Reality was Janet Blaven's stern features when she bade Mistress Moodie goodbye. The woman disapproved so thoroughly of adultery that Elspeth was at a loss to understand why the spinster lady had any part in aiding her to cheat upon her husband.

Another puzzling feature of her relationship with Michael was that James did not, at any time, construe her visits to Miss Blaven's cottage in a sinister light. He was suspicious of everyone; yet his hatred of Matt Sinclair, his fixation on the wrong 'rival', flourished like a poisonous plant.

Miss Blaven had drawn up a set of rules which Michael had promised to obey. The woman was adamant about them. No writing of letters each to the other. No meetings upon the moor or anywhere else, apart from Preaching Friar. No impulsive 'visiting' on Elspeth's part, the rendezvous to be by prior arrangement only. Miss Blaven believed that one fine day James Moodie would crash through the little door of her cottage and the sinful couple would be shamed and hounded and exposed.

But October dripped into November and November into December and, with the weather holding mild if wet, the weekly 'visits' continued without check. It was not until close to Christmas that Miss Blaven sent Elspeth a note in which she stated that it would be best if Mistress Moodie would not call for several weeks. No explanation was offered, no reason. Elspeth fretted, was tempted to write a letter in return, to break the promise she had made to the spinster and roll up to Preaching Friar in the gig, unannounced. But she chose to obey Miss Blaven's instruction out of gratitude for the woman's charity to her and for the fact that she had aided the lovers at all.

Elspeth did not even know that Michael was ill.

Four weeks passed without a word from Preaching Friar, four weeks without Michael, four weeks in which she suffered James's peculiar moods which contrasted darkly with the cheerfulness of the festive season. Her loneliness, highlighted, was harder to bear than before. As New Year came and went and January slipped away, Elspeth's impatience turned to desperation and she wrote a letter to Miss Blaven asking if she might call upon her soon. No reply was forthcoming.

Eventually, on a crisp, frosty day three weeks into the month Elspeth could contain herself no longer. She instructed Kerr to tell Tolland to have a gig ready. Wrapped up warmly, she took the reins from the horse-boy and rode along the rock-hard, ringing road between the villages, arriving at Preaching Friar a moment or two before noon.

The sun shone on frost-furred fields and painted the south-facing hedgerows a vivid green, cheating in its suggestion that winter was over. Everything that forenoon was so clear and so bright that Elspeth's gloom lifted and she felt exuberant and sure that Michael, at least, would welcome her.

She tethered the pony in the narrow lane, went through the kitchen gate and walked around by the flagged path to the front. Roses which graced the trellis had withered completely and hung in puckered bundles from the wiry thorn. In the garden, dung had been strewed thickly upon the beds and the air was tainted by its barnyard smell. In an upstairs window there was a trace of a light or perhaps the reflection of sun in the oval mirror in the corner of the bedroom. Eagerly she rapped with the iron knocker and waited, glowing with cold and expectation.

The servant girl who opened the door to her had the appearance of a corpse, with dark-circled eyes, drawn cheeks and a nose red and roughened by a heavy cold.

"Mistress Moodie, is it?"

"I've called to see Miss Blaven."

"She's gone out for a wee bit."

"Gone where?"

"Walkin'. She's hardly crossed the doorstep this past month, since Mister Michael was struck down."

"I believe," said Elspeth, "that I shall wait for her."

"Come in, then." At last the girl admitted her.

Elspeth said, "I did not know that Mister Michael had been ill. Is he . . . is he well again?"

"No, Mistress Moodie, that he's not."

The maid showed her into the parlour. It was as prim as ever, and less attractive, lacking the bowls of flowers and leaf-sprigs which, in other seasons, gave it vitality. No fire was lighted in the hearth, though the ash-pail stood there and a strew of twigs and kindling.

"Have I interrupted your work?" said Elspeth.

"I have other things I can be doin', Mistress Moodie."

"No. Get on with this room, if you've been so instructed."

"It's warmer in the kitchen," said the servant.

She looked fearfully unwell. Elspeth, in spite of her anxiety about Michael, spared a word of sympathy. "Should you not be in your bed?"

"I have been. I canna stay away any longer."

"Hasn't Miss Blaven given you a medicine?"

"Aye, an' it fair helpit. Smothered my cough and eased my chest."

The day-maid had been kept discreetly occupied during Elspeth's previous visits. If the servant had guessed what had been going on, she gave no sign of it. To her, Elspeth Moodie was just another oddity, like Miss Blaven herself. She pretended respect because her wage depended on it.

Elspeth said, "How long has Miss Blaven been out?"

"About an hour, Mistress Moodie. She'll no' be o'er long in arrivin' back, though, since she has the young man t' feed."

"Perhaps," said Elspeth, "Mister Michael would welcome a little company."

The servant shook her head. "I canna say if he's well enough. I'm not to be goin' in there, disturbin' him."

Elspeth said, "I'll go up. If he's asleep, I'll not waken him."

Still the servant seemed unsure. But Elspeth's anxiety had increased and made her reckless. There was in her an appalling fear, a fear that the small signs and unusual occurrences had more significance than Michael had led her to believe. Memory of them came crowding upon her and leaving the girl where she stood, sniffing by the cold hearth, she went up the short staircase to the upper floor of the cottage where Michael's bedroom was situated.

She paused before the door, breathless now with an overwhelming fear of what she might find within. She knocked, did not await his response, turned the knob and entered.

It was neither candle nor lamp which she had seen from the path below. Herbs smoked in a tiny wire basket hung over a glow of charcoal on a round brass tray. In the sunlight which streamed through the leaded panes the wisps of smoke from the pannier were like ill-formed ghosts. In the grate the fire was banked high and the room was warm, warm and fragrant as a summer's afternoon. It was as if Miss Blaven had known of her coming and had prepared a pleasant indoor bower for love-making. Only the appurtenances of the sick-room indicated that this was far from the truth.

Elspeth noticed a muslin-shrouded pot, compresses hung to dry upon a rack by the fire, medicine bottles, spoons and invalid cups on the table close to the head of the bed, and that a broad, ugly, earthenware bowl which was propped against the bolster was stained with sickness and blood. A curtain of yellow lace had been fastened above Michael's face to keep the winter sunlight from striking him, as if he were too weak to bear its weight. For a moment Elspeth assumed that Michael was asleep. She approached quietly, leaving the bedroom door ajar, a ridiculous gesture of modesty.

Physical desire had gone out of Elspeth. She felt as she had done four years ago when her mother lay close to death, changed in the nature of her love. She loved Michael at the last as she might have come to love him in old age, with a closeness which the stolen hours locked in his arms could not provide, for she understood now that Michael was dying and that nothing, not even love, could save him and draw him back to her.

Elspeth threw off her cape and bonnet, stripped off her gloves and flung herself down by him, her body gently laid across his chest. Nothing in her life upon the Nettleburn, none of the pretend pain of young love and its disappointments, not even the callous strain that infected her as part of youth, had prepared her for the anguish of that quarter-hour alone with Michael, alone with the unassailable knowledge that she had never needed to fear the future for the future had been no longer than a few cherished hours snatched from the autumn days.

There seemed to be so little of him. It was as if he had reverted into childhood. His skin was smooth, fair and unblemished so only the ivory-yellow tint hinted at that fatal disease which confused a promise of growth with the certainty of decay.

"Michael, my dear Michael," she whispered.

She could hear suspirations in his chest and throat, imagined that she could feel his thready, stabbing pulse. He stirred, but only a little, lids flickering to show her dull, unappreciative pupils leeched of colour. His hand was all bone. He did not respond when she clasped it, gave no sign that he knew who she was. It appalled Elspeth to realise that five weeks ago she had lain with him in nakedness and had detected no trace of malignant illness. In helplessness there was anger, anger at Janet Blaven for using her, for not informing her that Michael had been marked by God to leave them both. If she had known how it was she would have loved him more, loved him back into life.

Elspeth the pragmatist, the girl who had dug the rigs of the Nettleburn, was lost now. She placed her brow upon Michael's chest and prayed for a miracle of healing; a year, a six-month, a season of health for Michael, whom she had loved but had hardly known. She was still upon her knees when Janet Blaven quietly entered the room.

The first Elspeth knew of the woman's presence was a hand upon her shoulder. "He cannot hear you, child."

Elspeth started and glanced round guiltily. She was shamed at being caught there in prayer. Perhaps, and the thought did not stick, it was her wickedness which was being punished.

"Come up," said Janet Blaven. "We'd best leave him to rest."

"Is he. . .? Say that he isn't . . . Tell me, please."

Janet Blaven shook her head. She still wore an outdoor

garment, loose and ill-fitting like a horse-coat, still had a round straw bonnet tied with a scarf of purple wool upon her head. She too had aged. Sobbing, the girl clung to the woman.

On the bed, for a moment, Michael stirred once more, giving a moist, voluble cough, followed by a small convulsion. He did not open his eyes, however, and appeared oblivious to the women at his bedside.

"He's in no pain," said Miss Blaven. "I can promise you that I'll not see him suffer."

"What have you. . .?"

"Simple herbs. Strong remedies. Opiates. There is," the woman drew a shuddering breath, "no more that I can do for him now."

"What right have *you* to keep him here? Why do you not summon a proper physician?"

"No physician can save him; nor surgeon either."

"You don't *wish* him to be cured. You want him for yourself." Hysterically Elspeth thrust the woman from her and, swaying this way and that, cried, "*Michael! Oh, Michael!*"

Miss Blaven gripped the girl by the arms and led her from the white bedroom into the beamed corridor at the top of the staircase. She kicked the door shut with her foot. "Stop it. Stop it this instant."

"Let me stay with him," Elspeth pleaded. "I'll make no sound. *Please* let me be with him."

"No, Elspeth." Miss Blaven was firm. "Soon, very soon, I must send for his father and brothers. I had not wished you to see him again. I would have preferred you to remember Michael as he was."

"To hear that he was dead, without preliminary, without warning?" said Elspeth. "How can you be so heartless?"

"Lower your voice. My servant's trustworthy but she's not made of stone. The less she knows the better for all concerned. Come in here. We must talk privately."

Miss Blaven ushered the distraught girl into a second bedroom. Hardly more than a closet under the eaves, it was almost bare of furnishing except for three or four chests and a truckle bed. Miss Blaven closed the door carefully, leaned her back upon it as if to prevent Elspeth's escape. There was no evidence of sympathy in the woman now. She was implacably logical.

She said, "I did not anticipate that Michael would fall into the final phase of his illness quite so soon. But there's no predicting this fearful disease. It takes its own unfathomable courses."

Elspeth did not think to ask the name of the disease. She was shaking as shock caught up with her.

Miss Blaven said, "You must be exceptionally strong, Elspeth. You must compose yourself, return home to your husband. He must have no inkling of what has happened."

"How can I. . .?"

"I – we – have done all that we can. But it is not quite over for either of us. You, however, must put Michael from mind henceforth. It was, and you must so regard it, an interlude of love and no more. Your husband suspects nothing, does he?"

Sobbing, shaking, Elspeth answered, "Nothin' at all."

"Then we have all been very fortunate," said Janet Blaven.

"How *dare* you say such a thing with Michael dyin'. Is that your good fortune, Miss Blaven?"

Once more the woman caught Elspeth. Her hands were as strong as a man's. She held the frantic girl by the shoulders, forcing her to listen.

"Hear me out. Listen and understand. Stop behaving like a spoilt child. You're a woman and must behave responsibly with fortitude and courage. *For Michael's sake.*"

"Michael's sake?"

"His reputation can still be damaged."

"Ah!"

"By what stroke of luck the predatory tattle of servants and village folk has failed to alert your husband, I cannot say. Apparently he suspects nothing and regards your visits to Harlwood as having been harmless."

"I don't care about James. I don't care about myself."

"Think of Michael," said Miss Blaven loudly.

"You're worried about your own good name."

"Naturally," Miss Blaven admitted. "I'll live here with the memory of Michael. I'll never have him far from my thoughts, believe me. But I am not anxious to have memories tarnished by recriminations and slanders. If Michael had not been as he was, I would have sent him packing from the Lennox before I would have become his collaborator and your accomplice. But there was no time, do you see? No time for wounds to heal. He needed to taste love."

"I believe, Miss Blaven, that you have used me," said Elspeth stiffly, anger replacing grief for a moment. "You'd no thought or regard for me at all. Even now you canna spare my feelin's."

"No, I'm not so – Michael did not belong to either of us, Elspeth, least of all to you."

"I loved him. I love him still."

Miss Blaven said, "Yes, and he loved you."

The weeping fit was sudden and soft.

Elspeth bent her head and covered her face with her hands. At last she was reconciled to the inevitable loss. She had never really doubted it, not from the moment she had seen Michael. It was, and had been, a malicious device of Janet Blaven but it too had been advanced out of love. Elspeth understood that now, found that understanding tilted her grief, made it – almost – bearable.

The truth was that she had fallen in love with Michael's loving, and had been drastically opened to emotions that she had shut within her strange marriage. Fleetingly she convinced herself that Michael was not dying at all but simply leaving, passing not unto his Maker in Heaven but out of her life. It was a concept she could grasp, a comforting notion which erased betrayal and bitterness. Michael had loved her. She would love him always, no matter what befell her as James's wife. Suddenly, with perfect clarity, Elspeth understood what Janet Blaven meant. She must cherish Michael's memory to preserve the love that had existed between them. It was her duty. She must, indeed, be strong enough to let him go.

She wiped her eyes with a handkerchief.

"I'll do as you ask," Elspeth said.

"It will be difficult to do nothing, say nothing."

"Let me say goodbye to him."

"Yes."

In the bedroom the sun had slipped down the diamond pane and spilled light like watered wine upon the curtain. Michael had not stirred. The drug had pulled him down into painless depths where vitality mattered less than ease. It was not sleep but opium that held him from her but she spoke to him nonetheless, stooped over, her lips brushing his brow. It was how beloved children died, not young men, not the person who, only a handful of months ago, had strode upon the open moor, had found joy in wild country and had loved her under the rush of the high yew hedges in the October night.

It seemed that she, like Michael, had run her span in one rapid and ecstatic episode. She was glad now that the woman had kept the truth from her.

She shed no tears when she left him. Touching her lips to his she found them to be without taste and without warmth, a sign that she could not, no matter how she willed it, draw him back again.

The woman waited by the top of the staircase and preceded the girl down into the hall. The servant skulked, sniffling, in the kitchen as Miss Blaven followed her 'guest' out into the garden.

"How long will Michael . . . be with you?" Elspeth asked.

"Three days, four at most."

"Where will he be put to rest?"

"By the side of his mother and sisters in Glasgow St Cyrus."

"I assume it would be advisable for me not to visit the grave?" said Elspeth.

Miss Blaven inclined her head.

"In that case," Elspeth offered her gloved hand, "I will bid you goodbye."

"Will you not call on me, Elspeth, when the spring comes?"

"I think not," said Elspeth.

"Perhaps, for the sake of it, I may call upon you at Moss House?"

"For the sake of what?"

"Appearances."

Elspeth gave no answer.

She walked down the path by the reeking flowerbeds to the place in the lane where the pony was tethered. She unhitched the reins and climbed into the little conveyance and snapped the pony into motion. She looked back only once, from the crest where the lane opened on to the road.

Behind her, Preaching Friar lay bathed in the winter sunlight, calm, immaculate, pink-tinted. But the light in the window was too bright, her tears too profuse, for Elspeth to take it in, so she rode on quickly, rode back to the sober comfort of Moss House and, since she had no one else, to James.

SIX

The Fool of Quality

The most vociferous opponents of small-still whisky were teetotallers, clergymen and pig-rich Tories who sucked up to the Crown. Smugglers – a generic name for all who diddled the Treasury of its rightful dues – came in for some heavy whacks in the columns of national journals and in the sermons of the 'unco guid', those to whom the word 'economy' meant maintaining a status quo of hardship and repression in the labouring classes.

Padric Tomelty did not see it in that light. He thought of himself as a friend of the people, who dispensed at great personal risk the fine brown malts. Pad was not afeared of prison, fee-fines or of being shot at by King's musketeers. He dwelled in a haze of alcohol, worshipped by his womenfolk, employees and his customers alike. Public howls about the effects of whisky-drinking – social degradation, sloth, destitution and moral degeneration – fell off Pad's back like water from a duck. Crop-raisers made money by selling grain to Pad. Innkeepers made money by buying a keg of untaxed whisky to mix with their own puny waters. Old crones, fit for nothing but crow-scaring, earned keep by carrying cannikins of Pad's whisky under their skirts to sell at fairs and cow-markets. Padric kept money spinning for many folk and if, in the process, he made himself quietly rich, who was to know of it or care.

Eardmore was the hub of Pad's activities. His stills were portable, of course, would not be found within four walls but buried in caves and mole-hill bothies on the moor. But he stored grain and made malt in Eardmore and, carefully buried behind a hog-sty, kept a reserve of ten anchors of matured stuff against a drought. It was at Eardmore too, once in a while, that Pad Tomelty threw a jollification for his agents, clients and friends, for Eardmore was a safe howff far out on the moor, which belonged to a wild old Whig named Kaye who never bothered to visit his property except to gather the rents and take a tithe of thirty gallons of best malt each Lady Day.

Pad did not reside in Eardmore. He had the rent of a foul wee cottage at the back of Balnesmoor where Babsie, Pad's whiskery wife, kept her brood in check and Brigit, when she was not tumbling in a hay-loft with some lad or other, spent her nights. Tonight, however, Pad would be making a pay-out and hosts of Tomeltys would congregate at Eardmore, slinking in cliques along the secret tracks that led to the hollow of black ground where, like a fungus, the hamlet had grown.

Brigit first took Matt Sinclair to Eardmore. It was a sharp night towards the middle of January when, accompanied by Kenneth McDonald and three Tomelty cousins, they sneaked past Moodie's sheep-pens at Dyers' Dyke on to the long rock ridge that lay below the sponge of the high moorland waste.

Matt was not seriously 'in love' with Brigit Tomelty. She was hardly the sort of lass to foster airy-fairy notions in a man. But he found her amusing and lively, in and out of bed, and had no need to 'pretend' when he was in her company. He was aware that she had a vindictive streak and that it excited her to be stealing the attentions of her best friend's husband. But he learned more from Brigit about the state of affairs at Ottershaw than ever he learned from Anna and knew more now about the habits and character of the new laird than his father ever would.

Giggling, gossip and horseplay whiled away the trudge over the open moor in no time and it surprised Matt when the lights of Eardmore appeared below. Though it was January, cattle still roamed the lean pastures and sheep cowered under isolated rowans. For all its bleakness there was a touch of magic in the scene and the freezing night air was wrinkled with the strains of music and merriment as if the hillside had split open to reveal the hall of an elfin palace. Eagerly Matt wrapped his arm about Brigit's waist and louped down the hill after Kenneth McDonald into the long, low byres which already throbbed with folk.

McDonald had informed him that Pad had something particular to celebrate. The Revenue Commissioners had jumped the duty yet again, demanding an annual tariff of seven pounds sixteen shillings for each gallon of a still's contents, with a levy of six shillings and sevenpence more on every gallon produced.

Licensed distillers would be hard pressed to pay the swamping tax. Quality would deteriorate and Tomelty's Best would fetch an extra threepence or so per pint from discerning palates. Perhaps that was the reason that Pad seemed in such high fettle, lording it like a king over his court of reprobates.

Stationed in front of a huge open fire to the right of the doorway Pad was perched on a barrel with a jug in one hand and a rib of beef in the other, his eyes gleaming with delight as he conducted the jig played by fife and fiddlers. Weltered about the fire were more girls than staffed Ottershaw and hardly a face among them that Matt recognised. Brigit's arm tightened about his waist and she administered an impudent jab to his backside.

"They're no' for the likes o' you, Matt," she warned.

"An' why are they not now, if they've a fancy for me?"

"I brought you, did I not?" Brigit answered. "So you're mine for the night."

"Aye, an' you're braw, Brigit, braw as any ten gypsy lassies, though a bit too snugly clad for the company, eh?"

"Is it this ye want t' see, Matt?" She loosened the ribbons of her bodice and, as her shawl fell back, exposed the fullness of her breasts. "For wee mannies to be restin' their heads on when they tire o' boozin'."

"I'll not tire, Brigit, not o' booze – or anythin' else. I'll see you off your feet e'er mornin'."

"I pray that ye will, Matt Sinclair. Indeed I'm hopin' ye'll not leave me standin' upright for more than a half-hour."

"Brigit, m' love, m' cushat." Pad had sighted the new arrivals. "An' have ye brought young Matt wi' ye, indeed? An' who's that skulkin' shy there? Why, if it's not the grand man himself! Welcome t' ye, McDonald, my soul. And welcome t' you also, Fitter."

"An' here's Willie an' his lass," said Brigit, dragging forward a male cousin and a small, dark-haired girl who seemed to Matt to be not much more than a child. "Willie from the Blane."

For an instant Matt was distracted by the presence at his elbow of a stranger, the man Pad had called Fitter. He was not so young as most of the people who had made the trail across the hill though not quite so old as Pad Tomelty himself. In fact, when Matt glanced at him, he found it impossible to gauge the fellow's age. He had a queer look to him. A thin pointed beard and curled moustache made his appearance stranger still, like a Spaniard or noble Frenchman, though his clothing was plain enough and the sly wee smile he gave in response to Pad's effusive welcome was like a fissure in granite.

Matt experienced a shiver out of nowhere as the man's eyes met his and the smile became broader and colder still.

"Crack her long bones, son," Fitter murmured.

"Eh? What's that you say?"

"Dance the bold one t' death."

"Aye, aye, so I will."

Matt moved closer to Brigit who was smacking kisses all over her father's puckered features and embracing him as if she had not seen him in a twelve-month.

How often, Matt wondered, did Pad engage in such revelry? They were safe enough here, he supposed, but if King's Officers did manage to sneak up on them, they would fill the jail at Stirling to the very gates and stifle the smugglers' trade for months. Pad was at ease, though, so Matt accepted that there was no risk of a raid and, at Pad's beckoning, found a jug before the cask, filling up the vessel to the brim.

From this position Matt could see that the whores on the straw were already soused. Cheeks aflame, their skirts were flung up to show their legs. Brigit was by him, though, nudging him impatiently with her shins. He handed the jug up to her and filled another for himself.

"Here," Pad cried. "A toast t' my bonnie lassie, Bridie, an' to this busy lad."

Nobody paid much attention but Matt clicked his jug with Pad's and then, as if dismissed from audience, found himself being tugged away to make room for Fitter. When, several minutes later, he glanced round again he saw that Pad had climbed down from the barrel and was engaged in what appeared to be grave discussion with the bearded stranger.

"Who is he, Brigit?" Matt asked. "The Fitter mannie."

"A carrier," Brigit shrugged.

"I've never seen him before."

"He carries round the Campsies. I know him hardly at all." She drank from the jug. "Never heed him, Matt. Come wi' me. We'll find a neuk where we can tipple in peace."

Stalls were screened with rotting sackcloth. Behind the swags, lovers engaged in noisy couplings. Matt glimpsed the kick of naked feet, heard the unmistakable gasps of a woman at the climax of pleasure, the deep baying laughter of a man. It was not private here. Matt had no stomach for public love-making in a stinking cow-stall. He was surprised how the prospect shocked him.

"Brigit, it's o'er busy here for my likin'."

Brigit seemed astonished at his reticence.

"I'll find a place." She nuzzled up to him and kissed him with dragging touches of her lips. "I'm needin' you now, Matt. Sore needin'."

Out of the firelight, her breath sharp with whisky, Brigit seemed less attractive than he had formerly thought. No, Bridie Tomelty was not attractive at all. She was no better than the whores, waiting for whoever would take them. Matt closed his eyes and opened them again, hoping that he might see Brigit differently. But it was not in Pad Tomelty's daughter that the fault lay, it was in the son of the grieve of Ottershaw.

Sensing his withdrawal, Brigit quickly hauled aside the canvas which hung over the last stall in the row. She had no modesty, no care about who might be within. At first Matt could not see clearly then as he stepped closer, made curious by Brigit's sudden start, he recognised the Sylas sisters there within.

The dummy was propped like a great scarecrow in a corner, a candle of red wax in a water-dish in her lap. Her mouth was scooped into a long bill, her lips pursed, panting and cooing, while her sister lay covered by a man as old as Matt's father, head sprigged with grey hair, his breeks about his knees. Past the old man's shoulder, Matt had a sight of the girl's face, flat and expressionless, her hands folded upon her breast. Her response to the male's passion was less than a hundredth part of that which her mute sister displayed, as if one took the pleasure from the other in some devilish act of transference.

Brigit dropped the canvas curtain instantly and clutched at Matt's shoulder to pull him away. Nervously Matt forced a half-laugh but the fear in Brigit's eyes smothered it and he yielded, turning too.

There, only feet behind them in the nether region of the byre, stood Fitter outlined against the fireglow, smiling.

"What d' you want wi' me?" Matt snapped.

"Crack her bones, son," Fitter said.

"Come awa', Matt. Come awa'. We'll find another stall, later on."

Brigit was jerky with tension all of a sudden, though it could not have been her sense of propriety which had been offended. It was something about the sight of the dummy in the deep stall. Something that Matt did not understand. He did not understand either why the bearded man should cause such a stab of fear in him or why, just at that moment, he was suddenly as cold as ice and longed to find a great banked roaring fire at which to warm his limbs.

Giving in to Brigit, Matt hurried after her down the length of the long building, back out of the musty gloom and into the proximity of the open fire, feeling heat bathe and soothe him almost at once. He put his arm around Brigit Tomelty's waist and hugged her to him, but she cuddled against him without desire, as a child would.

When he dared to look back Matt found that Fitter had vanished. The man from Kilsyth did not reappear, not even for the paying-out which took place about ten of the clock before everyone became too drunk to count the bounty that little Pad Tomelty dispensed.

Anna did not think of herself as a thief. She behaved, however, as cunningly as one, receiving considerable thrills from her successful raids upon the larder and a sense of triumphant relief when she cleared the house and escaped into the trees with her booty.

She began by removing a couple of slices of flank mutton from a leftover plate. She had no need to hide them since she ate them at once in the security of the back staircase. Next came a particularly succulent piece of hare, three 'backs' of which had been larded with bacon and braised in cream and white wine. Randall had returned one with expressions of regret that he could not quite polish off all of Mrs Lacy's wonderful offering. Again Anna scoffed the meat in the seclusion of the stairs before carrying the tray down into the kitchen. It gave her an odd intimacy with Randall to consume his leftovers, to partake of the same rich food as he did, from the same plate too.

The first thing which Anna sneaked out of Ottershaw was a fist-sized end of red venison pudding which came down from Randall's midday dinner one afternoon in December. Anna's scheme was daringly simple. She removed the pudding piece from the dish, licked it clean and popped it into a pocket which she had sewn into the back of her skirt. All afternoon she had gone about her routine tasks with the pudding pressing against her, her nerves tingling. What triumph and relief when Mr Hunter duly dismissed her and she slung on her bonnet and shawl and went out, not too hurriedly, into open air and skipped away from the mansion. How exquisite the deer-meat pudding tasted when she finally ate it, with some ceremony, at her own fireside. She did not share it with Matt or leave any trace of it for her husband to discover.

One thing led to another. Soon Anna was hiding cogs of cherry trifle and apple-crumble on a shelf high above the landing door, a place neglected by the maids and as safe as anywhere. Late in the day she would retrieve the cog, hide it in a pouch in her skirt and slip away home with it. The game was thorough, complicated and stimulating. It occupied her attention throughout most of the day and diminished the terrible tedium by testing her nerve and ingenuity. Naturally Anna would no more have thought of lifting a candle-stump or a wash-clout than she would have of breaking into the silver and would have shunned any servant who stole trinkets to sell beneath the barrel at a local fair. The difference between one sort of 'crime' and another was crystal clear to Anna. She even managed to delude herself that she needed the leftovers to keep herself nourished, which was, of course, nonsense.

Secretiveness was a most alluring element. When she sat at table in the cramped, dirty kitchen of Pine Cottage she would imagine that she was Randall's guest in Ottershaw, would converse with him as she snipped her beef or toyed with a slice of pie. Wittily she would parry his compliments, give sparkling rejoinders – all the while trying to ignore Jacko's chatterings and smoke from potatoes on the hob.

If Matt got home before her she would hide the day's haul in a box in the closet in the bedroom and consume it only when she had the cottage to herself again.

On one particular Saturday in late January Anna was unexpectedly robbed of the pleasure of pretence. She got home about half past six o'clock. It came as no surprise to find that Matt had not yet returned. She extracted the bowl from its pouch and carefully put it on the table. Cinnamon custard, thick, yellow and speckled with raisins, gave her an appetite. She did not immediately take off her shawl and bonnet but raked and built up the fire, filled the kettle from the pail and hung it over the crackling sticks. She laid out a clean dish and a spoon, took off her workaday garments and, drawing a stool up close to the hearth, hunched over it in a moment of luxurious anticipation. The custard waited. She could smell its aromatic goodness. The first wisp of steam curled from the kettle spout. Anna sighed contentedly. She did not know where Matt was or when he would return, nor did she care. It was pleasant in the kitchen, warm and quiet.

Indeed it was quiet. Even Jacko was silent.

Tensing slightly Anna glanced up at the wickerwork cage on the rafters. She could see the animal within. It lay on the floor of the cage but not at all comfortably.

"Jacko," she called out sharply. "Jacko."

The monkey did not stir.

Anna got to her feet and stood below the cage. She could smell the damp acrid stench of the straw in the cage bottom.

"Jacko? Do you want a nut, Jacko? See here."

There was no trace of movement, not even the rise and fall of his sides, fur prickling with each breath. Puzzled and apprehensive, Anna climbed on the stool, took the cage in her arms and gave it a shake.

"Oh, God! God save me!" Anna exclaimed.

She unknotted the ropes, brought the cage to the floor, snapped open the door and stuck her hand inside. Grabbing the long, elegant, impudent tail, she gave it a tug. The tail uncoiled hardly at all, just enough to expose Jacko's face. The upper lip was lifted, showing yellow teeth, the eyes were fixed half-open, sightless.

Poor Jacko was dead.

She dragged out the corpse, shook it like a dolly, forced herself to extend the limbs, turn the monkey over and very carefully examine it, even to peer into its mouth, wondering if it had choked or strangled. Nothing indicated how the creature had died. Even so, Anna was terrified. At any moment Matt might stamp across the threshold, crying for his pet. All he would have would be a stiffening corpse. Anna knew her husband only too well. His grief would be violent. He would blame her for the monkey's passing. Matt, finding no cause, would surely accuse her of murdering the brute.

Tears flooding her eyes, Anna lifted the capuchin and rocked it in her arms, sobbing. "Why did ye have t' die? Why, ye stupid creature?"

Outside, she heard a mongrel growl. She released the monkey immediately, dropping it without ceremony on the floor, flung open the cottage door and peered into the darkness.

"Is that you, Matt?" she shouted. "Matt, answer me."

But it was not her husband. When she stepped indoors again the sight of the animal's corpse sprawled upon the flagstones brought her up sharply and, in that instant, Anna was seized with an idea which – at the time – seemed rational and brilliant.

Quickly she replaced the cage upon the beams, tied it fast, opened the door of the cage and left it so. Next she took away the bowl of custard and hid it in the closet then returned to the kitchen, picked up the monkey and carried it in her arms out of the cottage and around to the back. She found an old peat-cutting spade propped against the hut gable and, putting the monkey down by the spade, went indoors again to light a lantern. Mercifully there was still no sign of Matt's return. Anna went on with her scheme more confidently. If he came back and found her gone, it would help to confirm her tale, her lie. She intended to tell Matt that Jacko had run off. It would not be the first time that the capuchin had scampered out of the cottage, disported himself in the trees for three or four hours while Matt had tried to coax him back to the leash. In the past Jacko had always returned when he was hungry, lured down by a bowl of scraps. This time, though, Jacko would not return. Jacko would be 'lost' for ever.

It did not strike Anna as ironic that she chose the track to the Nettleburn. The Nettleburn was a long way from Ottershaw and still scarred by the slurry of rock and mud that the great autumn flood of 1809 had dragged down the hillside. Ruins of Mammy's little house protruded from the hummocks over which bracken and coarse grasses had rooted and spread.

The ground was hard and it cost Anna an hour of vigorous effort to howk out a hole. She worked without the lantern, having just enough light from the frosty sky, and dug the hole deep. She folded the capuchin's rigid limbs up to make him neat. He still wore the little vest and breeks that she had sewn for him. She shed a few soft tears as she slipped him into the hole. She packed the earth, replaced the turves, finally manhandled three big stones on to the raw digging, lit the lantern and checked the grave.

There would be frost after midnight, a coating of bristling white hoar would cover the site completely. By chance a dog might sniff out the spot but she doubted it and, soon after the thaw took hold, poor Jacko's bones would rot into the soil.

Lantern in hand, spade across her shoulder, Anna took the field corner route to the Ottershaw track and returned to Pine Cottage. To her relief Matt had not come back in her absence. Now she felt sure that he would be exceedingly late and welcomed the opportunity to compose herself for inevitable conflict. She would simply confront him with 'the truth', tell him how Jacko had skipped away through the half-open door and scrambled into the pine trees, how she had searched in vain for an hour or more. To substantiate her tale she placed a platter of fat bacon on the stoup and roped the front door so that it lay ajar.

In fact, she was being kind to Matt by giving him hope. In due course he would reconcile himself to the loss of the one thing in the world he truly loved, his damned monkey.

About midnight, Anna went into the bedroom. Seated on the mattress, she scoffed the cinnamon custard and hid the cog away. She snuggled down under the covers and, wearied by her exertions, soon fell into a deep sleep.

When she awakened it was broad white daylight and Matt, thank God, had not yet returned home.

Dunn moved smartly from the doorway and pulled out a chair for the gentleman who had already been relieved of hat and cloak at the hall door. The boy rushed around the table as soon as the guest was seated, and held the chair for his master, very patient and careful. Randall adjusted his leg, then, with a smile, said, "I trust you did not find the road too icy for your carriage, Mister Moodie?"

"Not at all. It's most dry and pleasant for this New Year month. Quite unseasonably so, in fact."

"Good weather for the ewes," Randall said.

"They grow, if anythin', a little too fat."

"February, even March, might rub that excess away, I'll be bound," said Randall. To the boy he said, "See what Mister Moodie will have to fill his glass, Dunn."

"Aye, sir."

"A little wine, if you like," said James.

"Your wife, she did not feel able to the journey?"

"She sends her apologies," said James. "She's a trifle under the weather."

"It is not a serious malady, I hope."

"A minor indisposition."

The men did not speak as Dunn manhandled the big decanter from the side table and poured wine into the glasses. He did it dextrously and, without spilling a drop, returned the decanter to its tray.

James expected the laird to make some passing mention of his sister-in-law who was now a servant under this roof but, to his relief, Randall said not a word about the embarrassing situation. As it was Sunday, Anna Sinclair would not be on duty at Ottershaw.

"Did you attend the kirk this morning, Mister Moodie?"

"I did, laird, but in Harlwood, not Balnesmoor."

"Harlwood?"

"Candidly, I cannot abide our new minister.'

"Yes, I believe that the Reverend Eshner is noted for palpable piety pompously promoted."

"Appropriate alliteration, sir," said James.

Randall grinned and James relaxed a little. It was possible, after all, that the laird was simply showing friendship to a neighbour, though James continued to have his doubts. He had kept abreast of events at Ottershaw and had learned that Gilbert was to be sent packing and that Randall was in process of making changes. Changes cost money. Capital would be required, and he, James Simpson Moodie, leased three hundred acres of grazing along the skirt of the moor and had made improvements, at his own expense, to the hillside pasture.

Randall came to the point. "I hear, Mister Moodie, that you have taken your Cheviot flock off the slopes of Drumglass and replaced them with Blackface. Might I ask why?"

"The flock did not thrive well enough on the higher ground. I have taken the Cheviots to another pasture, near Kilsyth."

"For more protection?"

"Aye, an' better grass."

"Is there not money in finer wools?"

"Indeed there is," said James. "Though the per pound price

for Cheviot pack tumbled last year to nine pence, it promises to rise again in the coming season. Trade with America an' custom of His Majesty's government keeps it up for the time being. Of course, competition from foreign imported wool is much reduced because of the war."

"What of the day when the war is brought to a conclusion?"

"My prediction is that preference will change in favour of a quality combing-wool."

"Hence, sir, you do not ignore the little ugly Blackface breed?"

"I ignore nothing that trots on four pins an' bears a fleece," said James.

"Is it combing-wool which supplies your looms at Kennart, if I may ask?" said the laird.

"Not entirely. I supply a mixed market."

"I trust you are not offended by my direct questions?"

"You have given me no offence, as yet, laird."

"You see, Mister Moodie, I have a proposition for you."

"Propose away."

"I wish to sell the Ottershaw Cheviots."

"Includin' the rams?"

"Down to the last tup."

"Send them to Stirling come the back end," James advised.

"Do you have no interest in a private transaction?"

James said, "In a fallin' market, laird?"

"Come now, Mister Moodie, the market is not going to plummet overnight. Apart from the fleeces there's money to be made from the mutton."

"Aye, your lamented father would turn in his grave to hear you speak so," said James. "But I grant you the flock might be sustained in the traditional manner by shearin' an' slaughter at the fourth year."

"I assume you know the flock well?"

"Four hundred horns," said James. "I do not know how many ewes are in lamb or how they are presently conditioned."

"Oh, they have not been neglected. Sinclair would not allow me to let them run to rot, even if I was inclined to be wasteful of a precious asset. You have my word that the Cheviots are in prime condition."

"Do you not wish to take the crop of lambs, laird? Sell come September, split the breedin' and rearin'? It's what I would do."

"Now, Mister Moodie – as it stands."

James heard himself laugh, ruefully. "To drove four hundred fat Cheviots any distance in winter weather is a fearful bit of a risk. What if there was blizzard on the road, to give an example, or tardy spring growth? Any man who took purchase now would be gamblin' on so many unpredictable factors."

"You've wintered Cheviots on Drumglass, have you not?"

"I have indeed."

"Successfully, too," said Randall. "The Cheviot is not a particularly soft breed. The breeding-rams are pure and the blood has been kept uncontaminated by Leicester crossing. Taken as a foundation flock, the Ottershaw Cheviots are valuable, Mister Moodie. Almost, I am tempted to say, an investment."

"Put them in the auction pen, in that case."

"How much would you pay?" Randall came out with it.

"Three thousand pounds."

"Preposterously low."

"I'd have grass to find, the drove to cost, an' the chance of a poor lambin' from unsettled ewes," said James.

"You lease the long stretch from the Dyke to Drumglass at a thirty-year fixed price," said Randall. "My father was, alas, not far-sighted in that respect."

"Might I point out, laird, that I've scattered money on to the ground, have paid out of my own pocket for drainage an' re-seedin' an' have started to cut back the bracken line?"

Randall shifted in his chair, leaned his elbow on the table and drew himself to the weaver. He might have spent the best part of his life in other pursuits but the Bontine strain was not so easily subsumed, and he had his father's love of and sharpness in dealing.

"I can break the lease, Mister Moodie."

"I doubt it, laird."

"Ah, but I can."

Randall spoke with such assurance that James was stunned into silence. His original striking of the clauses of the lease had been done in the traditional manner, though, of course, he had had his legal agents peruse the document before signature. Old Sir Gilbert had done nothing by way of individual amendments or addenda and, though the document was long and wordy, James found it difficult to believe that some loophole had been left for the new laird to wriggle through. The truth was, however, that the weaver had never expected to be dealing with Randall but with Young Gibbie. If he had foreseen that the soldier son might one day be in command of Ottershaw then he would have studied the terms of the lease in even greater detail.

"No, Mister Moodie, you haven't neglected anything," Randall said, correctly interpreting his visitor's perplexity. "But I have only a twelve-month to execute the terms of my father's will, and my father was exceedingly generous in his legacies. I have been obliged to make substantial payment to my stepmother and to my full brother, to Gilbert, and to collect for the payment of certain other legacies to the rest of my father's children."

"But you're the sole inheritor of Ottershaw house and lands, are you not?"

"That is so."

"Then you must also inherit the obligations of the leases."

"True, but clauses fixing the terms of endurance of leases are governed by a necessary privilege to renounce, in certain very particular circumstances."

James said, "I've never heard of such circumstances."

"My lawyer, Mister Angus Hildebrand of Dumbarton, has done more than hear of the circumstances. He has isolated them and applied them to my present situation."

"I took on the tract of land from the quarry to the slope of Drumglass, which included the Nettleburn patch then leased by Cochran, on the understanding that I would have it for thirty years. I've sunk much into improvement."

"For which you will be entitled to partial compensation."

"Partial?"

"At the will of an arbiter or, if that does not suit, on the word of a Judge Ordinary."

"Proceedings, do you mean?"

"Come, Mister Moodie, let's not take ourselves to war just yet," said Randall, resting his other elbow on the table and bridging his hands. "Be assured, however, that I'm not lying about the legality of it. Briefly, as Hildebrand has discovered, Ottershaw's inheritor may declare 'necessity' in respect of any portion if it is incumbent upon him to sell a portion to raise the sums for legacies. It's a protective measure, a very sensible one, to prevent an heir being forced into bankruptcy by malicious relatives."

"Would you sell a portion of Ottershaw?"

"Only as a last resort. If I am unable to sell the Cheviot flock, I'll sell the three hundred acres half-hill strip from the quarry ridge to Drumglass – the stretch you presently lease."

"I'd buy it," said James.

"No, Mister Moodie, no, you would not buy it."

"Could you, laird, prevent me if it came upon the open market?" said James, then shook his head. "Naturally it would not come upon the open market. How would the sale be made?"

"On paper only, by private agreement with my brother Gilbert."

"I see," said James. "Written off against the debt to Gilbert, defrayed perhaps until such time as you could buy it back from him?"

"Hildebrand's quite sure of the legality of the proceeding."

It was James Moodie's turn to grin ruefully.

In spite of the pressure of worry upon him, and the burdens of fear that he bore, he could still appreciate a clever stroke. He did not doubt for a moment that Randall spoke the truth. With longing, he thought of the land and the Ottershaw flock, both of which he would dearly love to possess, though he would have no sons to pass them on to, only Elspeth. How would she feel if the grounds of the Nettleburn and of Dyers' Dyke belonged to her, not as tenant but as owner? Surely it would give her great satisfaction and a feeling of accomplishment.

"Would you consider a sale of both the flock and the half-hill grazin's?" said James, knowing full well what the answer would be.

"No, Mister Moodie. But I'll sell you the flock, if we can agree a fair price for it, and I will thereafter honour to the letter the terms of the lease of the grass as settled between my father and yourself."

"I'd pay a top price per acre, laird, to purchase it."

"I'll not cut pieces from Ottershaw if I can avoid it," said Randall. "The land's mine on trust for my sons, if I'm fortunate enough to have any. If not I owe it to my full brother, for Gibbie, as you cannot have failed to notice, is a most successful breeder of children."

"Can I not persuade you?"

"No, Mister Moodie. But you may make me another offer for the Cheviots in the light of the knowledge I've just imparted."

No Cheviots, no grazing land in Balnesmoor; that was the kernel of Randall's negotiation, a tidy piece of extortion but one which would not disadvantage him. On the contrary, possession of the Ottershaw flock would, if the price was right and his deft touch had not deserted him, be a valuable asset in both the short and long term. That was the beauty of Bontine's blackmail. Randall, it seemed, was no addle-pated officer fit only to drink and wench and rattle a sabre. The old laird would have been proud of his son, though perhaps a mite distressed at his lack of ethics.

James said, "What price did you have in mind, laird?"

"Six thousand guineas."

"No, that is really too much," said James. "Not for me but for anyone. Perhaps after lambin' —"

"How much would you pay, now?"

"Assuming the condition of the flock is satisfactory —" said James; he took a long breath, "five thousand an' five hundred pounds — with a proviso."

"What is the proviso?"

"That I may graze the flock in your parks until midsummer."

"Will you pay for the grass?"

"I will," James said.

"In which case I'll accept six thousand pounds for the flock and give you the grazing at no fee until the last September market," said Randall. "I'll also instruct my flock master to attend them as he does now. Six thousand pounds, however, is my bottom price."

"If that's your last word," said James, "I'll agree to pay what you ask. I'll have a note for the full sum delivered to you tomorrow."

The men shook hands to clinch the bargain. Each understood, however, that the handshake would not be the seal on the arrangement, that James would draft a contract of sale, setting out in minute detail the conditions to which the laird had agreed and that, in turn, the terms of the lease would also be revised. But that was lawyer's business and James felt oddly satisfied. He still had the hill strip, which was dear to him, and had acquired the best breeding stock of Cheviots in the west, and at reasonable price too. First thing tomorrow he would send Macfarlane down to examine the lambing ewes and to prepare extra feed in case the weather should suddenly turn hard.

James left Ottershaw with the feeling that the laird and he would rub along well together and that Ottershaw, whatever the tattle-tales said, was in excellent hands. It did not unduly concern the weaver that he had laid out a large sum from working capital and that, if disease or blight struck the flock, he would lose a fortune. He was used to taking such risks. What worried him more was Kennart and the Cunninghams and, though he had made light of it to Bontine, the state of Elspeth's health which, this past fortnight, had become unusually precarious and delicate.

It did not occur to James, who had no experience of such things, that depression and dyspepsia were quite natural conditions in a woman who was eight weeks gone with child.

"Och, Matt, it's hopeless. Let's go home. It's near dark an' I'm frozen."

Anna kept her distance, peering from behind a beech tree, ready to make a dash for it if Matt's temper erupted. His brother and two of his sisters had been about but they had finally wandered off, leaving her alone in this part of the straggle-wood with her husband.

"Perhaps Jacko's found his own way back."

Matt had dragged in about one o'clock in the afternoon. He had said not a word about where he had spent the night but it was clear that he had been drinking heavily. He looked ill, with burnt-cork circles about his eyes and a whey-like complexion that aged him by twenty years. He had been so unwell that he hadn't noticed the platter of food scraps on the doorstep when he reeled into the kitchen.

Anna had blurted out the bad news at once.

To her surprise Matt did not tear his hair or lumber out into the pines. He had slumped at the table and growled at her to make him hot tea and porridge. He had choked down a bowl of thick oatmeal and two cups of scalding tea before he had heaved himself to his feet and, barking at Anna to follow him, had stumbled out in search of his precious monkey.

Sinclairs had been roused from the grieve's cottage to aid in the hunt and Anna was despatched to the foresters' hamlet to see if the creature had been spotted there. McDonald was in bed, though, so ill with drink, said his wife, that he could not come out.

All afternoon Matt scoured the woods and parks, up to the stubble fields that bordered the turnpike, even as far as Balnesmoor itself. Sandy, Matt's young brother, was packed off to Kennart, but returned without news of Jacko. Anna dawdled behind thorn bushes, rested out of the rising wind and gave only a token shout from time to time, "Jacko, Jacko, where are ye?"

Matt addressed the leafless boughs and tangled hedges constantly. But even his cries grew weak and plaintive as the sun dropped behind the hills and the air grew cold.

"He'll come home when he's ready, Matt," Anna said.

"The night air'll kill him."

"He's a monkey. He'll be used t' stayin' out."

"He's a brown capuchin, from the heat o' the jungle."

Matt had brought out a dog to help in the search and the mongrel bayed and snatched at the leash, almost jerking Matt from his feet, as a squirrel fled across the leaf-trash and shot into hiding up a gnarled elm. Matt gentled the dog, did not curse at him. He got down on one knee, shakily, and badgered the brute's ruff, rubbing his unshaven cheek against the wet muzzle.

"Where's Jacko, then, eh? Can ye not find wee Jacko for me?" he begged, hugging the dog to him.

Anna stood back, watching in disgust as her husband sought comfort from the half-wild mongrel which, in response, licked the man's ear consolingly. She could not bear it. She went forward and put her hand on Matt's shoulder.

Furiously he shook her off.

He was weeping as if his heart would break.

"Get awa' from me, Anna," he cried. "You hated him."

"No, Matt. No. He was a wee nuisance at times, but –"

Matt got to his feet. His hair was tousled, his coat prickled with old straw and leaf particles. He smelled as if he had slept in a pig gutter and his despair was pathetic.

She wanted him to cling to her as he had clung to the dog, to seek comfort from her.

"If you're so damned heartless, Anna, awa' ye go back t' the fire. Leave me alone. I'll find him myself."

"He's –" Anna started, then checked. "He's been found by somebody, perhaps, an' you'll get him back tomorrow."

"I think he's dead," said Matt.

He had his back to her again, scanning the dark shadows that had accumulated over the underbrush and that stole in about them stealthily and silently.

"I think I've lost him for ever."

"Matt, please, Matt."

"I loved him so," said Matt Sinclair, crying again.

"I'll buy ye another monkey, Matt."

"Buy! Buy! Do ye think my wee Jacko can be replaced? Och, it hurts. It hurts me t' think he suffered, that he's sufferin' now an' I canna help him."

Weeping uncontrollably, the young man stumbled forward, flinging himself into the thorns that spiked the banking and, with the mongrel trailing at his heels, went up towards the foresters' track, leaving Anna, helpless, behind.

She no longer felt sorry for him, or contrite.

She just wished to God that she had told him the truth; for once, the truth, no matter how much pain it caused.

Cold and hungry, Anna trailed back to Pine Cottage alone.

It was a cold, bleak day for riding out but so great was her husband's enthusiasm that Alicia agreed to accompany him, without promises, on the six-mile drive along the Fintry turnpike.

Alicia was still set against leaving the House of Ottershaw. Even with Randall so indelibly installed and so much in command, Alicia clung to the foolish notion that the new laird might relent and agree to share the mansion with his brother's family. Now, however, there were only a handful of months before the will must be finalised and, with Randall in possession of sufficient funds to pay everybody off, Alicia had been forced to bow to the inevitable.

She had heard, of course, of Strachan Castle. It was no castle at all in the romantic sense of the word, just a plain manor house which, at one period in history, had been gently fortified. It had once been part of the estates of the Longmuirs, wealthy burgesses of Stirling, but they had abandoned it in favour of the large and more habitable Cremanan where they had made their family seat for a century now. In the past hundred years Strachan Castle passed through the hands of many gentlemen farmers and merchants, the last of whom had been the proprietor of a small cotton mill in Fintry, which had mysteriously failed and led to a bankruptcy. For the last seven years Strachan Castle had been inhabited only by an auld wife and her son, caretakers installed by the bank to whom the building belonged, on paper at least.

The situation of the castle was not displeasing. It had a high wall to keep it from falling on to the road, a ring of handsome trees of some antiquity, and a dowelled gate above which, on a shield, was carved a date, 1547. Slightly mollified by the historical connection, older than Ottershaw and the Bontines by a goodly stretch of years, Alicia perked up a little as the carriage rolled into the littered driveway and, bouncing over the frozen ruts, gave her a view of the castle. Her heart sank immediately.

It was hardly more than a rectangle, eighteen or twenty feet wide and some sixty feet in length, graced with a mass of irregular projections and a multitude of windows of all shapes and sizes. It was the lack of neatness, of trimness, that there and then turned Alicia against poor Strachan Castle. She could tell at a glance that she would never be able to plane and pare and polish the building to her satisfaction and that, short of pulling most of it down, it would never have the chiselled regularity of an Ottershaw, that noble architectural profile which was essential in a gentleman's domicile. Indeed, the solid, ramshackle appearance of Strachan Castle was just what Alicia would have expected a burgess of Stirling to build and choose to live in.

"Does it not look homely, dearest?" said Gilbert, at her side. "Can you not see the children frolicking upon the lawn?"

The lawn was being grazed by two dun cows whose droppings had coagulated the carpet of leaves and whose hoofs had chopped the grass into a quagmire. Nose high and eyebrows higher, Alicia gave her husband no answer. She dreaded the thought of beginning a new life here. It seemed so very, very far from Ottershaw, though a fit young shepherd could have walked it in an hour.

"A round tower too," said Gilbert, as the carriage stopped and the foot-servant leapt to check the horses. "I always think that round towers have a pictorial advantage over the square variety."

The round tower, to Alicia's eyes, was hardly bigger than a candle and seemed to be affixed to the corner of the south front only by creeping ivy.

"It leans, Gilbert," she remarked, since her husband obviously required some sort of comment from her before he would be at peace.

She was helped down from the carriage, so muffled in clothes that she could hardly move her knees or elbows and could not feel Gilbert's arm about her as he escorted her towards the doorway which lay flat to the drive and had a gap beneath it large enough to admit a deerhound. The door opened at the Bontines' approach and the caretaker, followed by her mutton-headed son, emerged cautiously as if she expected Gilbert to begin beating her with a stick there and then.

"Ah! Mistress McAndles?"

"Aye, sir."

"I believe Mister Taylor of the Merchant Banking House of Falkirk indicated that we would be calling upon you."

"'T' tak' the hoose awa'," said the auld wife, in an accent almost unintelligible. "'T' tak the roof frae' o'er oor heids."

The son, who was taller than Gilbert and as broad as an elm, grunted threateningly.

Gilbert released Alicia and glanced back at the driver and foot-servant from Ottershaw, who braced themselves in case of a squabble.

Gilbert said, "It's not my intention to take Strachan Castle away, Mistress McAndles, but rather to occupy it, to bring my family to live in it."

"Wi' a wheen o' servants skitterin' aboot ma feet," the old woman mumbled.

In issues small as well as large Alicia's response to being obstructed was immediate and consistent. She pushed past her husband and squared up to the woman.

"Out of my way or I shall have my driver throw you out, you and that male person who's hiding behind your skirts."

The male person sank swiftly into the gloom of the hall and, in the course of the hour that followed, did not show himself again. It was a tiny thing, but valuable to Alicia Bontine, this prospect of evicting the old woman and her lumpish son, throwing them out along with musty bedding, broken stools and warped panels! It would be her first act should she become mistress of Strachan Castle.

Alicia, with Gilbert following, stalked into the castle like an invader. Her mood had changed. She experienced an angry determination, a response to challenge which had little to do with the castle itself. Indeed, she might almost have preferred it to be in a worse state of repair than it turned out to be, for it was sound enough and surprisingly dry, though it had not been thoroughly fired for many years. Alicia did not invite the old caretaker to show her about the apartments and corridors. She trotted on, chin up, eyes glittering.

"So this is where he would have us live, is it?" she snapped. "So it is to this pile that Randall would condemn us."

"I don't believe Randall –"

"Out of his sight, out of his caring."

"If you don't like the place –"

Alicia's voice echoed in a stone-arched tunnel that led down towards the servants' hall which, suitably, thought Alicia, was buried deep beneath the house, a large, stone-walled, stone-floored cellar with larders and pot-cupboards and a warren of small rooms off it. She sniffed at the cooking-fires, the ovens and the tubs. She recoiled from the interior water-closet, gave a scream of sheer revulsion at the sight of the caretakers' cubby. It would necessitate a woman to exercise a will of iron to make the barren building into a proud home.

Round the stone stairs and up again, through the long, not ill-proportioned dining-hall, up the main flight to the first floor of bedrooms and other appointments and above it still to a clutter of little attics and turret rooms, Alicia went, expressing her despair of ever making the place habitable and fit for a noble family.

"Open it, Gilbert."

Gilbert, who had said not a word to interrupt Alicia's flood of protest and disapproval, fought with the iron ring of the tower door; at least he thought it was the tower door for, so rapid had been his wife's tour, that he had lost his bearings. The door cracked open, creaked on mighty hinges and admitted light and cold air. He drew it inwards with all his strength and let Alicia poke her head outside.

"Roof," she said.

The door opened from the east side of the tower. A short flight of stone steps led down to a balustraded walk that gave access to the ramped tile of the roof or, more accurately, to the roofs.

"How convenient!" Gilbert said.

"It must be locked fast to prevent the children straying and falling," said Alicia and brushed past Gibbie and set off downstairs once more.

A quarter of an hour later Alicia emerged on the run from the main door, the old caretaker bowing and scraping obsequiously as the lady flurried away.

Alicia walked straight past the waiting carriage and half-way down the untidy drive, then swung round so suddenly that she might have been trying to catch the castle unawares, sticking its tongue out rudely at her back or winking its assorted eyes.

Breathlessly Gilbert caught up with her.

"Well, dearest?" he ventured.

"Is it for sale?"

"It is available on a ninety-nine-year lease."

"What do we purchase, in that case?"

"The lease."

"Ninety-nine years? Will that be long enough?"

"For what, Alicia?"

The woman snorted, amused at her own little joke.

She said, "Have it examined from top to bottom, Gilbert. If you find that it will not crumble in the first blast of storm or sink beneath the weight of our feet, attend to the lease."

"Take it, do you mean?"

"Precisely."

"Alicia, are you sure that –"

"I am sure that we will find no better on our pittance."

"Oh, I imagine that there are –"

"No better, closer to Ottershaw."

"But you have neglected to ask me –"

"I assume that we can afford it, Gilbert, or you would not have brought me here, beaming and gleeful as you are. I am left to conclude that you are in favour of acquiring this dwelling?"

"Yes, I think so. Yes."

"When may we occupy it?"

"Almost at once," said Gilbert.

"As your wife I have little say in the matter, I suppose. If you are content to bring us here, I shall not impede you."

"Alicia, we are partners in marriage and in life. It's not my intention to take you to a place where you will be miserable."

"It is not Ottershaw."

"I cannot give you Ottershaw."

"Then this old castle will suffice," said Alicia, "until such times as we can reclaim your rightful inheritance."

"Ninety-nine years?" said Gilbert.

It was now Alicia's turn to miss the point of the joke.

In spite of herself Anna was concerned about her husband. She had enquired from the stable lads if they had seen aught of Matt on Sunday night, if, perhaps, he had stolen a bed in the hay-loft, but the boys met her with an insolent blankness. Questions to the horse-men received no more informative replies and it was not until she encountered Brigit Tomelty upon the back stairs that, from an unexpected source, she found out that Matt had spent the night at McDonald's and had gone directly to work.

"How d' you know, Brigit?"

"I heard. From m' daddy."

Anna suspected nothing. Brigit was famous as a fount of information. "Would ye happen to know if Matt was wi' McDonald on Saturday night as well?"

"Drinkin'," said Brigit, inscrutably. "I hear the monk ran off an' got lost. Matt would be fair grieved."

"Aye, he was," said Anna.

"You never likit the beastie, though, so it canna have hurt you much, Anna."

"I wouldn't have wantit to see it dead."

"So it's dead for certain, is it?"

"It wouldn't survive the nights, so Matt said." Brigit's questions made her uncomfortable. "But I expect that daft man o' mine will search 'til summer comes."

"I canna imagine carin' for anythin' as much as that," Brigit remarked and, hoisting up the blankets which she had brought from the master's room, went on downstairs.

Anna's allotted task that Monday morning was menial but not strenuous. She would trim all the candles in the corridors and collect the parings for melting and remoulding. At least she would be on the same floor as Randall and would not be supervised.

During the course of the morning she saw nothing of the laird. Three of Mr Gibbie's children stampeded down the long west corridor at one point but they ignored Anna as if she were only a piece of furniture and even the nursery-maid said not a word as she hurried past in pursuit of her autocratic charges.

At first Anna's thoughts turned on the events of the weekend. If Jacko's body was discovered Matt would assume that she had murdered the wee brute and would whip her without mercy. In fact Anna attributed to her husband a far greater degree of viciousness than he possessed. He had slapped her only three or four times, leaving bruises but no injury. Wives in the villages suffered far worse than Anna from hot-tempered husbands and not a few were treated hardly better than cattle.

The corridor turned into a sort of cul-de-sac where a tall window overlooked the park. There was one iron holder bracketed to the wall holding a single, hardly-used tallow. Anna shaved the caked rim of the holder, then, with bowl in hand, stood idly by the window gazing out at the view.

Cheviots clustered under the boughs where dry crests of crop might be found. Pheasants strutted near the oaks, safe in the home park where shooting, even by the laird, was considered unsportsmanlike. It was a strange, sad sort of day, missing the russet sunshine. Mammy would have revelled in such January weather. She would have got her girls active and packed them off to repair fences or hedges or turn the potato drills. Anna would have felt fresh and strong and would have had an appetite like a tigress. After supper, though, by the flicker of the fire she would have been all pleasantly dozy and Mammy would not have scolded her but would have let her nap undisturbed in the chair.

Anna sighed. Life as a young girl on the Nettleburn seemed, in retrospect, more contented than it had been at the time.

She wondered what her sister might be doing right now; not wicking candles, whatever else. Elspeth would probably be taking morning tea, Kerr serving her from a huge silver pot while 'Pet swanned on the sofa with a new novel on her lap.

Anna sighed again.

"Sinclair, Sinclair." Dunn's shrill summons shook Anna from her reverie. "Master has need o' you."

Dunn had become quite high and mighty of late and had even tried to lord it over Mr Hunter until he got a clout on the lug to remind him of his place. Even so, Anna laid down the candle stuff on the floor and hurried to the door of the library.

"Tak' awa' the dinner-plates," Dunn told her.

"Is he in there?" Anna mouthed.

"Aye, the laird is in residence."

Anna went into the library.

A hot fire roared in the hearth to dispel the gloom of the winter's day and the laird was standing before it. Watching her. Anna flushed as she transferred plates and cutlery from table to tray. A dish of potatoes had hardly been touched and there was a joint of prime roast beef with a bone-handled carving-knife stuck in it. Pink gravy oozed from the blade and formed a succulent little puddle about the base of the roast. Anna had a ridiculous urge to tear off a piece with her fingers and stuff it immediately into her mouth. Instead, she dropped a curtsy to Randall and, treading warily, carried the tray out of the room. Dunn closed the door behind her.

Anna glanced left and right. The corridor was deserted. She leaned forward and touched her tongue to the plate, sipping the delicious gravy as a kitten will sup milk.

She carried the tray to the back stairs, opened the door with her hip, slid through. She put the tray down on the step, fished on tiptoe for the cog she had hidden on the shelf over the door, then changed her mind. She had no need of the cog. She cut four slices from the roast with the carving-knife, licked them clean and inserted them into her secret pocket. What a fine feast she would make of them tonight. Lifting the tray she made her way down into the kitchen.

Mrs Lacy was busy with pans at the fire. No other servants were in the kitchen. Anna did not notice Hunter at first as she made on towards the pot-room where the crocks were washed.

She did not reach the pot-room.

Mr Hunter was suddenly before her, barring her escape.

Anna, with a stab of pure fear, realised she had been caught.

Cook glared at Anna, her fat upper lip twisted in disgust.

"Put the tray down, girl," Mr Hunter told her.

She wanted to throw the tray at his sleek head, to dart away through the yard door and flee into the trees. She could throw away the bloody roast beef. Nobody would be able to prove that she had been stealing. Hunter caught her arm, swung the tray and laid it on the baking-table.

Still holding her fast, Hunter stooped, peered at the beef and sniffed it as if the very aroma were measurable.

"I'm surprised. I am surprised," the steward said. "The

daughter of Gaddy Patterson, a thief. The kin of our dear grieve, a pilferer."

"I don't know what you mean," said Anna defiantly.

Somehow she kept her hands from flying to the secret pocket. She planted her fists on her hips and met Hunter's melancholy eye challengingly.

"Candidly, I thought it was Tomelty. It would not have surprised me if it'd been Tomelty. But you, Sinclair!"

"Are you accusin' me of somethin', Mister Hunter?"

"Do you think comestibles grow on trees, lass? Do you think I do not know how much is prepared an' how much consumed? Do you deny that you have been stealin' food?"

"I do deny it. I've no need t' steal food."

"The beef was put out as a trap at the laird's suggestion."

"At the laird's –" Anna made herself silent.

"Clever mannie," the cook interjected. "Mister Hunter, here's the scale."

In horror Anna watched Mrs Lacy hold out a measure bowl manacled to a thin chain, the chain to the balance. Three small dairy-weights were already in the dish. Without awaiting Hunter's instruction the cook lifted the roast from the platter and placed it in the empty bowl.

Mrs Lacy extended the scales between finger and thumb. For an instant beef and brass weights held in perfect apposition then the weighted dish sank with a clink, leaving the roast high above it.

"How much, Mrs Lacy?" said Hunter gravely.

"Four slices'd be my estimate."

"Where are they, Sinclair?" said Hunter.

Anna did not answer.

"Have you eaten them already?"

Anna pursed her lips.

"Take her upstairs," said Mrs Lacy.

"If you've concealed them on your person," said Hunter, "it'd be wiser, lass, to divulge them here an' now."

"The laird said he'd deal wi' her," Mrs Lacy reminded the steward.

From the mouth of the servants' hall Anna heard giggles and whispers from other maids and, in that period of extreme tension, heard Brigit's thick laughter; even Brigit, her friend, took malicious pleasure in her downfall.

"What – what'll happen to me –" Anna stammered, "supposin' I had been stealin' food?"

"We'll let Sir Randall decide your punishment," said Hunter.

"Very well," said Anna. "Take me t' the laird then."

Gasps from the corridor, shocked faces, blurs of white in the gloom; Hunter turned Anna by the shoulder and pushed her towards the back stairs.

Anna was afraid of Hunter, afraid of the cook, afraid of Alicia Bontine and even of Drayer, the senior parlour-maid who had been at Ottershaw longer than anyone. But she was not afraid of the laird.

"Watch what ye do, Mister Hunter," she snapped at the steward as he pushed her with his knees. "What if the laird finds I've done nothin' wrong?"

"Sinclair, I've had ye markit as a spoiled brat since first ye marrit young Matt," Hunter told her, without the benefit of his polite accent. "Ye'll not get slippit o' this piece of mischief, I'll promise."

She fought him, seizing his arms, asked the question straight to his face. "What can you do t' me? Throw me out? I wouldn't care a toss if ye did."

Hunter was relieved of giving answer to an awkward question by the appearance of Dunn at the door to the landing.

"The laird's waitin'," the boy said gloatingly.

Seconds later Anna was bundled into the library and released from Hunter's hold.

She flounced and straightened.

Randall stood before the fireplace, a thin cane in his left hand. He leaned his weight slightly into it. He had on a frilled shirt, open at the throat, and a leather half-vest. Breeches of heavy grey linen, hitched high and tight, showed the contours of his body. He looked as smooth and hard as a stone from the Nettleburn.

"How did the scales tip, Hunter?"

"Meat has been taken, sir."

"She did not filch the whole roast then?"

"She's too wily for that, sir. Just a few fat slices, so it seems."

"Has she confessed?"

Anna threw the laird his answer. "I have nothin' to confess."

"Has the meat been discovered, Hunter?"

"As you ordered, sir, the culprit was brought here t' you."

"Has she not been searched?"

"No, sir. Shall I be sendin' for Mistress Lacy, or Drayer?"

"She shall not be searched. It smacks too much of criminal arrest, and this is only a crime against the good order of my house."

"What shall we do, laird?" said Hunter.

"Leave her with me," said Randall. "I shall persuade her to tell me the truth. If she is properly repentant then I shall mete out a just punishment, one which will not deprive her of her position, however, or bring shame to the Sinclairs."

"Beggin' the laird's pardon, would it not be for the best to send for the grieve, let him stand with you while the truth is uncovered?"

"No, Hunter. Not for the world would I subject Sinclair to such an ordeal. It'll be enough that he hears of it when it is resolved," said Randall. "It will be over and settled in a matter of minutes if the girl is honest and open."

"Speak up, you." Hunter dug Anna with his elbow.

Anna jerked away from the steward. What Hunter might suspect in the laird's personal intervention in domestic drama Anna knew to be a fact. She surmised that Randall wanted power over her, wanted her to submit to him as she had done once before.

"I have nothin' to say," Anna declared.

"Leave us, Hunter. Take Dunn downstairs with you."

"Beggin' the laird's pardon," said Hunter once more, "but I'm afeared I must take it upon myself to enquire what it is you intend, sir, since it is incumbent upon me to look out for the welfare o' the female servants."

It was courageous of Hunter to speak out. Old Sir Gibbie would not have needed to be reminded of the tradition that the steward of a house was responsible for protecting servants against masters, as well as the *vice* and the *versa* of it. It was a duty so little exercised that Tolland, for example, would not have considered it at all.

"No harm will befall her, Hunter, you have my word. I am no Caligula, you know."

Hunter, never having heard of the mannie to whom the laird referred, looked as blank as a piece of slate.

"Leave us, Hunter."

Steering Dunn by the shoulder, as if he were a culprit too,

Hunter left the library, closed the door and made a loud enough noise in the corridor to indicate that he had heeded the laird's command to the letter and had in fact gone downstairs.

Randall made no move towards Anna. He contemplated her for a moment or two, head on one side, then he seated himself on a lidded log-box which flanked the hearth.

"I spoke with your brother-in-law yesterday," said Randall, quite casually, while Anna stood on the carpet by the table and tried not to appear reckless. "He's such a sensible fellow."

"Aye, he can afford t' be," said Anna.

"You're not poor," said Randall, "nor are you ill-sustained. Did you steal titbits from my tray?"

"Aye, laird."

"Including the delicious roast beef I lunched upon this noon?"

"Aye, laird."

"Have you eaten it?"

"I took a taste, that's all."

"Come now, Anna, a taste would hardly tip Mistress Lacy's scales."

"Was it your – the laird's idea t' set a trap?"

"Oh, Hunter came to me in such a fly of feathers, clucking like a damned hen about pilfering – he's still used to having Mistress Alicia count every morsel, I expect – that I had to show myself cunning. It wasn't at all a bad ruse. Saw it used by a quartermaster-cook in a barracks in Perth some years ago. But, of course, the soldier was hungry. And the punishment far outweighed the crime."

"What – what happened t' the soldier?"

"Shot," said Randall without the trace of a smile.

"Dead, sir?" said Anna. "For stealin'?"

"He could no longer be trusted, do you see?"

"Well, you'll not be shootin' me," said Anna, who was not naïve enough, as some of the maids would have been, to be at all frightened by the laird's story of rough military justice.

"But you admit to stealing?"

"To takin' a wee taste of the leftovers, aye."

"I swear," said Randall, with a sigh, "that you are making it unnecessarily difficult for me to get to the bottom of this business."

"You could dismiss me from service," Anna suggested.

Anna too had relaxed a little. She was inclined to believe that the scheme had been naught but an excuse for him to get her alone, to speak with her in friendly, bantering fashion. She remembered the kiss, however, the sensuality of it and how this same man had taken advantage of two young girls for his pleasure.

"Is that what you wish me to do? Send you back to the dairy, or to field work? Do you prefer the byre to the house, Anna?"

"No, laird."

"Very well. Where is my beef? Do not pretend that you ate it all. I know that to be a lie, unless you swallowed it whole, like a python," Randall said. "It's my guess you've hidden it."

Bathed by the warmth of the fire Anna felt hot all over.

"Come here," Randall said.

She moved without reluctance so that she stood close enough for him to touch her without stretching far.

Quietly he asked, "Do you want me to search for it? Do you want me to find it?"

He placed his hands about her waist and drew her to him. His knees brushed against her thighs and closed slightly, pinning her. He put a knuckle under her chin and tipped her face up so that she was looking straight into his eyes.

"I think you've a secret, Anna, a little secret pocket and that if I look I shall find it," he murmured. "Is that not so?"

"Aye."

"Where then is it?" Randall said. "Is it here?" He placed a hand softly upon her breast. "Is it here, perhaps?" He placed a hand now upon her stomach, touching her with a little more pressure, a brushing stroke, not quite intimate. "Must I search more closely still?"

Anna leaned against him. "Stop it."

She had intended to be furious but his caress had drained her of determination. She had dreamed for four years of this moment without ever really believing that it would become a reality. She longed for him with every fibre of her being.

"Stop it," she whispered. "Please, don't make a sport of it."

"Ah!" Randall exclaimed. "You're not a child now, is that it?"

"I know what you want of me but you mustn't make a sport of it."

"What do I want of you, Anna?"

"To – to love me."

"What do you say to that?"

By way of answer Anna pressed herself against him, arms about his shoulders. She sensed shock in him as her lips fastened upon his and her fingers touched his hair.

He drew back sharply.

"I do want you, Anna. But you've taught me a lesson. It cannot be a command or a punishment or a foolish piece of play. I've thought of you, yes, so many times – the girl in the woods, eager and bold and young."

She kissed him again, with a release of passion that swept away calculation. His body was lean, not thick like Matt's, his hands quiet and gentle upon her, not grabbing and rough.

"I've thought of you also, night an' day," Anna confessed.

"But you have a husband."

"Under this roof," said Anna, "I've no husband, no master but you."

"In conscience, Anna, think for your own good what you are doing."

"I dinna care."

"Tomorrow you might care very much."

"Do you care?"

"Anna, if you bore me or displease me, I'll soon be rid of you, make no mistake on that score."

"What if I never bore you, never do anythin' but please you?"

Randall got to his feet. He snuggled his arm about her waist and held her against him.

"Do you not mind what they'll say about you?" he asked.

"No."

"In which case," said Randall, "damn them."

"But – but what'll Mister Hunter –"

"Do you wish to wait, to put it off, Anna?"

"No."

"Then let Hunter think what he likes. Let them all think what they like. To the devil with them and the consequences."

"Where are you takin' me?" Anna asked.

"To bed, of course," said Randall Bontine.

SEVEN

Chance and Necessity

Winter came late to the Lowlands of Scotland. In the first few days of February tales of heavy snowfalls and piercing frosts filtered down from the north. Scarf, in the course of his duties as James Moodie's agent, was in contact with trade travellers and heard the stories at the mart in Dunblane. He made certain that Mr Moodie was informed immediately in order that the weaver might prepare his holdings for the siege that would surely come.

Feed was bought from those daft enough to sell it. Straw was baled up for warm penning. Shepherds who tended Moodie's flocks were ordered to draw the muttons off the upper slopes and cluster them within reach of habitation. Some early ewes, those that grazed the floor of the strath, were due to drop in three weeks, a process which could not be left to nature if blizzards were in the offing. James did not stand about in the face of the reports wringing his hands and praying that his small pocket would be spared the punishments that snow and ice could inflict. He made sure that he and his hirelings were ready for the worst.

James had been out all day long, not in the gig or cabriolet but on horseback. He hated riding but found it convenient to get about the grazings at a gallop and change mounts at various stations along the circular route he had mapped out before he left Moss House. He was wrapped in heavy woollens, thick and cumbersome as armour, which chafed his skin and added to the discomfort of licking over bone-frosted roads and tracks. There was no sense of manly adventure in the trail, not for James Moodie, though he did not shirk or delegate this necessary duty.

The mere sight of the weaver thundering down the path was enough to stir the most lax of hired wool-growers into a fever of activity for fear that he would be stripped of shearing fees and lose his 'arrangement' on the spot. Mr Rudge could be cajoled from too close an inspection of flocks and premises by a tankard of mulled wine or the attentions of a pretty young lassie. Mr Scarf could be won round by spinning a tearful yarn about illness and disaster. But James Simpson Moodie's heart was as flinty as his stare and he brooked no excuse for laziness and indifferent tending. Besides, he appeared so rarely on outlying patches that a visit from him was like having Apollyon swoop down into your yard on wings of fire.

Even the best of herdsmen and breeders felt their bowels clench with fear when the cry came, "God, but it's Moodie! Aye, but it's Moodie himsel'." In Kennart too the advent of the master created a bit of a stir. Within the long building fingers flew a little faster and the chuckle of bobbins, chatter of shuttles and the slap-whack of battens increased with the whisper that Moodie had crossed the bridge or climbed the stairs to Rudge's office.

On that February afternoon, however, James did not ride into Kennart to whip up his weavers. Only a handful of womenfolk even knew that he was in the vicinity for he arrived at the Cunninghams' shop by the quiet path round the base of Rowan Hill.

Veterans of the Glasgow markets, George and Trina were well aware that large profits could be made in periods of scarcity. Against the sting in winter's tail, therefore, the couple had piled all the stock they could afford. Cottage and shop groaned with barrels, jars, boxes and sacks. Even the couple's bed in the half-loft was padded like a redoubt with containers.

The folk of Kennart had quickly grown accustomed to fine fare and the women blessed the Cunninghams for easing their burden at the stove, even if it did cost money. With each passing week more and more weavers' chink found its way into the Cunninghams' coffers. One commodity – naturally – sold better than all the others put together; and that commodity was drink.

George had acquired a licence, through the offices of his landlord, James Simpson Moodie, though he had dispensed whisky and gin without the benefit of paper quite happily. Tomelty's malt sold like wildfire, a generous dram for a penny, a price not matched by the Ramshead or the Black Bull or even by the Bell Tree in Drymen. What was even more appealing was that spirits could be purchased on credit.

Women as well as men took full advantage of the slate and would gaggle about the lighted shop at all hours and dare each other to consume cup after cup of gin. Several times Baynham had to break up brawls between members of the fair sex, a chore which he did not relish since he usually got his face raked or his shins kicked and could not bring himself to use his mallet on a lassie no matter how sorely he was provoked. Young men thought it a great laugh and egged the girls on, buying them more tipple on credit in the hope that they would toss all their inhibitions aside and grant free sexual favours indiscriminately.

Some stolid craftsmen frowned on this debauchery and made formal complaints to Mr Rudge. But Rudge was a sensualist and viewed the goings-on with indulgent interest and had even taken advantage of them now and again. It was not the complaints of a handful of moral-minded weavers that brought James to Kennart but a letter that had been delivered to Moss House, a letter penned by Mr George Cunningham no less, one of several.

Cunningham was serving behind a wooden counter which barred the front of the shop when James arrived. He wore the familiar pea-jacket and muffler, had his pipe in his mouth. Four wives and one old man were gathered before the shop sampling wee tin cups of 'blue ruin', unfiltered gin. Some of the women were also nibbling almond cakes, hot from Trina's oven, but within seconds of James's arrival the customers had vanished down the road to the village, leaving the area of the shop deserted.

"It's yourself, is it, Mister Moodie?" boomed George Cunningham. "How kind o' ye to drop in."

Stiffly James dismounted and tied his horse to a post.

"Aye, seems we're in for a grim spell," said Cunningham. "Come in by an' warm yoursel', Mister Moodie."

James slipped through the 'gate' by the end of the counters and threaded his way through the sacks and boxes.

Cunningham had erected an iron brazier at the back of the shed with a chimney vent above it and the fire in the grate's belly burned yellow and inviting. On a griddle hooked close to the brazier were two big tin jugs and, in a twinkling,

Cunningham had concocted a steaming cup of whisky-toddy which he handed over to the weaver. James drank it gratefully and accepted a second, holding it in his fingers while the warmth seeped into him.

From the tiny doorway into the cottage Trina Cunningham appeared. She looked more robust than ever, with her sleeves rolled to the elbows and all covered in flour. Her cheeks glowed cherry from her efforts over the oven fire indoors and, even to James, the establishment at the bottom of Rowan Hill had an alluring atmosphere of plenteous comfort to it, an oasis in the leaden landscape.

"Pie, Mister Moodie?" the woman chirruped.

The weaver, hugging the fire in the rear of the shop, shook his head. He drank the second toddy and returned the cup to Cunningham. "I'm here in response to your letters, particularly the last."

Trina Cunningham came forth, wiping her hands on her sackcloth apron and taking from a tray a nip of gin which she knocked backward into her mouth as casually as she drew breath.

"We are, as you can see, sir, well settled here," said Cunningham. "Our wares are verra popular wi' the weavers."

"Much savin' they make on fuel an' on time," put in Trina.

"I gathered as much by the sum you sent me through Mister Rudge. I take it that you didn't smear the figures. I have no means of checking your profits, of course, as you are well aware."

"Did it seem niggardly, Mister Moodie?" Trina Cunningham asked, with a slight note of acerbity. "Did it seem we was smearin' the figures?"

"Was that the reason you asked me to call?"

"No," said George Cunningham. "It has to do wi' the impendin' hard weather which, if you'll cast your glance to the door, you'll see has commencit."

It had, indeed, begun to snow.

"Come to it, Cunningham," James growled.

"We have a slate o' debtors," said Cunningham.

"If you give credit, that is not my concern."

"It cheats you o' profit too, Mister Moodie."

"Och, they pay," said Trina. "Most o' them."

"But?" James asked.

"But we could benefit them more if we could extend their credit further," said Cunningham.

"Extend? I don't take your meanin'," James said.

"Trina, fetch the slates."

There were four boards, long, rough-edged slabs of roofing slate, bought perhaps from the quarries near Balfron or from one of the pedlars who carted such material from the north. Chalk markings were thick upon the surfaces, like runic commemorations. There was, of course, nothing mystical in the meaning of the signs. George Cunningham could decipher them with ease which he proceeded to do, tolling off in a dry voice the names of Moodie's employees and the sums they owed.

"Aye, I've a picture of what you mean," James interrupted. "But what does it have to do with me? I'm not responsible for how you run your trade, Cunningham."

"One week's wage on average is our allowance," said the woman. "It's all they can be trustit for, ye see."

"But they don't pay us as they should. They don't pay a standin' week all at once," said George Cunningham. "In consequence o' which we have to deny them their provisions and touches o' pleasure."

"Meaning drink, I suppose," James said.

"Can ye deny them as works so hard a touch o' warmth in this bitter weather?" said Trina.

"Do you want me to supply drink, is that it?"

George Cunningham took the pipe from his mouth, spat into the brazier, then laughed. "Aye, you'd be a memorable master if ye did that, Mister Moodie. But no, what we have in mind t' suggest is that we give the slate every week t' Mister Rudge and –"

"Deduct the owing from the family's earnings?" said James. "I envisage nothing but animosity and bitterness coming my way from that. I'd be accused of paying them with one hand and taking it away with the other. They'd forget that they had supped well, had their taste o' whisky or can of ale. They'd see only pennies in their hands, think of the labour and convince themselves I had somehow cheated them of their entitled earnings."

"We'd see nobody starve," said Trina. "We'd extend their borrowin' week upon week, as needed."

Emphatically James shook his head. "I've never approved of such systems. They're but a step from not paying out coin at all."

"Many o' your weavers are paid by the piece, are they not?" Cunningham asked.

"Of course."

"Then they will surely work the harder an' slip more cloth from the treadles."

"See, Mister Moodie, how you'll gain from both ends."

"You've been in Kennart but four short months and already you're tellin' me how I should run my manufactory. Damn it, did I not give you all that you asked for? It isn't to be enough, it seems. Now you insist that I introduce a barter system and encourage my workers to indulge themselves beyond their capacity to pay, so they can shovel money into your pockets."

"An' your pocket too, Mister Moodie," Trina reminded him.

"The truck system works fine in big cotton mills," said Cunningham. "It's the accepted method in the coal-diggin's. I've heard men say they prefer it."

"I question if they prefer it," said James. "I suspect they're so enthralled by it that they do not realise how it makes slaves of them. God, but men are foolish enough to trade their souls for immediate satisfaction of an appetite."

"Souls!" snorted Trina. "If they have souls at all, sir, they should be barterin' wi' a minister an' not wi' honest shopkeepers like ourselves."

"Is this the point of all your letters to me, to force me to agree to the establishment of a truck system, committing my workers to spend their wages at your shop?"

"It's here they spend anyroads," said Trina.

"I feel you'd do well t' consider our suggestion at leisure, Mister Moodie."

James said, "Have you spoken to Rudge?"

"Nah, nah!" said Trina. "He's but a lackey."

"Mister Rudge is my appointed agent in Kennart."

"Maybe so," said Cunningham. "But I doubt, sir, if Mister Rudge understands commerce as we do. I doubt if he ever trudged the city's streets when he was a raw lad, peddlin' his wares round the keepers' an' the backs o' inns an' taverns."

"As you had t' do, Mister Moodie," added Trina, in case the weaver had missed the point.

"Very well," James said. "But now you have spoken with me on the matter – and I've given my refusal. I shan't change my opinion of the truck system, even on reflection."

"Ye might, Mister Moodie," said the woman, "if ye saw that it benefited the poor an' needy an' those poor weak creatures who fall into sore distress."

"I cannot see it," said James. "I see only how it would benefit you, Mistress Cunningham."

"Perhaps your lady wife – Miss Elspeth – perhaps she could explain it to ye," said Trina.

"She knows nothin' of such affairs."

"Then she's lucky," said Trina.

"Understandably protectit from the harsh realities o' life," said Cunningham. "But if she had seen what we have seen, she might favour any system which gave succour when it was required."

"It pains us t' send awa' a hungry lassie," said Trina Cunningham.

Apparently the thought was painful enough to require another nip of gin imbibed at lightning speed.

"Surely," said James, more cautiously, "you do not need my answer immediately?"

"Afore the snow comes would be welcome," said Cunning-ham.

Snow had already come, winding down over the ridge of the hill and washing out the line of the trees a half-mile distant. James's horse shivered, stamped, sneezed and tugged at the post-rein as if it wanted away from Kennart and into shelter before the fall thickened.

Cunningham took the pipe from his mouth again. He rested his buttocks against a box of Macready Import tea which saddled two sacks of rice and a small dump of sugar. "Perhaps, sir, I could tak' a stroll up t' Moss House tomorrow morn – if the weather permits – an' explain how it is wi' poor folk."

"I need no explanations," said James.

"To your wife – Miss Elspeth," Trina said.

"Mistress Moodie. She's married to me."

"Sure, it's a natural mistake, Mister Moodie," said Trina, "arisin' from a natural confusion."

"However slight her interest in commerce," put in Cunningham, "I'm certain she'd be interested t' meet somebody who knew her dear departit mother."

"Two peas in a pod," said Trina. "Mother as pretty as daughter, though she's been dead these twenty year, poor deceived lassie, dead an' buried under a flat stone, like as not, in some parish kirkyard."

"A stranger's grave," said Cunningham.

"How unfair, when Bell was no stranger at all."

Crossing and cutting, the flakes and ivory shadows of flakes swirled thick and fast on fluctuating wind. The bare-branched rowans quivered in the blizzard mist which, steadying again, hung like a massive curtain across the land, shutting out all sight, all sound.

James took up a third hot tin cup from the griddle by the brazier and drank the contents while he stared out at the snow.

By his left hand, stuck in a coil of black tobacco, was a sharp little dagger, honed on both sides of the blade. By his right hand, where he could pluck it up without stretching, a sack-grapple lay on the counter, its flattened hook fit to smash bone with a blow. James's fingers trembled as he brought the cup to his mouth and stared out at the muffling silence. One blow with the grapple and Cunningham would fall at his feet. Then the knife, plunging into the side of the fat woman's throat, ripping this way and that until her pig-squeals ceased and the snow ate up the moans.

He closed both fists about the cup.

Hollowly he said, "How — how would the system be run?"

"Simply, sir," said Cunningham.

Implacably James Moodie listened while, in a matter of a minute or so, George Cunningham explained how he would rook the poor weavers and their wives through the office of Mr Rudge and the services of McAlpin. Implacably James Moodie nodded.

He said, "Perhaps, after all, a trial would be feasible; a trial only."

"Shall we say a quarter, Mister Moodie?"

"Yes."

"An' you'll tell Mister Rudge?"

"Yes."

"A taste more toddy, afore ye ride home t' your wife?"

"No," said James. "No, thank you."

And then he left the couple, mounted the wet saddle and guided the horse down on to the snow-shrouded track to the village, to Rudge's office where he must humiliate himself before the manager and the manager's clerk by passing off the Cunninghams' orders exactly as if they were his own.

Since the last Sabbath in January, when she had attended kirk with James, Elspeth had not crossed the doorstep of Moss House. Her indisposition had furnished her with a ready-made excuse for low spirits. She had not been silly enough to ascribe the pangs and pressures that stirred in her body to a broken heart, however. She was only too well aware that she had conceived and that the baby must be approaching the third month of its growth.

As befitted a young woman who had been well educated, Elspeth had gone quietly into James's library and had consulted a book which detailed the meaning of the changes and explained the signs and symptoms of pregnancy. Knowledge rendered her less uncertain, less afraid. In a month or so her abdomen would show a swelling to match that of her enlarged and tender breasts. At least she was spared the need to hide her condition from James who had never looked upon her unclad figure.

The pregnancy distracted her from the misery that followed Michael's death. There could be no shadow of doubt that Michael had fathered the baby. He had come into her life as lightly as a gadfly and had gone out of it in a similar manner. She could not convince herself that he had gone from her for ever, such had been the scattered manner of their friendship.

Janet Blaven had informed her by letter that her nephew had died and had been carried for interment to St Cyrus kirkyard in Glasgow. There he was laid beside his beloved mother and the little sisters who had preceded him into God's abiding peace. One day, Elspeth promised herself, one day in the spring season she would find an excuse for travelling alone to Glasgow and would kneel by Michael's grave and pour out her heart to him, would tell him about their child, knowing that he would be glad. It was the only ray of consolation in that time of sorrow, the knowledge that Michael, not James, had fathered her child.

Soon, very soon, she would have to confront James with the truth. She had no inkling as to how he would react. In the past few months James had become unpredictable and Elspeth realised that she would be placing her husband in an appalling dilemma. How could he cast her from him, disown the child as a bastard, without admitting to the world at large that he had failed in his husbandly role? Only James and she shared the secret that he could not claim paternity because he had never fulfilled the marriage vow.

Gradually at first, then swiftly, Elspeth became excited by the prospect of having a child of her own. She was tempted to seek out Anna, whom she had not seen for many months, and confide in her sister. But Anna would be sure to tell Matt who would tell his father who, unwittingly perhaps, would steer the news back to James. Also, how could she explain to Anna that she had valid reasons for keeping the pregnancy secret from her legal husband? Anna's curiosity could draw as red and all-consuming as a furnace and she was afraid lest her sister wheedle the whole truth from her. Not to be able to talk of Michael, not to be able to talk of her child, it was small wonder that Elspeth settled into depression and hardly left her bedroom for the whole of that month.

When she awakened on the morning of the day of the snow, however, she felt well again. The wriggling bands of nausea which had tightened beneath her ribs and breasts were absent. Her revulsion at the very thought of food had been replaced by healthy appetite. She sent Kerr down to the kitchen with orders to prepare a breakfast to be served in the dining-room and with a request to her husband to join her there, but word came back that Mr Moodie had gone out early and was not expected to return before dusk.

Elspeth rose and dressed. She had never permitted a maid to clothe her and was glad of it now. Groomed and smart she went down into the dining-room and did justice to a large breakfast. When she had finished she went up to call on Mother Moodie upon whom she had not clapped eyes for almost a month.

Elspeth was not prepared for the sight that met her in the old woman's room. Mother Moodie was tied to the throne-like chair by two soft leather cross-straps and hung against them while the nurse, Betty, tried to feed her with pap from a bowl.

Though sweet herbs had been strewn upon the fire the chamber smelled acrid and awful. Elspeth had brought a novel, intending to sit by the old woman for a while, but she could not bring herself to stay for more than a few minutes. There was nothing she could do for Mother Moodie. The sight of the woman's decayed condition disturbed Elspeth, as if age might be a disease of contamination which would infect the child in her womb.

"How does she live at all?" Elspeth asked.

Betty answered, "Only God can answer such a question. His ways are verra mysterious, times."

"Does she suffer much?"

"Bit pain in the belly," Betty said. "Thinks she's carryin' a bairn, so she does."

Tolland, who had remained in the room, said sharply, "That's enough, Betty," then put a hand on Elspeth's arm. "Come away, Mistress Moodie, this is no place to linger in your condition."

"My condition, Tolland?"

"After bein' ill yourself," said the steward.

Elspeth was grateful to Tolland for giving her an excuse to leave the sick-room. It had been a mistake to come at all. Death was too near Mother Moodie and clouded Elspeth with memories of Michael. At least he had been spared this sort of indignity. Perhaps there was something to be said for dying young. She thought also of Gaddy, felt sorrow gnaw at her heart, and loneliness. She went downstairs once more but exuberance had gone out of her and she could find nothing with which to occupy herself, nothing that would lift her depression.

In the drawing-room she tried to busy herself with a piece of embroidery which had lain untouched in the frame for months but the threads seemed stiff as rope and her fingers clumsy on the needle. She gave up, wandered through the house, looked out of the back door to the garden and the moor. She returned to the library and did her best to bridge the gap between noon and tea-time by browsing through books.

It was into the afternoon when she roused herself and rang the handbell.

Kerr appeared at the door, crumbs at the side of her lips.

"Fetch me my riding-coat an' shoes, Kerr."

"Will ye be needin' the gig too?"

"No."

"Are ye not goin' to see Miss Blaven?"

"No, Kerr. I'm goin' out walking."

"I'll be comin' with you."

Elspeth resented being constantly trailed by servants. "You will stay indoors."

"The menfolk say it'll snow."

"I'm not an invalid. Besides, I intend only to walk to the head of the village."

"I'll fetch your coat."

"Do."

Kerr would tell Tolland and Tolland might try to dissuade her from going out alone. Why did servants seem like gaolers? If she had been a byre-maid or labourer's daughter they wouldn't have cared what she did with herself. Had marriage to James transformed her into an object made of porcelain or spun glass? Tolland did not put in an appearance, however, and Elspeth put on her outdoor garments in the hall and, leaving her anger behind, hurried out of Moss House and through the garden to the road.

She had no particular destination in mind but a trace of morbidity, mingled with sentimentality, drew her to the kirkyard to wander in solitude among the stones.

Elspeth was not, after all, fey enough to converse with the handsome monument that marked the place where Gaddy lay or to question the flat, sequestered tablet beneath which the identity of her natural mother was hidden.

Here Lies a Stranger
Died November
1791

In her present peculiar mood, though, Elspeth found herself close to tears. So much had changed that a span of twenty years, stretching back into a previous century, seemed an eternity. It came upon her abruptly that she was older now than her mother, the stranger, had been when she stumbled into Balnesmoor all those years ago and, protecting her infant to the bitter end, had succumbed to cold, exhaustion and neglect, to the terrible loneliness of the outcast. Gaddy had been near forty in 1791 and if her real mother had lived she would, even now, be a good eight or ten years younger than James.

The calculations gave Elspeth pause. She got down upon one knee, took off her glove and placed her hand upon the rough surface of the tablet but she could induce no feeling of rapport, or of empathy. She could not imagine face or feature, think of the girl as young. If they had to meet here and now she would be hard put to recognise the poor creature, let alone communicate with her. Rising, she walked the few yards to Gaddy's monument but felt distanced from it and did not stoop to touch it.

Turning, Elspeth looked over the blunt steeple that crowned the old kirk, up to the unleafed trees and misty white line of the hill that stepped up to Drumglass. She felt calm now. The liberating irresponsibility which Michael had brought into her life, the feeling of being at the centre of a glitter-wheel of possibility, had left her. She was moved by a different destiny, by the fact of her pregnancy. In winters to come she would no longer be alone. However James chose to punish her, she would be protected by the need to protect her child.

Snow had rolled westward from Balfron, swallowed Kennart and billowed suddenly into Balnesmoor. Elspeth fastened her scarf over her bonnet and hurried out of the kirkyard into the Bonnywell.

Slated roofs were already white and thatch, stiffened by hoar, had taken on a granular transparency. Smoke coiled on the rising wind, snaked down into the lanes and backs. From behind the congestion of cottages came the clash of a pump and the grunting of hogs. Two small lads lugged a butter-churn along a lane, splashing and slipping on the carpet of new snow and laughing at the exhilaration of the blizzard.

A timber-wagon trundled from the top of the brae where the road forked and split again into field-crossings and steading tracks. The wagon was a high, slat-sided cart that was pulled by a single horse. It bristled with deadfall. Elspeth recognised McDonald at the reins. As the cart passed she saw that the man seated on the tail-board was her brother-in-law, Matt Sinclair.

It had been several months since Elspeth had last encountered Anna's husband. She had harboured ill-feeling towards him since the time of Gaddy's death. Today, however, she was not displeased to see him. She would not call out to him, though, or wave a greeting, for she felt he, in the company of other foresters, might be embarrassed by her attention.

Matt, however, spotted her. He was off the cart in an instant. McDonald reined the wagon to a halt. Matt jogged round to the big fellow and spoke with him, gesturing over his shoulder with his thumb. McDonald nodded, grinned and clicked the horse into a walk again, leaving Matt standing on the road.

Matt looked thicker and coarser than she remembered him. He had lost his boyish handsomeness. The padded garment and bulky breeks contributed to the impression of stolidity. He demonstrated a pleasure in the chance encounter which took Elspeth by surprise. What had changed him? Was it Anna's promotion to house-servant? She had heard, through Kerr, that Matt was a friend of Pad Tomelty.

"My, but you're lookin' unco' bonnie, 'Pet."

His heartiness did not seem feigned. Had he been tippling down at the wood? If so, liquor had certainly sweetened his disposition.

"You look well yourself, Matt."

"We're deliverin' fuel to the Ramshead. I'll crack wi' you a while, if you've no objection, since it'll give me an excuse t' avoid strenuous labour."

"Will the big man not object?"

"Not him. It's the fifth load for the inns this week. God, but there's hardly a scrap o' hearth-wood left in the neighbour-hood. I swear if we'd had t' length an' split the bloody stuff we'd have been at it 'til Whitsun." Matt prattled on, "He's keen t' make money, our new lairdie. He'd have had the whole plantation sold an' shorn if my father had not intervened."

"Does he heed your father's advice, then?"

"In some matters," Matt answered. "Did you hear I lost the wee monkey?"

"No," said Elspeth. "When?"

"Three weekends since."

"Did it run away?"

"Chased away, more like."

"Will it not come back again?"

"Be stiff by now." Matt shrugged. "Foxes or fummarts'll have gobbled him up."

"You'll miss it."

"I do that."

"Can you not buy another?"

"Nah, 'Pet. There'd be none as gentle as Jacko. I've done wi' animals. They're more bloody bother than they're worth."

He had been tippling. She could smell the reek of whisky on his breath. If the grieve caught a man in drink during the hours of daylight he would roast him, shouting so loud he could be heard all over the Ottershaw parks and half-way up Drumglass. Lachlan Sinclair would not spare Matt simply because Matt was his son.

"I hear Anna's workin' in the big house."

"Anna?" For an instant Matt seemed to have forgotten who Anna was. "Och, aye, she's a day-maid. Dawn 'til dusk."

"What does she do there?"

"Dances on bloody Randall just the way my father danced for auld Sir Gibbie. Anna thinks the bloody grass grows green where the lairdie plants his hin' end."

"She'll be bringin' in more money, though."

"A shillin' or two more, I suppose."

"Still, it's better for Anna than slavin' in the dairy these cold mornings," said Elspeth, who was beginning to find the conversation disconcerting.

"Aye, whenever Anna gets cold, the laird heats her up."

"Matt, what are you saying?"

Sleet-snow had turned dry now and clung to every surface, formed little white whirlwinds along the road.

Matt reached out and caught her arm.

His cheeks were matted with stubble, flushed. In his eyes was a glitter of liveliness as if he had wakened from a daze. He reminded her a little of Peter Docherty who had once worked the Dyke for her father. Peter had fallen foul of the bottle, latterly.

"I'm not goin' yet," Matt declared. "Come, lass, an' we'll shelter in the close there an' finish our chat."

Two cottages, joined by a narrow arch of timber and sod, formed a roofed lane hardly wider than a man's shoulders which led into the pens at the back. Gated, the lane sometimes gave shelter to a sow and her farrow but today it was open and empty. Beyond it the view of the hillside might have been etched in soap on a blown mirror.

"I must get home, Matt."

"Are ye frightened what Jamie might say? T' the devil, Elspeth, I'm your sister's man."

Reluctantly Elspeth let him draw her across the road into the lane.

"Did ye not know that the fine an' honourable Randall Bontine has taken my wife for his pleasure?"

"Matt, I canna believe –"

"Oh, it's no fantasy. It's dinged about the byres an' stables. Every tongue from here t' Blanefield has touched the story."

"Who – who told you?"

"Nobody told me. Nobody had the stuff t' come up an' tell me. Maybe that's as well since then I'd be expectit to make a fool o' myself by challengin' the laird to his face. Can ye see that, 'Pet? Matt Sinclair standin' up to a laird?"

"Has your father –?"

"I canna say. Perhaps he's heard an' pretends he's deaf. He's damned good at that trick."

"How long?"

"Three weeks. Four."

"I think," said Elspeth firmly, "it's naught but malicious gossip an' you should take no heed of it."

"Anna hasn't denied it."

"But has she –?"

"Informed me about it? Embellished it with interestin' details? Hardly!" said Matt. "I see so little of her these days she'd barely have leisure t' tell me anythin'."

Surprisingly, Elspeth felt sympathy for him. He was gruff and selfish but, if what he said was true, he was a victim of Anna's flightiness.

Elspeth remembered only too well the incident by the Lightwater and Randall Bontine's swaggering arrogance. She did not suppose that he had changed much. She remembered too how Anna had mooned over the soldier for months afterwards.

"Is Anna the only one?" Elspeth asked.

Matt pushed himself away from the wall, scratched his chin with his nails. "Huh! I never thought o' that. Aye, it may be that Anna's only one o' a whole stable. I'll ask Brigit."

"Brigit?"

"Brigit Tomelty. She's a new servant too, strange as it might seem."

"Will she tell you the truth, Matt?"

"What has Brigit got t' gain by fibbin'?"

"Perhaps if she's one of –"

Matt threw back his head and laughed. "Nah, nah. Bridie's no' for the laird 'less he's no better than a ram leapin' daft about the ewe-field; though she would give him a fair warmin' if he'd the wit t' realise that the strongest spirits come in the plainest bottles."

Elspeth was not shocked by Matt's analogies. She had been raised on the Nettleburn, had consorted with field-hands and cottagers all of her life. What caught Elspeth off balance was Matt's meek acceptance of Anna's infidelity. Could it be that he was proud to have his wife picked by the new laird? She doubted it, not with Sinclair pride. Perhaps he simply did not know how to cope, short of dragging Anna out of service and locking her away in the cottage in the woods. That, Elspeth thought, is what many a man in Balnesmoor or Ottershaw would do, and add a whacking with a willow switch for good measure. Under the law of Scotland a husband, whether employed by a master or not, could demand as his right the return of his wife's person; a servant was no slave, obliged to tolerate grossness and impropriety. Anna had probably encouraged the soldier-laird. There was that to it; the quarrel was not between Bontine and Matt but between Anna and her husband. Elspeth understood the confusions and implications which Matt, for all his pride, had chosen to ignore.

Matt said, "I could tak' her away. He could do nothing t' prevent it. Anna's mine an' must follow me where I choose to lead."

"She might – she might not want to leave Ottershaw."

"Damn it, Elspeth, do you think I'm not aware of that?"

"Do you wish me to speak to Anna?"

"She'd pay no heed t' you. The truth is I'm not for bein' chased out o' Ottershaw by anyone. I'm fine an' settled here. With or without Anna, I prefer to stay put."

"Why are you tellin' me these things?"

"You're her sister. You've a right t' know what's goin' on."

"Is that the only reason, Matt?"

"If there's a public scandal, it'll reflect on yourself."

Elspeth smiled sardonically. Scandal it seemed again was dogging both Gaddy's daughters.

"What of you, Matt?"

"What of me?"

"Does it not hurt you when they laugh behind your back?"

"God, 'Pet, they know better than that. Besides, I have certain consolations."

"Drink?"

Matt chose not to answer. He changed tack. "You'll have heard how Gibbie an' his bairns are on the move t' Strachan Castle come the May month," he said. "God, but I don't envy him the runnin' o' that heap o' stones. There's only a hundred acres wi' the buildin' so he'll soon dribble through his inheritance wi' nothin' much to cultivate for income."

Elspeth had heard Tolland and James discussing some such affair but she had been too depressed to take much interest. Even now she felt no quickening of curiosity.

"Randall'll have Ottershaw to himself," said Matt. "He'll ruin the place inside three years."

"Is that your father's opinion too, Matt?"

Again Matt ignored her question. "Aye, then he needn't be secretive about his sport. He can have lassies in by the bloody bushel flittin' naked about the halls."

To Elspeth's surprise nothing Matt had told her touched her very deeply.

"Aye, when he's used her an' had enough pleasure from her, when he tires of her craikin', I expect he'll discard her," Matt said. "Then she'll come whimperin' back to me to beg forgiveness."

"Matt?"

"Then we'll see what's the best road out o' Ottershaw and what the world has t' offer us. I'll be wealthy then and she'll see me for what I really am."

"Wealthy? How will –?"

Matt tapped the side of his nose with his forefinger. "So long as ploughmen an' graziers have dry throats I'll make money. Did ye suppose I was the sort who'd work for a shillin' an' doff my cap in gratitude for the privilege o' servin' some high-born rake like Randall Bontine? Not me. Not Matt Sinclair."

"Do you mean the work you do for Tomelty'll make you wealthy?"

"Rich as sin."

"Matt, be careful."

He put his hands on her shoulders and bent his head so that his face was close to hers. She could smell whisky on him most powerfully now, a clean odour in contrast to the damp, animal smell of the padded garments.

"Aye, 'Pet, it's you I should have marrit, not bloody Anna."

She felt nothing, no twinge of regret, none of the longing that had once possessed her to be the wife of Matt Sinclair. A great gulf had opened between them. She pitied him, that was all. She pitied his despair, his conceit, his naïvety. How could Matt believe that Anna would ever come back to him, that a few ill-earned guineas in a purse would change Anna's attitude towards him? Elspeth knew her sister too well to suppose that she would settle for Matt Sinclair when her boldness and her good looks might give her value in the eyes of men like Randall Bontine. Matt had taken refuge in the illusion that he might win back Anna's love.

"Give's a kiss, Elspeth."

"Don't be so bloody daft, Matt," she told him.

She pushed him away but he held her.

"Would you not run away wi' Matt Sinclair if he was rich?"

"I – Matt, let me go."

He did not insist. He planted his lips on her brow, pushing back her bonnet.

"Better than the man ye've got, love."

"How dare you, Matt Sinclair! James is –"

Unable to devise a simple lie from her confusion, she pushed away from her brother-in-law and hurried out of the close into the road, into the sheeting snow, adjusting her bonnet as she went.

Laughing, Matt came after her, hands on hips.

He did not pursue her but stood idly watching as Elspeth disappeared down the road towards Moss House; then he turned on his heel, thrust his hands into his pockets and, head down, trudged away to the Ramshead to join McDonald.

Neither Matt nor Elspeth noticed the man on horseback, motionless by the elm at the head of the Kennart road. But the man had noticed them.

If chance placed James at the head of the Kennart road at precisely the wrong moment, what followed seemed no more than a logical, if tempestuous, yielding to necessity.

Elspeth barely had time to enter the house, to allow Kerr to take off her coat and bonnet, before her husband, his clothing caked with snow, came stamping up the corridor from the kitchens with a harassed Tolland trailing behind him. James shouted to her to join him immediately in the library.

Elspeth looked at Kerr who shook her head and swiftly took the garments away to dry, leaving the young woman stranded.

Tolland had gone into the library, leaving the door wide open. He emerged a second later carrying the weaver's great-coat and hat in his arms, his cheeks scarlet. Elspeth could hear her husband shouting furiously.

"Elspeth."

Her feet were sopping wet and moisture had seeped up her ribbed stockings almost to the knee. She would have preferred to go to her room and change before answering her husband's summons. Good sense and a measure of fear prompted her not to delay, however. She hurried across the hall and into the room.

Realising that a scene was in the offing and wishing to preserve a modicum of privacy, Elspeth closed the door behind her, then turned to face her husband whom she had never seen so livid with rage.

"I take it that you are no longer indisposed?"

"I'm better than I have been."

"Well enough to trot out on a filthy day like this."

"I felt the need for a breath of air and a little exercise." She would not bow to his anger.

It occurred to her that James had discovered her secret. She knew that he had been riding around remote grazings; had he heard from some sly farmer that she had visited Preaching Friar not to call upon Miss Blaven but to sleep with her nephew?

"Exercise of an immodest kind, eh?"

"I went to the kirkyard, if you must know."

"Oh, the kirkyard, is it? Is that where you keep your assignations, among the gravestones? On the grave of your mother, perhaps? God, girl, but you are so like her, in spite of all I've done for you."

Elspeth was too disturbed to take in the import of her husband's accusation.

"Perhaps I should have asked your permission, James, to walk out in Balnesmoor."

"My permission to sneak into the pig-yard with your lover," James shouted. "Do not deny it. I saw you with him."

"With – with him? Matt? Do you mean Matt?"

"Aye, damned if I don't. That whelp, Sinclair."

"My lover? Are you – have you lost your reason? Matt's my sister's husband."

"So that makes it a family concern an' relieves you of guilt, does it?"

"I met him by chance. He wished to ask after my health an' to tell me about Anna."

"Did it take him a quarter of an hour, hidden in the pig-yard?"

"We only sheltered there out of the snow."

"Do you deny that you've been meeting Sinclair in secret?"

"I deny it most emphatically."

Elspeth had so far kept her distance lest James forget himself completely and strike her down. Now she came forward, placatingly. She had always known that he was proud and jealous but had not imagined him to be completely irrational. The chance meeting with Matt would make her eventual confession almost impossible. Any hope she had nurtured that James would understand vanished.

She said quietly, "James, I don't care for Matt Sinclair. He's nothin' to me except Anna's husband. I haven't seen him for months."

James caught her by the nape of the neck. He shook her violently, so violently and unrelentingly that her ears rang and her teeth chattered and whorls of red danced and flickered in front of her eyes. For an instant she thought he might break her neck but suddenly he flung her from him with such force that she fell to the carpet. James Moodie's madness was a poison in the air. It took hold of Elspeth too. She imagined she felt forming limbs shrink softly within her and heard the anxious cry of the unborn. She clasped her forearms across her stomach and struggled to her feet.

She had no temper to speak of, not like Anna, but she was caught in James's fury and hurled words back at him at the pitch of her voice. She no longer thought of the servants, of Matt or Michael. All the pent-up frustrations and in-turned guilts of the past eighteen months burst forth in a torrent.

"What if I had?" she screamed. "What if I had deceived you? Have you not deceived me? Am I not your wife? Am I not young and – pretty? You've never loved me, no, nor wanted to love me."

"I told you before, I cannot."

"You should have told me before you proposed marriage, before you let me wed you."

"I gave you no –"

"You made me a false promise."

"No promise of – of *that*."

"Would it not be understood that in a marriage I would share your bed, that we might have children?"

"Do not say it, Elspeth."

"Is the thought so abhorrent to you?"

"I've provided you with –"

"Everything except what marriage means."

James shouted, "Do you need to be taken, like a damned ewe in the season?"

"I'd hoped I would be worth loving. If I had found a man who found me worth loving, would I be wrong to respond? God, James, but if I've learned how to deceive, I learned it from you and no other."

"So you admit Sinclair –"

"What if it *is* true?" Elspeth cried. "If Matt Sinclair has played husband with me, it's more than you've ever done."

"But I *am* your husband.'

"You are not. You find me abhorrent."

"Elspeth, I love you."

"Aye, James Moodie, you have to shout it because you never will whisper it while you hold me in your arms."

Something in that remark stung him, swung his mood into irrational fury once more.

He stepped quick and caught her arm, swung her round and caught her hair, pressing her down, shaking her with even more violence than before. Again Elspeth felt a shrinking inside her. She screamed, twisted, caught his wrist, twisting in a frenzy, and bit the pad of flesh at the base of his thumb.

James uttered a groaning sigh as if she had kissed him, giving pleasure and not pain. But he did not release her. Blood weltered her lips and still he held her. She had never lost control before, had never experienced such emotions, black and alluring. But as Elspeth dug her teeth into the weaver's flesh, she felt as if she were snapping a cord, biting it apart as midwiving shepherds did with lambs.

At length the pain became too much to bear. James shook her free. Blood poured from the wound, dripped to the carpet. He brought the hand up to his face, looked at it and then at Elspeth. For a fleeting moment she exulted in a sense of power over him. The little babe lay safe and secret still in her body. Memories of Michael were preserved like rose-petals in her heart. She was, after all, a lass from hard hill country and had the strength of a hill-child in her. James could not destroy her, short of murder.

She dabbed at her lips with her sleeve.

Motionless, James stared at the ooze of blood from the tear in his hand, his madness apparently discharged.

Then pain came into Elspeth, sweeping through her stomach and loins. Nausea rose behind her breastbone. She retched, holding on to the sofa, retched again. The sudden grip of the sickness shocked her into sweat.

James barely seemed to notice her distress or, if he did, remained indifferent to it. He rotated his bleeding fist, staring fixated at the coagulating blood. He glanced at Elspeth then returned to contemplation of his injury with a puzzled little frown.

"James. Help – me."

"What ails you?" he asked, casually.

"I'm – I'm unwell."

He tutted and, shaking his head, stalked to the door of the library.

He called out for Tolland, who came swiftly.

"My wife appears to be ill. Assist her to her bedroom and have – what's the girl's name –"

"Kerr, is it?" said Tolland.

"Aye, have Kerr attend her."

"Will I send for the physician, Mister Moodie?"

"Over-excitement, that's all it is," said James.

Without offering assistance, he watched Tolland, aided by Kerr, get Elspeth to her feet and out of the library into the hallway. From the door he watched them escort her up the staircase. He watched the bedroom door close.

It was dark in the house now, though falling snow seeped a ghastly grey light into the library. Out of the tunnel of the kitchen corridor came a maid-servant bearing a taper from which to light the candles about the place.

At the top of the stairs Tolland appeared. He picked dainty steps through semi-darkness towards the taper which the maid-servant held aloft. Tolland waved the girl away into the dining-room and advanced towards the master who, still with one hand cradled in the other, waited at the library door.

Tolland made no comment about the wound which bled obviously and profusely, blood making a soft pat-pat-pat upon the polished boards.

"The mistress is lying down, sir, but she's in great discomfort an' is weepin' sore."

"The maid's with her, is she not?"

Tolland paused. "It's a doctor she's needin', Mister Moodie."

"A doctor?"

"I have seen such events before."

James shook his head as if to clear it. The violence of the past few minutes seemed to have stunned him and robbed him of his ability to concentrate. "What 'events', Tolland?"

"I think, sir, she might be in danger of losin' the bairn."

"Bairn? What bairn?" James Moodie asked.

Tolland had turned the colour of old milk. He stammered, "I mean – I mean – I mean the fever may affect the mistress when it comes to bearin' a child."

"I didn't know you were expert in midwifery, Tolland."

"Shall I not send for Mister Carstairs?"

"In this weather an' at this hour? No, we'll wait until morning, by which time, I'm sure, my wife'll have fully recovered."

"Mister Carstairs –"

"No more of this nonsense, Tolland. My wife's upset because I had cause to reprimand her for wilfulness."

"I beg your pardon, Mister Moodie."

"Bairn, indeed!" James lifted his wounded hand and displayed it to the steward. "What you may best do is fetch me a bowl of clean water and a cloth. I'll be in my room. Also, I think, a pair of dry hose an' breeches."

"Aye, Mister Moodie."

"And where are the lights?" James shouted. "Bring me a damned light this instant."

Elspeth was conscious when Tolland slipped into her bedroom. She had never seen the steward harassed before. He behaved as if she were already dead.

Finger to his lips, Tolland whispered, "He'll have none o' the doctor, Kerr. I'm thinkin' he's gone loony, at last. God, but it's like a hospice here. How is she now?"

Kerr leaned over the bed.

Elspeth lay on her back on the top of the clothes, legs drawn up a little and knees parted. She had taken off her damp outer garments but still wore petticoats, shift and bodice. It was warm in the bedroom for the fire burned brightly, casting animate shadows about the chamber and flickering reflections in the window glass.

Tolland glanced behind him as if he expected the master to storm into the room at any moment. It was not a place where a steward should be found, not with the mistress of the house in such immodest condition.

Kerr said, "Are ye feelin' better?"

"I'm cold," Elspeth whispered.

"I'll get ye under the blankets in a minute."

Tolland approached. Elspeth looked up at him.

"Did you tell my husband I need a doctor?" she asked.

"Aye, but he'd have none of it."

"Didn't you tell him I was ill?"

"Tomorrow, he said that tomorrow'd do."

Elspeth felt a little easier now, though she could not get warm and the heavy pain on the insides of her thighs remained.

Tolland held his head to one side, trying not to look at her. He said, "Did you not tell him?"

"No."

"Why ever not, Mistress Moodie?"

"I wanted t' be sure first."

"How far are you gone?"

"Three months, close to."

"A bad time, a bad time," said Tolland.

Kerr said, "For a man wi'out a wife, you seem well versed in female secrets, Mister Tolland."

245

"I was the first o' nine bairns. I saw my mother cast three and I can remember it clearly. I know what it is, Mistress Moodie. But if you lie very quiet an' still for a while it might knit and settle again."

Kerr snorted. "Ye missed your callin', Mister Tolland. I'd never have guessed at such knowledge."

"Guard your tongue, girl," Tolland said. "Put your hand to her brow, see if she has sweat."

Kerr placed a calloused palm on Elspeth's brow. Even the touch felt soothing.

James may have abandoned her but she had not been deserted by those of her own kind. All the anxieties which had troubled her had been swept aside as her mind fixed on the realisation that she might lose Michael's child, that nature, in recompense for sin, might rob her of the only thing that she had ever truly wanted. The need to bear was as fierce and hot in her as fire in a forge. She knew that she was being shaped and tempered by it. She must not give in, not to pain, not to James, not to anything.

Tolland and Kerr whispered by the fire. The sound seemed unrelated to the travail of the past hours.

Elspeth turned her eyes, not moving her head, and saw firelight in the uncurtained window and, drifting thick against the glass, the blue-white snow. She felt pain ebb, become duller, hardly an ache and, as she looked out at the whirl of flakes against the sky, felt her body grow warmer and heavier, her lids heavy and sleepy. The sound of the servants' voices was like a lullaby, like hearing again the crooning talk of Coll and Gaddy in the cosy corner by the hearth.

Elspeth could not converse with a cold upright stone in a kirkyard in the broad light of day but, as she slipped down into sleep that night she was child enough still to murmur, "Mammy, help me, please."

The cotton shift was pasted to Anna's limbs with sweat. It wrinkled about her thighs as she lay against the bolster in the monstrous four-poster which, Randall had told her, had been a breeding-ground for three generations of Bontines. She felt heavy and sated. She had been with Randall in the soft feather bed, its brocade curtains closed, for two hours or more. She had pleasured him with sinuous tricks which nobody had taught to her but which, as far as she was concerned, were the birthright of any full-blooded young woman.

Randall was experienced and the couplings in the late afternoon had become the pivot of his day. He had never believed that breeding was the sole purpose of love-making but neither had he believed that he might be entrapped by it, drawn into a dangerous emotional need for one woman, a drover's daughter at that.

"What's the hour?" said Anna.

Pouring wine from a bottle, Randall stood naked by the fire. Anna admired his cord-like muscles, his lean, whipped-down build. She never tired of admiring him. It was not just that he was strong, but also a thoroughbred, as fine and well-glossed as his own stallion, quick too and tireless. They played on each other, the laird and the girl, caught in a skein of physical desire from which neither could escape, nor wanted to.

"Long after dusk." Randall lifted himself precariously on tiptoe and peered through the small breast-high casement. "God, but it's snowing with fair weight now. I hope my instruction was obeyed and the Cheviots brought to cover."

"How long after dusk?"

"About six of the clock, I reckon."

Anna laughed. "Tonight Hunter'll not swallow any tale at all. I came to help Dunn brush cloaks an' overcoats in your cupboard, remember."

"Dunn will be fast asleep in the library, curled up in front of the fire."

"With the key turned in the lock?"

"For sure."

"He's jealous of me, ye know."

Randall brought a glass of wine to the bed and handed it to Anna. As she reached to pluck it from his fingers he slipped his hand beneath her breast caressingly.

"Dunn has every reason to be jealous, don't you think?"

"Och, let me have my drink in peace, Randall," Anna purred. She sipped from the glass. "What sort of stuff is this?"

"Claret."

She slid out her tongue, touched it to the surface of the wine and rubbed it upon her upper lip, wetting it, then she leaned forward and kissed him upon the chest.

"I'll have to go, Randall."

"Not until I dismiss you, Sinclair."

"My husband'll be waitin' for his supper, fumin', no doubt."

"Will he make love to you tonight?"

Anna drew back in mock horror. "What sort o' question's that for a gentleman to ask a lady?"

"Will he?"

"Perhaps."

"Will you enoy it?"

"Mister Bontine, I prefer t' be discreet, if you've no objection." She drank again. "I trust you're not invitin' me to make comparisons."

"I've nothing to fear from comparisons," said Randall. "Have I?"

Anna pushed the wineglass at him and rolled from the bed. "Enough of this, sir. I'll need to be awa'."

Randall watched as she padded to the chair where she had thrown her clothes.

"If you were forced to make a choice, which of us would you choose?" he said.

Anna said, "Neither."

"Neither?"

She sat on a rush chair and furled her stockings over her legs.

"If I was a spinster after a husband," she said, "I'd be makin' up to – let me see – to somebody of the calibre of Mister Rudge."

"Rudge? Who is he? Oh, yes, Moodie's manager. Why, in Heaven's name, someone like Rudge?"

"He would keep me in style. An' he would appreciate me."

"I appreciate you."

"But I'm just a servant t' you, an' nothin' will ever change that."

Randall sat up. He was silent for a moment, deploying a variety of answers, choosing the correct one. Behind him – he glimpsed the movement out of the corner of his eye – Anna had stopped dressing. She glanced at him expectantly.

Randall uttered a little grunt, pushed himself to his feet, walked to the fireplace and turned to face her. Hastily Anna resumed her toilet. Her shift was tucked up into her lap and displayed the full, smooth thighs, pale above brown stockings.

"No," he said. "Nothing can change that – for the present. Particularly as you already have a husband."

"Husband or not," said Anna with a sigh, "I'll still be just a servant o' the laird, at your beck an' call. When I get too old t' please you, you'll send me out to the fields an' hoist another young lassie from the dairy for your pleasure."

"Of course I will."

Randall grinned.

"Devil, so you are," said Anna.

"No, Anna, you're the devil. You have me thoroughly bewitched. There's no help for our situation, however, and I would be grateful if you would not tease me on that score. God knows, I've a careless attitude to opinion but I am a landed gentleman."

"Aye, I know it."

"Even if I did decide to throw discretion to the winds, you'd never be accepted as a lady."

"Because I'm a dirty tyke from the servants' hall, I suppose?"

"Because my position entails obligations."

"Obligations t' who?"

"Society."

"What society? There's precious little society worth the name round here. You dinna hob-nob wi' the Edmonstones or the Duke."

Indicating that the turn in the conversation irritated him, Randall went to the chair where his clothes were folded and began to dress.

Anna stepped into her skirt, hopping.

"You can always send me back t' my husband," she said.

"Do you imagine I like having to share you?"

She flaunted her hips and tossed her head. "Better a bit o' me than –"

"In Spain," said Randall, "I could have bought you."

"Made a slave of me?"

"There are no slaves in Spain. For a few *pesetas*, you could have been mine."

"What would 'society' have t' say to that?"

"I would have had a handsome, upright lady for my wife, of course, and she would have borne me children in wedlock and have behaved with extreme modesty and decorum."

"While you an' your bought woman –"

"Scotland is not, alas, Spain," put in Randall.

"Do you believe it would have been the same between us if you'd bought me?"

"I'd have paid a high price for you, Anna."

It was Anna's turn to be irritated.

"A thousand gold guineas wouldn't be enough," she said.

"You have a good conceit of yourself."

"Is there not a sayin' among soldiers that a volunteer is worth a thousand pressed men in the heat o' battle?"

"I've never heard it," said Randall. "Pressed men learn discipline. Pressed men suffer no illusions. Now I think of it, it is volunteers who most often desert in the face of the enemy."

Fully clad now, Anna came close to the laird to share the oval mirror with him, primping at her hair as she fitted it tidily under the servants' mutch. Randall was grooming his side-whiskers which, Anna noticed, had a trace of grey in them here and there. He was not old, of course, but in comparison to Matt, a man of considerable maturity. As a lover she could imagine no better.

Randall glanced at her.

"You are not intending to desert me, Anna, are you?"

She leaned and bumped her brow gently against his.

"No, because you're not the enemy," she said.

He took her in his arms and kissed her.

"I've no other woman, Anna, and need nor want none."

"I'm glad t' hear it."

"Even though I am the master of Ottershaw and possessor of an inherited title, however, I can't do as I wish."

"What do you wish?"

"I wish that I might marry you."

"Words come cheaper than slaves in Spain, I think," said Anna.

"It's true," Randall assured her. "I'd have you as you are."

"Would you?"

"I swear I would. But you already have a husband and I doubt that young Sinclair will divorce you, no matter how hard he is pressed to do so."

"Pressed even by the laird?"

"Particularly by the laird."

"Aye, that's true."

Randall had taken the subject as far as he dared. He released her, spun her round and patted her behind.

"Go back to Hunter now. I'll waken Dunn."

"But the coats haven't been brushed at all."

"The coats do not need brushing. I haven't had one of them on my back for months. Go, Anna, before your husband comes in search of you."

"He'll be still abroad wi' his drinkin' cronies, like as not."

"Pad Tomelty's messengers, I presume."

"What do you know of Pad Tomelty?"

"Only that he sells excellent whisky at a reasonable price. That my foresters are paid more by the Irishman than they are by me, which is, perhaps, fair as they appear to spend more time working for Tomelty than for the benefit of Ottershaw."

Anna laughed and shook her head.

"Aye, you're a funny one for a laird, Mister Bontine."

"No insolence, Sinclair."

"Tomorrow?"

"If it can be discreetly negotiated."

Randall Bontine kissed her once more, unlocked the bedroom door and let her out into the corridor. He noticed that the candles had been lighted and wondered which of the servants had stolen along the passageway with the taper and what that servant had heard.

To his surprise he found that he did not much care.

Damn the servants, damn her husband. He must have her at whatever the cost; he needed her now like a drug.

"Good night," she whispered from the door at the top of the stairs.

"Good night, my love," said Randall.

Matt was not at the Ramshead or Black Bull boozing with disreputable associates, nor was he skulking at home in Pine Cottage. Matt, in fact, was hunched on a stool in the kitchen of Ottershaw House where, for an hour or so, he had been lying in wait for his wife.

Field-hands, men from the yards, and relatives of resident servants were forbidden to cross the threshold of the house. But Mrs Lacy, with a wee twitch of malice, had persuaded Hunter that Lachlan Sinclair's boy was an exception to the general rule and welcomed him in to warm himself until such time as Anna had completed her duties and was dismissed. Mrs Lacy did not waste time. She put little questions to Matt, trying to discover if he knew what was going on between the laird and his good lady wife.

Matt, who had taken more liquor at the inn, felt quite at ease. He was astute enough to realise that Mrs Lacy was a prying old bitch so did not rise to her questions. He kept his head down and supped the bowl of soup that was served him and did not appear to be in the least concerned that his wife was not in evidence.

When Brigit Tomelty flitted through the kitchen from the tub-room, which was as cold as the North Pole that afternoon, Matt merely grunted to acknowledge her greeting, though he eyed the swish and strut of her hips as she went down the corridor.

If Mrs Lacy had been less bound to the big house she might have heard village gossip and have kept a closer watch on Matt when the Tomelty lass was about, might have intercepted the one direct look each gave the other and the little wink that was exchanged between them. Mrs Lacy, however, had given up on Matt by that time and had marked him down as even more dour than his father.

Hunter, on the other hand, felt obliged to offer Matt sympathetic excuses every now and again, at the risk of making matters worse.

"She's brushin' coats. It takes a fair time if it's done thoroughly," Hunter explained.

"Aye."

"There's only her an' a lad at it, do you see?"

"Aye."

And later, "Mister Gilbert's wife must have checked her, I fear."

And Mrs Lacy, "Aye, or the laird."

And later still, Hunter said, "It'll soon be time for his dinner. I'll need to find out if he wants it up or down."

One of the two young kitchen-hands who were peeling apples in a corner of the kitchen sniggered. Mrs Lacy shouted at her to keep her mouth closed and her fingers busy if she didn't want a smack with a spurtle.

Throughout all this Matt waited, warm by the hearth, with

an expression of inscrutable innocence – or stupidity – upon his face.

It was almost a quarter to seven before Anna burst into the kitchen from the back stairs and, already chattering excuses, was confronted by her husband.

Matt rose, pushing himself up with hands on thighs.

Mouth agape, Anna froze.

"What – what're you doin' here?"

"I came in early, since it was snowin'."

"Oh! How – how long've you been here?"

"Long enough."

Wreathed in steam from a braised-beef pan, Mrs Lacy observed the meeting with delight. She could imagine what bruises Anna would receive when Matt got her home and, as there was no love lost between the cook and the upstart girl, Mrs Lacy hoped that he might leather her so hard she would lose her attraction for the laird, at least for a day or three.

Matt, however, was smiling.

It was a pleasant smile too, and did not, to the cook, seem insincere.

"Did you not see Sir Randall?" Mrs Lacy had only recently begun to use the title which the soldier had inherited, without apparent merit, from his father.

"He looked in. Took Dunn away with him into the other room," said Anna.

Hunter had had enough of manoeuvring and petty intrigue. He had a dinner to see to.

"Tomorrow, Sinclair," said Hunter, as the young woman wrapped herself in her shawl, "leave early from your house so you're not late."

"Aye, Mister Hunter."

"Good night to you, Sinclair."

Matt grunted and, ushering Anna before him, went out of the kitchen and through the tub-room and into the corner of the kitchen yard.

To Anna's surprise snow lay thick as fluffed fleece and was falling steadily as if it might forget to stop. The air had a muffled, anticipatory quality, a true winter's night, not nipping cold but liquid-thick in the mouth and nostrils.

With Matt's hand on her shoulder, the couple strolled home by the path that cut the angle of the back lawns and the vegetable garden and forked into the pines. There was a road to cross, which carriages used, and then the path narrowed. Matt steered her ahead of him. She felt comfortable in her weariness, stimulated by the snow, by changed shapes and altered contours, by the heaviness of pine boughs laden and sagging. Even so she had her guard ready to pull up, lies prepared, ready to fob Matt off, convince him that any stories he might have heard were just hall gossip.

But Matt said not a word, did not scowl and tut at the embered fire or the cluttered state of the cottage. He lifted the lid of the soup pot and stuck his head down to sniff the coagulated substance within and then shook the kettle to see if it needed filling and knelt by the hearth and soon had kindling crackling and split logs ready.

It was over an hour before broth bubbled and a shank of mutton knocked on the lid of the big, round, iron pan. Anna had a fresh piece of cheese for him, though, bought from Mr Hunter since that was one privilege day-servants had, to save them fretting about shopping for provisions. It was a generous wedge, enough for two at least. Anna put it out with bannocks that were not too pale with age. By now it was after nine o'clock, the fire had burned up and the room was hot.

But Matt did not peel off his jacket and his vest, did not even remove his boots. He ate in his outdoor rig, drank whisky and hot water while seated in the box chair with a splinter of wood in his mouth to loosen meat tabs from between his teeth. He looked restless as if he were one of those birds that could not roost but flew about all night long and slept only on the wing.

"Are ye not o'er warm, Matt?"

"I'm fine."

"Sit back."

He ignored her.

She would have touched him, stroked his brow, but feared a rebuff or worse.

It was three weeks since he had taken her to bed, then it had been almost by accident since he was fuddled with drink and hardly seemed to know who she was.

For some minutes Matt sat staring into the flames. The three big unstripped logs burned with a hiss, bark peeling in ornate patterns.

He got up abruptly, making Anna, still at table, start.

He paid her no heed whatsoever but kicked round the box chair and climbed upon it and took down Jacko's cage from the rafters. He stepped to the floor with the wicker cage in his hands, the little door, untied, swinging sadly on its hinges. Though his back was to her, Anna sensed that he was weeping undemonstratively. She cowered at the table, afraid that he was about to round on her. Had he found out about Jacko? Oddly, that little crime – of which she was innocent – tormented her worse than adultery with the laird.

Elbows cocked, the muscles of his wrists thickened. She heard the dry crackle of wicker as he tore the wooden sides from the box. Even beneath his heavy jacket she could see his shoulders grow massive with effort. Then the joinings made a crisp tearing sound and the cage expanded like a concertina. Matt slammed his fists into it, flattening it, roof and floor sliding up and down, then he lowered it, trod on it, crushed it until it was no shape at all.

Anna did not move.

Matt stretched and, oblivious to scorching flames, set the wreckage firmly on top of the logs.

"He won't come back," Mat declared. "Even if he does, I don't want him now."

"Och, if he came in the door, lookin' for –"

"I don't want him, d' ye hear?"

"Aye, Matt."

He swung round. His cheeks were fiery. But he did not roar at her as she expected. He spoke positively, in a manly sort of tone.

"How much did you pay the packman for him?"

He had never asked that question before.

"I'd some money from Mammy. I never stole from the keep."

"I dinna care where it came from. How much did you pay the bloody packman?"

"I –"

"Tell me, Anna."

His brow was dappled with sweat and his eyelashes moist with tears. He wiped his palm across them, then looked straight at her.

She said, "It was – Matt, I gave Jacko t' you as a gift."

"Aye, Jacko's all you ever gave me, Anna."

"Ten shillin's. I paid ten shillin's."

Matt nodded, turned and went out of the cottage.

She realised that he had not left her, that he would return, though she could hear nothing of where he went or what he was doing at the back of the cottage. She watched snowflakes fall, staring at them until it seemed that they formed an impenetrable fabric, like bridal lace.

Matt came back with a half-gallon keg under one arm which Anna had never seen before. He set it on the table, took out his grafting knife and prised off the lid. He tipped the keg like a jug and spilled coins across the table. Shillings, florins, crowns large and glittering among humble brown pennies and shy sixpences; Matt rummaged among the coins, deftly picking out ten shillings. He lowered the keg level with the table's edge and, with the crook of his elbow and flat of his hand, swept the rest back into the container. He punched the lid down with three blows of his fist. Ten shillings remained upon the table.

"Paid," he said.

Anna hesitated. "Why?"

"Because now I owe you nothin', Anna."

"In that case," she reached out, lifted the coins and closed them into her palm, "in that case, Matt, I'll take them an' give you thanks."

Matt nodded again, curtly, and with the keg under one arm swept his bonnet from the nail on the door and walked out of the cottage carrying his treasure with him into the snow.

EIGHT

Paying the Piper

Later, when it was all over, Elspeth could not make up her mind whether James had hoped that she would miscarry or if he had already entered that state of mental confusion which would manifest itself so horribly in the autumn months. For whatever reason, James did nothing for her during the eight days of the snow.

Long days they were too, though not tedious. She needed much concentration to keep herself relaxed, to check the frantic concerns which entered her thoughts and which might affect the tranquillity of the foetus within her. She had a vision of it, not as a mass of ganglion and tendons like thrown calves and lambs she had seen in byre and pasture, but as already quite human in appearance, a tiny perfect infant floating in a sac of milky fluid. She believed that it was already cognisant of her thoughts and feelings and that if it sensed ill-will or hostility through her then it would whimper and mew and drown itself, somehow, and she would expel it dead from her body.

During the course of the snow, when the villages were locked in on themselves by drifting on the turnpikes, and not even a horseman could struggle from Balnesmoor to Ottershaw, let alone to Harlwood or Balfron, she saw little of James. She knew that he was avoiding her, keeping away from her bedroom. He made one brief visit each day, carefully choosing the noon hour so that he might appear in outdoor togs and claim that he had important 'business' to attend to so could not stay long with her. He would remain for five minutes only, not even sitting down and he would not allow Kerr to leave the room, thus preventing unwelcome confidences between him and his wife.

"How do you feel today?"

"Somewhat better, James. But I'll stay in bed a while longer."

"This weather's treacherous. Bed's the best place. It would never do if you got up prematurely an' contracted a chill. Believe me, there's nothing to get up for."

"I usually like snow."

"Not in your present delicate health. Have you eaten? Did you have breakfast?"

"Cook sent up a bowl of rice an' milk, which I enjoyed."

"I'll find you a jar of honey, if I can."

"Where, James? Can you get out far in this weather?"

"Rudge is stuck at home but McAlpin forged his way up from Kennart yesterday to assure me that all's well at the mill."

"And you, can you ride there yet?"

"Dear me, no! But there's a way by foot, apparently, down the line of Ingram's wood, where the trees have kept the snow thin. I'm to go along the river-bank, for a drift of snow as tall as a plough-horse has blocked the brig on this side."

"How will you cross the river?"

"On the ice."

"James, please take care."

"Have no fear for me, Elspeth."

He would kiss her on the brow and she would sense the tension in him, read in his eye the sullen fear that their sham marriage would soon be shattered. He kept his promise, however, and brought her a tub of honeycomb next morning and on the following day a box of dried apricots. But he came only once in the day, never in the evening. It was as if dusk brought a special darkness to his heart, a darkness which Elspeth could no longer dispel. She missed him, in spite of her fear of him.

Tolland stood in for his master, showed genuine concern and sympathy, fussed over her during the eight days of doubt. Kerr too proved a loyal friend, as if, in separation from James, Elspeth had drifted back into the circle of labourers and servants, common folk to whom trouble was indigenous.

On Wednesday Elspeth awakened to the drip of thaw. She lay on her side for a while, listening, then popped her head above the blankets. The wind was strong but now it beat from the west, and had chased away the easterly's dry cold. She heard the spat of sleet upon the pane, wet and clinging, and a hiss of snow sliding in a lump from the slates. She sat up, hugging the blankets, but found that the bedroom was warm though the fire had died.

At that moment Kerr entered.

"Kerr, is it thawin'?"

"Och, so you're awake. Aye, it's a lovely runnin' thaw, thank Providence. If the wind holds warm it'll free most roads by evenin', so Mister Tolland says."

"Open the curtains, please."

Kerr pulled back the drapes. Almost forgetting that she had taken to bed in considerable pain, Elspeth eased herself to the floor and walked across to the casement.

Cloud scudded over Drumglass and trailed mist across the moor. The Orrals looked like slabs of pudding, ribbed with pouring cream. She saw, to her delight, red deer heading upwards from the dwellings, a sign that thaw would soon expose crop for them on the safety of the hill. On the Dyers' Dyke Macfarlane had let out ewes to stretch in a fenced paddock that hung on the slope below the farm.

After Kerr put a robe about Elspeth's shoulders and slipped kidskins on to her feet to keep her warm she left her by the window while she cleaned out and kindled the fire. Experimentally, Elspeth walked about the bed while Kerr, pretending not to, kept a weather-eye on her mistress.

When the maid went downstairs with the ashes-pail Tolland was waiting for her in the corridor.

"She's up and seems fine," Kerr reported.

"Even so," said Tolland, "if he doesn't fetch Carstairs today t' make certain then I'll have Luke McWilliams ride over t' Harlwood tomorrow wi' a letter for the woman."

"Is Miss Blaven back from Glasgow, have ye heard?"

"I haven't heard," said Tolland. "From what you've told me, if she's at home she'll make every effort t' come here."

"Because it might be *his* bairn?"

"None o' that, Kerr. Not a blessed word about that," Tolland said sternly. "We've neither the right nor the evidence to go leapin' to such conclusions."

"But I saw him," Kerr insisted. "He was keepit out our way but I did see him once – and he was more than a laddie, I can tell ye, Mister Tolland."

"Whatever he was, the poor chap's dead an' buried and

that's the end of it," said Tolland. "Miss Blaven's the only person who might help the mistress."

"Shall I tell her upstairs?"

"Certainly not," said Tolland.

All day long the wind sloughed from the west. Sleet turned to heavy rain and the drifts shrank, washing the roadways with mud and swiftly filling the rivers. Mr Rudge managed to ride down from his house in Drymen to begin parcelling three large consignments of tartan cloth for shipment to Jamaica, via the Glasgow agents of Pirie & Ure. To Rudge's gratification McAlpin, in his enthusiasm, had already begun weighing and had checked each piece through against its pattern, for the folk in Kingston, Jamaica, were said to be very knowledgeable about strict Highland fashion.

James had been abroad early. Again he was obliged to go on horseback for the roads would certainly not accommodate a carriage, even a gig. As had become his habit, he went alone and without informing anyone where he might be found.

First he rode to Ottershaw and, without troubling the laird, looked over the Cheviot flock to see that it had survived the blizzard, which it had, admirably. Relieved that Sir Randall had not given him short weight in the matter of tending, James took a path through the woods on to a wind-scoured little ridge which led him to the flats by Wrassle's farm where, as he had anticipated, he encountered young Wattie McGowan on a shaggy, hoof-sure pony, with the Drymen postbags strapped about him.

From his greatcoat pocket James extracted a sealed letter which he had penned the previous evening and handed it to Wattie who glanced at the address to calculate the rate.

"Kilsyth, Mister Moodie. Aye, it might be a day or two afore we can get there since the snow's still dense behin' the Campsies."

"Whenever you can, Wattie." James paid over the postage charge. "There's no great urgency."

"Will ye have goods goin' out the day, Mister Moodie?"

"If the thaw continues we'll try a load for Glasgow tomorrow."

"It's bad beyond Blanefield. Eight days we lost. Daddy went out yesterday an' never got further than the tilt beyond Ottershaw."

Weaver and carrier rode together for a half-mile, following the thread of brown mud which exposed the crown of the road. They parted in spitting sleet. James swung north towards the mill which he could see, smoking like a dung-heap, around the river bend.

Sleet and then rain drove him to shelter for the rest of the day in Mr Rudge's office. He spent time upon the walks of the mill itself chatting, amicably enough, with weavers whom he thought of as companions in the craft, though they thought of him in other less charitable terms. Throughout the afternoon rain undermined the snow and washed it down into the ground where the frost sat deep and hard in the grassroots and the whole of the Lennox thrummed with the sounds of thaw and the mill-wheel thrashed in the lade like something demented.

In the dusk James went up over the bridge, which had been shovelled out to clear a route for the cloth-carts, and up the Kennart road to Balnesmoor. On arrival at Moss House he did not go upstairs to look in on Elspeth nor did he enquire of the steward as to his wife's state of health. He retired immediately to the study off the kitchen where Tolland brought him a change of clothing and a bowl of hot broth and, with no exchange at all between master and servant, left the weaver to brood until supper-time.

The following morning, as soon as James had gone out, the steward dispatched Luke McWilliams on a stout pony to Harlwood with a short, informal note to Miss Blaven of Preaching Friar.

At noon, awkwardly riding side-saddle on a hired mare, the formidable Miss Blaven arrived, mud-spattered and scowling, to call on James Simpson Moodie's wife.

Widow Trotter, who had once been a wet-nurse to Randall, was one victim of the blizzard. Sinclair made certain that she had the best of attention. He ordered the foresters to clean out the corner of her one-roomed cottage, where a pile of rubble had fallen in through the roof, and mend the beams with seasoned timber.

At noon Matt tipped a wink to McDonald and received a nod of sanction. The foresters would soon be hiding out to eat their dinners and drink a tot or two and Matt would not be missed.

Matt took himself along the road to Pad Tomelty's cottage which was tucked away like a midden behind the more respectable dwellings. The door was not only closed but barred and sackcloth curtains hung untidily over the two spyglass windows. Matt knocked boldly. After some shuffling and whispering within a youthful voice asked who was there. Matt gave his name loudly. The door was unbarred and a small, square, bellicose face peered round the jamb at him. This, Matt knew, was Colm, one of Pad's sons. The ten-year-old had the features of an adult wise already in the ways of the world.

"Whit're ye wantin'?"

"Is your father in?"

"He's verra much occupied."

"I'll not keep him long."

With manifest reluctance young Colm Tomelty allowed Matt to squeeze into the cottage.

The place did not smell of humanity, of bedding and broth, but reeked of solder and flexion which told Matt that metalwork was being done upon the premises.

Pad seemed delighted to see his protégé and had Colm fetch meat and whisky for refreshment. A stool stood before the fire and a low table at which Pad sat cross-legged like a cobbler. It wasn't a brogue or a patten which occupied the last but a sheet of thin copper.

The remaining parts of the assembly required for distillation were scattered about the room; stillhead, receiver and worm. From under the cooking-pots on the fire protruded the handle of a brazing-iron. A bowl of tiny rivets chittered on the hob. It was typical of the Irishman to waste no time but to prepare for the coming season when barley would again be plentiful and he could extend his 'dumps' back towards Aberfoyle from whence, a year or two ago, he had been routed by King's officers.

"Tell me, Pad, what it would take to learn how to make the vital waters, as you do yoursel'?" Matt said.

Colm, at ten, snorted. He had already learned that smugglers were born not made. His father silenced him with a tap from the hammer, gentle enough, on the side of his head.

"Patience," said Pad, "an' nerve."

"An' money?"

"Aye, that too."

"But it's not somethin' beyond the average man?"

"Oh, there are secrets to it." Pad put down his hammer, lifted aside the beaten panel which would soon form one third of a still. "Secrets to the makin' of whisky a man can drink wi'out re-gorgin' it on the spot."

"Would you teach me?"

Pad cocked his head. To some he would have seemed merely impish but Matt had been with Brigit often enough to recognise slyness.

Pad said, "Teach you t' abandon your prospects as a grieve an' take into the hills wi' me an' mine, is that what you ask, Matt Sinclair?"

"No," said Matt. "I'd wish t' buy an assembly from you, everythin' required t' distil a potable whisky on my own account."

"Heh, have ye such a big drouth then, lad?"

"I have a drouth for makin' money, Pad."

The smuggler shook his head. "But this's no trade for that, Matt. Do ye suppose I'm wallowin' in filthy lucre?" He waved his hand. "Does it seem so from the evidence o' your eyes?"

"Perhaps not, but you're a wheen richer than any tree-planter, an' don't pretend otherwise."

"Can ye face prison, if needs be?"

"Eh?"

"Prison, the jail at Stirlin'."

"Have you faced prison, Pad?"

"I've been shut awa' three times."

"I never knew that."

Pad shrugged as if it were not something worth bragging about. But he paused to smile and ruffle Colm's hair for the boy was beaming up at his father in admiration. To have suffered in a dungeon was, for the laddie, the true mark of manliness.

Pad said, "Did Brigit no' tell ye?"

"No, she did not."

"Tighter an' tighter the noose draws," said Pad.

Matt laughed uneasily. "Aye, Pad, but you canna convince me there's no profit t' be made in good liquor."

"It's not the makin', it's the sellin'."

"I've learned a bit about that already, have I not?"

Pad did not deny the young forester his conceit.

263

"I could build ye a still, all that'd be required," Pad ventured, "for a fair price since I know ye so well an' you're a close acquaintance o' my daughter."

"What sort o' price?"

"It's no' everybody who can construct such an intricate device as a whisky still," Pad went on. "It requires t' be dismantled at the double now an' then, packed neat for swift carryin' over rough country."

"How much, Pad?"

Pad leaned his elbows on the low table and squinted up at the young man. "There's only room enough for me an' mine in this part o' the world, Matt. I couldna impart wisdom an' sell a tangle o' gear t' a man who'd cut away the very foundations o' my livelihood."

"Compete wi' you?" said Matt. "I wouldn't have the gall. Nah, nah, it's away from here I'm wantin'."

"Easy t' make a mouth about it," said Pad.

"I'll take an oath on it."

Pad crept forward until the stool was canted and his shoulders had come so high that his elongated earlobes rested on them. He cupped chin in palms and contemplated the curved copper sheet before him as if it were a scree-ing glass. "What is it that ye really want, Matt?"

"Liberty t' journey where the wind blows me, an' make a decent shillin' on the way."

"Foresters can aye find work, here an' yonder."

"I'm no bloody forester," Matt declared. "Foresters have no respectability."

"Is it respectability or freedom you're after acquirin'?"

"Can I not acquire both?"

"Smugglin's hardly a respectable profession."

"I could be in one town today, another tomorrow, turnin' a guinea in each passin' spot."

"Matt, if ye heed an old man's advice, given in faith for the sake o' my daughter, you'll make your peace wi' Ottershaw an' give up this notion."

"That I'll not do, Pad."

Pad Tomelty clacked down the stool's hind leg. A girl child brought in a whisky jug, another carried a round tray with a platter of boiled fowl upon it. There was no seasoning, apart from a pick of salt, and the pieces of fowl dripped with greasy water. The strong brown taste of the whisky flavoured the bird, however, and with the platter between them forester and smuggler fell to.

Munching, Pad said, "What sort o' payment did ye have in mind, Matt, if I was to impart all the tricks o' the distiller's art?"

"An' supply the assembly?"

"Bright an' shiny," Pad promised.

He no longer looked even passing paternal. He had, after all, made one bid to dissuade young Sinclair from sticking his head in a noose. Now the price was there for him to grasp.

"What is it worth?" said Matt cautiously.

If Matt ate beef as he ate the boiled chicken, Pad Tomelty thought, it was small wonder he needed to set his aim at a rich man's income.

"Twenty pounds," Pad said.

"I dinna have as much."

"How much do you have?"

"Thirteen pounds."

Pad Tomelty ruminated on a fragment of fowl.

He swallowed and said, "It's not enough, Matt."

"What would be enough?"

"I'll sell ye the gear for fifteen," Pad said, "but it would be doin' you precious little good wi'out the knowledge."

"What's the price o' the knowledge?"

"Work for me, as you do now, for a year wi'out payment an' I'll instruct you in all the skills attendant on makin' a decent drop o' whisky."

The bargain was wholly fallacious. There was little enough to be learned about the process of distillation. Any Highland crofter could have shown Matt the ropes in three or four hours, given him the recipe; would have too, for a guinea in the fist.

But Pad Tomelty had no more scruples than his daughter. He was as well with the daft boy's money as anyone else, particularly since it was his efforts and energy that had generated the cash in the first place. In addition – Pad salved the slight itch of conscience with the thought – by binding the grieve's son for a further year he might prevent Sinclair doing something rash and irreversible. What Sinclair needed, Pad reckoned, was a pastime to take his mind off his wife's infidelities with the new laird of Ottershaw. Fifteen pounds was not an unfair price to ask for such a service.

"Will you make me a still at the end o' the time?" said Matt.

"I'll make ye the finest still there ever was, Matt," Pad Tomelty said with such sincerity that Matt felt as if he had been promised a kingdom.

He had seen with his own eyes how folk of all persuasions clamoured for illicit tipple, how Pad Tomelty throve in the providing of it. Matt felt as if his troubles were nearly over, the burden of woes which marriage to Anna Cochran had dumped upon his back would soon be lifted away, leaving him fleet and free as a stag on the high hills.

"I'll bring twelve pounds tonight," Matt said.

"Tonight?" said Pad.

"I want t' get started at once."

"Then here's my hand on it, young Matt."

"An' mine, Pad, an' mine."

As soon as Kerr was dismissed from the bedroom and the women were alone, Miss Blaven got up from the chair by the fireside and stalked to the side of the bed where Elspeth, dressed in a day-jacket and propped up by pillows, lay.

"You *are* pregnant, are you not?" Janet Blaven demanded.

"I am."

"What induced your house steward to send for me with such urgency?"

"Nothing," said Elspeth.

She had been astonished to see the woman from Preaching Friar, and not at all pleased. It had not taken her long, however, to deduce the truth. She could not blame Tolland and Kerr for conspiring in such a manner or question their good intentions. She too had thought, seven or eight days since, of sending for Miss Blaven who had the sort of knowledge of the body and its malfunctions that could only be found in the Killearn midwife, a person with whom Elspeth wanted no truck:

"Do you still have it?" The woman leaned over her, peering with steely spinster's eyes into her face.

"I don't understand what you mean?"

"I mean, girl, did you shed the foetus?"

"Miscarry?"

266

"Call it what you will; has it gone?"

"No."

"Are you certain of that?"

"Of course I'm certain. I'm not entirely ignorant in these matters, Miss Blaven."

"Has there been no doctor to see you?"

"I did not deem it necessary."

"It was hardly for you to choose, girl. Perhaps it is as well that Carstairs wasn't summoned since he would only have bled and dosed you with nitre. You've more chance of carrying your term without that young idiot's ministrations."

Carefully Elspeth said, "If my husband wishes Doctor Carstairs to attend me, of course I'll agree."

Janet Blaven scooped up her skirts and plumped herself down on the bed, so close that the clothes were tugged tight across Elspeth's body.

Miss Blaven spoke with whispered urgency. "It's Michael's child, is it not?"

"The child is my husband's, not Michael's."

The lie was more believable than the truth; it would prove so with everyone. Nobody would ever suppose that the marriage had been loveless.

Miss Blaven would not give up.

"When is the birth due?"

"In October," Elspeth lied.

The woman's lips moved soundlessly as she calculated.

Defiantly Elspeth kept silent.

"Are you sure?" said Miss Blaven.

"I can calculate from the night of conception."

"Hah!" The woman expelled breath as if she had been struck a blow to the diaphragm. "I thought – I'd hoped –"

Miss Blaven, Elspeth realised, would have destroyed her without a qualm to have saved Michael. She would destroy her mercilessly to claim the Blaven baby if the lie, like the pregnancy, survived its full term.

In that quarter-hour Elspeth saw how alike Janet Blaven and James Moodie were in several respects, how each used love for selfish ends. How well suited they would have been.

"Whatever you had hoped, Miss Blaven, I regret that the child I'm carryin' cannot possibly have been fathered by Michael."

"You regret –"

"Aye, I would have had part of him with me for ever."

"Instead you bear your husband a child."

"How can I help it?" said Elspeth. "I'm his wife. And Michael is dead. You've no claim on me, Miss Blaven, unless it's to reveal what occurred between Michael and me. I see no point in that unless malice for its own sake gives you pleasure."

"You were never a girl I would have chosen."

"You didn't choose me. Michael chose me."

"If there had been more time –"

"Speculation's useless, Miss Blaven."

"My, but you have a hard heart."

"No harder than your own."

"How dare you say that."

"To let me fall in love with him, be loved by him, knowin' that he would soon die."

"Is that what you think of me?"

"I think you did it for Michael, without a care for anyone's feelings."

"Time was so – so short."

"It may not seem so short for you now, Miss Blaven."

"I had you judged from the first. You did not love him. He was nothing to you but a diversion."

"Think what you like," said Elspeth. "I'm married to Mister Moodie and will quite soon be mother to his daughter or son."

Lips pursed, cheeks flushed, Miss Blaven pushed herself from the bedside.

"I could have helped you," she said.

"But only if Michael –"

"Let Carstairs earn his twenty guineas," said the spinster grimly. "I trust that we never have occasion to meet again."

"My maid will show you to your carriage, Miss Blaven," said Elspeth with rigid formality. "I give you thanks for callin' to enquire about my health."

Stiff-backed, Janet Blaven turned and quit the bedroom, leaving behind her, about the bedclothes, the dry aromatic odour of rue.

Elspeth was aware that the outcome might be disastrous but she had been steeled by the encounter with Miss Blaven and could delay no longer in breaking the news to her husband.

She kept herself calm, anticipated the worst, repeated under her breath a resolution not to reveal to him the father's identity, come what may. The news would not be wholly unexpected. Kerr had informed her of Tolland's 'indiscretion' in hinting that the mistress might be pregnant. James, whatever his faults, was no fool.

James returned home at half-past five o'clock. He would have repaired immediately to his study if Elspeth had not waylaid him in the hall. He was surprised to find her up and about, dressed in her finery, and followed her into the drawing-room.

He glanced at the wine, the plates of cake which, at Elspeth's request, Tolland had set out. "What's this? Are we expecting guests?"

"In a manner of speakin', James," said Elspeth.

"Explain yourself."

Agitatedly James prowled about, back and forth in front of the fireplace, the chair and sofa, his head turned in her direction but his eyes not meeting hers.

"I'm carryin' a child, James."

"Yes," he said, not loudly. "Yes, I had a notion that might be the case."

Elspeth kept very calm. "It's not, as we both know, your child. It'll be born in August, late in the month."

"So you can mark the date, can you?"

Elspeth was not deterred. "I think we must discuss the matter an' what you wish to do about it."

"I see, I see," James said silkily. "The father o' the bastard wishes me to take the blame."

"Blame?" said Elspeth. "It's not the word I'd choose. But, aye, since you've raised it, you must take the 'blame'."

"Have you 'discussed the matter' with your lover? What does he have t' say to it?"

"He has nothin' to say to it."

"Is he dumb? Is he a mute? Have you taken a mute t' your bed?"

"He has nothin' to say to it because he has not been told," said Elspeth. "In fact, he'll never know that the bairn is his."

"Who else have you told?"

"The servants have guessed." Elspeth hesitated. "Miss

Blaven called on me today, an' I think she guessed too, though I did not discuss it with her."

"Who else?"

"Nobody."

James put his arms behind his back, clasped his forearms with his fists and drew his shoulders forward. She had never seen him do this before for he was usually a settled man who would sit like a stone through any crisis.

Elspeth went on, "It wasn't my intention, ever, to deceive you, James. But then you deceived me. I expected true marriage. I wanted a child of my own."

"A bastard child!"

"I know that the baby's not of your blood, James, but in the eyes of the law and the kirk it need not be born a bastard. I'm your wedded wife and I'll say nothing."

"Aye, *you* might say nothing but what about *him*? He'll be clashin' tankards with his cronies, braggin' how he put horns on Jamie Moodie."

"No, he'll not. I promise. He canna."

"Can't you hear how they'll cackle, how they'll shout how the weaver couldn't spawn a bairn of his own on his spunky young wife?"

"James, nobody in Balnesmoor or elsewhere will hear such a thing. The man's gone."

"The devil he is!"

"Stop pacin' about," said Elspeth sharply. "Listen to me, please."

"I hear you, Elspeth. I hear your lies."

Nevertheless James ceased his frantic promenade and threw himself down upon the sofa, legs jutting out, fingers to his lips as if to check an uncontrolled tirade of recrimination.

Six months ago, before the Cunninghams crawled into Kennart to torment him, he would have been delighted at the prospect of becoming a grandfather. He would have feigned indignation but, in due course, he would have forgiven Elspeth, would have reared the child as his own. But the Cunninghams were coiled like vipers and would not allow him to rest with the lie, the standmark of incest which nurtured not love but corruption.

"If you wish me to leave you, then I'll do so," said Elspeth.

"An' go to join your lover, I suppose?"

"I canna."

"Because he's married," said James.

"Because he – because he's –"

"You'll take me for half my fortune in a separation, you an' him between you."

"I'd expect only enough to keep me alive until my baby's delivered an' I got strong enough to work."

"Work? You? In the fields, I suppose?"

James slid his hand from mouth to brow, covering his eyes.

How could he cast out Elspeth as he had cast out Bell? But it was not a matter of forgiveness. In marrying Elspeth he had professed his sin to the world, though his desire for her was that of father for daughter and nothing other. He felt as if he were perched on the edge of an abyss.

The lover, Sinclair, must know that the marriage had never been consummated. James hated Matt Sinclair, hated and despised the man who had seduced his daughter. Sinclair was a loutish, arrogant wastrel and would never better himself in life.

"James, are you ill?"

Elspeth's concern was genuine.

James groaned aloud without being aware of it.

She had risen and would have come to him but he had rendered her so afraid of intimacy that she did not dare.

Dry, rope-creak sounds came from James Moodie's throat. "I – I – I –"

He could not say outright that he loved her. It would have been better if Elspeth had died all those years ago, had slipped away into eternity under her mother's breast in the rank hut by the Nettleburn. He had tried to be rid of her, God knows he had tried. He had tried to be rid of her later too, but now he had his chance. He could, as she suggested, separate from her, send her packing, not to starve like Bell, but handsomely endowed with an allowance which would provide all the creature comforts that she and her child might need. The gossips of Balnesmoor, Kennart, Harlwood might leap to any damned conclusion which suited them. Ironically, they would tattle out the truth, that he was not the father of her bairn at all.

Tempted, James stared unblinking at his daughter.

He could not, could not do it, could not send her away.

"I – I – I –"

Pain gripped his head like the pincers of a vice, fierce physical pain. Tears welled into his eyes.

"James! Oh, James!"

Elspeth was on her knees before him. His daughter wept for his suffering. He reached out his arm and drew her against him, cuddling her to him.

"Dearest, dearest, I dinna mind about the bairn," James moaned. "It's not that, not you."

"I didn't mean t' hurt you."

"I know, I know."

Elspeth waited for him to ask the question which she could not answer, but he did not ask who the father was, not then, not later, not ever.

It did not dawn on Elspeth that James had not asked because he believed he already knew and that, already, he was planning how to be rid of the man.

Alicia was the only person on Ottershaw who did not know of her brother-in-law's scandalous involvement with a servant-girl. Gilbert could have told her, broadly, what was in the wind and the nursery-maid, Peggie, or any of the other poor wights who were obliged to attend the former lady of the house, might have deluged her with intimate details of the affair. But Alicia was not the sort who encouraged confidences. As a result she heard nothing of Randall's liaison with Anna Sinclair until it had advanced to boiling-point and had distilled into a queer kind of love.

Alicia had a castle to occupy her attentions and, by hook or by crook, she was already set on transforming the tumbledown old place into something not just habitable but positively grand. So single-minded had she become that she could not be bothered with trivialities like ensuring income. She did not blench when Gilbert tried to explain that, with a scant hundred acres and no rent roll, he would have to find another means of making money and that Strachan Castle would never be another Ottershaw.

"Have you spoken with Sinclair?" Alicia demanded.

"He'll not leave here."

"Offer him a higher wage."

"I've done so. He won't budge. I can hardly insist, Alicia.

272

There's no land to speak of at Strachan for Sinclair to manage."

"We must buy more land."

"There's no land to be had in the vicinity of the castle. In any case, Alicia, the last ten years have seen such a whaling rise in acre price that we could hardly afford to buy a kitchen garden, let alone grazings."

"Find something else then."

"But what?"

"I leave it to you. You are, after all, the head of the family."

"Alicia?"

"Gilbert, I have work to do, satin linings to measure for the seamstress."

Gibbie slunk away.

In due course he turned to his brother for advice and assistance in regard to a certain proposition which had opened to him and which might solve most of his problems, long and short.

Thank God Randall was not locked in his bedroom on that pleasant, sun-blink afternoon. Gilbert found the girl, Sinclair, in the library and she informed him that laird and grieve had gone out to the scrub acres by Fumarts Wood. Gilbert thanked the girl politely. It would hardly do to offend one who shared his brother's bed, even if she was a servant.

Gibbie found his brother and Lachlan Sinclair in the rough stretch of ground that flanked the wood. Sinclair's mare was tied to a sapling but Randall had no horse or pony with him. He preferred to walk his property, to strengthen his leg. Sinclair had a thick tablet of paper in the crook of his elbow and was busily jotting down measurements and neat drawings upon it in pencil, with Randall pointing with his stick as if he were planning an attack upon Kennart which lay across the bend of the river about a half-mile distant.

Soon after joining them Gilbert indicated that he wished to speak with his brother on a private matter and Sinclair, his measuring work being done for the present, mounted and rode off on other business, leaving the Bontines alone.

Gilbert noticed that his brother was exceedingly pale and had shed some weight. It was, perhaps, not surprising as he had spent most of the winter indoors. Though he was more

273

gaunt and vulpine than ever, he had lost, Gibbie thought, much of the nervous rapaciousness which had marked him upon his return from Spain.

Wasting no time Gilbert embarked at once upon the topic that had brought him out of doors.

He said, "I've been offered an opportunity to buy into a partnership which owns and operates the Farmers' Banking Company, and, Randall, I would value your opinion as to the advisability of accepting."

"What do I know of banking, Gibbie?"

"Probably less than I do."

Randall laughed. "There's no estate with Strachan Castle?"

"None to speak of," Gilbert answered.

"Therefore you require a source of income."

"In a word – yes."

"Who put your name forward for this singular opportunity?"

"Summerhays."

Randall murmured his surprise. "Well, that's something to be said in favour. Father, as you'll recall, had naught but admiration for old Nigel Summerhays."

"It's his share of the partnership that he wishes to sell."

"What do his sons have to say to that?" Randall asked.

"He has but one son, appropriately named Cotton."

Randall laughed again. He seemed, Gilbert thought, in an uncommonly good mood today. Sport with the servant-girl had certainly done his temper no harm.

"Cotton Summerhays is a director of the British Linen Bank. In fact, he has a great house in Tweeddale Court adjacent to the bank's property in Edinburgh."

"So," said Randall, "old Nigel doesn't wish to see his provincial bank gobbled up by the Linen?"

"Something of the sort," said Gilbert. "He has offered me, out of the blue, the whole of his share in the partnership."

"At what sort of price?"

"Seven thousand pounds."

"By coincidence," said Randall, "the exact sum that you have inherited from Father. I wonder how old Nigel got a nose of that."

"It's hardly a deathly secret," said Gilbert.

"Have you discussed this venture with Alicia?"

"No, not in detail."

"Why ever not, Gibbie? Is your wife not a wizard in finance as well as in law?"

"Alicia's preoccupied with preparing Strachan Castle for occupancy in May."

"Gibbie, let me ask you: are you more of a banker, d' you suppose, than you are a squire?"

"I think," said Gilbert without umbrage, "that it might suit my talents rather better."

"Can you make two and two come to five?"

"If I add a percentage of profit to the sum, aye."

"I gather that you have more than half a mind to stump up this back-breaking seven thousand pounds."

"It's appealing, certainly," said Gilbert. "But I'm not quite such a fool as you've always believed me to be, Randall. Unlike Alicia, I do not believe that you'll squander the living here on Ottershaw. I do not believe that I'll ever return here as laird. It is therefore essential that I shape a life elsewhere and Strachan Castle will do well enough."

"Why did you saddle yourself with such a wife, Gibbie?"

"Alicia's not without her virtues," said Gilbert.

"We are different laddies, Gib, which is as well. But you're right in your judgement that I'll not be losing Ottershaw on the turn of a card in a drunken spree in Edinburgh. Ottershaw is my burden, Gibbie, my fate. I've accepted that fact. But to return to the Falkirk Farmers' Bank; do you have seven thousand pounds?"

"I can raise it, even after my expenditure on the lease of the Castle and some imperative work of repair."

"But?"

"Will you write to Hildebrand and ask him to find out all that he can about the assets of the Farmers' Bank, and its foundation?"

"Hildebrand? Why, of course," said Randall. "Yon Dumbarton rogue will be able to tell you to a farthing what the partnership's worth."

"Will you do it?"

"With pleasure, Gibbie. It's very sensible."

"Within the month?"

"Immediately."

"I already know what the bank's main sources are – cattle

and sheep. It lays out notes against grazing herds and finances certain recognised drovers."

"Is it in wool-dealing too?"

"I'm sure it will be."

"In that case why not consult Moodie? No man knows the state of the wool markets better than our wee weaver mannie."

"I've another plan for Moodie," said Gilbert.

"Plan? What's this?"

"I shall be after his banking business if I take the partnership. Indeed, Randall, I shall be after business from Ottershaw too."

"Not worth having, old chatter-box," said Randall. "Truly, I'm on my uppers since I met all the legacies. Remember, if you will, that Mother had her third, apart from your own payment. I will be a borrower for twenty years, living on hard credit. I'm sure the Farmers' Bank will not want that sort of business."

"It might," said Gilbert, trying to seem sly.

"Moodie, however, is a hare worth the chase," said Randall. "I agree that capturing his banking business would be beneficial, a feather in a new partner's cap."

"If," said Gilbert, "I decide to become a partner at all."

"Hildebrand will steer you." Randall put his arm into his brother's and, still arm-in-arm, began to walk towards the house again. "But if I were you I would go after the business of another local gentleman, somebody who may be richer than any of us."

"Who might that be?"

"Pad Tomelty, of course," said Randall.

And the Bontine brothers laughed.

In the course of the next six weeks, while winter gusted into spring, it became generally known that Weaver Moodie had gotten his wife with child. It was predicted that having found the way, as it were, Moodie would soon see his lawns littered with squalling bairns and that Gaddy Patterson's eldest would rapidly lose her good looks and slender figure and become just as drab and dumpy as any cottar wife.

In accordance with the truce she had compacted with her husband, Elspeth appeared on James's arm at the kirks in Harlwood and in Balnesmoor, though she was on each occasion so swaddled up against snell spring winds that, as one wag put it, "She might be carryin' quadrupeds for all ye can see."

Distrust and suspicion were present in her relationship with James but at least she did not have to hide her pleasure in the pregnancy or her delighted anticipation of motherhood. Doctor Carstairs examined her and pronounced her well, the miscarriage a threat that had not increased, though care would be required to ensure that she carried to term.

It was the end of March, only weeks before the district went mad with lambing, before Anna called upon her sister. Since Anna did not even pretend to be a kirk person, in spite of her father-in-law's grousing about Godlessness, she had not seen Elspeth for many months, a lapse which neither sister felt keenly. The combative friendship of girlhood had evaporated, rivalry put to rest, at least to Anna's way of thinking.

'Pet might be married to a wealthy wool manufacturer but Moodie was just a common tyke compared to a laird, to a Bontine who could trace his ancestry back three hundred years. And she was the laird's true love and his lover and, if fate was at all kind, might eventually bear the next Bontine in line. If Anna envied Elspeth anything now it was the babe in her belly not the fine clothes on her back or wedlock to a dour and scowling weaver like James Simpson Moodie.

Anna had taken the precaution of announcing her intention to call at Moss House in the form of a letter. Elspeth was waiting for her and Tolland warned that Anna Sinclair was not to be kept on the step. James had made himself scarce. His absence did not bother Anna in the slightest. Nothing offended Anna these days. She soared higher than a hawk in her happiness for she knew, with that innate assurance which is the birthright of beautiful women, that she had secured Randall's heart and meant more to him, in spite of the scandals and deceptions, than passing amusement. She whitened the circumstances, felt lofty and grand, found that she could thole Matt quite well since he no longer bullied her and spent more time out of Pine Cottage than in it. She did not care a jot who Matt was with or what road he chose to take to perdition. She would be free of him soon, she felt certain.

There was less awkwardness between the sisters than there had been for years. They met like amiable acquaintances, relaxed enough but with a mature restraint upon them.

"Does it hurt?" was one of the more personal questions that Anna asked.

"It did at first," said Elspeth. "But it's only a wee bit uncomfortable now."

"It hardly shows in that frock."

"It's not due until August; there's time."

"If you're fortunate it'll be small."

"It doesn't feel small."

"What'll you call it?" said Anna.

"If it's a boy, it'll be James, I expect."

"What if it's a girl?"

It was something to which Elspeth had given no thought at all. She waved her hand. "After Mother Moodie, like as not."

"Mary Jean." Anna wrinkled her nose. "What a cheekful t' chew. Could y' not call it after Mam?"

"It'll be for James to decide."

"Call it after me, if ye like."

"I think it'll be Mary Jean."

"Please yourself," said Anna, thinking that one day Elspeth might be flattered to be related to a laird's wife, to be aunt to Bontines. The sheer impossibility of such a pass did not deter Anna from nurturing the dream.

Elspeth said, "Is Matt in good health?"

"Matt? Och, aye, he's never ill."

"I met him, as he'll have told you, on the day of the snow."

"Aye," said Anna glibly, "he did mention it."

Elspeth seemed to be waiting, with an alertness that disconcerted Anna. Matt had made no mention of a meeting with her sister and Anna did not feel constrained to pour out her heart to Elspeth.

"Is he still runnin' spirits for Pad Tomelty?" Elspeth asked.

"He just delivers an occasional keg. They all do, the foresters. McDonald's a bigger rogue than our Matt by a long chalk."

"Oh, I thought Matt was well set with Tomelty."

"Where did ye hear the like o' that?"

"I've heard other things too, Anna."

"Concernin' Matt?"

"Concernin' yourself."

"Is there nowhere in this damned country free from tattle?" said Anna, with a sigh of resignation.

"I heard how you'd become a – a favourite of Randall Bontine."

Anna laughed, brittle as an icicle. "I like that word 'favourite'. Are ye too mealie-mouthed t' come out with it, 'Pet?"

"Are you sharin' the laird's bed?"

"What if I am?"

"Good!" said Elspeth emphatically.

Anna was surprised. She had expected priggish outrage and a sermon on morality from her sister.

Elspeth said, "So it's the truth, is it?"

"I never said that. I only said I can do as I like."

"You've more courage than I'd have," said Elspeth.

"Meanin' what?"

"It's not as if you were single."

"Matt's too scared o' his place on Ottershaw to defy the laird. Randall Bontine's a match for anyone."

"Does the grieve know?"

"Old Lachlan? He was offered a post wi' Gibbie at Strachan Castle, though there's no estate there, so I hear. But he wouldn't leave his precious Ottershaw or abandon the true laird o' the manor. If I danced like Salome in the middle o' the sheep fank wi' Randall playin' the pipes, old Lachlan would look the other way. He's a bigger hypocrite – aye, an' a bigger slave – than anybody in these parts."

"Be careful, Anna, that you don't become the slave."

"Slave t' Randall Bontine would suit me fine."

"Is he – is he all you'd hoped for, Anna?"

Anna tilted her chin in an expression of arrogant defiance. "More. Much more. He loves me."

"So the other things don't matter?"

"What other things?"

"The satin gowns an' kidskin slippers; a carriage of your own with two chestnut horses an' a footman; all the things you an' I used to moon about when we were young."

"Aye, an' daft," said Anna.

"It's brave o' you to give up all for love."

"Give up?"

"Chance losin' your husband an' home."

"I'm not done dreamin' yet, Elspeth," said Anna, startled by her sister's interpretation of her affair with the laird of Ottershaw.

"Randall Bontine can never marry you, Anna."

"Since I'm marrit to Matt, do ye mean?"

"Even if you were free of Matt Sinclair, a laird canna marry a servant lass."

"Randall can do what he likes."

"A hundred years ago it might have been true, but no longer, Anna."

"God, how I hate it when you pretend t' be sensible."

"It's the truth, though."

"If I was free of Matt Sinclair —" Anna began.

"Convention would kill it."

"Randall cares nothin' for convention."

Anna was flustered and annoyed. What if she had no husband? What then? What if Matt no longer existed? That would be the true test; then she would be unprotected, without base. She would be forced to trust Randall or become an outcast, despised and reviled on Ottershaw and Balnesmoor.

Once more Elspeth had effortlessly, unwittingly, brought Anna to earth with a bump.

Anna allowed not a trace of confusion to show. She refused to give Elspeth that satisfaction. Some things did not change with the coming of maturity. The resentment between the sisters would never diminish but would rear up between them for evermore.

Anna got to her feet.

"Well, I've blethered long enough, 'Pet," she said without obvious hostility. "I must be gettin' back now. In spite o' everythin' Matt will expect t' be fed."

"It was kind o' you to call."

"May it go well wi' you an' the baby."

"An' may it go well with you, Anna," Elspeth said. "Take care."

Several years would pass before Gaddy Patterson's daughters met again, enmeshed in a tragedy that neither of them could have forseen for, come the autumn, Anna, like her sister, would be with child.

In April the first seed barley was put to the ground in fields along the Strath. Since Scotch barley was the fountainhead of whisky the hearts of those folk who were fond of the vital waters gave a bit leap at the sight of the sowers. In due course

Padric Tomelty would have his share of the crop to germinate on the floors of Eardmore and soon thereafter bottles of smoke-brown whisky would come clanking down from the moor.

Not the only producer of illicit spirits in the Lennox, there being a few dribble stills on outlying farms, Pad still had a monopoly on patch barley which government taxation had lowered in value and which could be turned to silver only by sale to a distiller. Fourpenceworth of malted barley would yield four shillings' worth of whisky in experienced hands. For that reason, and to keep his regular clients supplied, Pad risked storing grain as well as jugs during the winter months. But many sacks were wasted with mites and mould and not even Padric could mate supply to demand throughout the spring season. Prices shot upwards. Those who could pay got it all, the sore-afflicted being left to lick dry lips or make do with beer which, to a hardened whisky drinker, was like being put back on cows' milk.

The three four-gallon kegs that Matt Sinclair was assigned to deliver to the Cunninghams had, therefore, considerable value for all parties to the sale, not to mention slaves of loom and spindle whose tongues were hanging out for a dram, some of whom had reached a state of 'partiality' for liquor that a bottle a day could hardly satisfy.

The Cunninghams had acquired 'paper protection' against inspection by King's Officers, as riding officers of the revenue were locally known. A thorough search of the hillside behind the shop would have unearthed several anchors of whisky upon which duty had not been paid but waving licences and invoking the dreaded name of Moodie was quite sufficient to deter Johnston, the gauger from Drymen, from coming too close to Kennart.

Matt did not feel threatened by gaugers or the horsemen of the revenue. Left to his own devices he would have banged the kegs on to the cart and lugged them quite openly down through the Bonnywell and on to the Kennart Road. Pad, however, insisted on caution and Matt, though he had scoffed at the Irishman at the time, was soon to be damned grateful to him for concealing the containers beneath a load of pine logs.

The King's Officers sprang on him without warning. They came thundering out of a hollow a half-mile uphill from

Kennart bridge. Two were enough to cause the dray horse in the cart's shafts to shoulder left into the hedge and to turn Matt's blood to ice.

Cutlasses were drawn and raised.

Matt was addressed in a yelping English voice. "You there, where do you go? What do you carry?"

The officers seemed hardly older than he was but dashing broadcloth coats, three-cornered hats and alien accents brought Matt leaping to his feet on the cart board. It was all he could do to stop himself from jumping down and sprinting away across the field, abandoning not only the expensive cargo but the laird's horse and rig to confiscation by the agents of the Crown.

The officers rode with agility, jigged their mounts as if horses and men shared one brain. The head of the Ottershaw dray was held fast by one officer while the other tripped about the conveyance, a cutlass naked in his fist as if at any moment he might decide to strike Matt's head from his shoulders and let it bounce downhill into the Lightwater.

"Come now, you, what do you tote?"

"T – timber, as ye can see." Matt was too frightened to be impudent.

"Stealing it, are you?"

"Ste – Nah, I've t' deliver t' Kennart."

"Kennart?"

"T' the mill."

Matt did not know whether to keep his eye on the officer in front or to swing round to see what the devil behind him was about. The casks were covered by narrow logs of unbarked pine, boxed in by them; Pad had made sure that they could not be seen without shifting the timber.

"Are they weaving with wood now, these Highland savages?"

"It's for repairin' buildin's," Matt explained.

He felt vastly relieved when the rearward officer appeared by his side and transferred his inspection from cart to driver.

One officer spoke to the other. "What's your opinion, Cecil, shall we have him down and stripped?"

"Have him unload the cart," Cecil sniggered. "He's thick enough to benefit from the exercise, I would say."

"Step down, boy."

Matt climbed down by the wheel on to the road. Sleek horses towered over him, penned him in. Bending from their saddles the officers peered at him as if he were a piece of ordure.

"Take off the load."

"I – I –"

"Empty the cart to the boards, boy."

The blade of a cutlass was laid on his shoulder.

Matt flinched as the pressure of the cutting edge against his neck guided him towards the rear of the cart. He saw that the timber had shifted when the cart had tilted off the crown of the road. Removal of just three or four logs would expose the banded casks. Matt's mind clamoured for excuses. He would have blurted out names, delivered Padric Tomelty, Brigit, the Cunninghams, big McDonald, all and sundry, to the Crown Officers there on the Kennart road if at that moment a familiar voice had not shouted an interruption.

"What's goin' on there?"

From the hollow by the river-bank Lachlan Sinclair emerged. His coat skirts, breeks and boots were saturated with water and the mare, wet to the belly-band, snorted with the effort of the gallop into which she had been whipped.

"Why are you impedin' this man?"

The officers were startled, their arrogance punctured somewhat by the authority of the stranger on the mare.

Matt gave not the slightest hint that the man was his father. He was not out of danger yet; even the grieve of Ottershaw could not stand in the way of King's Officers if they had set their minds on trouble.

"What's this fellow to you?"

"He's a forester employed on the estates of Ottershaw and has been despatched along this road in the service of Sir Randall Bontine."

"You, who are you?"

"I am Sinclair, Sir Randall Bontine's grieve."

"Only a grieve!" the younger officer exclaimed. "You behave like a Lord Sheriff."

He sniggered but Lachlan urged the mare forward, slid it against the horse's crupper and, reaching, caught the young officer by the sleeve. He drew him round with such force that a less expert rider would have been pulled from the saddle.

"I'll stand no insolence, not even from a King's man," said Lachlan.

"Hold, sir," said the senior officer. "Do not be so quick to take offence."

The young officer wrenched his arm from the grieve's grasp. He skittered his mount five or ten yards downhill, to obtain a favourable stance in case he had to shoot his pistol or make a charge against the man who, after all, might be no grieve but just another smuggler.

Matt sidled against the cart wheel, pressed his back to it as if his body might further shield the casks beneath the logs. His mouth was dry, his eyes fixed on his father who had brought the mare close to the senior officer and managed a smile of sorts, a kind of Bontine sneer.

"I do believe you're searchin' for whisky," he said.

"Indeed, that's so. There are smugglers in the district."

"There's whisky here," said the grieve, "but it's paid for to the Crown and the suppliers have licences for its sale."

Matt was astonished at the range of his father's knowledge. He could better have understood it if his father had been a toss-pot but Lachlan had always been opposed to strong drink.

The officer said, "The shopkeepers in Kennart, do you mean, sir?"

"I do mean, sir."

"What proof have I that you are, indeed, this grieve fellow?"

Lachlan stopped smiling. "Suspicion is, I suppose, a requisite of your profession but I'd not have taken ignorance as a requirement."

"Ignorance? Explain yourself."

"I'll let Mister Rudge, manager of the Kennart mill, do the explainin'," said the grieve. "He's expectin' this load of timber, which has been paid for and is urgently needed for building work. Might I suggest you extricate the cart from the ditch an' ride along with us an' let Mister Rudge confirm who I am and what –"

The young officer shouted out, "Tell him to unload, Cecil. I have my doubts about this fellow."

"If you wish to count the logs then you must unload them yourself," said Lachlan Sinclair. "Aye, an' put them all back when you are done."

The senior officer had his cutlass across his knees and had

lost his erect and haughty seat. Without conviction he said, "We do not take orders from grieves, do you know."

"I do not take interference – for that's all it is – from casual riders, even if they do flaunt a Crown appointment."

The senior officer hesitated, glanced towards his companion who had kept his distance.

"Matt," Lachlan said, "mount the cart. See if it'll draw easy from the ditch or if we'll need to take off the load."

"Aye, Fa – aye, Mister Sinclair."

Vaulting up like a cat, Matt was on the board instantly. He was not rash enough, however, to slap at the big dray horse but coaxed it against the shafts so that the listing wheel rose, rolled and gradually found the solid verge. Behind him, pine poles chattered and squeaked. He whipped his head round expecting to see the casks laid bare, but did not; nor did the younger officer who had galloped briskly past cart and grieve and had turned behind the carrier, peering into it.

"Come then," said Lachlan Sinclair, "if you must have me identified, it can be done in Kennart where you may also watch the timber being unloaded. Follow us down."

The senior officer hung back. "It will not be necessary, grieve."

"I insist upon it," said Lachlan, to Matt's horror.

"Do not jib me too far, sir," said the officer, "or I might take it upon me to arrange a raid upon Ottershaw and a search of your cow-houses and sheep-folds. Be on your way with your timber."

Matt let out his breath. He was standing on the board and gave a yell to prompt the dray horse. He felt the cart dunt against him as its weight nosed forward and the wheels trundled on to the slope that would take it around the corner and on to the bridge. He held tense to prevent himself charging like a charioteer away from the King's Officers.

"Drive steady," Lachlan muttered, riding by his side. "Very steady."

The cart turned down the long corner. Kennart and the basin of the Lightwater lay below them like a harbour. Lachlan glanced quickly behind him.

"Are they – are they –" stammered Matt.

"No, they've stayed," said the grieve. "Now, tell me, what else does the cart contain apart from honest timber?"

"Whisky. Three casks."

"Good God, Matt!"

"Aye, it was fair lucky you came when you did."

"Fair lucky! Is that what you think of it?"

Lachlan Sinclair stretched and caught the check rein, drew the cart to a halt just short of the mouth of the bridge.

Up on the summit of Rowan Hill, distinctive against the sky, stood George Cunningham. His hackles had been instinctively stirred by the presence of Excisemen in the neighbourhood and he had come out to scan the road for sign of his precious cargo. Grieve and forester were aware of the figure on the hilltop though neither remarked it to the other.

"If I had not been makin' a survey by Fumarts Wood," said Lachlan Sinclair, "if I had failed to notice the officers ridin' towards the road, what would have become of you?"

"I'm in no mood for a sermon."

"You'd have been arrested, arraigned, tried and found guilty of transportin' illicit spirits."

"Aye, an' I would have been given a fine of money to pay an' my good, close friends would have paid it for me to secure my freedom."

"Matt, Matt!" said the grieve sadly. "What a trash you're makin' of your life."

"If that's your opinion why do you not dismiss me? Are you not the bloody grieve an' is Ottershaw not more important to you than I am?"

"That's not so," said Lachlan. "But, mark me well on this, I've a limit to tolerance. What can I do if you persist in these infamous associations?"

Blazing with indignation, Matt cried, "An' what of your damned 'associations'?"

"What do you –"

"Aye, you're loyal, fine an' right, Father. Loyal to a bloody fornicator."

Matt was as much shaken by that moment of revelation as by the threatening quarter-hour which had preceded it. He knew; the grieve knew. Matt slumped down hard upon the board, reins in his fists. No denial was possible; no doubt remained. His father was well aware that Anna was Randall Bontine's piece of amusement. It could not be hidden. Truth burned on his father's face.

"Is that why you'll not send me packin'?" said Matt. "Because Randall Bontine would lose Anna?"

"Get on, get on," Lachlan Sinclair snapped. He slapped the dray horse's rump to drive it forward. "Get on with your work."

Matt steered the cart into the bridgegate and over the span, into the sounds of the churning mill-wheel and din from the long buildings, shaken with the aftermath of his experiences on the road. He struggled to control himself for George Cunningham was scurrying towards him, so anxious that he had even taken his hands from his pockets and the pipe from his mouth.

"Was that King's men I saw?"

"It was," said Matt.

"What happened, lad? Did they no' search the cart?"

"I brazened it out," said Matt. "I told them who I was an' what they could do wi' themselves."

"An' the other chap?"

"Nobody of importance," said Matt.

Matt could not have guessed that his father had ridden into the scrub again to hide himself among the stunted growths of the water-meadow and, with a hand over his face, to weep in sorrow and in shame for the son he could not save.

The gaunt Alicia was gone from Ottershaw along with Gibbie and three children, those not yet sent to education, two servants indentured by agreement and every stick of furniture, piece of linen, every plate and glass that she might claim Gibbie had bought. There were also hampers packed with clothes, one of the carriages from the mews and two horses, though Gibbie had to negotiate for the last-named items and pay a price for their possession. If Gilbert had but known, Randall would have donated twice over just to see the back of Alicia and certainly did not count the woman's casual embezzlements as too high a price to be rid of her from his house.

It was the first of the warm, moist days with the air May-sweet and the sun so bright you could hear the grass grow in the pastures and the bubble of sap in the trees around the park. Moodie's Cheviots had lambed like champions. Bleat and blether came loud around the house along with the drone of bee swarms and choruses of sparrows from the stable yard.

To spring's awakening and new beginnings Alicia seemed oblivious.

Alicia was last out of Ottershaw. Sweeping grandly past the sweating men who had lugged out the portables and loaded them on three carts, she took her place in the carriage and snapped at Gibbie to make sure the children had attended to their little businesses because she had no intention of making countless stops along the route and allowing the carters excuse for dawdling. As usual the Bontine children were stowed away, this time among boxes and chests on the last cart. Two tear-stained, snuffling nursery-maids, their worldly goods bound in flop-eared bundles, penned in the darlings who were not at all dismayed at the prospect of dwelling in a castle now that they had been assured, by Gilbert, that there were no dungeons to which Mama might banish them.

Having dutifully checked on the children, Gilbert returned to Randall and shook his brother's hand, a signal that at least he bore no grudge, then, with a fat leather wallet full of important documents under one arm, he clambered into the chaise and gave word for the procession to start away for Strachan Castle.

The coach rumbled into motion, followed by the carts. At that instant, spontaneously, house-servants and yard-hands broke into a tremendous cheer, quite loud enough to cue herders and ploughmen in the fields, even McDonald's men in the forest, all of whom stopped work, flung their bonnets in the air and gave glad voice for the deliverance of their brethren below.

In the coach Alicia sought her husband's hand.

"Do you hear how they honour us, Gilbert, the humble labourers of Ottershaw? It is their way of saying that we will be sorely missed."

"Yes, dearest." Gilbert caught sight of a couple of gardeners in the shadow of a rhododendron performing a jig of obscene celebration. "Sorely missed."

In the kitchen yard at Ottershaw, where Gilbert had made his farewells to the laird, the cheering had grown quite hysterical. It was all Sinclair and Hunter could do to call a halt to it and shoo their sundry charges back to work.

Randall watched the carts toil up to the turnpike and vanish behind the trees. He sighed happily, rubbed his hands and looked up and about as if clouds had lifted from his rooftops and the beeches' silky leaves had sprung out bright green in the moment. "Now," he said, "now let us make the best of this beautiful day."

Randall already had a plan, something he had been saving for the day when Alicia finally left his ken.

"Dunn, tell them at the stable to bring out Sabre, saddled and bridled. Anna, come with me."

"Aye, sir." Dunn scampered off.

Anna hesitated, frowning slightly. "Laird, what are ye intendin' to do with the horse?"

"Try out my leg, Anna."

"On Sabre? Is he not o'er sparky?"

"Full of pith, Anna. But would you have me ride a pony? I am, or was, a Hussar, if you recall. It's the stallion or nothing. I prefer things with a bit of spice in them."

Anna gave him a glance that needed no interpretation.

The zenith of her life was approaching, a peak of experience against which she would balance the misery of her ebbing fortunes in the days ahead, and regard as worth the exchange. There would be other excitements in the span of that short summer but none to match the events of that May-day noon.

Discretion was thrown to the winds now that Alicia had departed. Anna accompanied the laird to his bedroom and there watched him dress himself in breeks of creamed cloth and a riding frock-coat with great gilded buttons which he wore over a flowing silk shirt, unlaced at the throat and without a cravat to spoil it. He pulled on a pair of hessian boots, old friends unearthed from his dunnage in the loft, and clamped about his leg a boot-garter of buckled leather which he spiked so tight that the girl protested that he would stop the blood in his veins.

Randall laughed. She had never seen him so gay, or so relaxed. It was as if Gilbert had taken away the memory of a striving childhood and Alicia, somehow, had lugged off all disappointments. Randall stood up, stamped the boot upon the floor, then, eager and swift, swept Anna into his arms and lifted her toes from the floor, carried her to the bedroom door with him, while she squealed and giggled.

He kissed her on the mouth.

"Today I'm going to ride my horse, Anna, while you watch me in admiration."

"If you do, Randall, I will."

They clattered downstairs, laird and servant-girl.

Mrs Lacy had come out of her kitchen, Hunter too, along with other house-servants, including Brigit, for Dunn had had the head horseman bring the stallion round to the terrace in the full fall of sunlight where the animal pranced and danced, dainty and dreadful, in expectation of a canter and perhaps a full gallop.

It rolled its dark liquid eye at Randall as he approached down the stone steps. He took the reins from the horseman. Anna came forward from the little crowd of servants who stood in the open doorway and joined Dunn, the privileged pair, advanced and acknowledged. She leaned against the acorn-shaped stone ornament at the base of the steps. She had eyes only for Randall as he gentled the horse, steadied it and, with feet together in the broad stirrup, hoisted himself lithely into the saddle. Anna had never seen anything so well done. She clapped her hands in delight at the performance.

No sooner was the laird seated than he had Sabre walking; he knew that the animal was more manageable in motion than at rest, for he shared with the thoroughbred an energy which was wellnigh uncontrollable at times. Randall flowed with the stallion's stride, comfortable, lyrical. If there was pain in the leg and thigh, his joy at being back in the saddle numbed it. Canter accelerated into gallop, mount and rider carried faster away, up the beat by the elms where lambed ewes were scant, rider and mount moving with such poise that the sheep were no more startled than they would have been by a passing gust of wind. If Ottershaw's more heavy-handed stable lads had damaged Sabre there was no sign of it, nor of his volatile temperament. He did not buck or weave, went straight down the length of the park and turned tight to the fist on the rein.

Anna marvelled at how well Randall rode, breeks clear of the saddle, weight into his knees. She should have known him better. Randall Bontine was strong, quicker than any stallion and came down towards the house like a charging lancer, then swiftly eased from gallop to three-beat canter and down again to a high-stepping, arrogant walk which brought him back to the steps of the terrace, beaming, hair tousled, coat peeled back from his chest. The reins lay across his fingers as lightly as spider threads.

The servants did not know how to express their admiration. They murmured warmly and stirred. It was left to Hunter to speak for them. "Well done, sir. It's grand t' see you fit again an' in such braw fettle." The domestics chorused, "Aye, aye, so it is, sir."

Anna alone went forward, not at all intimidated by the unpredictable horse, not while Randall saddled it. She put her hand upon the laird's knee and, while the whole household looked on agog, stared up at him.

"I love you," she mouthed. "Wonderfully."

Randall said, "Would you like to ride him?"

"I canna."

"Have you never ridden?"

"Only a pony, once."

"Take my arm, Anna. Hold to it tightly."

Randall stooped from the saddle. He put his arm about her back, his fingers fanned. She stretched on toe tip and let herself go slack, unresisting, as he swept her from the step and set her deftly across the saddle in front of him.

Sabre whickered loudly, fretted his hoofs but did not rear up and box his forelegs or toss his muscular neck or seek to dislodge the girl. Randall had command of him, was his master too.

"Lean close against me, Anna. Trust me. I shan't let you fall."

She was so high above the ground, elevated to the level of the terrace, staring straight into the astonished faces of the servants, including Brigit and the outraged cook. Anna sat still and slack, folded securely in Randall's arms as if it were the most natural thing in the world to be riding across the saddle with the laird of Ottershaw. She felt the vibrancy of the horse beneath her thighs, the flick of coarse hair as Randall coaxed up Sabre's head and its mane streamed across the backs of her hands and arms. It was as if she had boarded a great, high-prowed ship which went lifting and dipping through a big sea swell. Anna had never seen the sea but she had read of it, imagined it. This was how it must be, lofty and surging and strong, taking possession of you. She had never been more exhilarated and aware of her body.

Buffered by Randall's shoulders and safe in his arms, the stallion's rhythm undulated through her, rolling her at breakneck speed up the parkland away from the house. Just across Randall's collar she could glimpse the façade becoming smaller and smaller, terrace and servants receding, receding, receding, trees and ewes and contours of the hill of Drumglass swishing past in a spectacle of brand-new vistas and perspectives.

Randall was no harsh rider; he did not gallop Sabre, not even to impress Anna. But to the girl the canter seemed like a dash, faster than she had ever travelled before, even on a cart. The oaks and elms whisked away then closed again. She tucked in her head against Randall's chest as the stallion was reined up the banking to the broad track that led away to the west, across the pasture and the scrub to the meadow on the fringe of Fumarts Wood.

Suddenly Anna realised where Randall was taking her; to the tumbled willow where first they had met. So fast was the ride that Anna felt herself sucked back in time. By the overgrown tree she half expected to see Elspeth and Anna Cochran, startled and guilty, to observe herself and her pretty sister through the soldier's eyes, in all their knowing innocence. God, how it had fled, all of it except the daydream of being loved by Randall Bontine.

Randall lowered her from his grasp and slid after her to the ground. He tethered Sabre to a sapling and left the animal quietly cropping the lush grass. Taking Anna by the hand he led her towards the willow.

"Do you know where we are, Anna?"

"How could I ever forget this place?"

"Did you think of it when I was away?"

"Every day, every night, Randall."

The laird leaned against the slope of the big white willow, uprooted by a storm several years ago. He brought the girl to him, breasts against his chest, her stomach pressing his thighs. She had taken off her ribboned mob-cap and her dark hair fluffed about her face and neck.

"Is it not strange," Randall said, soft-voiced with a rare shyness, "that I dreamed of you when I was fevered? In a nunnery in the mountains of Spain. How far it seemed from Ottershaw."

"Why did you come back?"

"I was summoned. It was my duty. Besides, I was no use as a cavalry soldier with this." He clamped his hand upon his leg." No use to anyone."

"But you can ride again now," said Anna. "Will you go back to fight against the Frenchies?"

Randall laughed. "I have resigned my commission, Anna. In any case two miles upon Sabre's back is little enough. My limb would not stand the strain of a half-day's ride."

"Would you go back, though, if you could?"

"Aye, in an instant."

"Leave Ottershaw?"

"Ottershaw must always be second-best."

"Leave me?"

"Perhaps I might take you with me."

"Elope with me?"

"Abduct you," Randall said.

Pulling Anna closer still, he kissed her throat and mouth.

Anna responded, rubbing her body against his until, swiftly, he was aroused.

She drew him down upon the grass at the base of the white willow, lay under him while he made himself ready and bundled up her skirt and petticoats. He entered her with dominating force, a hard profane passion that made Anna cry aloud and arch herself up, knifed by astonishment, then, flowing with him, wrap her arms tightly about his back as he drove on through pleasure and sensation to a final effort of release.

Randall made love to her again that afternoon and often in the summer days that followed. But Anna was never in any doubt that it was during the coupling by the willow tree that her son by the laird was conceived.

NINE

The Wind on the Hill

A mutter of August thunder across the Campsie Fells brought Elspeth out of sleep. Without her knowledge and without James's permission, Doctor Carstairs had administered a tincture of laudanum via the jug of rice water that stood on the chest for the patient's refreshment, laudanum being the young physician's specific against most ailments, including those which might arise from childbirth.

Carstairs was not at all disposed to attend women in labour. He performed the task of male midwife only for families who insisted upon it and who would meet his exorbitant fee but then, in general, did exactly the proper thing by leaving nature to get on with it without excessive intervention in the process. However, he was a 'doser' of the new school and could not resist slipping a few drops of sedative into Mistress Moodie's drink in spite of the fact that the labour had been of short duration and the birth achieved without complication.

Threatened miscarriage early in pregnancy did not seem to have affected the infant in the slightest. She came slithering out into swaddles of warm linen and mewed petulantly when Carstairs inverted her to clean and to inspect. He judged her weight to be about seven pounds and found her well formed and apparently healthy.

"Is it . . . is it sound in all parts?" gasped the anxious girl from the bed, invariably the very first question to be asked by mothers high-born or low.

"Perfectly sound. Perfectly fine."

"What – what is it?"

"A female. A girl child."

The mother, of course, was young and sturdy and seemed exceedingly eager to embrace the responsibilities of motherhood. For an event as basically indelicate and disagreeable as a birthing it had all gone swimmingly. Carstairs lingered long enough to ensure that all was well then went downstairs to pass the news to the proud father in the library and to collect, there and then, his banknote for fifty guineas. He was off home again by two o'clock in the afternoon, a mere seven hours after his arrival, leaving mother and daughter in the care of trusted servants.

Naturally Elspeth viewed the matter rather differently from the doctor. But she had not found the pain unendurable and had clutched at the bedhead rail and screamed aloud only in the very latter stages. She was not so far gone in the grip of contractions that she did not feel just a tiny bit ashamed of her display with Kerr and Betty and the man doctor gathered about in the shadows. It had not been quite such a frightful experience as she had been led to believe it might be and her hours of suffering were amply repaid by that wonderful moment of empty relief, by the knowledge that she had delivered her baby alive, "Perfectly sound. Perfectly fine," and by the fact that it was a girl.

In the aftermath of effort, before she slept her first sleep, even before she held the little morsel to her breast for her first feed, Elspeth realised that all along she had wished for a girl in preference to a boy.

It seemed more 'right', more 'moral', that she had brought forth a child of her own sex, not a son who might resemble Michael, might in later years remind her too much of Michael. A girl would be more her own, would belong to her as she had belonged to Gaddy, close and intimate and easier to understand. Drifting into sleep, Elspeth felt that Michael at last was drifting away from her, drifting off like a light summer cloud. She did not regret it, not now that she had a baby of her own, a daughter upon whom she could shower her love.

Kerr awakened her about five o'clock with a glass of weak tea to heal her thirst. Kerr helped her move from the bed to a chair, changed bed-linen and Elspeth's night-frock, gave her a sponge before slipping a clean, sweet-smelling dress over her head. Elspeth, wide awake, was acutely conscious of Betty in the corner by the screen and the tiny discontented sounds that came from the lace-draped cradle. She had no patience with ritual preparations but endured them quietly because she too wanted everything to be just perfect, just right.

"Mister Moodie came up," Kerr told her. "He lookit in at

the baby. He'll come back up later, he says, when the wee one's had her nourishment."

Betty had control of the nursery while Tolland did reluctant nursing duty in Mother Moodie's sick-room.

Betty had no time for eighteenth-century fiddle-faddle. Though she had no children of her own, she had helped raise three sisters and had learned from her mother's 'sensible' approach to their care.

The Moodie baby was not to be swathed, swaddled or subjected to the perils of pins, except to affix its napkins. She was brought to Elspeth in Betty's arms, clad in a shirt of brushed cambric, her cross little visage framed in a cap of white linen and a bonnet of softest wool. Her toes and fingers, which Elspeth anxiously counted, wriggled, her activity not calmed until her mouth was guided to Elspeth's nipple and her cheek pressed against her mother's breast.

"Should she not be more still?" asked Elspeth as she felt the strong tug of the baby's gums for the first time.

Arms folded, Betty stood by the bed-end, no smile upon her lips but a warmth and tenderness in her eyes. "Nah, nah. She'll be still enough when she's filt hersel' up. She's as fine a wee bairnie as ever you'll see, Mistress Moodie, so dinna fret yoursel' otherwise."

"Is she gettin' milk from me, Betty?"

"See her cheeks chuff? She's gettin'. If she fails t' find suck she'll let us all know it right quick, so she will."

When the feeding was over the baby gave a satisfied little snort and instantly fell asleep, still at last in Elspeth's arms where Betty prudently left her for a quarter of an hour before putting her down in the cradle by the screen.

It had been a warm day, without sun but not oppressive. A small, guarded fire had been lighted in the hearth and Kerr swept about the grate and put on a few sticks to cheer the curtained room. Elspeth was inclined to ask for the curtains to be thrown back and a casement opened, to look out into the August evening sky; but she was afraid that a draught or chill would catch the baby and Betty was not quite so liberated as to suggest fresh air as a stimulant for a weary young mother, let alone a new-born infant.

James came at six, knocking very uncertainly upon the door and awaiting Kerr's permission to enter.

He had, Elspeth thought, dressed himself up grandly for the occasion. He wore a frock-coat of very best broadcloth and a snuff-coloured waistcoat with gold buffs and buttons, was smooth-shaven and groomed and as formal as a courtier. She could see, though, when he came first to the bed and bent to kiss her brow, how the cradle tugged at his attention, how he did not particularly wish to linger with her, not at first, but take himself to the screen and gaze down upon the girl child.

What was going on in her husband's head and heart was a mystery to Elspeth. She believed that she detected a shine of pride on him and he let his lips rest upon her forehead for a moment longer than usual. In spite of her uncertainty she felt a stir of affection for James. After all, she had deceived him, and he had stood by her. The baby was not his flesh and blood, yet he was proud of it.

Tongue-tied, James murmured, "Are you – have you – is it well with you, dearest."

"Aye. She's taken milk."

"Oh!"

He hovered, glancing behind him, embarrassed.

Betty had gone downstairs to eat supper and then to sit with Mother Moodie while Tolland scrounged through the kitchen to raise a decent dinner for the master. But the life of the household seemed distant to Elspeth. She trusted Betty, Kerr and Tolland to ensure that her welfare and that of the baby was not neglected.

"May I –" James gestured.

"Of course you may. She's –" Elspeth snipped off the remark; she was not his, not James's.

In time perhaps she might be able to dispense with such caution, when the baby had grown and been accepted and James had put the memory of her infidelity behind him. There would be no more children for her now. The future of the family must centre around her daughter.

James went to the cradle and stood for all of ten minutes, quite silent, watching the infant sleep. He did not croon to her or make any sound of affection but, from time to time, he would give a curt nod as if he were shaking the water of approval upon her brow.

Before James left Elspeth was almost asleep again. It was

all she could do to keep her eyes open, to smile at him when he gave her a parting kiss.

"Is she not lovely?" Elspeth whispered.

"Quite lovely," said James.

Betty had become Elspeth's clock. On the servant's return, Elspeth was awakened to give her breast to her daughter, two feedings in the hours between evening and full dark. Kerr would sleep in a cot in the closet, with an open door, and would attend both mother and baby, as required, during the night. Betty would not be far away, in her cramped room adjacent to Mother Moodie's room.

Elspeth, who had no hunger yet, only thirst, drank from the flagon of rice water that the doctor had left, then bid the maids good night and turned lightly – pleasantly lightly – into the pillow. All was safe, all was well.

She wakened two hours later. Suddenly.

She knew immediately that it was thunder. Panic gripped her, jerked her painfully from the bolster. Thunder. August thunder. She gaped towards the curtained windows, expecting to see a jagged flash of lightning, expecting the low sinister rumble to break into a deafening peal, to crack the rooftop and bring beams and slates crashing down on the cradle in the corner. Since the day of the great storm, the night of the flood when the hut on the Nettleburn had been swept away, taking with it the settled pleasures of her girlhood and youth, Elspeth had dwelt in mortal terror of thunder and torrential rain.

On the mantelshelf a night-lantern flickered. The fire had collapsed to grey ash and gave no extra light. By candle-shine, though, Elspeth could make out the rearing shape of the lace cowl of the cradle and imagined it, against all reason, to be some ghostly presence which threatened her baby with harm.

"Kerr?" Her voice had dried to a croak. "Kerr, where are you?"

But Kerr was young and slept deeply, head buried in the blanket in the confinement of the closet.

Thunder rippled again. Sense told Elspeth that it was distant, that she need not fear sound by itself. But her emotions were whirled about by fear and she had come so suddenly out of slumber that reality had the eccentric vividness of nightmare.

"Kerr?"

No answer, not even a snore, from the closet.

Shaking, Elspeth flung aside the bedclothing. She swung her feet to the floor. Her gown was damp with perspiration. She had not, at first, the strength to support herself. She clung to the side of the bed and dragged herself down its length towards the screen, towards the cradle. Her legs were like reed pith. Bare feet upon the carpet rolled as upon a sprinkle of tiny glass balls. But another grumble of thunder spurred her on. She let go of the support of the bed and struggled unsteadily to the cradle.

The position of the lantern had been arranged to keep direct light from falling into the cradle and lace diffused the candle's radiance and cast a strange, eerie aura about the baby's bed. Elspeth felt momentarily relieved. She had reached her new-born child, could protect her now. Her lips shaped into a little soft smile as she leaned forward.

The blanket was folded neatly. The flat silk pillow held in its centre the indentation of the little head. But the cradle was empty, her baby gone.

For once Anna knew where Matt intended to spend the night. He had told her – and had no need now for prevarication or lies – that he would be engaged in the running of a batch of still-whisky, assisting Pad Tomelty in a howff near Eardmore.

McDonald would see to it that Matt had a job of work in the forest which would allow him to slip off in mid-afternoon, make the long trail up the ridgeway before evening. It did not occur to Anna that Brigit, after she left Ottershaw, might also strike out for Eardmore to spend a few hours in Matt's arms. Anna had no clue that her husband and fellow-servant were erstwhile lovers. She had heard, of course, that Excisemen, abetted by a couple of King's Officers, were on patrol about the Lennox. But Brigit imparted very little hard information on the threat, just sneered at and scorned the inefficiency of the tax collectors and assured all and sundry that her father was far too clever to be laid by the heels – again.

Life within the house of Ottershaw had been reasonably placid during the summer months. With Gilbert gone, and his leg healed enough to enable him to ride, Randall was out and about for much of the day. He showed no inclination to involve himself in sporting groups or societies, a number of which courted his interest, or in the social round which was available to landed gentlemen, ponds flickering with eligible young girls whose mamas would be only too delighted to dower them away to a handsome bachelor landowner. Randall's predilection for more-or-less candid dallying with servant-girls put off all but the more ardent Dianas and his reputation grew charcoal-black as summer progressed and invitations and blandishments were not just refused but ignored.

Gilbert and Alicia had settled well into Strachan Castle, so well apparently that Alicia did not return to Ottershaw at all, not even to spy upon her brother-in-law. Gibbie turned up once or twice in the month to try to persuade Randall to make investment in the Farmers' Bank of Falkirk in which he, Gibbie, had purchased a partnership since Mr Angus Hildebrand had expressed guarded enthusiasm for the project. With the time of crop sales and the big autumn cattle marts approaching, however, Gibbie too had a press of business upon him and he did not show his face at Ottershaw at all in August.

It was the first full night that Anna had ever spent at Ottershaw. The arrangement was easily managed with the collusion of the redoubtable Hunter. A side door was left open; Anna departed at her usual hour, returned after dark. She was waiting for the laird when he came upstairs after late supper in the dining-room.

Love-making occupied the couple for a time, but the activity upon the bed was not now so prolonged or so fierce as it had been in the early months of summer. It was not that Anna had lost her enthusiasm or her longing to please the laird, or that Randall found her any less desirable; the plain, revealed fact of Anna's pregnancy made the relationship tender and more loving but less prolonged.

Unlike her sister, Anna had not kept the news of her pregnancy to herself for long. Almost as soon as suspicion of her condition came to her she had informed Randall. The laird, as was his way, had behaved unpredictably. He had not thrown her out or begun the process of disassociating himself from the relationship, both of which courses were open to a man in his position. Anna might have created a great fuss – but who would have paid her much heed? The 'scandal' was local and accepted. Those who could not come to terms with it pretended to ignore it. The advent of a love-child, in and of itself, would not spot the laird's reputation much worse than it was at present and all the little tensions and strains that the birth of a bastard might entail could be eased by parental practicality.

"Can you be sure that the child is not of your husband's making?"

Anna had answered honestly. "Not absolutely."

"How absolutely?"

"I think we made the bairn on the Monday of Whit."

Randall had laughed ruefully. "It would not surprise me, Anna, if we had made ten bairns on that day."

"It was that time, Randall, I'm sure of it."

"Will your husband imagine that the child's his?"

"Aye, he might. He's daft enough."

"I wouldn't wish that," Randall had said.

"What can we do?"

"I cannot possibly marry you."

"Aye, I know it."

"I mean, Anna, I could not marry you even if –"

"In two years o' marriage Matt never gave me a bairn."

"It's not the blood-line, Anna."

Anna, the dreamer, had quickly come to terms with reality.

"I want nothin', Randall, except that you keep me near you," she had said.

"What if – what if I decide, some day, that I must marry? I'm a Bontine, Anna. I might eventually feel that Ottershaw must have legitimate heirs."

"Do you feel that now?"

"I don't know, quite, what I feel now. No, I do not have any urge to seek a wife."

"What can we do, Randall?"

"Sinclair's the problem."

"Matt, do ye mean?"

"I was thinking more of my grieve. I wouldn't like to be without his services."

"Need he be told at all, about the bairn I mean?"

Randall had frowned. "If only –"

Anna was suddenly tense. "If only what?"

"If only we could be rid of your husband. He's the encumbrance to our arrangements," Randall had said. "If it was not for him, I could look after you. Aye, the child would be a bastard, no help for it, but you would be cared for, Anna, you and your babe."

"Can you not send Matt away?"

Randall had shaken his head emphatically. "I've no justification for it. What would be my excuse; that I want his wife?"

"What can we do, then?"

"Let me mull it over in my mind, Anna."

Now it was August, bordering September; Anna had grown quite plump, not so much about the abdomen but generally. Being Gaddy's true-born, she found her condition natural and had no fear of it. Fortunately she did not suffer many of the inconveniences of pregnancy, only increased appetite and a tenderness of the breasts. She considered it ironic that 'Pet should be so coddled, wrapped in wool in Moodie's mansion while she, bearing an heir to the Bontine family, was obliged to skiddle about her servant's duties and keep some sort of trim for Matt at Pine Cottage. At least she was not turned out to hoe weeds or for harvest gatherings, for Hunter drew the line at permitting 'his' staff to soil their hands with clay, eschewing the 'old ways' in these enlightened times.

Bitterness in Anna's marriage had dwindled. For somebody who doubted that sexual pleasure could be an enduring bond between a gentleman and a drove-wifie's daughter, then the attitude of Randall Bontine and Anna Sinclair to the impending event might seem cold-blooded.

The rough-hewn folk of the villages, let alone the doyens of Lennox society, could not have deduced how akin were the laird and the servant lass. The settlement which must be forged between them would contain few selfish advantages for either one, and the child, though not recognised, would never want for food and shelter. The bairn might have no civil rights, as would a lawful child, but would have Randall Bontine for father and Anna for mother and that would be enough natural material advantage for any son or daughter to inherit in the world. But there was Matt; Matt would surely be accounted father since Anna was his wife and had had connection with him within the period of gestation. For the good of her bairn's welfare and future, Matt Sinclair had to go out of her life.

That night, after love, Anna lay in Randall's arms in the huge island of a bed, not dulled by the exercise but with wits sharpened.

"Have you thought yet what we can do, Randall?"

"I've thought that we might – I might – confront him with the state of things and offer him a tidy sum to leave you and go abroad."

"America, maybe?"

"Well, hardly so far, Anna. Unless he wished it."

"We could concoct a rare story about that," said Anna. "Sayin' how Matt would send for me when he was settled. Even old Sinclair might believe it."

"No, not the Colonies," said Randall. "Perhaps Ireland. I could find him a position with my Uncle Alexander."

Anna sat up. "You're not thinkin' o' sendin' me there?"

"Calm yourself," Randall said. "I have no power, no inclination, to send you anywhere."

"All I ask is that I stay near you."

"What would this husband of yours take to leave Balnesmoor?"

"He'll resist. Not out of pride, out of malice," said Anna. "I know him. He'll do it for spite. He'll claim the bairn's his, though he'll know fine well it's not."

"How will he know?"

"Because I'll tell him."

"Do you hate Matt Sinclair so much, Anna?"

"Not hate; despise."

"Divorce, even if Sinclair could be made to agree to it, would take four years, after 'desertion' of husband, that is."

"Four years?"

"Your husband, of course, might divorce you," Randall said. "But then he would be obliged to cite a basis for the action and I fear that would be difficult to prove."

"I could show my baby t' the judges."

"Do you suppose that the child will bear such a striking resemblance to me that a judgement would be incontrovertible?"

Anna did not understand. She did not invite an explanation. She had condensed things down, simplified them with that high disregard for consequences which was her style. Anna had had an idea.

"I see little to chuckle about," said Randall.

The girl leaned across to touch the laird's scarred chest with her fingernails.

Outside the mansion thunder expanded the air over Drumglass and made the Cheviots restless in the park below Ottershaw, induced the ewes to bleat for their fat-grown lambs. It was not the panic roars that signalled that foxes were among the flock and Randall hardly registered the sounds, being intent upon Anna and her sudden skittish delight.

"Out with it," Randall murmured.

"My husband smuggles whisky for Pad Tomelty."

"So you've informed me. What of it?"

Anna dabbed a kiss on to her fingertips and planted it on the laird's lips.

"We'll turn him over," she said.

Randall sat up, hand on the girl's shoulder. "Turn him over?"

"To the Excisemen."

"Good God, Anna, that's harsh business, is it not?"

"Turn him over when we know he'll be carryin' kegs."

"I see no point in —"

"He'll sell the lot o' them. I know my husband. Matt'll tell all to save his neck."

"Smuggling's not a hanging offence, Anna, not unless he attacks an officer. At the worst of it he'll receive a sentencing to six months in Stirling jail."

"But if he peaches on Tomelty, he canna show his face near here again."

Randall took his hand from her shoulder and stroked his chin thoughtfully. "For fear of a reprisal from the smuggling gang?"

"Aye," said Anna eagerly. "An' you would offer him shelter."

"Where? In Ireland?"

"Ireland it would be."

"But he would wish you to go with him, would he not?"

"I would refuse."

"He'll never leave you, not if he thinks you're carrying his child."

"He'll not know, Randall. Don't ye see?" Anna said. "An' old Lachlan will thank ye for it too. I can stay on. Be near you, be here in Ottershaw for ever."

"It's a harsh thing, Anna."

"It could be so easily brought to pass."

Randall lowered himself to the pillows. He let his hand idly toy with her dark hair but did not at that moment meet her eye.

At length he said, "Let me enquire about the niceties of the law; that done, I'll consider it further."

"How long will you consider?"

Randall shrugged his shoulders. "Three days or four; a week at most."

Anna pursed her lips.

"Very well," she said.

But, always impulsive and quite obsessed with the brilliance of her scheme, Anna could not contain herself for one whole week. Before Randall could converse with Hildebrand, let the idea float, Anna had acted on her own account and unwittingly brought Matt into murder.

Elspeth's cry finally wakened Kerr who, rubbing her eyes, stumbled out of the closet and put her arms reassuringly about her mistress.

"She's – she's –"

"Ach, it's all right. Dinna be feared she's come t' harm."

"Where – where –" Gasping, Elspeth could not frame the question.

"Mister Moodie came in an' took her. About ten minutes since, that's all. He told me t' lie quiet an' not t' wake you since you were sleepin' so deep. He'll bring her back soon, I'm sure."

Kerr's arm about her did not much comfort Elspeth but the maid's explanation was credible and dulled the first shock of the empty cradle. It would be James, was typical of James.

"Och, but you're tremblin', Mistress Elspeth," said Kerr. "I'll awa' downstairs an' find the master."

"No," Elspeth managed. "I'll – you go back t' bed. I'll go down myself."

"You canna, in your condition."

"I'm not in any 'condition', Kerr." Elspeth sounded convincing. "I wish to go downstairs to join my husband."

"Let me fetch Betty."

"Kerr, will you go back t' your cot. At once."

Kerr hesitated. "Aye, Mistress Elspeth. If you're sure you'll –"

"Give me my robe."

Kerr held it out and Elspeth, hardly knowing how she supported herself, slipped her arms into the sleeves and drew the light garment about her. She was sore about the stomach but the initial weakness was passing. She was infused with a determination which stemmed from suspicion and, beneath it, a fear which she could not nominate at this hour of the muttering night.

Leaving Kerr, Elspeth opened the door and went out into the corridor. James had not gone downstairs. She needed no more guidance than the band of light beneath Mother Moodie's door to tell her where her husband had taken her child.

Fear grew in Elspeth again, pushing aside her debility. She went along the corridor and paused. She could hear her husband's voice and, very faintly, the tiny, fractious cry of her baby. She opened the door and slipped into the old woman's sick-room.

A battened screen with pastoral tapestry studded to its frame defended the area of the door, keeping out unwelcome draughts. Elspeth stood behind it, shoulder-blades pressed for support against the wall. She could see the blaze of a candelabrum, the impish flicker of firelight upon the ceiling, hear James clearly.

"Mammy, Mammy," James crooned. "Can you see her? Is she not bonnie? Would she not break your heart, being so bonnie?" He sang a snatch of a psalm tune, throaty and soothing, then said, "Aye, she's as bonnie as Bell was. My Isobel. She's her mother's fair features, though, as ye can see. Look, Mammy, please look at her. Your blood. Your great-grand-daughter. My grandchild."

Elspeth did not take in the import of James's address. She was listening nervously for some response from the old woman, for a voice to come out of the corpse-like bundle that would be propped in the chair or in the wooden bed. They went past her comprehension, the words that James had uttered and their true meaning. He did not repeat them.

Instead there came a faint whimper, not from the baby but from the old woman. It was the first sound Elspeth had heard Mother Moodie emit in eight or nine months that might not be other than random coincidence. She strained her ears, leaned heavily upon the wall to brace herself. She did not know what to do. Should she show herself, join James in the dark, proud exhibition of a grandchild to Mary Jean Moodie? Should she remain hidden by the screen or slip away now that she had established that her baby was safe? Yet Elspeth did not, in her skin and nerves, believe that her baby was safe in her husband's arms. The ritual of this night-showing distressed her, the thought that James might hold the new-born forward to be kissed by the raddled, spit-dribbled lips of the crone, trying to force his mother out of dementia in one final, talismanic moment of love.

"James."

Elspeth propelled herself away from the wall and came around the screen.

The sight that met her eyes inflamed her fear. It was not anything untoward in the scene, for the infant was snug in a shawl in James's strong arms and not close to the withered figure in the bed. Mother Moodie, who could not breathe while lying down, slept in an upright position, huge straw bolsters thrusting her chest forward and those vile leather straps around her, even at night, restraining and supporting the frail body. Her wig had been removed. Her hair was as scant and close to the bone-white scalp as lichen on a stone. Her eyes were wide open, wrinkled lids affixed. She stared – perhaps – at the little form in her son's arms.

The lips did move. Words did come; not words but sounds, just sounds, no more shaped and no more meaningful than the noises that the baby herself might make in a week or two, and hardly stronger.

"*Ba – ba – ba – bah.*"

"Baby, Mother," James urged, oblivious to Elspeth's presence. "Aye, a baby. Baby Moodie. A wee lass. See. See her."

"*Fa – fa – fa – fath.*"

"Aye, aye, Mammy. Speak."

Riven, silent, Elspeth watched the struggle for communication. She could not believe that Mother Moodie had made any real connection, only that the insistence of her son had sparked a moment of energy in the dying brain. Her tongue was a dried leather thong rolling in the half-open mouth, language itself forgotten.

"*Fath-th-fath-tay.*"

"Say it," James urged. "Say 'father'."

He stepped closer to the bed, turned the baby in his arms and held her upright like a doll.

"See her. She's ours. Can you not say 'father'?"

Elspeth could stand no more of it.

"James, stop. Please stop."

Whatever half-spell James had woven was broken by the girl's interruption.

Mother Moodie's eyes flickered and closed. As if exhausted by the effort she seemed to fall instantly asleep, head flopping against the leather straps, a bubble of saliva at the corner of her lips.

James swung round. He did not seem awkward with the baby but lowered her lightly into his arms again, cradling her. She fretted slightly, her little fists bunched by her chin. He inclined his shoulder over the bundle as if to indicate that he would not yet relinquish her, not even to Elspeth.

"How long have you been there?" James snarled.

"I just came."

"Should you not be asleep?"

He was angry with her for intruding. It had not occurred to him that he had given her a horrid fright.

"What did you hear?" was her husband's next question. "Did you see? Did you see how Mother knew me?"

"Yes, I saw."

"Leave her with me, then. Let her stay here with me."

"James, for God's sake, give her to me."

He glanced from the child to his mother and then, querulously, at his wife, his daughter.

"I must feed her," said Elspeth.

Her heart was palpitating. Her legs trembled under the robe but she would not show him weakness. It did not seem to strike James that she should not have been here at all, that he might harm her in this vulnerable period. Elspeth's fear shifted its axis, but she was outwardly calm and reasonable.

"Give her to me now, James, because it's so late. You can bring her to show to your mother tomorrow."

He crouched, almost dwarf-like. The fire flung his shadow in a grotesque, bent shape across the far wall of the room. Then, gradually, he straightened, became calm and concerned too.

"Did the thunder waken you?"

"Aye," said Elspeth.

"You should not be on your feet. You might do yourself injury, Elspeth."

"I — I am tired."

"Come." James put an arm tentatively about her, holding the baby snug against his chest. "I'll carry her to her crib. Lean on me, dearest."

James appeared to be himself again, kindness itself. He was concerned for her health and contrite about his thoughtless behaviour in removing the baby without her knowledge and permission. He escorted Elspeth back to bed, saw to it that Kerr settled both mother and infant.

Elspeth watched James go out of the room, heard the creak of the boards as he went away, not to his bedroom but downstairs to the hallway. She was shaking, sweating, but all notion of sleep had gone. Across the hills thunder still muttered but it had come no closer and Elspeth hardly heard it now.

"Kerr."

"Aye, Mistress Elspeth?"

"Kerr, bolt the door."

"But —"

"Bolt the damned door when I tell you."

Startled, the servant did as she was ordered without daring to question the reason.

Four days later, in the middle of the morning, Mother Moodie lapsed into unconsciousness and, before noon, was obviously and mercifully dead.

Celebration turned to mourning in Moss House.

And September began with rain.

Attitudes towards James Simpson Moodie and his executives had changed during the course of the summer, creating divisions which had not been recognised before the arrival of George and Trina Cunningham and the establishment of the shop under Rowan Hill. For reasons which Rudge could not fathom the Cunninghams were protected by old man Moodie. By extension they were part of the circle of authority, on almost an equal footing with Scarf and he – not a situation that Rudge wore lightly.

The shopkeepers were discreet in the manner of 'tapping

cash'; that is, they did not actually turn up at the manager's office on Saturday afternoons to claw off their owings in person. But it was because of the Cunninghams that paying days became fraught with tensions, because of the Cunninghams that Baynham the smith was obliged to stand by the table while the count-out was in progress.

Weavers who had ignored their wives' spendthrift habits, who had enjoyed good meat three or four times in the week, lads with a large capacity for whisky, coffee and tobacco addicts might well find that their dip from the oblong box on Mr Rudge's table had been reduced to a mere copper or two or even to nothing at all and, when shouting for dues, would be politely shown the ticket which had come down from the shop and reminded that credit was not unlimited.

When credit stopped, a man was condemned to a week or fortnight of gnawing on the knuckle, to hearing his bairns whimper from hunger, to humping his pride and scrounging on neighbours who had been less profligate than he. Boozers took it hardest of all. They believed that they had a right to special treatment, that the tap should not be turned off for them.

What galled Rudge most of all was that the Cunninghams never refused a customer credit over the counter and seemed, by inference, kind and generous friends of the workers. He, on the other hand, was put in the invidious position of doing their collecting for them, of saying *No*, of appearing to be a flint-hearted villain. He received glares, ugly insults, temper fits in the Cunninghams' stead while the couple remained snug in their shop, safe from the sordid business of debt collection.

If it had not been for the looming presence of Smith Baynham there would have been fisticuffs and brawls in or about the office and men would have been dismissed on the spot, making more work for the managers and causing even more ill-feeling. Baynham no longer played constable to the Cunninghams. He refused to patrol the stretch from the road-end to the shop; that, the smith claimed, was not Kennart and what went on there was none of his concern and must be sorted out by the traders.

On four or five occasions during June and July, Rudge had broached the problem with James Moodie. He had found the owner less than responsive, hardly receptive and not at all supportive. Moodie, with his rake-away from shop profits, had always been a man who believed in acquiring wealth by any means. What respect Rudge had nurtured for the self-made weaver faded like the blue of poor calico in summer weathers. By August he, Rudge, felt that he was the main prop of the weaving hamlet, its cornerstone against collapse.

George and Trina were not ignorant of the narrowness of the line which separated them from their just desserts. They had chestfuls of notes and coins buried here and there about Rowan Hill. Their expenditure on stock did not come near their income and, in the months of field-work, the shop drew customers from all around. Beer and spirits pulled in the pounds. A touch of extra salt or mustard in meats and pies did not harm the palates of tillers and sowers, hoe-women and harvesters, who came to the counter for refreshment.

George and Trina did not fear the accumulated wrath of the folk of Kennart. They had the protection of James Moodie and might twist the screw on him a good bit yet and, if trouble threatened from another quarter, might turn it in the direction of the owner's door without a qualm, knowing that Jamie would stand up for them against any odds since he had even less choice in the matter than he'd had before his dear young bride got filled with child.

On hot nights, when the long day's labour was over, George and Trina, worn out by affability, would top a jug with gin and lemon and carry it out to the stump at the front of the shop. There they would sit, buttock to buttock, staring up at the stars scattered along the blue edge of the afterglow. They would share the liquor jug, turn about and philosophise on Providence and Sin and let their imaginations wander to the future.

"She'll drop any day now, I'm thinkin'," Trina would say. "I've heard she's heavy."

"How did ye hear that, my love?"

"From yon lassie who sparks wi' Luke McWilliams."

"Luke McWilliams?"

"Moodie's young coachman."

"Oh, aye. Is it Stewart Murray's daughter he's makin' cow-eyes at?"

"The same. She tells me how Moodie's wife has not been

seen 'cept about the gardens this last month and how she's big as a barrel at the front."

"Is it this month, though?"

"It canna be much longer, unless she's droppin' a pair."

George would laugh, sip from the jug. "Twice as much grief for the weaver mannie, eh?"

"If they're his at all."

"Now, now, dearest! How could they be otherwise than his since she's not reputed t' be the 'independent' kind? Have ye heard t' the contrary?"

"The bairn's his, George. Who else could have done it?"

"By God, it's disgustin'."

"Waitin' twenty year t' find another Bell."

George would shake his head, pass the jug, suck on his pipe, stare up at the stars. "How can a man do that?" he would ask the heavens.

Trina would sigh, wheeze, drink. "When the bairn's a year, we'll bring Moodie in on the rope, eh? I've no taste for all this space, George. As ye know I'll be fell glad t' get back to my home town again, t' the city."

"Rich, Trina, rich. We'll go home rich."

"Rich enough, I suppose," Trina would say, since her definition of riches was not limited by surfeit any more than it was by necessity.

During spring and summer the Cunninghams crossed not a word with Mr Moodie, glimpsed him only at a distance. Monthly payments due to the mill-owner were punctiliously reckoned, changed into banknotes and despatched to Moss House in the bag of one of the mail-delivering McGowans. No receipt was expected or received.

George might have settled for Kennart, might have dug his roots in deep. Eventually he might have employed a lassie to do the cleaning and baking, a lad to heave sacks and take turn at the serving-counter. But he knew Trina too well to believe that they had taken their last cart-ride together. Trina would work with a will; it was not laziness but restlessness which would eventually drive her out of the rustic haven and back to the bustle of dear old Glasgow. George laid his plans accordingly.

In eighteen months or so he would offer the shop as a going concern, sell the 'business' to Mr Moodie. Mr Moodie would not quibble over the price or the cash value of the 'goodwill' that they had laboured to build up. Money thus earned added to money diligently saved would be invested to provide a comfortable income. And if they ever ran short they might return to Balnesmoor for a visit and approach their benefactor, James Simpson Moodie, in the sure-fire knowledge that he would grant them a 'loan' to tide them over.

The birth of a Moodie girl child, the Cunninghams believed, added strength to their schemes. George composed yet another flowery letter in which he offered congratulations and conferred finest blessings on mother and daughter. Unfortunately for him the letter arrived on Mr Moodie's dinner-plate on the day that his mother passed to meet her Maker; George could hardly be held to blame for that piece of ill-timing.

Details of the Moodies' doings travelled swiftly to the shop-keepers' ears. Matt Sinclair was an excellent source of news, for the young forester was garrulous when in drink. Luke McWilliams, who had served Moodie for years and had never forgiven the weaver for discarding him from Moss House when the wife arrived, slipped down to Kennart now and then in pursuit of Stewart Murray's daughter and would stop for a dram at the shop where he would pour out intimacies ten to the dozen.

It was from McWilliams that the Cunninghams heard how Mother Moodie had been buried with all the pomp and ceremony usually reserved for a queen. Jamie Moodie had followed the carriage from Moss House to the kirk, walking alone in advance of the other mourners. Old Jamie had a face on him like a thunder cloud, so furious and severe that no-body hardly dared speak with him even to offer the hand of condolence. It was a manly funeral with a big procession. The laird was there, Gibbie from Strachan Castle, Rudge, Scarf and even McAlpin; the notables added to by thirty or forty strangers in from all parts, men with whom Moodie did trade and who did not want to offend the producer of quality cloths.

"How did he comport himself? Did he weep?"

"Moodie? Nah, not him! He ground his teeth like millstones but never shed a tear."

From Matt Sinclair the Cunninghams heard how Gilbert Bontine returned to Moss House a few days after the funeral, stayed for half the morning and went away all chirruping and smiling; how the Ottershaw flock of Cheviots had been gathered up from the parks and shepherded along the turnpike and up the lane on to clean, cleared pastures on Dyers' Dyke; how parcels of new-bought Blackface began to arrive on Ottershaw soon after. From Matt the Cunninghams also learned that Moodie appeared as proud as a bloody peacock of his new-born daughter and was forever strutting about the house with the shawled baby, showing her off so much it was a wonder the poor infant didn't split at the seams with so much handling.

Neither McWilliams nor Matt Sinclair, however, brought the Cunninghams news of the letter that Mr Moodie despatched to Kilsyth, the last in a series, or of the rendezvous that was arranged between the weaver and a man named Fitter for an evening hour in the disreputable parlour of the Old Thorn Inn on Glasgow's outskirts. Matt would surely have recognised the features of the said Mr Fitter for it was a face you were not likely to forget. But nobody at all learned of that meeting, which lasted only a quarter of an hour, or of what passed there between the men.

If the Cunninghams had heard of it, being of a sly sort of disposition themselves, they might have twigged that something unpleasant was afoot, though not even George and Trina could have guessed that Mr Moodie, through the agency of Mr Fitter, planned to be rid of them, not just from Kennart but for good and all.

At one time, not so long since, Matt Sinclair might have been as puffed up as a bantam cock but he was not entirely stupid. The encounter with the King's Officers in March had badly shaken him. Nonetheless he was committed to a lawless course and could not very well demand his twelve pounds back from Pad Tomelty. Pad would be sure to let everyone, including Brigit, know that the grieve's lad had no stomach for adventure, had shown himself to be a coward. Rather than lose face Matt continued to smuggle whisky from the Tomelty stills. In fact he only felt secure when he was buried in Eardmore or crouched in a hole in the hillside by Pad's side, choking on the reek of peat smoke and watching the distillation drip-drip-drip from the lip of the worm. On the open roads, though, with kegs in a cart or flagons clinking in his saddle-packs Matt was as edgy as a cat in a kennel.

Mostly Matt moved his quotas of whisky by night and, where possible, discovered unused paths to carry him unseen to the backs of the Ramshead or the Bull or down to Rowan Hill. In summer he forded the Lightwater rather than risk appearing on one of the bridges, locations where Excisemen might be lying in wait. Gone was the carefree conceit that had drawn Matt into Tomelty's circle. He had finally begun to question his ability to cope with the stresses of being a whisky smuggler, to view the tedious existence of an estate manager as, perhaps, a more worthwhile end.

Matt Sinclair was the key to the riddle of what exactly took place at Kennart on a blustery night in mid-September in the year of 1813. No enquiring genius emerged to put all the pieces together and not constables nor King's men nor even the Sheriff of the county acquired a sufficiency of facts to do more than pick at the truth. James Simpson Moodie might have supplied a fat portion of fact and Anna Sinclair another, and the two, together with Elspeth, might have concluded that Matt was not only key but victim. But there was to be no family conference afterwards, no meeting of the three, and motives suggested in the Sheriff's Report were vague, flavoured with hints of political plotting.

The wind from the hill was gusting strong. Oaks shook and elms creaked. Pines in the plantation set up a massive brushy clash, which contrasted with the round howling of the wind across the open moorland and its scything hiss over the pastures of the Strath. Matt picked up the loaded pony in cloud-heavy twilight. The walk up from Ottershaw into the teeth of the wind had wearied even him and he was glad to rest for a quarter of an hour in the old black barn in Eardmore where Pad Tomelty waited.

Pad was considerate enough to have brought him a dish of boiled mutton and a half-loaf of bread. Matt ate hungrily, washed down the food with mouthfuls of whisky then hoisted himself into the saddle which was strapped to the pony's back. In swollen saddle-packs were two dozen blue glass flagons, each of which contained a quart of new-run whisky, the bottles swaddled in sackcloth and padded out with heather to prevent breakage.

The pony was large for the breed, arch-necked and sturdy. In daylight it might have trotted down the moor ridge in an hour and been at Kennart in two, even with a load. But night travel was hazardous and Matt would not risk the broken track that descended steeply over the shoulder of Drumglass. He would go round by Rossbridge, turn down off the moor miles east of Harlwood, cross the Endrick and then the Lightwater behind Balfron and come at Rowan Hill, about the hour of eleven, through the coppice on the long, long route; nobody would expect him to fling so far out from the stills. Besides, the tracks were flatter, less exposed to the half-gale that belled across the Lennox and showed no sign of abating before morning.

Pad Tomelty opened the barn door. Holding on his bonnet with one hand, back pressed against the boards, Pad shouted, "Tread wi' care, Matt."

"I will. I will."

"If it blows too fierce, lie up."

"I'm goin' by Rossbridge."

"Aye, then there's Miller's place t' shelter in, if needs be."

"I know it. Can he be trusted?"

"He can," said Pad. "Listen t' me, son, ye can bide here if the weather has ye worrit."

"The Cunninghams expect me tonight."

"They can wait."

"Nah, nah! On a night as wild as this," Matt shouted, "all the bloody Excisemen'll be indoors."

Pad laughed, shook his head and slapped the pony's rump.

Matt trotted out of the shelter of the barn into a crosswind which, blowing up to a gust, made the pony sway for a moment until it found balance and, tucking down its head, clopped forward steadily.

Eardmore was soon behind. Matt forged on, stooped over the feathery mane to offer less resistance to the flooding air. He was warm enough, for the wind had no bite yet. His belly was snug with the supper Pad had provided. He settled to the ride attentively, though the pony knew the road better than he did and, even packed, was sure-footed and game.

As he drove over the Fintry road the freshness of an unmown clover-lay tickled Matt's nostrils and the vicinity of Harlwood brought him the fermentations of dung and compost strew and a corn harvest half taken in. Smoke from crofts and steadings, the whiff of a hog-sty, a multitude of smells woven in the wind told Matt where he was, while the pony picked tirelessly on, wheeling nearer and nearer to Kennart.

Matt was neither fearful nor apprehensive. He sincerely believed that the riding officers of the revenue, Georgie's appointed bully-boys, were weaklings who would not brave strong weather for the sake of duty. Nor had he Anna's infidelity on his mind, the frustration which thoughts of his wife with the laird engendered.

Anna had been informed that he would be gone all night. She demanded no explanation. Casually he had told her that he would be making a drop to the Cunninghams. She did not ask why he would not return to Pine Cottage, did not care a fig. If Anna chose to spend the night in Bontine's bed it was no skin off Matt's nose. He would find solace and satisfaction in one of the hay-sheds by the backs of Balnesmoor, with Brigit. Yet he had lost the hunger for Brigit that once had been so keen. He did not wish to be shut up in a cottage somewhere with her; nor did he wish to escape into some travelling future. Matt had arrived at a static state, neither free nor bound. He wanted nothing much but a long rest after the job was done. If Matt had been a shade more nervous, if the wind from the hill had not blunted his caution, he might have spotted the rider who had dogged his tracks all the way from Eardmore.

The wiry, nimble figure was seated on a pony no less sturdy than Matt's own beast but the stranger's mount was free of pack or saddle-bags. Quicker to the rein, it stepped and halted, tripped on swiftly again in response to the touch of the rider, a bearded man who had lain in wait in the rocks above Eardmore since sunset. Not until it became certain that Sinclair could be bound for no other place than Kennart did the stranger break off his shadowy pursuit. He galloped down a dip below the coppice and, reining again, rolled slow and quiet through the mill hamlet, past the darkened mill buildings and the sleeping cottages and up the path to the Cunninghams' shop.

Hugh Fitter from Kilsyth was not the only stranger in the vicinity of Rowan Hill that gusty night, however.

Crouched in the bracken by a straggle of hawthorn just above the shop was the gauger from Drymen, Kerr Johnston by name. Johnston was heart-in-the-mouth nervous. After all he was only a humble gauger, a measurer and calculator, who had never before been on a raid with the riding officers. He was not, strictly, riding with them now. He had no horse or garron and had been instructed to leg it down to Kennart in advance of the mounted patrol and put himself in a scouting position before sun set behind Ben Lomond. He had been warned that if he gave the show away, if the Cunninghams twigged to his presence, it would be as much as his job was worth. Soon after dark six mounted men arrived in a glade a quarter of a mile away, protected by the hedgehog hump of the hill. By then Johnston was cold, tense and hungry. He cursed the sender of the anonymous letter which had been slipped beneath his door very early that morning, damned to hell the vindictive swine who had peached on George and Trina Cunningham in terms too detailed to ignore.

At first Johnston had considered ignoring the tip, burning the single sheet of paper on the fire. But he feared that his superiors might learn of his neglect of duty and dismiss him from service. He raged and wrestled with his conscience for an hour or so and then hurried out to the livery stable at Buchanan, hired a fast horse and able young rider, at government expense, and despatched the original letter and a missive of his own devising, under seal, to Gartmore where two revenue officers were currently billeted.

Five hours later, about one o'clock, Ronald Cecil ambled into Drymen, posted his horse outside the gauger's house and went inside. Though Cecil was English, there was nothing unusual in his appearance to rouse suspicion in the minds of those who were sympathetic to smugglers or in the pay of Padric Tomelty. Within the gauger's house, however, the plan was made, Johnston's part in it made clear. If the letter was not a simple mischief, and it did not seem so, then a delivery of hill-run whisky would be made after dark to the Cunninghams of Kennart. A raid would catch the culprits, buyers and sellers, red-handed.

Ronald Cecil and his cohort, John Barnes, had borrowed

four experienced militiamen from the Duke's brigade and had them in readiness, eager and armed to the teeth, in a deep wood behind Buchanan. They would advance stealthily to a glade by Howe's gate close to Kennart to await Johnston's signal that the smugglers had arrived, then the six mounted men would move in upon the shop and net the transgressors. In Cecil's opinion there would be no blood shed.

So Hugh Fitter came on the unencumbered pony, tethered it off the path some distance below the shop and crept up to the cottage with all the stealth of a hunting stoat. Expecting at least one pack-animal, Johnston did not notice the arrival of the man from Kilsyth. It would have been better for Matt if he had, if the alarm had been raised prematurely.

It would have been better for the Cunninghams too, for before Matt rode up to the cottage some twenty minutes later George and Trina Cunningham were dead.

Betty bathed the morsel about half-past nine, lifted her like a troutling from the wooden tub before the nursery fire and dabbed her dry with a huge white towel. The baby, who had already acquired the name by which she would be baptised, Mary Jean, seemed quite at home in the warm water but did object to being coddled in a towel. She set up a girn of quite blistering temper and did not shush until she had been wrapped in her napkin and dressed in her fleece bodice and clean night-robes. Already, so Betty said, the wee thing had learned that the towel ordeal would be followed by a feed which was why she fell quiet and patient in the servant's arms and graciously permitted herself to be carried downstairs to the drawing-room where Papa and Mama waited.

Perhaps it was a cottar mentality that led James to instigate the odd little ceremony of the late-night feed. Elspeth did not object to it, since she had none of that sort of snobbishness in her either and did not believe that babies should, as a matter of course, be kept strictly out of sight or that the tending of them was something of which a mother should be ashamed. She suspected, however, that James enjoyed the paradox which the drawing-room's elegance made of the business of breast-feeding. The 'picture' must be pretty. Elspeth must wear her hand-stitched gown with an unfashionable separation of jacket and petticoat, wisps of sleeves and a drape which, for modesty's sake, she held across her breast while baby sucked. James also primped himself up; full evening dress, olive-suited, a white marcella waistcoat, even buckled shoes which he generally considered effeminate. While Elspeth fed the infant James would stand at a respectful distance, sipping coffee, head cocked, a smile hovering at the corner of his lips, chuckling now and then when the baby's greedy gurglings became too impolite to ignore.

The establishment of a nursery had been James's idea. He had executed it with his usual speed and thoroughness. The nursery had been Mother Moodie's sick-room. Only three days after Mother Moodie's departure, her tiny namesake was installed there. The room held ghosts, however, given substance by unpleasant connotations. It also separated Elspeth from her baby, though that was the style in 'society' and Betty was a tender and careful nurse. Wary of her husband, particularly in the days following his mother's death, Elspeth let him have his way, negotiating not at all for her wishes, concerned to draw a line only when the baby's comfort and welfare were concerned.

But James was a doting father; almost too doting. Elspeth could not rid herself of the feeling that James wanted the baby for himself, to claim and possess it. Certainly, he was in and out of the nursery all day long, often while she was having a nap in her bedroom or occupied with minor chores of housekeeping. He would 'walk' the baby, quite safely but in a manner that was alien to a majority of gentlemen, hugging her lightly, murmuring to her in confidential tones, showing her this and that object about Moss House, promising her that, come the warm days, he would show her his horses and his baa-lambs and the splish-splash wheel of his mill.

Little Mary Jean was seldom cross when she was in James's arms. This rankled with Elspeth, gave her prickles of envy and apprehension. A child so young required mothering, not fathering, but she put up no objection, seeing in James's attachment to the baby a relief from the grief of his mother's illness and passing.

Mother Moodie's chair was the only one of her possessions that James retained. Clothing, personal things, were parcelled tidily and taken away – taken where, Elspeth did not enquire – but the throne-like chair was carried into James's private study and installed there, though it seemed too large and looming for the small chamber.

James had written to his sisters, double-duty letters informing them of the death of their mother and the birth of his daughter. Neither sister had so far replied. In due course, perhaps, some formal little note would be brought by the post to Moss House, a gift of linen or a trinket for the new baby, but the Moodie sisters had fashioned their own lives and had long ago shoved James and Balnesmoor behind them. If James was hurt by their neglect he gave no indication of it. To Elspeth he seemed at peace with the world. He referred to little Mary Jane as 'my daughter' and promised a christening celebration that would shake the Lennox with its lavishness.

When not in the baby's company, however, James was indrawn and silent. He spent hour upon hour in the study. His trips away from home had been curtailed by circumstances but he seemed in no hurry to put on the mantle of management again. He did not even ride out to supervise the transfer of the Ottershaw Cheviots to Dyers' Dyke, left it entirely to the Macfarlanes. He had been gone from Moss House only once, for a half-day, and had taken the horse and not the cabriolet.

Gilbert Bontine had paid a call only a few days after Mother Moodie's burial, the arrangement having been made outside the kirk. Elspeth's question as to the purpose of Gilbert's visit was met with a vague reply, delivered with a touch of wry amusement. Gibbie had gone into banking, it seemed, and was unashamedly bearding customers for the Falkirk Farmers'.

"Will you give him your business, James?"

"Some of it, perhaps."

Anna had not come near Moss House, nor had she written to her sister or made any other attempt at communication. Elspeth wondered if Anna was jealous of her state of motherhood or if, for some other reason, Anna was deliberately slighting her. Of Miss Blaven she had seen nothing, heard nothing for months. She did not anticipate that she would ever have other than accidental meetings, if that, with the spinster again.

Moss House had become the hub of her existence, brought about with her daughter's arrival. She would probably bear no more children. Mary Jean must fulfil for her all that a family should be and for twenty or thirty years she would live the life that James arranged for her, without folly or adventure, and only the unfurling of her daughter's destiny to satisfy and console her. Perhaps it would be enough. Perhaps that was all there was. At least she had all the creature comforts that money could buy, a security and respect many a young wife would envy.

And then it all changed, changed with dramatic and devastating suddenness, as it had on the night of the great rain-storm which had drowned the Nettleburn and induced her mother's fatal illness.

Elspeth would never forget the moment, precisely recorded by the striking of the little Turkish clock on the mantel-shelf.

Eleven.

James turned his head at the sound. She saw her husband's profile, blunt and swarthy, and then, through a narrow gap in the drapes that covered the long windows, that queer, smudged glow in the middle of nowhere.

Hedges shut off the front of Moss Road. Trees were posted adjacent to the gate. Elms marched down the line of the Kennart road; yet there was a sight-line, an unsuspected optical deception which revealed, even in the autumnal season, the lift of the hill above Kennart.

Mary Jean nuzzled against her breast, tugging on the nipple. Elizabeth could not leap to her feet.

"James?"

The Turkish clock was still chiming.

"James, what's that in the sky?"

The smudge of reddish-yellow light waxed and waned. Across it, without dimension, danced the shapes of leaves flung about by the wind.

"Hm?"

"There, across the fields." Elspeth nodded.

She had shifted position on the chair, instinctively tightening her grip on the baby, drawing her forearm across her little legs.

"Do you see it?"

She glanced from the gap in the curtains and for a split second read in James's expression a mingling of guilt and foreknowledge that reason could not later erase. It was as if

322

he had been expecting something to happen. He strode to the window, flung back the curtain and, with arms raised, pressed against the glass.

"Good God, it's Kennart!" he said. "Kennart's burnin'. Someone's fired the mill."

Matt reined the pack-pony and straightened in the saddle. His back was stiff, his thigh muscles ached and he was no longer relaxed. In the window of the Cunninghams' cottage a lantern showed its light, an agreed sign that all was well, that George was ready to unload the flagons and stow them safe away. Matt respected the Glaswegians, though he did not much like the fat woman. They were an experienced pair, though, and clever at manipulating the laws, had licences and permissions to deter the gaugers if they were pushed to an inspection.

Since that day in March there had been no reports of King's Officers in the neighbourhood. Pad had told him that two of the devils were billeted in Gartmore to raid down into the forests around Loch Ard, breaking the small still trade that flourished in the hinterland. Riding for the revenue was work only for ruthless, devoted young men, those with no affection for impoverished brethren or love for the native drink itself, a natural employment, in other words, for Englishmen anxious to rise in esteem. Pad promised Matt that Kennart, Balnesmoor and Ottershaw would be safe from serious harassment since the parish was protected by the good names of Mr Moodie and Sir Randall Bontine.

Pad Tomelty's assurances notwithstanding, Matt stood his ground for two or three minutes on the crown of the path. He was aware of every sound, every stir in the brush, but the air was alive with noise and movement since the wind found a funnel in the narrow glen.

Matt took a deep breath, pinned his attention on the dab of colour that was the lantern and gave the pony a touch of the heel.

Wooden shutters which closed off the shop rattled on rope hinges. Matt brought the pony to the lee of the shop and dismounted. He ached so much that at first his legs would hardly support him. He stamped his feet to restore circulation before tying the pony to a hitching-post. The animal sagged its head in search of a few leaves of grass or weed-bite along the bottom of the wall. Matt rubbed his palm affectionately along its shoulder; the wee beast had done well and made fine time considering the weather.

Flexing his back muscles, Matt walked around the shop frontage to the cottage's low-lintelled doorway which was barred by a pine-board door.

Again Matt paused. Still stiff, he whirled his arms about his head in a windmill, grunting as the tensions eased.

Beneath the door light showed.

Matt knocked, waited, then thumbed down the latch and pushed the door inward. It was surprising that Cunningham had not come out to greet him. George Cunningham was usually eager and alert. Perhaps the windy din of the night had muffled the sounds of his arrival.

"Mister Cunningham."

Stooping, Matt entered the cottage.

"George? Are ye there, man? I've brought the –"

If Matt had been of short stature, Pad's size, say, the cheese-wire would have snapped clean about his gullet, he would have found his breath cut off and been strangled where he stood. But Matt's breadth of shoulder and his posture deceived the attacker. The wire loop snapped on his shoulder, ruching up his jacket, and became embedded in his collar flap.

Instinctively Matt reared up to full height. He thumped his forehead on the beam at the kitchen entrance but hardly felt the blow. He stared into the deserted kitchen, lit by firelight and lantern-glow. A stool had been overturned, crockery smashed, a gin bottle spun languidly on the hearthstone.

He bellowed, "GEORGE."

Somehow he knew that his assailant was not George Cunningham. Cunningham was too bulky. The impression was of a wiry man, somebody small and nimble. He must have been positioned behind the buckram curtain which closed off the lead to the shop.

Matt felt the man's hand tear at his cheek and jaw, striving to jerk his head back and work the wire under his chin. Matt buried his chin in his chest and in that same instant pitched himself backwards with all his might. Caught by surprise, the attacker rammed into the post of the shop lead and had the breath knocked out of him. He released his grip on the handle of the cheese-cutter, snatched at the buckram curtain, fell through it and was lost for a moment behind its crackling folds.

The tiny hallway confined the struggle. It was like fighting in a coffin and Matt, terrified and furious, plunged about like a bull, flailing his fists into the bulging curtain. The man came out low, head low. He butted Matt in the pit of the stomach, winding him in turn and charged him backwards into the kitchen.

"GEORGE. GEORGE."

Trina Cunningham lay on the far side of the hearth. She was clad only in an undershift, stockings wrinkled like snakeskins about her thick calves, her mountainous stomach protruding obscenely. Her head was craked round, eyes popping, tongue, black, lolling from a gaping mouth. Attentive even in death, George was close beside her, stuffed into the corner, head and arms hanging over the rush-bottomed chair with which he had been propped up.

Piled about the pair, like a martyr's pyre, were sugar sacks and baskets, sheaves of dry corn all drenched in oils and, by the stink, in spirits. Blankets and the mattress from the half-loft had been hauled down and added to the pile and it was into this snarl that Matt toppled, with the murderer on top of him.

Matt did not see the knife. He hardly felt the dart of the little vee-shaped blade across his cheek, nor the stab of it into the muscle below his collar-bone. He was astonished when blood flecked the mattress, flung out by the violence of his motion. Pumped up by fear, the little man was no match for Matt's power. When the hand darted in again Matt caught it with his right hand. The knife, a short, two-edged dirk, flickered close to his right eye and he flinched his head back from it, fearing for his sight. But now he could see his attacker's face and recognised the stranger, Fitter, whom he had encountered at Eardmore. Forked beard and sallow complexion were unmistakable.

Tomelty, Pad Tomelty had sent this hireling to destroy the Cunninghams, to destroy him. Tomelty must be behind it. Realisation burst like gunpowder in Matt's brain. He roared aloud with the pain of it. No longer inhibited by fear, his rage was raw and red. He had been betrayed into a violent plot, into murder. He would make Tomelty pay for his twelve-pound treachery.

Sensing the change in his victim's mood, Fitter scrambled

to escape. Desperately he lashed out. His forearm struck Matt on the bridge of the nose, dazzling the forester with pain. But Matt continued to cling to the knife-arm. He used it to drag himself to his feet and, in the same movement, to draw Fitter down into the mattress. When he was upright, Matt twisted and wrenched at the man's arm. He heard Fitter cry out in agony. With all his force he hurled the murderer across the kitchen.

The knife skittered and pattered loose over the floor. Fitter rebounded from the far wall, close to the window. Sinclair was too physically strong for him. He had failed to catch the young man by surprise as he had done Cunningham and the woman. Sinclair would not buckle, would not give him another opportunity to strike. Fitter groped for the lantern on the window ledge and flung it at Matt's head.

Matt fended off the lantern. He did not see where it fell. It thudded into the straw pile close to Trina Cunningham's body. The candle bobbed out. Thin petals of flame caught the edge of a frayed sheet, puffed into pale blue scallops and burrowed with a fierce little crackle into the strew. The warmth of the hearth-fire had partly evaporated the fuels which Fitter had sprinkled on the pyre. Flame spread in a series of soft sighs. Matt did not notice the rapidity with which the stuff ignited. He was intent upon nailing Fitter.

The man had retrieved the knife from the floor. It was a tool, not a butcher's blade. He had not intended to use it as a weapon. He had been instructed to feign an accident. Fire had been his weapon, fire and the cheese-cutter which, together, would leave no positive traces of foul play. He had, however, underestimated Sinclair. Now he must leave the job only two-thirds done. Fitter crabbed towards the door. Matt lunged at him. Fitter parried at him with the dirk. Ignoring the danger, Matt caught his arm again, swung him violently against the wall and fell against him, fingers fastened about the bearded jaw. Fitter pumped the blade into Matt's flesh but the knife was too short to do stopping damage. Matt's fingers tightened, his thumbs found the windpipe.

Specks of red and black whirled in the air. A shimmering veil of flame outlined Sinclair's head. From the corner came a loud crack as a thin glass bottle shattered in the heat and spread more oil into the blaze. Smoke sucked over the hearthstone into the draught of the chimney, followed by ribbons of red flame. Fitter struggled frantically to break Matt's grip. He drove his knees into the young man's stomach and Matt slackened for a moment. Choking, Fitter dropped and butted Matt in the mouth with the crown of his head.

Matt staggered back, dazed. Blood oozed from the puncture wounds in his leg but he was not seriously weakened and had no thought for the injury. He wanted to wring from Fitter due confession, to have Fitter name his master.

The door delayed him. Fitter could not hold against Matt's strength for long, however. Knee braced against the post, both fists on the handle, Matt strained and hauled until Fitter, on the outside, was forced to yield. He let go suddenly. The door flew inwards and Matt again went sprawling.

On his left the kitchen was a mass of flames and coiling smoke. Air from the open door fanned the blaze. Though Matt could not see it, the chair against which George Cunningham was propped was burning and the shopkeeper's clothing smoked and smouldered, his features turning black. Fat Trina's arm wore a bracelet of fire and her shift was laced with flame. Beams and boards had ignited and as soon as the gusting wind found openings, cottage and adjoining shop would bellow swiftly into a furnace of heat and light. Nothing much would be left upon which to build a tale, truth would be lost with the evidence. Beneath his anger, Matt realised it. He thrust himself out of the cottage into the night and set off down the path to Kennart in pursuit of the man named Fitter.

Four minutes had elapsed since Matt had brought the pony to the lee of the shop. Unknown to the young forester, Mr Johnston, the gauger from Drymen, had been most active in that time. Identifying the pack-pony and guessing at the contents of the saddle-sacks, the gauger had crawled out of his hawthorn hide and had set off like a rabbit down the back side of Rowan Hill to rouse the riding officers.

There had been talk of flares and signals but in the end Revenue Officer Cecil had decided that a combination of stealth and speed would trap the smugglers effectively. He had split his force. Barnes and one militiaman would gallop down to the Kennart road to stopper that avenue of escape while he led the others into the narrow glen. Cecil had calculated that it would take Johnston five minutes to raise the alarm, that three or four would see the horsemen out of hiding and into sight of the shop. No cargo could be unloaded in less time than that, particularly as the smugglers would not feel pressed.

Johnston had his nose towards the glade. Weaving among the trees, he did not see the fire break out. Cecil and Barnes, however, caught the first hint of the conflagration which would reduce the Cunninghams' property to greasy mounds of char and debris; a shower of sparks, sucked through the cottage chimney, soared high over Rowan Hill.

"What the devil!" Barnes shrilled.

"Looks like the lum's awa'," said one of the militia.

"Chimney be hanged," Cecil snapped. "That's a roof at least."

Urged on by his superior, Barnes sawed his horse round and, with one of the militiamen behind him, set off at a gallop for the curve of the hill. Cecil wasted no time in leading his group past the alderbrake and on to the sheep pad down which Johnston would appear. Gauger and riding officer met some hundred yards from the base of the hill.

"How long have they been there?" Cecil shouted.

Rasping for breath, Johnston got out, "Only – only minutes, Mister Cecil, sir."

"How many of them are there?"

"One man an' a pack-animal."

"There must be others, hidden somewhere."

"Only – only the one, sir."

"Did you recognise him?"

"No' – no' verra well."

A plume of flame, decorated with sparks, curved high over the hill-top ahead of the revenue officer and his men. Cecil opened his mouth to question Johnston further but the gauger had clutched his side and fallen into a sitting position on the bank. The situation had begun to twist out of the shape that Cecil had intended for it and he was suddenly possessed by a fear that the smugglers had somehow outwitted him. With a wave of his arm and a wild shout he led the horsemen on, as fast as they dared ride, into the ramp that sloped up to the tight-headed little glen.

He was no longer steering blind for the burning cottage gave enough light to guide him through thorn bushes and willow shrubs. But he had seen something else, something that caused him to spur his horse with reckless urgency; the shape of a man running hard down the path towards Kennart.

Cecil should have ridden on in pursuit of the fugitive but pity constrained him to check on the pad outside the cottage. The building was well alight and, even as he watched, fire slithered and expanded deep within the recesses of the shop. Through warped shutters he could see its suffusion, hear the slump and hiss of comestibles turning to flame. Sight of the pony roped fast to the hitching-post by the gable arrested the revenue officer. He would curse that few seconds' delay. But the pack-animal was kicking and bucking and in sheer terror and he could not quite trust the local men not to leave it to suffocate, to ride willy-nilly after him.

With his cutlass he gestured.

"You, be quick. Free the beast before the wall falls. I need the evidence on its back."

The militiamen were brave and two ducked against the waves of heat that emanated from the cottage and were not an instant too soon in pulling the pony away. The shop, being built mostly of wood, broke and collapsed inward without warning.

Embers and hot fragments wafted across the riders, making their mounts too unmanageable. The militiaman who had charge of the two vacant saddles found himself with his hands full. Being unable to do much else, he permitted the animals to prance out of range of the spume from the blaze into the turn of the Kennart track. Several minutes of chaos ensued. Thrusting and pulling at the reins in a vain endeavour to control his horse, Cecil could not forge a way past the refractory horses. At length the revenue officer found room and, leaning forward, gave his mount its head. But he did not charge far along the path. The night was bright with flames and the shape of the man on the path was obvious. So quick did Cecil come upon him, though, that only skilful riding, a striding jump, prevented the body being crushed by flying hoofs.

From Kennart the first of the weavers arrived, young men and eager boys, cheering for some weird reason, as if the fire were part of a festivity which old George and fat Trina had laid on to promote their wares. Visible above the ranks, slashing and bulling through them without regard for the labourers' skins, came Barnes and his companion.

For a second or two Cecil was at a loss what to do. He realised immediately that the fugitive could not have run off by the path to the mill. Barnes would hardly have let him slip unchallenged into the crowd; not even Barnes would be so foolish as to ignore a man sprinting in the wrong direction.

"Damn you, keep back. Keep away," Cecil cried. "Barnes, hold them where they stand."

Cecil cocked a leg across the saddle and slid to the ground. Holding the horse by him, he stepped across the path to the prone figure, knelt.

The officer had no need to make an examination.

The fellow was clearly beyond all mortal aid.

The deer-horn handle of a dirk protruded from his throat. Blood dappled his chest and trickled from his lips, matting the queer forked beard.

"Who is this man?" Cecil demanded.

Nobody in the gathering crowd answered him.

For nobody knew.

Until he waded into the Lightwater Matt was oblivious to the extent of his wounds. He had been driven by panic, blind panic. He had supposed that the King's Officers would thunder on to him, trample him underfoot like a rat or an otter. He did not, however, immediately surrender to a fate that seemed inevitable. He had got what he wanted from Fitter. Cold and hard as an icicle in the centre of his fear that knowledge stood.

Fitter's answer had stunned him so much that he had released his hold on the assassin and been stabbed again for his stupidity. There had not been enough fight left in Fitter, however, to check Matt's furious retaliation. In a brief, split-second scuffle, the blade had been driven through Fitter's gullet. He had slumped against Matt, gagging and vomiting. Matt had lowered him to the ground, afraid that somehow he would be pinioned by the hard, grasping hands, be held in the dying man's grasp. He was scared away from the body by the appearance of horses flying down the glen. He had turned and headed for Kennart, for cover, leaving Fitter on the path behind him.

Out of the cottages, like bees from a bank-hive, weavers and spinners emerged as Matt broke from the shrubs at the mouth of the path. Fire capped the hill. The smell of it, billowed on the wind, had been enough to rouse the mill-workers from their beds.

How many of the vanguard had spotted him, let alone recognised him, Matt could not be sure. He was not one of them, could not appeal to their sense of fellowship, put himself with them against the King's men. He veered to the right, stumbled across the lumpy road that wandered out of Kennart and straggled uphill towards Drymen. He crashed through a sparse hedge and down on to the patch of marshland that bordered the river. Hubbub, fire, shouting drove him on. Temporarily safe in the darkness of the vale, the river black against black before him, he did not hesitate, but waded down into the water and struck out for the far bank above which lay Fumarts Wood.

Initially the water revived him; then all the wounds that Fitter had inflicted began to smart, ache and leak blood. Shock caught up with Matt, making his belly gripe. Treading water in the deep channel, he let the river support him while he retched in spasms.

The Lightwater was not particularly deep or wide and Matt needed to make no effort, apart from keeping afloat, to cross it. The current dragged him twenty or thirty yards downstream and nudged him against a barrow of silt and mud. He crawled up it on all fours, still retching, grabbed the roots that overhung it and pulled himself on to dry ground again. Drained, he could do nothing but rest under the protection of the bank, while the fire-glow spouted volcanically from the hill and scribbled its reflections upon the water at his feet.

He had killed a man. In fight or not, he had murdered a man. Matt felt no shame, no remorse, only hopeless despair. He would be hunted down and caught. Tried, convicted, hanged. He would bring shame to his father and mother, to his brother Sandy and his sisters. He could not, even now, undo it. His enemies would rejoice at his downfall, that doom which he had courted and brought upon himself and his family in a measure out of all proportion to his trivial crimes.

Anna and Bontine would laugh at his capture. They would be free of him. Once he was dead they might marry if that was what the laird desired. Pad Tomelty would not defend him, in court or out of it. Pad would have news of the burning, and be away across the hills, forsaking his stills and grain-stores, wife and children. Brigit would spurn him too; he had gone too far even for her.

But of all the folk in Ottershaw and Balnesmoor who would bless the outcome of that violent night, James Simpson Moodie was the one Matt hated most of all.

"Tell me who sent you. Tell me or I'll throttle you."

Fitter's gesture of malice was the confession itself.

He grinned. "Weaver Moodie sent me."

"Moodie? Who paid your bloody fee?"

"Weaver Moodie."

"But why? For what purpose?"

"To have you killed, all three."

"To murder me too?"

"Aye, you most of all."

There no longer had to be logical reason for Jamie Moodie's behaviour. Matt had a glimmer of motive behind the weaver's plotting, a glimpse of the subtle stuff of guilt and jealousy of which he grew more certain as he cowered under the river-bank.

Across the Lightwater he could make out the King's Officers as they trotted across the road, riding hither and thither. One had a lighted lantern on a pole, another a pine torch. About them milled the weavers, prying and laughing, crying back news to the shawl-wrapped women and children who stood about the cottage doors.

Matt stirred himself. He hoisted his chest over the bank and rolled himself into the weeds.

Crouched, he scuttled forward into the shelter of the trees and started at a run through the wood, not in search of sanctuary or escape but towards the turnpike, bound for the head of the village and Moss House.

TEN

The Lost Man

Long after midnight Elspeth was not only awake but up and about. She had seen to it that little Mary Jean was settled in her cot and Betty installed in the nursery to meet with any crises which might arise, then had gone into the echoing upstairs parlour which was seldom used for any purpose at all and had joined Tolland at the window there.

Steward and mistress were not the only ones who looked from Balnesmoor upon the fire and smoke that wreathed the crown of Rowan Hill below. Servants huddled in the gardens and, in the loft of the coach-house, grooms and stable hands crowded like pigeons. Bold Luke McWilliams had begged the use of a horse to ride down after his master to see what was truly amiss at Kennart but his request had been sternly refused. If the presence of servants was required by Mr Moodie then Mr Moodie would find a means of sending for them.

It did not take Tolland and Elspeth long to conclude that it was not the mill that had caught alight and that the fire did not seem to have spread from its original source, though whether it had been contained by reason of bucket-labour or simply the whim of the wind they could not, from such a distance, deduce. Unusual sounds floated up from the valley. Faint shouts and cries added to the half-heard, half-imagined crackle of the fire itself. What it meant, the occupants of Moss House would learn only when the master returned. By a quarter to midnight there was little left to see; just a dust of embers in the darkness which flickered slightly as the big gusts tumbled over them.

Tolland chased the servants to their beds, locked all doors and windows, saving the kitchen door which he left unbarred against Mr Moodie's return. Duty done, the steward brewed tea in one of the kitchen pots, toasted and hot-buttered slices from the day's loaf at the grid of the oven and, relaxing formality, asked Mistress Elspeth if she would care to join him for a late bite of supper. He had judged, rightly, that the young woman was agitated and might be glad not only of refreshment but of company.

Elspeth followed Tom Tolland downstairs into the servants' domain. She never lingered here since her presence intimidated the girls. But she made her tours of inspection with a certain wistfulness, attracted to the long, low-beamed kitchen and its cosy warmth. Perhaps she would have been happier as James's housekeeper. Such an arrangement would have saved him embarrassment, the deceit necessary to ensure that she did not share his bed or any sort of intimacy.

Seated at the baking-table, Elspeth and Tolland speculated on what might have caused the fire and which particular dwelling had been destroyed. They concluded, again, that it might be the new shop, the store managed by the Cunninghams. Tolland waxed eloquent on the disservice they had done to Kennart by bringing drink and credit to the villagers. He did not so far forget his place, however, as to criticise Mr Moodie for permitting the Glaswegians to settle in the mill-hamlet and kept to himself much of the gossip that had come his way concerning the pernicious influence that the Cunninghams seemed to have over his master. Elspeth felt her restlessness begin to wane. Perhaps, she thought, she soon would go upstairs to bed, leaving James to find his own way in or, more probably, for Tolland to sit up until the master returned.

Neither of them caught the series of noises that, on a calmer night, would have had Tolland reaching for the heavy-handled broom. But the wind was loud off the Orrals and boomed about the back of Moss House as well as the front. It confused even the dogs in the stable yard so that they lifted their heads from their forepaws and frowned but did not bark an alarm.

The crash of the door from the kitchen yard brought Tolland to his feet. He had taken two steps towards the corner where the broom was kept when the inner door, into the kitchen itself, flew open and Matt Sinclair stumbled across the threshold. The young man was barely recognisable. Soaked to the skin, smeared with blood and close to collapse, he reached out and braced himself against the table-top.

"Wh – where is he? Where's the bastard Moodie?"

Tolland glanced at Elspeth, then moved softly, skirting Matt. But the young man was sharp and wary.

"Stand still, you, where I can see ye."

Tolland said, "Mister Moodie's not at home."

To Elspeth Matt said, "Is that the truth?"

"Aye, Matt."

Matt leaned on his forearms on the table. Droplets of watery blood stained the stone floor.

Tolland would have moved again but Elspeth shook her head, ordering the steward to be still.

Elspeth said, "James rode out, over an hour since, to the fire at Kennart. Is that where you've been, Matt?"

"Fire? Jesus God!" Matt said. "It was no fire at the mill done this t' me. It was your damned bloody husband. He did it."

Tolland said, "We saw fire."

"The shop, the Cunninghams'."

"Matt, will you not sit down an' let me look to your hurts?" said Elspeth.

"Look me int' the jail an' up the damned gallows."

Tolland said, "Gallows? Why do you talk of gallows?"

"I kilt a man," said Matt.

Elspeth said, "Who did you kill?"

"He went for me."

"Was it a weaver?" asked Tolland. "Or a gauger, perhaps?"

"No. A stranger. Your damned husband sent him."

"James? Sent who?"

"A man. To do awa' wi' the Cunninghams – which he managed to accomplish."

"Do you mean t' tell us," said Tolland, "the Cunninghams are dead?"

"Aye. Both o' them."

"Burnt?"

"Throttled first."

"Did you –"

"Nah, nah. I was marked as third victim."

"Whose victim?" said Elspeth.

"The man's victim. Your damned husband's victim."

"Matt, will you not sit down? Please," said Elspeth.

Tolland interrupted. "Are you, by chance, bein' pursued?"

"Aye."

335

"Who's pursuin' you?"

"Revenue officers. Militia."

"Ah-hah!" said Tolland. "So it is smugglers' business, is it?"

"For God's sake, find me somethin' t' drink." Matt kicked out a kitchen chair and placed his knee upon it.

"Was whisky involved?" said Tolland. "A raid by the revenue officers?"

"Your damned master told the revenue officers. They were waitin' for us. For me. But he was there first. He kilt them both in cold blood before I arrived on the scene. He was hidin' in the cottage t' kill me too."

"But you –" Elspeth began.

"He had a knife."

"What weapon did you carry?" said Tolland.

"No weapon. He died by his own blade."

"You fought, did you?"

"Aye, we fought. First he tried t' throttle me then to gut me."

"Where was James? Did you not see James?"

"Moodie paid him, paid the man."

"How do you know, Matt? How can you be so sure?"

"He told me, wi' his dyin' breath he told me."

"The murderer told you?" said Tolland. "Told you he was an agent of Mister Moodie?"

"Aye."

"He was lyin'," said Tolland. "He was lyin' his way into hell."

"The murderer, Matt, what was his name?"

"Fitter."

"Fitter?"

"Aye."

"Are you certain?"

"I met him once at Eardmore. It's no' a name you'd forget."

"Was he also one of Tomelty's gang?" said Tolland.

"I know naught o' who he was, 'cept he had instruction from bloody Moodie to do what was done tonight."

Elspeth's apprehension increased. She had heard the name of Fitter once before. Some years ago, when the cattle on Dyers' Dyke had been poisoned by bad oil, it had been a packman named Fitter who had sold the jars to Peter Docherty,

Peter who had taken the blame. But she recalled vividly all that Peter had told her: *I'll swear Weaver Moodie was at the back o' it. But bear that name in mind, Elspeth. Dinna forget it. Fitter.*

At the time of the enquiry, however, no proof had emerged to support Docherty's claims. Elspeth had managed to push aside the implication that James had planned and seen executed the callous slaughter of her mother's herd just to lay hands on the grazing acres of Dyers' Dyke. She could not accept that James Moodie would be so sly and ruthless. Fitter: the unusual name had floated into her life once more in connection with violence and disaster, again linked with that of her husband. Matt had no knowledge of that long-ago business and nothing to gain by deceiving her.

"Do the riding officers know *you* killed the man? Is that why you're runnin' away, Matt?"

"I was not seen t' do it. But they'll know my name by now. Your bloody bastard of a husband'll have informed them."

Tolland said quietly, "Sinclair, you must leave Moss House. It isn't safe for you to tarry here."

"First let me bind your wounds, Matt. You've lost blood an' will lose more if –"

Matt drew in a sharp breath. Since he had blurted out the truth, however garbled, the fury in him had dwindled. He had no reason, save that she was wed to Moodie, to doubt Elspeth's integrity but he had developed a great distrust of wives in general and would not give in to her at once.

"It's a horse I need," he said, "not bloody nursin'."

"I can get you a horse," said Tolland.

"Matt, why did you come to Moss House?"

"To confront Moodie. For answers from Moodie."

"It's fortunate for you, lad, Mister Moodie isn't at home," said Tolland. "You're in no fit state to challenge a man of his strength. He'd overwhelm you, lock you in the cellars and send at once for the officers."

"Aye, or kill me wi' his own hands," said Matt, "if he's man enough t' do his own filthy work, which is somethin' I doubt."

Elspeth said, "Tolland, fetch me cold water in a basin an' hot water in a bowl. Clean towels from the cupboard, an' bandages."

"I've fresh black sticking-plaster, lint an' styptic waters in the back pantry," said Tolland. "That'll staunch the flow o'

337

blood. Do I have 'permission' to fetch the medications?"

The steward referred himself to Matt who, peering down at his thigh, saw that indeed he was losing blood.

"Aye, go an' fetch the stuff," Matt growled.

Without another word the steward left the kitchen.

"Drink," Matt said. "Give me a drink, 'Pet."

He eased himself on to the wooden chair and stretched out his legs while Elspeth poured tea from the pot on the hob and laced it with brandy from a bottle on the cook's special shelf. She held the cup out to her brother-in-law who grabbed it and swallowed the hot liquid in one gulp. She refilled the cup and put it by him and, coming round the table, knelt to examine the puncture wounds. The cloth of his breeks had been driven into them by the force of the blows and the thick fibres had aided coagulation.

"Shoulder too," said Matt.

He adopted a peculiarly lordly pose, quite unwittingly, and gave up the ferocity of manner which he had brought across the fields with him.

Tolland returned with a basin of cold water, drawn from the pump, and four clean towels under his arm.

"The servants," said Elspeth, "are they up?"

"Asleep," said Tolland. "They heard nothing, apparently."

The steward set the basin upon the table and poured hot water from the kettle into a soup bowl which he placed on the table too.

"Cut the cloth," Tolland advised.

He handed Elspeth a paring-knife with a thin sharp blade.

Matt winced as Elspeth slipped the blade along the seam of his breeks and tore it open down the length of his thigh. In the heat of the kitchen his clothing had begun to steam and his fair hair, plastered to his scalp, had half dried and stuck up in tufts like thistles. With finger and thumb, Matt peeled away the trousers. Four deep, narrow wounds marred the white thigh.

Stooping, Tolland inspected the damage.

"Lint an' sticking-plaster will seal them."

"An' bandages too," said Elspeth. "The dressin' must be thick if Matt's to ride far tonight.'

"Aye," said Tolland dryly. "A horse."

"If you bring plasters and lint," said Elspeth, "I'll fashion a dressin' while you go to the stables an' have a horse saddled an' brought round."

"The stable lads'll be curious," said Matt, "when they see me."

"They'll not see you. They'll do what I tell them," said Tolland. "Tomorrow will be time enough for us t' answer questions."

"Why are ye doin' this?" Matt addressed his sister-in-law first and then, challengingly, the steward. "What am I t' you?"

"You're Anna's husband," said Elspeth.

Matt snorted in derision.

"An' you're Lachlan Sinclair's son," said Tolland. "I'm aidin' your escape only for your father's sake. I admit, though, I'm inclined to believe you got caught in some evil not of your own makin'."

"Somethin' of your damned master's makin'."

Elspeth said, "If this man Fitter was, as you claim, a hireling for murder, Matt, then you canna take his word as Gospel truth. He might have lied, might he not, about James?"

"Whether he lied or otherwise," said Matt, "the fact of it is I kilt him. I ran for it, too. God, but the King's Officers will have my neck in a noose, since no court in the land'll show mercy to a smuggler."

"That's true," said Tolland.

"I'll need t' get out o' the Lennox," said Matt.

"Go south into England," Tolland advised. "Take a new name for yourself an' lie low."

"I will."

"What about Anna?" said Elspeth.

"Damn Anna!" said Matt. "The bloody laird can look out for her. It's how she wants it, anyway."

Impassive as usual, Tolland said, "Shall I go an' fetch a horse now?"

Elspeth's touch had soothed Matt's anger and suspicion. He did not object when she gave the steward permission to leave Moss House. If Elspeth trusted the servant then he, Matt, must do the same. It also occurred to Matt that it might not be to the Moodie family's advantage to have him brought to book, no matter how confused and despicable the crime. If the weaver was involved at all then the weaver would not want an enquiry. Better a fugitive to carry the blame away with him, to keep the mystery mysterious, than a trial which would expose everything.

Tolland went out of the kitchen, closing the door behind him.

Styptic water nipped Matt's wounds. He bit his lip against the sting. With lint, plaster and a garter of bandages the bleeding would be stopped and he would heal well enough. There were other wounds and abrasions to attend to, however. He stripped off jacket and shirt so that Elspeth might dress the injury to the flesh of his shoulder. Cuts on the neck and face were superficial, required no medication except washing.

"Matt, do you really believe that James had the Cunninghams –" Elspeth could not bring herself to complete the sentence.

"Somebody did."

"Fitter himself?"

"For what possible reason?"

"A reason unknown to us," said Elspeth.

"Nah, nah!"

"Perhaps it was Pad Tomelty sent him. You thought yourself you first saw Fitter at Eardmore."

"Why would Padric wish the Cunninghams done t' death?"

"Did they not pay their debts?"

"Aye, on the nail."

"Matt, are you certain you were an intended victim?"

Matt snorted once more. "Do ye think my wounds were inflictit by accident, eh?"

"Perhaps you disturbed Fitter in the act."

"Damn it, 'Pet, he was waitin' for me. He could have fired the cottage an' been miles awa' across the fields. He waited only t' kill me too."

"I canna believe James would condone such a thing."

"Given reason, your weaver mannie'd do anythin' that brought him gain."

"Perhaps I'm the reason."

"You?"

"He was jealous of you, Matt."

"Dinna tell me he thought we were –"

"Aye, I think he thought we were lovers."

Matt laughed. "As if you'd have truck o' that sort wi' a mere forester."

340

Elspeth was tempted to tell Matt that she had encouraged James's false belief. But her brother-in-law was confused enough and had enough anger in him still, perhaps, to turn on her. She did not mention her baby. She must, she supposed, share responsibility for what had happened to Matt – if James had acted against him, as Matt so vehemently claimed.

"I haven't always been Moodie's wife," said Elspeth. "Besides, you're more than a forester. You're a Sinclair. The name's respected here in Balnesmoor."

"My father's name, no' mine."

"Why did you take up with Tomelty, Matt?"

"I needed a life o' my own."

"Did Anna push you into it?"

"She was never happy. Nothin' could make her happy."

"Anna's always been – different."

Matt appeared to have no interest in discussing his wife, in finding excuse for his own behaviour in err infidelities. He put his hand on Elspeth's shoulder while she laved his wound. They were close to each other in that quiet moment in the warm kitchen but there was not the slightest physical attraction in their intimacy.

Matt said, "Did old Jamie really think we were lovers?"

"I've never known what goes on in James's mind," Elspeth answered, evasively.

"He tried to bribe me to quit Balnesmoor, once."

"But you wouldn't go?"

"By God, I'd quick enough go now," said Matt. "It's my pride or my bloody neck, 'Pet. I'm o'er young t' swing from the gallows, do ye not think?"

"Matt, be careful."

"As soon as I'm on the horse, I'll –"

The knock upon the front door of the house was hollow and echoing, like the clang of some great cracked bell in a tower.

Matt pushed Elspeth away.

"Your bloody steward! He never intendit for me –"

"Hide, Matt. Hide in Tolland's pantry. I'll get rid o' them, whoever it is."

"What if it's Moodie?"

"He would not knock so." Elspeth pushed the medications at him. "Take these. Hide them too."

She did not wait to see Matt safely into Tolland's cubby but

341

hurried out of the kitchen and into the hallway to answer the knocking before the servants could gather their wits. Perhaps Matt had put his finger on it. She trusted Tom Tolland but had she trusted him too far? These past months it had seemed to her that Tolland's loyalty had shifted its axis; yet he was, after all, her husband's man.

She wiped her hands on her dress, tidied her hair and tried to appear unruffled.

"Who is it? Who calls at such an hour?"

"My name is Barnes, girl," came the answer. "I am an officer of the Excise in search of a fugitive from the King's justice."

The speech was delivered in a shrill English voice. Elspeth glanced behind her towards the kitchen corridor.

"Fetch your master at once, girl."

Elspeth unslotted upper and lower bolts, turned the iron handle and pulled upon the door. It opened, allowing the wind to swirl past her and extinguish the single branch of candles which lit the hallway.

The young man on the step had a lantern in one hand; in the other hand, a drawn sword.

Elspeth did not step back to admit him.

"You, fetch your master."

"I am wife to James Moodie, mistress of the house."

"Moodie? Is this Mister Moodie's dwelling, do you say?"

"It is. What do you seek here at this ungodly hour o' the night?"

"I did not realise it was Mister Moodie's house."

"Realise it now, sir!"

"Have you seen sign – you, or your domestics – of a man?"

"A man?" said Elspeth haughtily. "Do you suppose I would admit a man to my house at dead of night? My husband shall hear of this, sir, an' you'll answer for your impertinence."

Barnes was nonplussed. Behind him, at the gate of the garden, his horse pranced in the care of another mounted man.

"Did you not see the blaze at Kennart?" Barnes asked courteously.

"Ah!" said Elspeth. "You seek a fire-raiser, do you?"

"We seek a young man, Sinclair by name. You know him, do you not? Matthew Sinclair."

"He's my brother-in-law. What has he done?"

"He has done murder."

"Murder? Matt Sinclair would not –"

"He was seen and named, Mistress Moodie, by your husband."

"Did my husband send you here?" said Elspeth. "Did my husband order you to disturb his house?"

"I am instructed to ensure that Sinclair has not sought refuge in the village."

"This dwelling has been locked tight all evening."

"Your steward –"

"My steward's asleep."

If the light had been stronger Elspeth might have noticed suspicion on the face of the English officer. But it was a passing phase, a response to improbability. Stewards did not sleep through dead-of-night intrusions. The riding officer, however, did not persevere. He had fulfilled Moodie's insistent charge that someone ride at once to Moss House and ascertain that all was well there. The young woman, the wife, did not seem distressed. Barnes hesitated. He would have welcomed an invitation to enter, to search the premises, but that would have led to all manner of complications. He did not believe that a murderer and fire-raiser would be foolish enough to hide in the house of the man who was willing to name him as guilty.

"Have you not seen my husband, sir?"

"I – Indeed, I saw him at Kennart."

"Where is he now?"

"He may be still at the mill, or riding out with my companions in search of –"

"When will he return?"

Barnes was intimidated by the young wife's forceful questioning. He had done only what he had been told to do, yet felt that somehow he had obliquely offended the person who had given him the command in the first place.

James Moodie had been on the scene rapidly. He had inspected the blazing cottage, had given his smith sanction to bucket water from the lade to drench the flames, though it was far too late to save the building or any of its contents; more, he had examined the corpse on the path and had been unable to put a name to the dead man. But he had seen a familiar figure fleeing the mill-hamlet and had shouted out the name at the top of his voice to Cecil. "*I saw Sinclair runnin' away. Matthew Sinclair.*"

The crowd of weavers had been silent, not amazed by their employer's revelation. Most of them knew only too well that Sinclair was Tomelty's runner. The hue and cry had begun. The revenue officers would not rest until Sinclair had been caught or, as was often the case, slain in a fight to avoid capture. Prudently, Barnes kept all this to himself.

He answered the young wife's question with a shrug. "When he is ready to return, Madam. When the fugitive is caught."

"In that case," said Elspeth Moodie, "I'll bar the door an' will not open it again until I see my husband's face at the window."

"Your steward –"

"Good night to you, sir."

Barnes bowed and stepped back as the heavy front door slammed shut.

He swung on his heel and returned to the gate. He did not, however, immediately ride away from Moss House. Preceding the militiaman he trotted his horse some distance along the road to Harlwood and looked back into the pale-patched stables to the east of the weaver's house.

Lights were visible in the lofts but no apparent activity, nothing to suggest that Sinclair had raided the stables and had stolen himself a horse. Though he was not entirely satisfied, Barnes was too inexperienced to press an enquiry in the face of Mistress Moodie's defiance. He lingered for three or four minutes then wheeled his mount and headed for the main street where the other militiamen were rooting out the villagers and shaping a raid on Tomelty's cottage. Perhaps they would be more successful there and Sinclair, the butcher, would be laid by the heels before daylight flung the search out into the surrounding hills.

In Moss House the servants had peeped out into the corridor. Elspeth snapped at them to return to their beds at once, and assured them that they were not threatened, that the disturbances of the night did not concern them in any way at all. Betty had come out on to the staircase but Elspeth instructed the maid to return to the nursery and not to leave Mary Jean's side for the rest of the night, no matter how many King's Officers battered on the door.

Elspeth then hurried into the drawing-room and, hidden by the drapes, watched from the window as the English officer mounted and rode off towards Harlwood. She did not trust the man; nor, she realised, did she trust James. She had hidden her shock well, too well. It seemed that James had indeed betrayed Matt, that her husband was deeply and pervertedly involved in the calamitous events of that night. She watched the shadows of the horsemen vanish behind ornamental hedges but did not quit her vigil just yet. In all probability they were circling by the lane to the stables. Where was Tolland? He had been gone for so long, too long. Would he be caught red-handed leading a saddled horse to the kitchen yard?

To Elspeth's relief the horsemen reappeared after a few minutes' lapse of time, galloping back towards the village. As soon as they vanished, she ran down the corridor into the kitchen.

"Matt," she hissed. "Matt, they've gone. You can come out now."

She pushed open the door to Tolland's pantry.

There was no sign of Matt, no response to her urgent call. The half-open door into the kitchen yard told the story, told Elspeth that Matt had taken fright and fled through the garden on to the moor.

A quarter of an hour later Tolland returned, not on horseback but driving the gig. By his side was Lachlan Sinclair, the only person, Tolland believed, who cared enough to save his son and who had power to deflect, at least for a time, the cutting edge of justice.

The clatter of hoofs on the cobbles of the yard brought Hunter leaping from his bed.

"Open. Open. I must speak with the laird."

Wrapped in one of the old laird's handed-down dressing-gowns, a muslin nightcap askew over one eye, Hunter appeared at the door with an ancient brass-belled blunderbuss in the crook of his arm, his heart pounding.

"Who creates such a row at this hour?"

"James Moodie. I must talk with Sir Randall."

Dunn, out of his cot, came scuttling downstairs with the speed of a ferret, not so rapidly, however, as to blow out the candle he had snatched from a bracket at the head of the stairs.

The stillness of the mansion, with Alicia, Gibbie and the children gone, magnified the voices. But this was Ottershaw, not Moss House, and none of the servants, not even Mrs Lacy, dared leave their sleeping-quarters for fear that they would be reprimanded by Sir Randall who, surely, would be disentangling himself from his bedclothes and whatever else might be in his bed.

Weaver Moodie did not dismount. He was not a neat rider, could not swing himself in and out of the saddle without effort. He preferred to remain on the back of his chestnut mare, a pliant enough beast, stationary before the kitchen door. With Dunn's arrival – and the candle, before the wind outside snuffed it out – Henry Hunter was able to identify that the rider was indeed James Moodie. He laid the blunderbuss on its stock just behind the door.

"What's amiss, sir?" he asked.

Dunn, all eyes and bare legs, crouched behind the steward as if, like a guard-dog, he might spring and affix himself to the weaver's ankle at a command.

"Where's the laird?"

"The laird's here, Mister Moodie."

Wearing nothing but a pair of trews, Randall appeared at Hunter's side.

"Fire has been raised at Kennart," James Moodie said.

"The mill?"

"No, not the mill itself. The store. It has been burnt to the ground, taking the occupants with it."

"Indeed a tragedy," said Randall. "But what, Mister Moodie, does it have to do with Ottershaw?"

"There has been a murder."

"Yes, the shopkeepers –"

"Also a stranger," said Moodie. "The murderer has been recognised."

Randall, Dunn and the steward were all motionless.

James Moodie did not await their questions.

"One of your foresters. Son of your grieve."

"Sinclair, do you mean?"

"Aye, sir, Matthew Sinclair. He's the murderer and, by the evidence, the setter of the fire."

"Matt," muttered Hunter. "God in Heaven!"

Randall shivered and rubbed his palms across his naked

346

chest. "I see, Mister Moodie. I assure you that Sinclair is not at the house here."

"His cottage an' his father's house must be searched."

"Indeed," said Randall. "But why do you ride alone?"

"Militia, led by King's Officers, are searchin' the village, in particular the abodes o' the whisky-dealers."

"Is Tomelty involved?"

"Sinclair, it seems, was runnin' whisky for Tomelty."

"But," put in Hunter, "is it proved Matt did murder?"

"Proved enough," said Moodie.

"Was the stranger, then, a revenue officer?" said Hunter. "Are there militia dead too?"

"The shopkeeper an' his wife are burnt to death in their beds," said Moodie. "Another man, so far unknown by name, has a knife in his throat. Is that not slaughter enough for you?"

"Was Sinclair seen?" said Randall.

"Aye, sir. He was seen," said James Moodie. "Now, if you would be good enough to stir yourself an' gather your men, I would appreciate it if a party could be formed."

"Has Sinclair fled? Are we to give chase?"

"He has, it's believed, gone to ground. He canna have got far from Kennart. It's thought he came over the Lightwater an' even now might be lurkin' about your parks or buildings."

"Not if he's wise," said Hunter.

"Be quiet, Hunter," Randall snapped. "Dismount and come in for a moment, Mister Moodie. I'll dress myself and rouse men for a search, though we have little enough chance of unearthing the fellow until daylight, I think."

"No, Sir Randall. I'll not tarry. I must ride back to Balnesmoor."

"Very well, Mister Moodie."

"I trust that you'll not protect this murderous devil?"

"I have only your word that Sinclair has done murder."

"Believe me, Laird Bontine," Moodie shouted, "Sinclair is guilty of terrible crimes an' must be brought to justice."

By the laird's side, Hunter muttered, "Better we find him, sir, than the cutlasses, eh?"

"Yes," said Randall to the weaver. "I'll attend to the setting of a watch upon Pine Cottage and his father's house too. I will also muster men to scour over the parks and plantations. You may leave the search of Ottershaw to me."

"How far, Sir Randall?" James Moodie insisted.

"What?" Randall said. "Oh, to Blanefield. As high as the pass between Drumglass and Dumgoyne. To the Lightwater and the boundary of the Blane."

"I'll ride to Wrassle's farm then to give them warning."

"Would it not," said Randall, "be more appropriate to carry the dreadful news first to Lachlan Sinclair?"

"He is your grieve, sir. I leave that onerous duty to you."

"If Sinclair is apprehended –" Randall began.

The chestnut mare tripped close as Moodie moved angrily in the saddle. "He *will* be apprehended, laird. By God, he will. If he resists, he may be brought back dead."

"Yes," said Randall Bontine softly. "I understand, Mister Moodie. Sinclair must be taken – somehow."

"I'll ride by again at dawn," Moodie threatened and, slumping his thighs forward, urged the patient mare into a trot which turned him back on to the curving drive which would take him to the turnpike and Balnesmoor.

Laird, steward and boy watched the weaver out of sight.

"Hunter, close the door."

"Aye, Mister Randall."

"Dunn, be quick, lad. Dress yourself warmly and go to Pine Cottage. It's a dry night, if windy. Look carefully into the cottage, very carefully."

The boy started away towards the corridor that would take him, flying, to the stairs.

"Wait."

"Aye, Mister Randall?" said Dunn, pausing.

"What are you to do there?"

"See if the murderer's in residence."

"And what if he is, Dunn?"

"Come back here an' tell Mister Hunter."

"You must not show yourself to Matt Sinclair. Do you understand?"

'Aye, sir. I'll wait in the trees, will I no'?"

"Wait in the trees, yes, until I send for you." Randall waved the boy away. "Hurry now."

Hunter waited, agitatedly. He had sufficient experience of the new laird's ways to know that the soldier's brain would have arranged all the facts and would already have formed from them some strategy. He had a queer feeling in the pit of his stomach, foreknowledge of what the laird would expect him to do.

"Hunter, dress and go to the Sinclairs' house."

"What! Shall I tell them the truth?"

"Tell them only that Matt has escaped from a raid by King's Officers and is being sought by them."

"Not about murders or fires?"

"No, not a whisper. If Sinclair wishes to ride out with us in search of his son, you must contrive a means of preventing it. I do not want Sinclair to leave his house. If he insists, bring him back here with you."

"What of his wife, Aileen?"

"She must be comforted through the waiting period, of course."

"The boy, Sandy, he's old enough, and sensible."

"Fetch one of the women; somebody known to her."

Hunter said, "Not Mistress Anna?"

Randall said, "No, Hunter, not her."

"What if Matt's already hidin' at the house?"

"Detain him there."

"How, laird? Lachlan'll never stand for it."

"Carry your blunderbuss. Leave it hidden by the door. If it comes to it, restrain both Sinclairs at barrel-point."

"I dinna care for this business, laird."

"I care for it even less, Hunter."

"Do you think Moodie speaks the truth an' Matt did do for the shopkeepers an' this stranger?"

"I think it's a matter of no consequence," said Randall. "If he's caught, guilty or innocent, I fear he'll swing."

"It's not what I asked you, sir."

"It's the only answer I'm ready to give. Now, go on with you, Hunter. And take care."

Lifting the blunderbuss, Henry Hunter hurried off to his closet to jump into his clothes and be about the unpleasant task of bearding the grieve at home.

Cold now, Randall went through the kitchen and up the back stairs to the bedroom where Anna waited.

Unlike Tom Tolland, who had entered her life only a handful of years before, Elspeth had known Lachlan Sinclair all her born days. In fact, he had stood as her godparent, along with

Doctor Rankellor, at a time when every hand in Balnesmoor was turned against her mother. Once she had been much in awe of the grieve of Ottershaw, not only because of his position in the community but in response to his air of authority and dependability. She had thought of him as strong but fair. It had seemed to Elspeth as if nothing would shake the rock of the grieve's character and it pained her to see him so broken by events over which he had no control. The straight back was bowed by grief, the handsome face wrinkled by weeping. He sat on a chair by the table, sobbing at the news that Matt had gone, had struck out into open country where, Sinclair groaned, he would surely be tracked down like a fox, come morning.

Tolland had been less sparing of the grieve's feelings than Henry Hunter would have been. He had expected fortitude from Lachlan. He had informed him of all the circumstances, including the allegation of murder, which had brought Matt into hiding at Moss House. But Lachlan Sinclair had not brought his wits together, had not forged some practical plan which would save his son. Lachlan Sinclair had gone to pieces.

All during the ride along the rough track that bordered the moor, with the gig leaping and swaying in the wind, Sinclair had held his head in his hands and moaned; Tom Tolland had realised that he had erred in bringing the grieve into it at all. His kindness had blown back on him. He hoped, however, that Matt would be able to draw his father to him, wring sense out of him, and was dismayed to find, on arrival in the kitchen, that Matt had fled.

"But why? Why did he run away?" Sinclair cried. "Did he know I was comin'? Is that the reason? Did he run before me? Was he shamed? Did he not think I would give him my aid?"

"The Revenue Officer at the door," said Elspeth, "put him in a fright."

"He didn't know I had gone for you, Lachlan," said Tolland. "He'd have waited, if he'd known. It's my blame. I should have told him."

"Och, Matt would put himself in jeopardy, face the swords of King's Officers rather than me. I know him. He has always been afraid of me."

Seated, rocking, the grieve clasped his hands to his chest and beat against the bone in self-punishment.

"Does he not know I love him?"

"Aye, he knows. He knows," murmured Elspeth.

"Could he not wait for me?" Sinclair parted his hands and leaned forward, fists on thighs now. He stared at the stone floor beneath his chair. "Is that Matt's blood?"

Elspeth had swabbed the kitchen floor with wet rags but had not had time to be thorough, had neglected a few spots of blood by the table.

She put her hand on Sinclair's shoulder.

"He'd torn his leg. I bound it for him."

"Did they shoot him?" Lachlan Sinclair clutched at her wrist, his eyes massive with grief. "Tell me, lass, is Matt dead."

"Man, man!" said Tolland. "We're not deceivin' you. Matt made a run for it. You can hardly blame him, with Excisemen hammerin' at the door. Come now, Lachlan, draw yourself together, I beg you."

Elspeth said, "Matt will escape them yet."

"Where will he go? Ottershaw's all he knows. He'll be lost in the world. Alone in the world." Lachlan clasped Elspeth's wrist again. "*She* did it to him, you know. *She* changed him. *She* turned him wicked."

"Matt isn't wicked," said Elspeth placatingly.

"He would never have done all this but for his marriage to that girl."

"It – it wasn't Anna's fault," said Elspeth.

"Aye, aye, it was *my* fault. I should never have allowed the marriage. She was not for our Matt. It was not made in Heaven, that bond. She isn't like my Aileen."

Elspeth felt sympathy for the grieve but also a certain annoyance at his self-pity. Lachlan Sinclair had not accepted his son because his son was not a model of himself. How that arrogance must have rankled in Matt, shaped him into the weak and indecisive husband that he had proved himself to be. Behind the failure of Matt's marriage loomed the shadow of his father's domination, stern not kindly. Love unspoken was almost as bad as no love at all.

She drew her arm away from the grieve.

"Perhaps Matt *has* gone home," she said. "I canna be sure what route he took after he left the garden here."

"What's that you say?"

"Aye," put in Tolland, who also was embarrassed by Lachlan Sinclair's collapse and, like Elspeth, wanted rid of the grieve now. "Aye, perhaps Matt's gone back to Ottershaw. Where else would he go but home?"

"He'll find no wife there."

"He'll come to you, Lachlan," said Tolland. "I should have thought o' it before."

The grieve cocked his head to one side as if he had caught a distant strain of sweet music. The wrinkled, tearful expression eased from his features. His mouth became set and proud and hard. "That's what he'd do, aye."

"If he finds no armed militia there," said Elspeth.

"He'll come to me."

"To Ottershaw," said Tolland.

"He knows I'll speak with the laird."

"Sir Randall?" said Elspeth, startled.

"The laird'll protect him."

"But –"

"I've served the Bontines boy an' man. Matt's one of mine an' I'm the Bontines' servant. It's incumbent upon the master of Ottershaw to protect his own."

"We must hope he realises it," said Tolland, as astonished as Elspeth at this curl in the grieve's thinking.

Lachlan Sinclair slapped his hands to his thighs and got to his feet. "If he *has* done wrong, Matt must pay for it. But I'll see to it, with the laird behind me, that he receives justice."

"Shall I drive you back, then?" said Tolland.

"If you'd be so good." Sinclair nodded. "I'm grateful to you, an' to yourself, Elspeth, for fetching me. I was not myself before."

"If I had known –" said Elspeth.

How much had Lachlan Sinclair grasped of the situation? Did he truly expect Randall Bontine to exercise his power to protect a young servant accused of heinous crimes, a young man, moreover, who was husband of the laird's mistress? Lachlan had stepped into not one trap but two and would surely be caught in one of them.

Elspeth glanced at Tolland who pursed his lips, shook his head. It was not wise, the steward seemed to indicate, to try to force sense upon a sensible man.

"How could you know, Elspeth?" said Sinclair, with infuriating magnanimity.

Lachlan Sinclair had not, the girl realised, seriously questioned his son's guilt, doubted the bald facts of the crime.

Elspeth allowed him to leave without conscience. She was relieved when the door closed on grieve and steward.

Lachlan Sinclair's moral blindness presented her with a miniature of her own failing, of her husband's culpability. Doubt boiled within her. She needed to be alone to do what had to be done. She watched the gig jounce on to hard track behind tossing hedges.

When it had gone, Elspeth walked resolutely into Tolland's pantry and took down the big iron ring on which the steward kept all the household keys. She found a candle and lit it, stuck it firmly in a holder and went out of the kitchen and across the corridor to the study in which James spent so much of his time in brooding retreat.

The door which protected the room's secrets naturally was locked. Patiently Elspeth fitted a key into the lock, a second, third and fourth; a fifth at last engaged and, when she turned it, allowed the door to swing inward upon its hinges. Extending the candle before her Elspeth went into the room.

It was furnished as she remembered it from the two or three occasions upon which she had been permitted, in James's presence, to cross the threshold. She had not been curious about these matters of business and the profound thoughts which occupied her husband in his privacy. But she was curious now. Instinct prompted her to hope that James would have some record, some letter or paper scrap which might validate her belief that he was capable of hiring a murderer, that, in some obscure way, he was only protecting her and her baby from harm.

Desk, chair, decanters, a bare mantelshelf over a dead fire, an oil lamp, a silver dish with flints, a row of ledgers on the board floor, and a chest to hold them straight; above the chest was a window neuk draped with a curtain. She knew where the key would be, on James's watch-fob. She placed the candle-holder on the desk and returned to the kitchen and, in the cupboard where utensils were kept, found a stout skewer. She took it back to the study, closed the door and knelt again before the chest.

Bound with bands of iron, pimpled with rust, the chest seemed stout and secure. But its lock was a small, brass, heart-shaped affair. Without compunction Elspeth stabbed the skewer into the aperture, leaned her weight upon it, boring and levering until the casing snapped and wood splintered. With the point, she worked the lock loose, thumbed the catches and lifted the lid.

No fat bundles of letters, no tangible trophies of the past met her gaze, only a sad little bag of dried lavender which lay like the corpse of a vole on top of a couple of ledgers. Elspeth was disappointed. In worn roan bindings, the books seemed no different from those on the floor. She put the lavender bag to one side, lifted out the volumes and carried them to the desk. She lit the lamp from the candle and in its circle of mellow light opened the uppermost ledger.

James's script; in places it was hasty and spidery, in others careful and formal. The ink had faded. Elspeth had to peer to decipher the words. It was, she realised, a logbook of sales made twenty years ago, in the days when the Moodies had conducted trade from the cramped cottage in the Bonnywell, opposite the manse. Sums paid in recompense for cloth pieces seemed pitifully meagre, profit measured in pennies not pounds. Still disappointed, she flicked over the pages at random.

It was in the fold of pages dated 1791 that Elspeth discovered the first in a series of inserted leaves, letters and notes. The sheet was innocuous enough, a page trimmed from the Balnesmoor kirk records: *November, 11th Day Thereof, 1791. To pay for a coffin for a poor starved woman, Who was a stranger . . . 6s 8d.* Written in James's 'official' hand, the entry obviously referred to her mother, her real mother, not Gaddy.

Elspeth thought it queer that James had never shown it to her or even mentioned it, queerer still that he had defaced the kirk register at a time when she was nothing to him but a foundling brat, and Gaddy naught but a troublesome stranger.

Penned in dark ink, bold in the margin, was an additional entry, a name. *Bell Harper.*

Oblivious to the chill, to the blundering wind, Elspeth seated herself on the ladderback chair and, trembling, began to read the history of passion and threat, subterfuge and guilt which had been her husband's torment for two decades.

* * *

Anna met the laird as he emerged from the top of the back stairs. She had crept from the bedroom in response to the disturbance and had crouched at the top of the main staircase from which position she had caught enough of the conversation to pick up the gist of the night's events.

"Randall," she said, "it's Matt, is it not?"

Clad only in an indecently short shift, Anna padded behind the laird as he strode into the library.

The fire flickered in the hearth but the candles had been extinguished and Randall ordered her curtly, as if she were a mere servant, to put a taper to the wicks at once.

Anna did not obey.

Hands on hips, she snapped, "Will ye not tell me what's happenin'?"

Randall ignored her. He tugged open a recessed cupboard, dug inside and brought out his tunic, his sabre in its scabbard and a swagged leather belt with side buckles. He flung the equipment behind him on to the floor, dug deeper and came out with a heavy, oblong box.

"Light me a candle, Anna."

"Not 'til ye tell me –"

"Damn you, girl."

He caught her by the arm and swung her bodily towards the hearth. Anna gasped but no longer dared defy him.

Swiftly she stooped, lit one of the tapers and transferred flame to the candles in the brackets over the hearth.

Randall placed the box on the floor, knelt by it, opened it and took out a stubby Spanish pistol. Expertly, in moments, he fitted a flint to the percussion screw, held the weapon at arm's length and full-cocked the powerful mainspring. He pressed the trigger. Starting away, Anna involuntarily covered her head with her arms. Even without powder and ball, unloaded, the pistol made a deadly, wicked clack as the flint chopped down into the flashpan.

Anna gave a little scream but Randall paid her not the least attention. He took a chamois bag from the box, deposited into it a small powder horn and other necessities for the firing of the weapon then, standing, dragged the tunic to him with his foot and began to dress.

Anna had had enough. She strutted to him, caught at the

355

tunic sleeve, pulled it tightly, drawing the laird off balance. He rounded on her.

"Why did you do it?" he snarled.

"Do what?"

"Peach on your husband."

"I never did."

"Do not lie to me, Anna."

"I had nothin' to do wi' burnings an' murders."

"Perhaps not, but did you not inform the Revenue Officers that Matt would deliver illicit spirits to Kennart?"

"What proof is there I'd –"

"You told me, Anna."

"An' you said –"

"I said I would give you an answer in due course. But that wasn't sufficient for you. God, girl, do you not see what you've done?"

"Matt *was* runnin' whisky."

Randall buttoned the heavy tunic across his chest, fitted the belt about his waist and clipped the scabbard to it.

"What – what's that for?" said Anna. "The sword?"

"You disobeyed me," said Randall. "You acted without a thought for consequences –"

"I can be yours now, Randall. Whatever's happened at Kennart t'night, Matt's to blame for it an' we'll be free o' him, come what may."

"Come what may!" Randall shouted. "Come what may! You bitch. How can you condemn your husband to death? For that's what you have done."

"He'll get off, you'll see," said Anna uncertainly.

She was close to tears. Nothing had gone as she had planned. It should have been clean and quick, Matt either slain by the King's Officers or arrested on the spot. She could not understand why the building had been fired or some stranger knifed to death, nor could she quite fit Matt into the violent pattern of events. It was not contrition or concern for Matt that brought tears to her eyes but Randall's cold anger and the realisation that she had alienated him.

Now another thought entered her mind. She clutched at Randall's sleeve again.

"What if Matt comes here, comes in search o' me for vengeance?"

"It would be no more than you deserve, Anna."

"You're not blameless," she cried. "You needed no great coaxin' t' take me from him."

"That much is true," Randall admitted. "But my capacity for vindictiveness is not equal to yours. Do you think I would have allowed you to peach on him?"

"What if he comes here t' kill me?" Her fear was genuine.

The laird hesitated then said, "He'll have more than enough to do in escaping the hunt."

"You dinna know Matt as I do. He'll come here t' cut my throat if he can."

"In which case," said Randall, "it's imperative that I run him to earth before anybody else finds him."

Anna wiped her cheeks with her wrist and squinted quizzically at the laird. "You'll ride alone?"

"Where will he go?"

"Why the sabre, Randall, why the pistol?"

"To protect myself."

"Against Matt?"

"Where will he take refuge?"

"If there's a fight, if Matt resists –"

"All will be solved."

"Aye, an' nobody will ever blame the laird."

"Where?" said Randall.

"Eardmore," Anna said.

Desperation dropped away as Matt left Balnesmoor behind and climbed through the gullies of the Orrals on to the high moor. For the sake of speed he had been tempted to cut across the pastures of Dyers' Dyke on to the ridgeway but it provided the only path for horsemen and he had an image in mind of an army of his enemies pouring along it to outstrip him and hack him to pieces.

Alone in the midst of the windy wasteland, however, Matt's confidence began to return and with it a certain thin optimism. Pad would still be at Eardmore. Pad would help him to escape. Pad would provide him with a horse – the first essential – and food and perhaps a little money to see him through his long journey across the border into England. Hue and cry would have its limits. If he could be out of the Lennox by morning he would have a struggling chance of escaping free and clear of the pursuit.

Going to Moss House, for whatever muddled motive, had been to his advantage. The bandaged leg hurt hardly at all and he was losing no blood. He wished, though, that he had taken a moment to filch a dry shirt and breeks from the steward's cupboard. He had been too hasty in his flight, too moved by mistrust of Elspeth. She had done him no wrong nor given evidence that she supposed him capable of murder; yet the squawk of that English voice at the front door had rubbed up his panic like shavings in a tinder-box and he had been out of the kitchen and across the garden before he could control himself. He had not even had the foresight to arm himself with a carving-knife or scrape a half-loaf or piece of beef from the larder to keep his strength up.

Ribbons of cloud skimmed over the skyline but there was moonlight to steer by and he had ride-knowledge of the terrain and enough sense not to trot lest he step into one of the green, seeping bogs or trip and twist a limb on the tough hag. He walked at a steady pace, concentrating on the ground ahead of him, stopping to take a bearing on the hill shape every now and then and, he believed, making such headway that he would be into Eardmore long before the King's Officers could forestall and outrun him.

Panting, Matt came over the last hunch of the moor on to flat ground that bit like a wedge into the hillocks behind the remote community. He could see the black outlines of dwellings but nary a light; which was all to the good. Eardmore might be Pad Tomelty's kingdom but Matt did not trust the inhabitants there any more than he trusted the folk in the villages of the strath.

Wryly he thought of Jacko, how his pals had liked Jacko, had roared with laughter at the wee beast's antics but how not a one of them would turn out to help when Jacko had got lost. Perhaps it was as well that Jacko had departed. He would have been obliged this night to steal back to Pine Cottage to burden himself with the wicker cage during his jink out of Scotland; he would not have left Jacko behind.

Flagging a little, Matt made his way across lumpy grazing to the broken-down barn. At any moment he expected one of Eardmore's scrofulous mongrels to yap warning of his approach. But none did. The dwellings seemed as deserted as if he had been gone for half a lifetime and Eardmore had at last been cleared and left to rot. The barn door was roped on the outside. Matt untied and pulled it open enough to allow him to slip inside.

The wind harped in warped rafters, drummed through buckled boards and spun chaff in whirligigs across the earthen floor.

"Pad. Pad, it's me. It's Matt come back."

Pad was not in the barn.

It was dark as a pit and at first Matt could see nothing. He groped to a pile of sour hay and thrust his arms into it. He was seeking the solidity of kegs stored there, the flagons of ripe whisky ready for delivery. He found nothing. He stepped into the loose hay, trampled on it as on air, discovered not a trace of barrel or bottle.

Fear snared him again, pinching his stomach, closing his throat. He gave a choked cry and bolted from the barn. Padric Tomelty had shifted out the whisky, for no reason other than the trouble which had erupted far, far below in Kennart.

Three hours, more, since he had confronted Fitter; it would take the King's Officers that to ride round by Harlwood. But somebody, some sneak from Kennart, had been on pony-back almost before the knife had entered Fitter's gullet. Which of the weavers was Tomelty's spy, so sharp and swift that he had known what was what from the instant the confusion broke out?

Matt stood uncertainly by the side of the barn, head raised, sniffing and sighting round the crude square of cottages. Not a light, not a sound; the village had been 'cleared'.

They would all be up there in the hills, in one of the sheltered dells of sweet grass, wrapped in shawls and blankets, drams from a tapped keg to keep them warm, their animals about them, moved far enough from the hamlet not to be heard by revenue or militia. Tomelty's stocks of whisky, trundled behind a pony, would be deeved away in the autumn bracken or tucked in niches in the crumble-rock.

Pad had heard the news, perhaps had known all along what would happen at Kennart. Back the thought came roaring that Tomelty had betrayed him, that the stranger – Fitter – had died with a monstrous lie on his lips. Jamie Moodie might not have been the contriver after all. It gave Matt no consolation; he had already survived an excursion to Moss House. He had climbed to Eardmore to be safe, to find protection and friendly assistance. Had he stumbled headlong into a trap?

Paralysed with doubt, uncertain of his conclusions, Matt edged again into the shelter of the barn.

Were they here?

Were the King's Officers in position?

Watching him? Waiting! Ready to pounce?

Matt strained his ears to catch the tell-tale whinny of a horse or the clink of a bridle but the wind that flooded the moor bore too much volume for small sounds to be audible. He heard the horse only when it appeared, sight and sound linked. The huge, towering animal stepped high and dainty out of the north-west wind into the square.

Matt fell back into the barn. He dropped to all fours, crawled across the earthen floor to the hay pile and burrowed into it. One man meant others. One horse, one rider would not be considered enough to corner a dangerous fugitive from Georgie's justice. If they saw him, he would be done for. He lay motionless in the stinking hay, arms over his head, his face peeking out.

The door battered and clacked as if it were shouting a warning to the riding men, betraying him. One minute passed, then two, three. No alarm was cried and nobody entered the barn. Matt did not move. His eyes had grown accustomed to the darkness and he could see, just, a broken trestle by the rear wall. Wood would provide a weapon, a club. He must arm himself, make a fight of it. If he had to die here in Eardmore then he would die on his own terms, like a man.

The hay whispered as he rolled through it and came to his feet, crouched. He darted to the broken trestle and groped about it, found a suitable length of wood to make a club, then closed his hand against a hard, metal object. A rusty scythe-blade without a handle. He wished he had light to see by for he felt sure that the shaft would be lying about too, but the clop of hoofs at the door of the barn forced him to improvise. He uncoiled the muffler from about his throat and wrapped it quickly around the bottom curve of the blade. Blunted though it was, the scythe made a fine weapon and he chose it in preference to the club. He had a notion that he might be able to immobilise the horses with it if he could work close enough in the dark. Matt had no opportunity to dwell on his fancy, however. The barn door opened wider, patching the floor with a pearly moonlight. Matt knelt by the trestle, hidden, the blade held in both hands.

One horseman only, tall and elegant in the open doorway; the man eased the stallion forward and halted on the threshold. The animal, Matt saw, was a handsome grey, familiar in its grace and vitality.

"Sinclair. I have seen you. Come out."

Matt was too foxy to fall to such obvious tricks but it startled him to be summoned by Randall Bontine, added another strand to his confusion.

"I'm alone, Sinclair."

A lie, of course; the laird had been sent for by the King's men, had led them here. Anna would have told them where he might be found, though Eardmore was hardly a secret among the villagers who knew Pad Tomelty. It no longer seemed to matter who had turned the hunt in his direction, who had given information to the revenue officers. For all Matt knew, or cared, Bontine was at the back of the plot to bring him to the gallows.

"You have precious little time, Sinclair, if you are to be away before daylight," Bontine shouted. "I can see the streak in the sky to the east already."

Still Matt said nothing. He was directly in front of the doorway. He would have preferred to come at the stallion from the flank. Bontine was shrewd. He would not bring his mount into the dark interior of the barn where he would lose the advantage of mobility. Matt held the scythe ready, listening to catch sounds of other riders who were perhaps circling the barn.

"Sinclair, I give you my word that I'm alone."

Matt shouted, "Aye, an' what worth is the word o' a man who has stolen my wife?"

"Anna has naught to do with what's between us now."

"Come in, then, come in an' step down."

"I'm not the one the revenue officers seek, Sinclair. No, nor am I entirely stupid. What do you have, a knife?"

"Come in an' see, laird."

"By God, I believe you think you can best me."

"Are you truly alone?"

"Yes."

"How did ye know about Eardmore?"

"Anna told me."

"Then I'm not to be taken alive."

"I give you –"

"Your word, laird? I'm a fool in your eyes, perhaps, but no' such a fool as that."

"I've no wish to kill you. I'm here to help you escape."

"Hah!"

"Do not force me to come for you, Sinclair. I'm armed with sword and pistol and might do you serious injury."

"Have ye not done me that already, Sir Randall?"

"She was never yours, Sinclair. I did not steal her from you. Besides, Anna is no man's possession."

"Under law she was my wife."

"Do not let pride, of all things, bring you down."

Sabre had grown impatient with the exchange and shook his head, uttering a snicker of temper and stepping sideways in the doorway.

Matt lifted the scythe blade to his shoulder as the laird backed the horse out of the door. Sir Randall had roped the door back at some point, Matt realised, for it no longer rattled and flapped in the wind.

Matt rose and crabbed quietly to his left out of the spill of half-light. He sprinted across the angle of the barn to the inner wall, then, having found volition at last, pivoted around the post and almost collided with the stallion.

If it had been the laird on foot, Matt would have swung the blade and cut him down. But he could not bring himself to mutilate the stallion, the huge, energetic creature which he had tended during Mr Randall's years in Spain, which he had ridden so proudly into the rain to Glasgow on the night of the old laird's death. He had admired the thoroughbred too long. He gripped the pad around the blade tightly with both fists and willed himself to strike. It would have been simple to slice the rusty metal, smash the stallion's pastern bones and lame the beast, drive the point up into its belly. But he could not do it to Sabre. The scythe stuck in his hands while the horse pranced hard by him.

Matt ducked to one side. He kept the wall of the barn close so that Bontine could not run him down. The laird was occupied in controlling his mount, shifting and cajoling with the rein.

Mad at his own squeamishness, Matt tore around the gable into the mouth of the wind. He could not escape now. He had beggared his only chance of taking revenge against Bontine for all the ills the laird had brought down upon him, for loyalty squandered and love stolen away. He could not challenge Randall Bontine in fair fight, man to man, upon the ground. With the scythe slung over his shoulder like a token of his class, Matt ran away.

Bontine was out of the saddle. He held the rein in his left hand to keep the stallion from bolting. The back, not the cutting edge, of the soldier's sword pinned Matt to his knees. Matt waited for the expert stroke that would sever his head from his body.

"Take him," Bontine said.

He was offering the rein, the stallion.

"But –"

"He knows you. He'll ride for you, Sinclair. Take him."

"So you can murder me as a horse-thief?"

"I need no excuse, Sinclair. I have the power to kill you as a fugitive without much fear of reprimand."

"Do it then an' stop tormentin' me."

"I'm no butcher. Here, take the damned rein before I think the better of it," said Randall. "Sabre's strong as well as fleet. He'll carry you out of the Lennox. I suggest you ride towards Edinburgh, across the Carron Water, and keep off the turnpikes until you are beyond Stirling."

"An' what then?"

"Do not try to sell the stallion. It's too fine an animal and will draw attention to you."

Matt said, "I could leave it at an inn with instructions it had t' be returned t' Ottershaw."

"Yes," said Randall. "Give the inn-keeper or ostler money and promise a second fee at Ottershaw."

"I wouldn't be wantin' Sabre fastened to a dung-cart on some mangy farm," Matt said.

"Get up."

Matt scrambled to his feet.

Randall retreated a yard from him and gave Sabre a nudge with his elbow, extending the reins towards Sinclair. The stallion reached out its muzzle, sniffed at Matt, snickered and showed teeth. Tentatively Matt accepted the leathers. He noticed that Randall Bontine had not sheathed the sword, however, and when the laird slid his right hand into the breast of his tunic, Matt half expected to be shot or struck down with a knife.

The laird brought out a leather purse and tossed it to Matt.

"Silver," he said. "Ten pounds in coin. A guinea to an ostler, or to a carrier if you do not trust an inn. Do not ride Sabre until he's blown and do not leave him wet."

"Why are you doin' this? Is it for her?"

"For Anna?" Randall Bontine laughed. "God, Sinclair, she would have you dead."

Matt gave a snort. "Aye, but you'd not, since then ye might fall victim t' her too, eh?"

"I'm not as you suppose me to be. Take Sabre and ride away, Sinclair, before I forget who I am."

Matt put up no further argument. He did not care if he had been made party to a cynical trade, had been given his life in exchange for his wife, with horse and purse thrown in as make-weight. He swarmed into the saddle and brought Sabre round to face the east, on to the same path he had taken with the pack-pony only hours ago.

It was short of sunrise but the wind had lifted cloud from the horizon and the shapes of the hills, outlined against the bands of yellow, were tinted red as turning leaves.

"Was it you sent the Revenue Officers t' raid Kennart?"

"No," Randall Bontine replied.

"Was it Anna?"

"Be away with you, Sinclair, before I lose patience. What's done's done. Those of us who stay behind will knit up the truth if we can."

. "Aye." Matt gave Sabre just a touch of the heel. "Never fear, laird, you'll not be bothered wi' me again."

Horse and rider merged with the charcoal landscape, then, coming from the grazing, were framed distinctly against the dawn flush.

Randall brought the Spanish pistol, primed and loaded, from his tunic. He drew the action to full cock. Gripping right wrist with left hand he raised the gun and took steady aim upon Sinclair's back. In the shrill wind he could almost make out Anna's voice insisting that, for her sake, he squeeze the trigger. But Matt Sinclair was out of range, out of harm. Randall lowered the weapon and stuck it back securely into his tunic. He picked the sabre from the ground, wiped it on his sleeve and sheathed it.

Bands of light were stretching. He could see mountains to the north raised out of darkness, the dropping moon all wan, rinsed for another night. Soon Tomelty's gang would creep out of hiding; he did not wish to be discovered by them, though they would not dare harm the laird of Ottershaw.

Turning up his collar, Randall set off down the ridge towards Balnesmoor and Ottershaw, ignoring his aches and hurts. He had done the right thing, the honourable thing. Now he must go further still and break with the girl he loved, not to punish her for presumption but to save what was left of his reputation and preserve the tradition of the house.

Gilbert would help him – at a price.

Anna, no matter how she railed, would have no choice but to obey.

It was dawn before James returned to Moss House. The expanses of moor and hillside had emerged with daylight and, as he walked the horse to the stable, he had a dreary realisation that Matt Sinclair might escape him yet; and with Matt Sinclair gone loose the rest had been futile.

The Cunninghams were dead. There would be no more letters, no more threats from those fiends; James had not one drop of remorse in him for what had happened to the shopkeepers. Indeed, if lying on the path with a knife through his throat had been Sinclair and not Hugh Fitter, then he would have been delirious with happiness, would have ridden the mare up to the stables with a whoop and a cheer, would have gone lightly along the path by the wall to the kitchen door, lifted his daughter into his arms and showered her with kisses. But Sinclair had evaded him and, though the day's search might dig the man out of hiding, Weaver Moodie had only been unburdened of one anxiety to be laden with another.

It was a quiet, reasonable sort of madness that possessed James Moodie. He still had sufficient control to practise its forms only in his own company, to let out the slack of rational behaviour only when he was alone.

The nearer James approached to Moss House, however, the further the madness receded, replaced by a slack, exhausted despair. He craved sleep, craved softness, the feel of his grand-daughter in his arms, to hear her innocent, uncalculating little cries which he would gently soothe. He would walk her about the corridors until he had worn away the last of his terrors, the fear that Matt Sinclair would not be caught but would haunt him with letters and demands for evermore.

Luke McWilliams was up and about. He took the sore mare from Mr Moodie. James said not a word to the boy and the boy had wit enough to ask no questions, though he burned with curiosity.

By the back path, between moor and garden, James came to the kitchen door and found it unlocked. He opened it quietly and stepped into the corridor.

Perhaps Tolland had stayed up, the steward faithful in ignorance. But there was no sign of Tolland in the kitchen. James headed for the study where, on the desk, he would find a decanter of brandy and a jug of water to melt the knot in his chest.

She was seated with her head on her arm, golden and hazy in the light of the lamp, a dream not a ghost, ledgers and papers spread out on the desk-top before her.

She had been crying. Her cheeks glistened as, at his ap-proach, she lifted her head. She stared at him with such anguish and revulsion that James felt as if his heart would stop.

Shame came upon him. Shame for all that he had done. Shame for the sins of omission, the neglect, the conniving, the unspoken lies. He had ruined Elspeth, destroyed her. He went forward, arms out, tears swimming in his eyes, to offer her, at last, love. But it was too late for healing, and his daughter was not ruined, not broken after all.

Elspeth got to her feet.

"What have you done?" James whispered.

"Found you out."

James nodded.

"And what have you found out, dearest?"

"Who you are. Who I am."

"They're dead."

Elspeth frowned. "Do you mean the shopkeepers?"

"All dead."

"Matt – he isn't –"

"Have no fear on that score, dearest. I'll have him. He'll not tell anyone."

With a sudden lunge James grabbed at the papers on the desk-top. His fists rose with paper in them, met and ripped the letters into tatters, scattered the fragments like snow into the air. Some fell into the funnel of the oil lamp and charred, sending wisps of blue smoke into the air.

"You may burn them all, James. I've read them."

"Liars, the Cunninghams. Damned liars."

He leaned his knuckles on the desk and pressed himself forward until it seemed that he was perched on toe tip. He looked huge, bull-like in the glow of the lamp.

"I know who you are," Elspeth said again.

"Well then, you know."

"Did you murder her too?"

"Murder? Why do y' talk of murder? I've murdered nobody."

"Only the Cunninghams."

"They were evil."

"What of Bell Harper? Was she evil too?"

"Bell?"

"My – my mother. Did you not slay her too?"

"She died because it was God's will."

"Your will, James."

"She had no right to come to Balnesmoor."

"She had nowhere else to go, had she?"

"You know nothing of such people."

"I know who you are, what you've done."

"Aye, lass, but do you know why?"

"All these years," said Elspeth. "Year upon year upon year, pilin' one lie upon another, James, until you'd smother us all beneath the weight of them. My mother, my real mother, Gaddy, me, an' now my daughter, Mary Jean."

"I'll care for her. I'll love her. She'll be a lady, wealthy an' refined. No stain will touch her," James Moodie said. "She's mine."

"No."

"She is mine, as you were never mine."

"*No.*"

"I tell you *yes.*"

"If I defy you, will you be shot o' me too? Because I offend you, threaten you? Be rid o' me the way you got rid of my mother, the shopkeepers, Matt. Matt did nothing –"

"He was your lover."

"He was never my lover."

"Even now, you defend him?"

"Matt Sinclair had no part in any o' this."

"I *saw* him."

"You saw nothing but a shadow of yourself."

"Do you think I'm blind?"

"Aye," Elspeth shouted. "Blind, blind. I do think you're blind."

James smirked. He flung himself back from the threatening posture at the desk. He spoke swaggeringly. "You canna deny me the child, Elspeth."

"I'm your child. Mary Jean is not."

"Who would believe it? You must keep silent. It would be a corruption, a taint on her all her life long if you spoke out."

"How can you put it on to her, generations removed from your sin?" Elspeth cried. "Is it not enough that you got me by lies?"

"How else could I have got you?"

"For God's sake! Could you not have told me the truth?"

"That I'm your natural father? Is it palatable, the truth, Elspeth?" James stepped back to the desk, head lowered. "Would you not have asked me about her, about Bell Harper?"

"Who was she?"

"A trollop."

"No, I dinna believe –"

"She let me, a common weaver, take her, did she not?"

"Perhaps she –"

"She could not love *me*. Do you think I was such a fool, even then, to be taken in?"

"God in Heaven!"

"A miserable cottage-weaver from the country. She would have let me do anythin' to her."

"She – perhaps she loved you."

368

"How could she? She did not know what I was, only what she supposed me to be, lost in the damned city."

"Why did you desert her?"

"She was trash."

"Ah! You deserted her because she wasn't fine enough for you."

"An elder in the kirk, a weaver who owed nothin' to a master. How could I burden myself with trash?"

"Did you know she was carryin'?"

"She dumped the brat on my doorstep, did she not?"

"I'm that brat."

"Aye, you are. My daughter. My flesh an' blood."

"Could you not own me? Take me in?"

"I took you in. I gave you my name."

"Twenty years after, twenty years too late."

"Now it's – it's well, though. Unless Sinclair escapes."

"Well?"

"Nobody knows."

"I know," said Elspeth.

"I have Mary Jean. She'll love me."

"I know the truth, that you're my father."

"In the letters. All in the letters, I suppose."

"Enough," said Elspeth. "You killed her through cruelty. My mother. Bell Harper. If it hadn't been for Gaddy Patterson, a drover's woman, you'd have let me be lost t' you forever."

"Only you know the truth," said James, as if the mouthing of the fact caught him by surprise. "Only you."

"Aye, so will you kill me as well?"

"How can I? You're –"

"For Mary Jean?"

"I must protect her at all costs."

"Protect her first from yourself, James."

"Do you *not* understand what I have *done* to protect her?"

"Weaver Moodie. Elder Moodie. The great James Simpson Moodie. God! I canna breathe in this house for the stink of your rotten hypocrisy. Let me out."

Elspeth emerged from behind the desk. But he could not release her yet. Confession and justification; he had to make her understand the magnitude of *his* sacrifice.

He caught her by the arm. Having experienced his violence once, Elspeth struggled, beating at him with her fists. He struck her with his forearm upon the side of the head, making a glare of false light blaze in her head. She swayed, almost fell, only her presence of mind saving her. She groped for the heavy roan-bound ledger, grasped it in two hands and swung it flat into her father's face.

James gave a little jump and clasped his hands to his nose. Blood trickled from one nostril. Dazed, he leaned against the desk. Elspeth walked past him into the corridor, along it and up the stairs to the nursery. Her head ached but she was improbably calm. Even when she heard him roaring beneath her she did not increase her pace, did not fly from him. Tom Tolland had not returned from Ottershaw and there was no man in the house to protect her and her baby. The female servants would be cowering in the hall. She hoped that James's bellowing from below would bring Betty to the nursery door. She refused to run from her husband, her father. Perhaps that was him in her, his strength of will, his defiant pride. But Elspeth could not relate herself to James Moodie in that manner. She was, and always would be, Gaddy Patterson's daughter; the corruption in James Moodie was a separate, alien thing, roaring below.

"What is it, Mistress Elspeth?"

Betty stepped on to the landing, a pair of brass coal-tongs raised in her right hand.

"My – my husband's gone – mad."

"Drink?"

"Aye," said Elspeth, seizing the simplest explanation. "Brandy in excess."

"Come in quick, then."

Elspeth slipped into the nursery. Betty threw the big bolt and turned the key in the lock.

The women stood back from the door as it shook with James Moodie's first pounding assault. The sounds were those a demon might make, wailing, snarling cries, fists and fingernails ripping at the woodwork. The door vibrated as if a malignant force sought entry.

White-faced, Betty glanced at Elspeth.

"Where's Mister Tolland?"

"Gone t' Ottershaw with Mister Sinclair."

"What – what's really wrong wi' Mister Moodie?"

"He's drunk, Betty, an' it has affected his reason."

The servant stepped back as once more the door shook and vibrated. The key waggled in the lock, fell clinking to the floor. In the night cradle Mary Jean woke and whimpered. The maid went to her charge immediately, standing with her back to the doorway as if to reject the violence there.

Elspeth faced up to it.

She was not afraid. James could not reach her or her child here in the nursery. Whatever madness took hold of her father had festered for twenty years or more. She saw in the outburst the poison of selfish pride, the innominate pride of the male who would be father and husband but could never bring himself to be lover, could never give love in case it weakened him in the role of master. James Simpson Moodie had been warped by un-loving. He had built an empire of wool-woven cloth to numb his pain. Small wonder that Gaddy had detested him and in turn he had both hated and loved the wild Highland woman who had come as a stranger from the glens.

In time the beating upon the door grew weaker, the cries became feeble and hoarse. The thump-thud-thump of his boot seemed childish and vain as he kicked against the panels. Elspeth would never open to such a man, would not yield to him no matter how he raged and wept and demanded his right to be forgiven because, by accident, he had fathered her. She sensed that he was still outside, slumped in exhaustion at the base of the door. But she had her baby to suckle and Mary Jean would not wait.

"Are ye reposed enough?" Betty asked when Elspeth lifted the baby from the cradle, breast already exposed. "It's said excitement curdles milk."

"I'm fine, Betty."

Elspeth seated herself on the nursing-chair, took the crying baby and held her soothingly while James whimpered outside.

"See how hungry she is," said Betty, pretending that all was as normal.

Elspeth touched Mary Jean's cheek, and gums and lips fastened upon her nipple.

Minutes later there was a fresh commotion upon the stairs. Tom Tolland's voice came to them. They heard him cajoling James to come downstairs again, to take rest. And, by the silence, James complied.

Uncertainly, Betty said, "Is – is Mister Moodie sick?"
And Elspeth answered, "Yes."

Anna kept her vigil by the library window throughout the night and into the broad hours of the morning. The big room was warm and she did not spare the logs – logs which Matt himself had cut, perhaps – or the candles that she had trimmed. None of the other servants came upstairs.

Anna's fears that Matt might sneak back to Ottershaw and take revenge on her for her treachery waned as daylight crept across the parks and uncoupled the sky from the hills. The wind too abated and there was the promise of September sunshine in the streaked cloud to the east. She refreshed herself with sips of wine from the laird's decanter and nibbled pickings from the supper dishes which had not been gathered away.

Below in the kitchen Mrs Lacy would be questioning the girls to discover what dreadful things had happened during the night and what the rumpus in the kitchen yard had meant. Servants from the hall would be eating a hasty breakfast and bustling, gossiping, to their duties. Brigit would not report for service. Unless Anna's guess was far wrong, Matt was by no means the only hireling in the parish and, with the King's Officers rampaging about, there would be a few 'catches' made and many a lad lying very low. The Tomelty family, Brigit with them, would have turned invisible, flitted away into nowhere as they had done more than once in the past. Padric would not confront trouble at any price. She would miss Brigit's chat and her impudence but that was small cost for being rid of Matt Sinclair, released from the bonds of a marriage which had threatened to strangle her.

Anna felt a certain uneasy satisfaction in the turn of events. Whatever happened to Matt, caught or slain, she would be free of him. That would have been a dab in the eye for her mother who – Anna could never forget – had forced her into the marriage in the first place. What Gaddy would have said to having a daughter pregnant with an heir to Ottershaw Anna could not imagine. She suspected, however, that Gaddy would have come to terms with it and turned it to benefit, for that had always been Gaddy's way.

Now that the wind had dropped, Anna could hear sounds from yard, stables and fields. No matter what doom or destiny intruded, the routines of the farm must continue. Even with Matt Sinclair fleeing from justice, and the laird riding hard after him, cows must be milked, stotts separated for marketing, butter and cheese made, late cropping continued to its conclusion. It would be months or years before Ottershaw would suffer from a lack of management, for the men who did the work from day to day would function like wound springs, without supervision.

Seated by the window, forehead against the glass, Anna tried to imagine what it would be like to be the lady of this place, to be more wife than lover to Randall. She wondered if he would change towards her when she mothered his son. She comforted herself with dreams and fantasy, stilling her anxiety about what was taking place in Eardmore or on some other corner of the moor.

It was after eight o'clock before the laird returned.

Anna had been on the look-out for the stallion. It surprised her when Randall appeared on foot among the trees by the park. He was limping badly and stooped. She had a sudden rush of panic at the thought that Matt might have bested him, might have stuck a blade into Randall too. All Anna's silliness evaporated. With a cry she threw herself back from the window, ran out of the library and down the main staircase. She burst from the front door, scampered down the stone steps and across the lawn, her dark hair tousled, her eyes glittering with tears.

The laird glanced up but did not stop. He did not even change direction. He limped on, dragging a diagonal line for the front of the mansion. Anna reached out her arms to him.

"Did you not find him?" Anna said.

"Yes, I found him at Eardmore."

"Randall, are you wounded?"

"No, only weary beyond belief."

"Is Matt dead, then, or taken?"

"Your husband's gone."

"Gone?"

"Escaped," Randall said.

"On Sabre?"

"I gave him the horse."

"Damn you, Randall, why? Now we'll have to wait four years t' be free of him."

"After what you've done, Anna, I doubt if you'll ever be free of him."

"Randall, I beg you –"

They had reached the stone steps which led up to the front door of the mansion. Hunter, who had returned from the grieve's house some while before, waited discreetly on the terrace.

"Has Sinclair been found, sir?"

"He will not be found, Hunter, unless he is very careless. You may inform Sinclair that his son got safely away from us."

"That's good news, laird."

"And fetch Dunn back from the pine wood."

Anna plucked at Randall's sleeve, demanding his attention, his reassurance. He pulled himself up the steps on to the terrace then stopped and turned to her, placed his hands upon her shoulders and drew her against him. Not without passion, he kissed her upon the mouth – then handed her over to the steward.

"Hunter, take her home."

"Home, laird?"

"To her family. To the Sinclairs."

With that final instruction Randall brushed past Anna, stalked, limping, into the house of the Bontines and closed the door behind him with his heel.

The wind had strewn the lawn with leaves and turned the bracken blond upon the fringes of the moor. By noon, however, the air was almost still again. Sunlight dappled the flanks of Drumglass and shimmered on the knuckle of the loch away beyond Kennart.

Elspeth had slept for three hours, lying dressed upon the bed behind a locked door. On waking, she found the house tranquil. She washed her face at the basin with water poured from the jug, then combed and pinned up her hair. She studied her features for a moment in the glass. She saw no trace of James in them, none that she could discern. She was as fair as her father was dark. Perhaps she resembled one of his sisters or had come into the world in her mother's cast. It mattered not. She could not change her thinking. She could not fit with the knowledge of her identity. She felt strangely calm and relieved, as she had done that day when Gaddy died.

She uncurtained the window and looked out at the weather then unlocked her bedroom door, glanced into the corridor, slipped along it to the nursery where Betty and Mary Jean were both wide awake. The baby, chuckling, was being petted in the nurse's arms.

Without waiting, Elspeth fed the baby while Betty, who had slept hardly at all, tidied up the room and prepared the day cot for Mary Jean's afternoon nap.

"Have you heard any news of Matt Sinclair?" Elspeth asked.

"Aye, Mister Tolland had word from Ottershaw just an hour since. Matt Sinclair, it seems, has got away. He stole the laird's horse." Betty, even the God-fearing Betty, giggled at the thought of Sir Randall left stranded. "Stole it an' rode awa' from Eardmore."

"Safe away?"

"There's no word t' the contrary."

"What else, Betty, did Tolland tell you?"

"There's been men here from Kennart about the burnt bodies an' the dead man."

"Has James gone out with them?"

"He wouldn't even see them. He's – pardon me – he's in no fit state for transactin' business the day."

"Where is he?"

"Downstairs. He's still drunk, I think," said Betty. "Tom Tolland sent the men awa' t' speak wi' Mister Rudge."

Elspeth nodded. James was above reproach. He was too wealthy and powerful, too cunning to absorb blame for what had happened to the Cunninghams or to the man named Fitter. She did not hate her father and would not, could not, expose his calumnies and crimes. How could she do so without revealing the most fearful crime of all and, as James had threatened, tainting her daughter's future with the shadow of an incestuous conception?

It mattered not that James had possessed her only as men possess daughters, with deceit but without passion. Convention would destroy them, all three. She had put that behind her immediately. She could not blind herself to James's evil connivances.

It had been in her mind like a crystal from the moment she grasped the import of the letters in the ledger. The Cunninghams' threats and subtle revelations must have twisted into

James's brain like hot wires. But the man, Fitter, had been employed before. She did not doubt that James had had the cattle poisoned to lay his claim on the pastureland and, perhaps, to pull her into his possession. She could not live in comfort with such a man whether he be husband or father.

"Betty," she said, when the baby was fed, "fetch out Mary Jean's overclothes an' wrap her up warmly."

The maid stiffened. "Are ye takin' her out?"

"Aye, the wind's gone an' the sun shines."

"In the garden only?"

"I'll take her down to Ottershaw. I must visit my sister."

"Ottershaw?" said Betty. "It's too far."

"I'll go in the gig."

"I'll come."

"No, Betty."

"Kerr, then. Take Kerr."

"Have the big brown pony put in the shafts. Bring shawls an' back-laced boots."

"What else?"

"Nothing else," said Elspeth.

"Leave Mary Jean for her sleep. I'll walk her in the garden later."

"No. It'll cheer my sister to see her niece."

Betty frowned. The servant was fond of the baby and with an almost maternal instinct seemed to sense the girl's intention. "Will ye be back for tea?"

"Of course I will, Betty. Now hurry, please, before the best of the day's gone."

"Mister Moodie'll —"

"I'll tell my husband where I'm goin', Betty."

A quarter of an hour later it was all done. The gig stood at the front gate, Elspeth was dressed in her warmest clothing and Mary Jean wrapped in a robe and sash over her flannel binder and frock, her tiny face framed in a cap.

With her, Elspeth carried not only the baby but a large muslin bag which she had packed quickly while Betty was downstairs. It contained baby-napkins, blankets, bedgowns and, in a kid-skin reticule, fifteen pounds in coin which had been saved from her inheritance; all that Gaddy had left her that could be counted in material terms.

"What's that?" Betty was even more suspicious. "You'd think ye were off for a month, Mistress Elspeth."

"It contains a few things for my sister."

Elspeth handed Mary Jean to the servant but kept the bag in her hand as she turned along the corridor to the kitchen.

Tolland was not asleep, though the steward too looked tired and drawn. He was seated at the kitchen table eating soup from a bowl when Elspeth disturbed him. He scrambled to his feet, buttoning his waistcoat.

"Where's my husband?" she asked.

"In the study, Mistress Elspeth."

"Is he – better?"

Tolland glanced round at the cook who was a notorious tattle and drew Elspeth out of the kitchen into the corridor. He had the key of the study in his hand and hesitated at the door.

"Did you not say that Mister Moodie was better?"

"Aye, he is. But I took the liberty of lockin' him in."

"Is he so enraged, Tolland?"

"He's not himself. I feared he would create a disturbance which he would soon regret. He's been at the bottle too."

"I see."

Elspeth was torn by indecision.

It would be simplest to run away without confronting James. She dared not tell him the truth, of course, but must convince him of her intention to visit Anna to offer comfort, and to return. If he guessed the truth then he would prevent her leaving Moss House that afternoon and would surely set some guard upon her and the baby, employing men like Fitter for the purpose if he felt he could not trust the servants to do his bidding in the matter. But Elspeth was not so heartless as her father and, though he deserved no kindness, felt a nebulous concern for his welfare.

"If you give me instruction, Mistress, I'll open it," said Tolland. "It's time, perhaps, he was roused."

"Yes, open it."

Tolland unlocked the door.

He stood back and let Elspeth enter.

The curtain was still drawn but there was enough light to show her the chamber. In the fireplace the embers of the ledgers and papers made grey and insubstantial ash and gave off the heavy odour of oil. James had drenched them from the bowl of the lamp, had burned everything, the records of his father's trade as cottage-weaver, his own history too. When the oil had run out he had used brandy from the decanter which lay empty by the hearth.

Tolland said, "I'll wait close, Mistress Elspeth. He's not himself."

"Aye," said Elspeth.

It had been vain, James's effort at destroying the past. On the other hand there had been a certain element of cunning in it, for the documents in that chest provided the only evidence of his connection with the 'agent' Fitter and of the hold that the Cunninghams had exercised upon him. James, even in despair, had been both practical and thorough.

Elspeth had leisure to inspect the scene for James was slumped in a drunken stupor in Mother Moodie's throne-like chair. He occupied it as she had done, had even loose-buckled the leather straps to hold him upright. Glass and bottle, fallen by his hand, indicated that he had drunk quickly, systematically seeking that numbed state which brandy could bring, the sick, uncaring slumber which followed it. His mouth was open and his cheeks caved in. He snored.

It seemed to Elspeth that in the past few days James had gravitated towards the condition which had claimed his mother in her latter years. His hair was thickly streaked with grey and he had reassumed the coarseness that tailoring and grooming had managed to disguise. She had never seen him asleep before, nor drunk. How long would it be before James entered the haven of muttering and demented indifference to the world as it was, until time dispensed its inevitable punishments?

Going softly forward she touched his hand.

"James?" she whispered. "Father?"

The man did not stir into wakefulness but slouched down further into his voluntary bonds and, with a harsh sigh, let his head loll forward.

Elspeth did not try to wake him.

Gently she kissed his brow.

"Goodbye," she murmured.

Turning, she left him in the closet room, alone in the darkness.

Tolland and Betty accompanied her down the path to the waiting gig.

The steward too seemed to have guessed what was in her mind but did not remonstrate with her or try to prevent her leaving.

"Tolland."

"Aye, Mistress Moodie?"

"Look after him –"

"I will."

" –until I return."

Betty, with tears in her eyes, handed over the baby and Elspeth settled herself on the board in a comfortable position with Mary Jean in the crook of her elbow, the reins in her right hand. Elspeth drew in a deep breath.

She snecked the pony into an easy trot, heading along the road into the village. She glanced at Moss House, clean and solid against the rolling quilt of moorland where, in another sort of existence, she had met Michael Blaven and before that had spent her childhood under Gaddy's loving eye.

Sobbing, Betty ran a few paces after the gig. But Elspeth did not turn round and Mary Jean, snuggled against her mother's breast, slept peacefully in the autumn sunlight, rocked by the motion of the wheels.

Six weeks later to the day, travelling in the opposite direction and under a sky which presaged rain, a narrow flat-bed cart pulled by a single horse creaked along the road past Moss House.

Unlike the great procession of Gilbert Bontine's family, the Sinclairs' 'flitting' was scanty, though their destination – Strachan Castle – was the same. A lifetime of devoted service did not amount to much when its accumulations, roped to a cart, added up to but a few sticks of furniture, a basket of clothes, a box of books and a handful of sentimental ornaments which Aileen, over the years, had almost polished away.

Sandy Sinclair was at the reins. His mother, red-eyed, huddled by his side. His sisters, tall girls, trudged by the side of the cart to ease weight on the axles and on the horse which would have to be returned to Ottershaw's stables tomorrow none the worse for wear. Without a high, handsome mare under him, aged by the events of the season, the former grieve of Ottershaw might have been taken by a stranger for naught but a tired old pedlar wending along to yet another fair. Seated on the tailgate, legs dangling, he stared at the ruts in the dirt which the wheel-rims unspooled behind him. By his side sat his daughter-in-law, Anna. Her condition was obvious, a fine swollen belly that she did not have the decency to hide.

The good folk of Balnesmoor did not turn out to speed the grieve, pillar of their enclosed society, upon his way. Like the workers on the Bontine estate they had skulked, embarrassed, indoors, ashamed of Sinclair's shame. But not a one of them, not even Lachlan himself, blamed the laird for relieving him of a position of authority which, under the circumstances and to all concerned, had become untenable.

Sir Randall had not been idle. Bargains had been forged and deals made, laws firmly laid down. Lachlan Sinclair had faithfully implemented the laird's instructions to the letter, without protest. Lachlan worked to terminate his connection with Ottershaw, if not with the Bontines, as if it had been his dearest wish. He found a tenant for Tomelty's abandoned cottage, a decent thatcher with a family. From Buchanan Sinclair hired a young forester who had plans to marry a lassie from Balnesmoor and was glad of employment and a cottage, Pine Cottage, to call his own. Lachlan even selected his own replacement, a progressive, energetic bachelor who had been depute-manager on Lord Rushing's cattle farm in Galloway and who was looking for advancement and a degree of freedom to experiment with breeds and feeds. On Lachlan's recommendation Sir Randall had agreed to take on the man for a trial period of one year.

For the sleepy rural community which gathered round Ottershaw it seemed that changes came thick and fast after the Kennart murders. Cheap free-run whisky was difficult to find since Pad and his clan had vanished from the Lennox and, it was rumoured, had gone to ground in the Pentlands with designs on the parched throats of the gentlemen of Edinburgh. Warrants for the arrest of the felon, Matthew Sinclair, turned dud. The stallion, Sabre, was returned to Ottershaw from a livery in Dunbar, many miles south of Edinburgh. It was assumed that the young man had wriggled out of Scotland

and found a hiding-place in England. With him, Matt took all the blame for events at Kennart.

It was predicated by officers of the Sheriff that the fire and murders had stemmed from a quarrel between smugglers. Hugh Fitter's history, such of it as could be unearthed, confirmed that he was a man of violent disposition and dark connections. Not one word of his contracts with James Simpson Moodie came to light, however, and Mr Moodie was left to get on with his money-making affairs without impediment or taint.

For all that he appeared blameless, James Moodie was never the same again. It was as if the firing of the shop under Rowan Hill had singed his reason. Certainly it frightened his young wife so much that he was obliged to send her, with his baby daughter, to reside with his sister in Perth. Or so the story went. Tom Tolland kept his mouth shut, Betty too. Even Kerr, who was inclined to gossip, was guarded in her slanders on that score. It was odd, though, that Elspeth Moodie had last been seen driving alone towards Glasgow and that her gig had been left in front of the inn at Blanefield, quite the wrong direction for Perth.

Anna, of course, imagined that she was privileged to know the truth. Moodie had been down on her, raving and ranting, with not a thought for the grief-stricken Sinclairs. But Moodie had been forced in the end to accept Anna's assertion that Elspeth had not visited her, had left no message, had run off without farewell.

The timing of Elspeth's departure suggested a tie with Matt's disappearance but no matter how she fitted it together Anna could find no feasible link. At that point Anna was not thinking too logically, overwhelmed by fear that the King's Officers might trace the letter which she had sent to the gauger in Drymen, the letter which had led to the conflagration at Kennart and, in all probability, to murder. With each passing day, however, the threat of exposure waned and by September's end Anna was inclined to feel that Elspeth had slighted and rejected her too, as had Randall and everybody else.

She had been bargained away and could do nothing other than agree with the plans that had been made for her, short of taking to the hills or following the old drove road into Glasgow, as Elspeth perhaps had done. Anna did not have the determination of her sister, nor, finally, the impetus. Though Randall would have no truck with her, the memory of his last kiss, given against the grain on the terrace of the mansion, nurtured in Anna hope that one day she might be brought out of exile and restored, with her child, to Ottershaw, close to the only man she had ever loved, or ever would.

Anna had no information on what it had cost Randall to find a place for her. The laird had been obliged to bribe Gibbie to take her. Gilbert's 'price' had been the financial business of Ottershaw, and a flock of notes of agreement and fund transfers had gone from Hildebrand's chambers, and from the library at Ottershaw, to dockets in the Falkirk Farmers' Bank, a 'catch' which enhanced Gilbert's reputation and the company's stock.

In fact Gibbie was only too pleased to have Sinclair at Strachan Castle for Gibbie had been swayed by Alicia and had begun to see himself in progress towards wealth, position and power; and land, no matter how he made his livings, was the ultimate possession, and the tending of land the ultimate Bontine responsibility. Lachlan Sinclair would be a valuable asset when the time came to expand the holdings of Strachan Castle. In the meantime the remaining son, Alexander, would earn his keep as a cattle-man and the girls and the wife would be set to work in the great rambling house under Alicia's hawk-like eye.

Anna Sinclair, his brother's mistress and wife of the notorious outlaw, was not welcome. But Randall had insisted upon it and Gibbie had finally surrendered on the point for the sake of 'business'. She could be kept out of sight in the kitchen or the little dairy shed, cared for until her child was born. Gilbert was wary on this score for he had a feeling that his brother was genuinely attached to the wild hill lass, for all her lack of pedigree and faults in character, and that Randall would not, in the long run, see her bastard starve in case the babe was his after all.

So Anna left Ottershaw with the rest of the Sinclairs on a lowering afternoon, and ground up on the cart through the village and on to the top road that led away to Fintry. She had lived with them for six long weeks, had endured Aileen's hatred and Lachlan's silent recriminations, the sneering jibes of Matt's sisters. She would endure more, much more, under gaunt Alicia Bontine. Yet they had taken her in, had fed and kept her warm and given her a bed to sleep in. She could not blame them for hating her since she had stolen away their son and, so they believed, had ruined him. There was no bargain struck with the Sinclairs. They obeyed only the ancient, immutable law that decreed that a family must take care of its own.

Miserably, Anna sat on the tailgate of the cart, no longer childish enough to weep and seek attention. In her, smaller though than the growing babe, was a tiny kernel of belief in the ultimate power of her dreams, that 'binding' which defied nature and family, which might bring her back to Randall.

Already she missed her sight of the laird, the sound of his voice, the touch of his hands upon her. Rocking in the rhythm of the cart she felt the first spit of the rain upon her cheek and raised her head and looked away towards the Orrals which were veiled with mist. And saw him there, saw first the gig with the hood raised and Tom Tolland, happed in a greatcoat and muffler, sitting as patient as a monument within; saw James Moodie standing on the mound of grass at the base of the sign that marked the limit of Balnesmoor, the sign whose arms pointed in all directions, to Harlwood, Balfron, Killearn and Fintry, and by extension outward into the world.

He came running, Moodie did, running with scuttering little steps, like an auld wife chasing hens. His hands were raised, his features pinched and anxious yet ingratiating as if he expected a rebuff as sharp as a whip snapped at his head.

"Stop, please stop," he cried as he came abreast of the cart.

Sandy, nonplussed, drew the rein and slowed the horse to less than walking-pace, hardly moving at all, but not halting quite for it was a far piece to Strachan Castle and dusk would come early with the rain.

Peering upward, James Moodie minced down the length of the cart, crying out, "Do you know her? Do you know her? Have you seen her?"

Turning, Aileen Sinclair appealed to her husband who, rousing himself from brooding, straightened and gave reply.

"Aye, Mister Moodie, we know your wife."

"Have you seen her, then, on your travels?"

"No, sir, we have not."

James was trailing behind the cart now, following at funeral pace along the road towards Fintry.

"You." He nodded to Anna. "I know you, do I not?"

"I'm Anna Sinclair."

"Have I seen you in Glasgow? Do *you* know her?"

"She's gone," said Anna. "Elspeth's gone. She's not wi' us."

Moodie stopped in his tracks. An expression of amazement opened on his face. "Gone? Where's she gone? Can I not find her?" He ran a few more steps, his hands against his chest as if in supplication, in the habit of the praying elder that he had been once in days too long ago to bear remembering.

"If you see her," he called out as the cart creaked on, "if you see her, tell her she will always be loved."

"Dear God!" Sinclair growled. "What has become of him!"

James Moodie raised his hand uncertainly, gave the Sinclairs a little wave, then, like a restless sparrow darted away to the hedgerow and, standing on tiptoe, called out across the misty fields, "*Elspeth. Elspeth. Elspeth,*" calling still until the echo of his voice dwindled and was absorbed by the air.

Anna could see what would become of him, how the weaver would waste his days in the dream of Elspeth's return, crying into the dust of the field-crossings, over the pasture and the tilth, crying into the time that was gone and never would return.

An unexpected sadness came upon Anna. Tears welled into her eyes. She had nobody to whom she could turn, nobody to care for her, to give her love, yet she did not weep only for herself but for Gaddy and for Elspeth, Matt and the poor lost man by the crossroads sign.

The grieve said quietly, "What ails you, lass?"

"I – I don't know."

"Here," he said, "lean on me for a while."

Awkwardly Anna put her arm about him, laid her head upon his shoulder and let Lachlan comfort her as the cart rolled on down the endless road to Strachan Castle and beyond.